LOVE UNEXPECTED
LOVE'S IMPROBABLE POSSIBILITY
BOOK TWO

LOVE BELVIN

MKT PUBLISHING, LLC

LOVE UNEXPECTED

from the *Love's Improbable Possibility* series

book 2

by Love Belvin

Published by MKT Publishing, LLC

Copyright © 2013 by Love Belvin

All rights reserved. This book may not be reproduced, scanned, or distributed in any printed or electronic form without written permission from the author. Please do not participate in or encourage piracy of copyrighted materials in violation of the author's rights. This book is a work of fiction. Names, characters, places, and incidences are fictitious and the product of the author's imagination.

ISBN: 978-1-950014-66-8 (Hardcover)
ISBN: 978-1-950014-15-6 (Paperback)
ISBN: 978-1-950014-11-8 (eBook)

MKT Publishing, LLC
First print edition 2013 in U.S.A.

Cover design by Marcus Broom of DPI Design

CHAPTER 1

I was in my cubicle when Munick came over and banged on the wall requesting an update on the Harrison case.

"So, you want a search warrant to look at Harrison's phone records?" Munick murmured tentatively.

"Yes, I can take it to Judge Warren before he leaves for vacation today if you can sign off right away," I answered, masking my exasperation.

"Is it imperative for you to look at those? Don't you have a CI or something you can work with?"

I knew Munick had still been reluctant to investigate his *buddy*, but he had to look past that and do his job. Darryl Harrison was a corrupt motherfucker who needed to be put behind bars with the rest of his hoodlum associates! Munick would just have to suck it up.

"The CIs I have cannot connect Harrison to Jacobs. They can only tell me about Jacobs' associates. I need more access to get the evidence." I omitted the truth, which was I hadn't been able to get anything on Jacobs either. I'd only had a statement from an incarcerated underling that Jacobs ran the operation and was partners with Harrison.

"Well damn it, Lombardi!" Munick screamed until he remembered the level of sensitivity needed for this case and lowered his voice. "...what evidence do you have to get the fucking warrant from the judge?" he continued, getting in my face. It was obviously forgotten that I am a competent and decorated detective. Though I may have been getting off to a slow start, with persistence, dots would start connecting in this case.

"I have an informant in custody ready to talk now. It's just a matter of using whatever intel he gives and adding it to what we find on the wire. You know how this game is played, Captain. Sometimes we have to pull the strings together for the shit to stick," I tried pleading with him. I really wanted this case bad. Harrison needed to be brought down.

Munick glanced down at his watch and then over to me with an angry scowl. "You have twenty-six more days on the clock. Not a damn piece of paper will get my John Hancock until you have something substantial. You can ruin your career by trying to make things stick, but I won't be going down with you!" Munick stormed off kicking up dust along the way.

Mother fuck me! This shit is going to be harder than I thought.

Back to the phone I went, having other sources to tap out before calling it quits. Daryl Harrison was going down and if this Azmir Jacobs was his pawn, he'd have to pay the piper, too.

Rayna

I flew to visit my brother, Keeme, in prison. Per usual, Michelle gave me a lift to the airport. As she hugged me goodbye she asked, "Are you sure you don't want to get a room and stay just one night? Would you consider staying with your family? You could do both, you know?" Michelle pleaded with me with her warm hazel eyes. "It pricks at me that you take these quick turnaround flights when you visit Akeem. Then, you're crazy enough to try and return right back to work!"

I rolled my eyes and gave her a parting embrace. "Shelly, I'll be fine. I'll text you when I land."

We went through the same ritual of questions every time she dropped me at the airport. And my answers never varied. She knew I only had one goal on my mission, which was to visit Akeem and resume my normal life.

Aside from that, I was holding a secret from her, and it was eating me alive. This wasn't the type of information I liked keeping from her. But my thoughts were that I'd bide my time and hold off on telling Michelle about my blow up with Azmir until I wrapped my mind around it myself. After all, I had to get through my visit with Akeem and didn't need a double dose of guilt on my shoulders when visiting him. I'd tell Michelle when I was ready.

I caught the first flight out that morning and five and a half hours later I was arriving at *Newark International Airport*. I rented a car, stopped to get a bite, and headed straight to *Caldwell State Prison*. I hated visiting my brother behind bars. The correction officers were so rude, treating even visitors as criminals. As we entered a corridor leading to the visitation room, they'd slam a cell door reminding us of where we were. This time I jumped and turned toward the cell door. The guard laughed, bringing unwanted attention to me. I reserved my feelings for my brother's sake. I always felt it was my fault he was in there. Had I not been involved with that damn O, he'd have no reason to defend J-Boog that night because there wouldn't have been a confrontation.

Akeem's appearance had changed. He was thicker and had more hair on his almond shaded face. He had grown into a man. He resembled our father so much it scared me; the similitude was hauntingly uncanny. My mouth dried as though I'd swallowed a handful of cotton balls. I must have worn my feelings on my face because as he sat down, he smiled in a blushing manner.

He picked up the phone, "What, woman?"

"Keeme, man, you look just like Eric!" I cried with widened eyes.

"Oh, yeah? It's funny because I said the same shit to myself the other day. It's crazy, right? What's going on with you, little mama?"

"Oh, nothing." I sighed, still reeling from his aging features.

"You know you got people asking about you and shit?"

"Who?" I hissed, trying to mask my paranoia. I've told him a hundred times to keep my affairs confidential.

"Moms, Pops, Grams, Nikki, Theresa...everybody."

"And what the hell do you tell them?" I quizzed.

"Ain't shit I can tell them. Shit! You don't tell me a goddamn thang! Na-Na, you don't even want me to know where you rest your head! That's fucked up!" His protest was obviously loud because the room seemed to have gotten quiet and the guy next to him lowered his phone and looked Akeem's way.

"We're not going through this again, Keeme. The last time I came we argued about this until it was time for me to leave. We're not going through this shit again! You don't need to know where I live until you get out."

"What if something—" he attempted, but I interrupted him knowing where he would go with that same sad song.

"What if something happens to me? Is that what you were going to ask, Keeme? What the hell could you do from here? Huhn? What? You can't do a damn thing. Like I told you before, if something were to happen to me, you'd be notified and compensated."

"Compensated? See, what does that shit mean?" His voice was so deep I had to remember my brother was a man now, not the young adolescent I used to argue with about stealing my food from the refrigerator.

"If the time comes, you'll know. If it doesn't then you won't need to, right?" I gave him an intense gaze. I didn't want to fight, I wanted to reconnect with him. "Keeme, what else is going on? I've missed you. I couldn't wait to come to see you." I tried to fight back the tears.

"Shit! Yo' ass should be missing me! I ain't seen you in a minute. What the fuck took you so long? I thought something happened to yo' ass! Now you talking all this crazy shit about compensating and shit! Did you finish school?" he pried.

"Yes, Keeme. I told you when I was here last year during my spring break I was graduating in May. I'm even done with grad school now. I've already started work in my field."

"Damn, girl! You really doin' ya thing. I'm proud of you. So, what you get your degree in? Getting ghost?" he asked, being facetious.

"I got my Master's in... You swear not to tell anybody, Keeme?" I asked with cautious eyes.

"Here we go with this secretive bullshit again. You better hurry up girl, we ain't got all day!"

I snapped my neck at him expressing my seriousness and forcing him to agree.

"Okay, girl!"

"I am a Physical Therapist. I'm even running a practice."

"Damn! That's whassup! You're finally done with school?"

"Yes, Keeme. What girls do you have coming to see you in here? Who visits you?" I asked out of curiosity and to change the subject. The guilt I felt from being responsible for my brother never being able to dream outside these prison walls was unbearable.

"Ain't no bitches coming to see me that you know of. I meet broads through my boys in here. But you know how it is, out of sight out of mind," he spoke somberly. My heart twisted in my chest. "Oh! Cousin Sundryia come through every now and then. She been a G. J-Boog sister Renee was coming to see me for a minute then stopped. They don't even send cards like they used to when I first came up in this bitch." Akeem snorted. That must be tough to chew on. "Grams brought Pops to see me for the last time last Christmas. That was funny as hell. That nigga didn't even know what to say. I was looking at him like *Yeah, nigga. I'm flesh of your flesh and blood of your goddamn blood. It's yo' muthafuckin' fault that I'm in this bitch.* He's a straight bitch, Na-Na. A straight bitch! I hate that muthafucka." I silently choked on my tears. I understood the sentiment.

"I wrote Grams and told her not to bring his gay ass up here no more. I ain't no damn freak show!" Akeem's features wrinkled; I could tell he was struggling with his next thought. "But he didn't look good. Grams said that nigga sick. I said good for his ass. Fuck-'em!" Akeem seethed. I hated seeing him out of sorts but discussing our father would do that to the both of us.

"What about our mother, Samantha? She been here?" I didn't know if I really wanted the answer to that question. I'd quickly figured out in my teen years our parents weren't the most supportive, and during the times they were needed the most they likely wouldn't come through.

"Yeah. Matter of fact, she was here like two months ago. She got Aunt Claire to bring her. All she did was cry. That was like her third time coming to see me and I been in this bitch—*what...like seven years?* Yeah, seven years, not including my time in the county waiting out my trial. You da only one who visit me like that. That's why I was like worried when I ain't see you in a while. You usually come around every holiday." Akeem was somewhat right. I would visit twice a semester and on breaks, which was primarily around the holidays.

"Yeah. Well, I'm here now. I don't let your commissary go empty, do I?" I teased.

"Nah!" His smirk was bashful.

"I know I don't. As a matter of fact, I'm gonna max your account today before I leave because I'll be short on funds until the end of the summer," I explained. The truth of the matter was I knew I had to focus on furnishing my house as soon as I hit the Pacific soil and that alone would wipe me out for a while. But no matter what, I always took care of my brother—even if it was with my last.

What he didn't say was *he knew* I was alive because his commissary stayed with a balance, and I wrote him often. The dummy never looked at the postmark on the envelope to figure out where I was. It was an endearing form of ignorance.

"How much longer do you have in here? I'd like to hug you soon!" I joked.

"On the up an up, I got like seven more years, but my lawyer is tryna' get that bitch reduced since I ain't been getting into no trouble or nothing. Oh, and thanks for keeping him on your payroll, Na-Na. I appreciate dat shit like a muthafucka. Every time I hear from him, I think about you 'cuz I know if it wasn't for you throwing a few dollars his way, I wouldn't even hear from that nigga."

"No problem. Keep me posted. I'm surprised he hasn't yelled it's time to go yet," I referred to the guard. My time there had always seemed so short. I turned to see the guards still surveying the room. When I turned my attention back to Akeem I smiled, still admiring his features and being overtaken by the only warm memory of my childhood. My brother. We were damn near twins and had been through so much together.

"So Rayna, where you going once you leave here? Akeem asked like a child not wanting to separate from its mother.

"To put some money in your account, fool," I quipped in an attempt to lighten the moment.

"No. For real, man!" he pleaded. I saw the desperation in his eyes, so I got serious.

"You know I'm getting on a plane, Keeme." I sighed not wanting to make my life sound so grand when he'd be left in a tiny cell to live vicariously through me. It didn't seem fair.

"Where, girl?" he demanded, causing me to relent.

"Let's see." I pondered my answer aloud. "Just know I'm going somewhere sunny where the wind blows easily. I'm okay, Keeme! For real. Don't worry. You got a birthday coming up in a couple of months. I'll be back to visit for your birthday, and I plan to give you something really nice." I tried ending the conversation peacefully and with a twinge of hope. I tried to make him smile.

I knew me not discussing my whereabouts bothered him, but I didn't trust that he'd keep it a secret. The last time I told him specifically where I was at school in North Carolina I started getting phone calls and mail from people I didn't want to correspond with, namely LaTavia. She sent me pictures of her baby who looked just like O. What shocked the hell out of me was it included a letter from O. He must have written it from prison and asked her to send it to me. He hinted over at the money in the account, but indirectly. If LaTavia got wind of that, he'd never hear the end of it. I ignored it.

Then my grandmother called with my mother on a three-way asking for money and apologizing for her indiscretions as a parent all in the same breath. Needless to explain why, I changed dormitories on campus, privatizing my address and telephone number. I knew they wouldn't visit. People in the hood never go anywhere. Since then, I've minimized the information I gave my brother. He didn't mean for any of them to reach me and was even willing to have his peoples who were in the same prison as O "handle" him, but I begged him to drop it. I explained how responding to it would confirm where I was, and I didn't want that at all.

I chatted a little bit more with my Akeem and left. It's always hard leaving him. He, along with Chyna, were the only positive references of home I cherished other than my grandparents. Everything else was gloomy. I hated the thought of Jersey. I stopped at a nearby outlet to do a little shopping to kill time. After an hour or so I headed to the airport. Now that I'd seen my brother, I couldn't be happier to leave.

On the plane ride home, I got comfortable in my seat and immediately tried to relax. My mind wrestled with so much. I had so much to deal with, specifically a line item labeled **A.D. Jacobs**.

Panting. Sweating. The cogs of my mind racing. I'd just awakened from another nightmare consisting of home—J-Boog, bullets, and my punctured heart. I hated them. Despised their haunting nature. I thought I'd escaped them each time I went long periods without them. But when they came, I was reminded that no matter how far from home I've physically traveled, I was still a slave to those deadly circumstances. To my fate. No matter how often I tried, it was clear I was meant to be alone. Exiled to a fucked up land called loneliness, solitude.

It was Sunday morning, five days after my blow up with Azmir. Often on Sunday mornings, in lieu of attending church like I did as a kid, I would reflect on my life—the good and bad. One thing I no longer had to worry about on my "bad list" was how I was going to have to repay Sebastian. That problem had weighed on me for a long time. Having it off my shoulders was certainly a huge respite.

That sense of relief brought my stream of thoughts to Azmir. *The man with the gold pocket watch.* That damn pocket watch flooded the forefront of my mind. My guilt had finally slapped me in the face. *Doomed to my fate.* I was perturbed by his benevolence, but he made it clear that paying off Sebastian wasn't a loan.

Wonder if he's changed his mind given my blow up at his job.

His gesture was generous and could only mean he was truly interested in me. *Had I cut off my nose to spite my face?*

Resigned to this fucked up land called loneliness.

Remorse set in. I looked at the clock that read six twenty-three. In an instant, I decided to bite the bullet and tell Michelle what had taken place. I picked up the phone and when she answered, I unloaded more forcefully than I'd realized I had in me.

After I finished with the office fiasco there was an expectant pause. I gave her room to reply. But nothing.

"Shelly, you don't have to tell me. I know I've fucked up," I admitted preemptively.

She immediately hissed, "...royally!" I braced myself. "I don't know what else to say. I actually don't think I need to because I can see you feel like shit. What are you going do to get back in his good graces is all I want to know."

"I was thinking more on the traditional repentant side. A few things have come to mind," I answered confidently, having given it some thought over the past few days.

"They all had better be superior because you really need to redeem yourself. And you've been on the clock for a few days now. I can't believe you haven't apologized yet. No. I take that back. I forgot who I was talking to," she supplied dryly. She was upset with my behavior. Worst of all, she was disappointed in me.

I spent the next few minutes revealing my plan to her. She helped me with a few recommendations. I had decided to woo my way back into Azmir's favor, baller style. My next call went to Petey. I needed inside help to bring my plans into fruition. Azmir was a busy man, and I could barely get a moment of his time when he was chasing *me*. Now that I am the one doing the chasing, I had to use every resource available to me. I needed interference with his schedule, and I knew Ice Queen Peg wouldn't be very cooperative. I made plans for a Saturday and Petey agreed to have all of his assistants clear his schedule for that day and he would try to do what he could from his end. Then the expensive part: planning an event that would impress Azmir Jacobs.

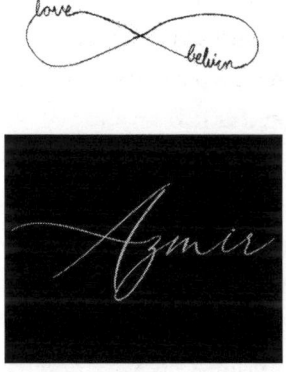

I was meeting with Big D when my phone alerted me of a text. I looked to find it was Rayna. I didn't know what to expect. I hadn't spoken to her since she spazzed out on me last week at the rec. I was beginning to think she was psycho. The only reason I wasn't fully convinced was because of her distance. Had she truly been a deranged woman she wouldn't have stayed away for so long.

Are you with her?

I was confused. Who was she referring to? Maybe she hit me by accident. *I'll play along.*

And she would be...?

My replacement.

I thought it was a cute attempt at breaking the ice. But she was going to have to come better than that. She was out of line that day at the rec.

Cute. What can I do for you? I replied in between conversing with Big D. I know it wasn't the most inviting response, but I had to see where all of this was going before making her think shit was all good.

Ouch. Well, I can see you're still salty with me. I guess I should just cut to the point. I'd like to apologize for my behavior and the awful things I said to you.

She was showing humility. A brother can't lie, I felt an immediate sense of relief and finally decided she wasn't totally crazy. *Good, because I really like Rayna.* In an honest moment, I would admit to missing her.

It's all gravy. Done deal.

No, It's not. My reaction and outburst were totally unacceptable. You didn't deserve that. Plus, seeing that we've made love I don't want our next encounter to be one of smashing.

Rayna tried to infuse a little humor and had a little game. Before I realized it, I had released a little snort. Big D looked annoyed. He gave me and my phone a once over, which said it all. I could see why he'd react. I'd chuckled like a little bitch. Even a fool could tell I was communicating with a woman. She had me intrigued and I was all in.

I accept your apology. Not sure about the lovemaking or smashing...don't want to choose the wrong method and have you come into the rec going postal and shit. I couldn't resist.

Haha. Really funny, Mr. Jacobs. ***extreme sarcasm here*** How soon can I see you? And don't tell me you'll get back to me after checking your schedule. I don't wanna be fit into your schedule, I want to BE your itinerary. How's tomorrow at 3PM.

She was aggressive. I liked it. But I still had to see if it was possible.

Indeed. Let me see what I can do in terms of moving things around. How long are we talking?

I had to know. I had just about every appointment for tomorrow canceled in the past three days. That has never happened before. It made room for me to catch up on things I'd been putting off because of work. Considering the fact I'd recently lined up a few flexible items when business plans got canceled, knowing the timing of this "meeting" would help a lot.

Plan to be preoccupied well into the nite. Meet me at the Irish Pub near LAX. See you then. She ended it there not leaving me room for rebuttal. She knew what she was doing. She had my attention.

After leaving the meeting with Big D, while Petey and I walked to the truck, I whistled an old jam: *"Sometimes I love her. Sometimes I love her not. I ain't letting her go."* I'm not sure where it came from, but it was on the dome.

Petey clowned me with, "This broad got yo' bitch ass singin'."

"What?" I asked but knew where he was going with it.

He continued to laugh with our muscle, Marcus. Petey was putting me on blast. I wasn't mad. As I've said before, this chick, Rayna, had me going.

"Yo, that thing with the goons in the "Wood" for tomorrow been pushed back. I told 'dem niggas not to holla at us until they got they shit in check," Petey informed me.

"I'm sure that didn't sit well with them. These young niggas are preemies. They lack patience and forethought. They want to go straight for power without learning the trade. I gotta feeling this youngin', Supreme, is gonna be a problem," I warned.

"I keep telling my little peoples that he fucks wit' to tell him to chill for a minute and he can have half those blocks. Word done been out for a minute that you retiring, I heard he threatening war and shit. You offering to meet with the little nigga should'a been all good, you know? He knew you was tryna' meet 'em half-way. I hear 'dem little niggas got arsenal," Petey informed.

"I'm tryna' bow out gracefully. Let them little niggas take shit too far. I got something for they asses," I declared.

"Yeah, 'dat's what I'm afraid of…killin' these kids. But this here is a game of honor. Fuck er'thing else." Petey agreed.

"Kid still fucking his mother?" I asked.

"Indeed."

"Let's keep that in our back pocket."

I felt in my gut something was going to pop off. I had a couple of entry level management individuals, also known as block captains, getting knocked and cuffed. I knew when a shake down by *One Time* was happening, which meant law enforcement was cracking down on street activity. I could also feel an adversary on the come up. Although these were damn near babies trying to run up on my territory, they were reckless. They shot first and recalled later when whatever substance they were high on had come down. They were worse than bitches. Bitches would cry immediately after causing irreparable damage. These young cats would wait 'til they entered the yard, become somebody's bitch, and *then* cry. I had seen it time and time again.

Call it my old age, but I saw how inner-city young black men all had the same ending—death or prison. This gang shit was out of control. I've always hated it but saw how it was an inevitable course for kids. They had no other options. Either kill for protection or be killed. I tried to offer a solution with my local basketball teams and funding a couple of *Boys and Girls Club*s. I also fund summer camps and overnight and day programs. I saw modest effects of it, but the young males had it hard. The game is fucked up and I was losing the stomach for it.

The next day I was headed for L.A. to see Rayna. I received a text from a number I didn't recognize. It read:

Hey, it's Trisha. I'm textin U from my friend's fone bcuz I left mine at the hotel this morning. Could U get it for me? xoxo

I had to laugh. This young ass girl thinks she's slick. I confiscated her phone before I sent her ass packing late last night. I do this often, especially with young girls because they love sharing pictures with their friends *and* on social sites. And this Trish chick wasn't any different. I met her at a *UCLA* basketball game a couple of months back. She sought me out through her girlfriend Wop had been involved with. Trisha was hot. Beautiful cocoa skin, long eyelashes, and a tight body. I could tell she knew she was dope, and I liked her aggressiveness. She kept eyeing me the whole time at the game and made her wishes known before we left the game that night. She told her girlfriend I reminded her of the first crush she had on an older guy, and she wanted to act out a few things she couldn't as a kid. She promised not to disappoint. *These young girls are off the damn chain.*

I gave her my number and we chatted a couple of times. Trisha had been begging to hook up, so I finally relented last night and got us a modest room. Shit, I was horny as hell. I ain't had no pussy in over a week and no good pussy since my time with Rayna in Phoenix. Good was an inoperative description—Rayna's pussy made me want to do things I couldn't admit to publicly. When we fucked in Phoenix, she let down all guards and offered herself to me wholly. She exposed her submissive capabilities and unleashed the beast in me. For the first time in my life, I'd made love to a woman. I can't explain what had gotten into me, only that we connected on a level I never knew existed. That experience demonstrated my needs of her no other woman could satisfy. It scared the shit out of me. Then she left me.

So, when this young and ripe Trisha came around, I was game. I figured she knew she had to come with it since she talked so much shit. I had Wop pick her up in my *Range* because his ride was being worked on. I'm sure he told her it was my truck. I know this because when I confiscated her phone while she was in the bathroom showering, I saw pictures of the inside of my ride. There were also pictures of the hotel room and the bathroom. She didn't manage any of me, but she did take a few of herself in the mirror with her bra and underwear on when she was getting ready.

I ordered room service and while we were eating in the dining area, she made all kinds of sexual gestures with her fork and spoon. She was twenty-one years old and drank like a damn sailor. I was cool with it just as long as she wasn't eighty-sixing everywhere. I'd been with young women her age and they rarely disappointed. She was another story. After all the teasing, she eventually fell to her knees and unbuckled my pants. When my jimmy popped out, she yelled, "Damn!" while staring at it and trying to figure out if she could handle it. It was downhill from there.

Her head game was whack and her sex was even worse. It lasted longer than I was prepared for because I couldn't bust. She had no rhythm and kept moaning like the shit was sexy. I was turned off. My dick started going down. I told her she was off the hook and to go shower. She must have seen I was disappointed and offered me head again. I declined and told her I'd call Wop to come and retrieve her.

I five fingered her phone when she left the room and that's when I noticed she sent out three texts. One had pictures of my ride, and the others were of the hotel suite. I don't know how she managed those, but she did. Needless to say, she wouldn't be seeing her phone again.

Reeling in my thoughts, I texted her back: **I'm not at the hotel. I'll have my man reimburse you for the phone. Peace.**

Okay, well it's a Droid. Thanks! xoxo

This dumb ass broad. That phone was some cheap ass sidekick. *Nice try*. That gave me a hearty laugh.

I was pulling up to the bar where I agreed to meet Rayna. It was an indistinct location and not a place I had ever known of people hanging out. I tossed my reservations and made my way inside.

When I walked through the door, I saw the place was half full. It smelled of smoke from people lighting up. The televisions were going and there was chatter from people interfacing. I saw no familiar faces in the place initially. I scanned the room until I saw Rayna, waving her arm patently caught my attention.

She sat at the bar and wore a huge grin on her face as I made my way to her. She stood to greet me, and I immediately noticed her cleavage. Her breasts announced themselves, they puffed like marshmallows in her halter dress. The dress was a wine color and cupped her breasts, fitted her waist, and fell down to her feet. I could tell she wasn't wearing a bra. She looked luscious. If she was trying to get back in good favor with me, she was well on her way. I gave her a hug and kiss on her forehead and noticed her inebriating fragrance. *Cool Water*.

The scent along with her soft feel carried a hint of familiarity of her sexuality. Her vulnerability. Her physical submission. Her emotional willingness. My heart stammered in my chest. *Fuck!*

"Look at you, all sexy...getting your grown woman on," I teased after we embraced, hoping to hide my excitement of seeing her.

She blushed, "You don't look half bad yourself. You're always dapper." She gave me a once over as she nervously brushed the back of her neck. "I thought you stood me up. You're usually very prompt."

"I know I'm a few minutes behind. Traffic is a bitch today," I explained. I couldn't help but notice her eyes. She kept batting them. That told me she wanted to present herself demurely, which was the exact opposite of what she had me believe during our last encounter. I was all in.

The bartender came with a glass of brandy for me. This meant she ordered in anticipation of my arrival. I took a sip and nodded in approval.

She leisurely informed, "You're going to have to gulp instead of sip. We're running late."

"Running late? Did I miss something?" With raised brows, I was confused. I thought the plan was for us to talk over drinks.

"You look baffled," she jeered with a cunningly sexy smirk.

"...because I am."

"I told you I wanted to apologize. I left out the part about making amends. Finish your drink. We're about to get started," she ordered.

I was definitely perplexed at this point. I took a minute to ponder what she said. *I hate surprises.* I took another nip at my drink. I wasn't good with others' acts of spontaneity. But with what Rayna was wearing, I was certainly game. It took a lot of internal struggles for me to fight off my arousal.

I looked Rayna square in the eyes in search of answers. I hadn't spoken to her in damn near two weeks. Where was she going with all of this? I didn't like being kept in the dark, but her confidence and excitement seemed unerring, so I conceded.

I took my last guzzle, "A'ight. I'm game."

With a knowing smile she collected her things from the bar, stood, and extended her smooth caramel toned arm to me and flirtatiously muttered, "This way, Mr. Jacobs."

I paused for a minute, once again reading her before accepting her hand and then following her.

We went to *LAX* and to say I was beyond perplexed would be repetitive. Where was she taking me? She asked if I had I.D. on me, which was senseless because any responsible adult would. Before I knew it, we were checking in at the ticket booth.

She has tickets for us to go to Santa Barbara? What the fuck?

We had a few minutes before boarding and decided to retreat to a restaurant to have another drink before ascending in the air. I couldn't resist, I had to ask, "Rayna...baby, where are we going?"

She laughed and with a bright smile she answered, "To dinner," as if it were no big deal.

"Shit. There are hundreds of restaurants near this airport. Why would we need to board a plane to get to one?"

"Because I want to experience something new with you. It's my way of making amends. Just relax. I'll have you back in town before the night's end." Through a warm and seductive smile, she assured me.

Against my comfort level, I went with the flow. A short time later, we boarded the plane and in forty-five minutes, we were in Santa Barbara. There was a car waiting for us. We took a ten-minute ride to a colossal sized ranch. The sun had begun to retire as we were seated in an outdoor dining area overlooking splendid nature. A beautiful view of the terrain was at our feet. The balcony where we sat was covered in cobblestone. And there was soft music playing, blending perfectly well with the backdrop as we sat in the open air. There were only a few other patrons there. You could tell this was somewhat exclusive. It was nice...real nice. Her game was tight.

The waiter approached our table, and after introducing himself and informing us of the specials, he asked, "May I start you off with something to drink?" Before I could answer, Rayna ordered me another glass of brandy and a cocktail for herself. I felt cared for. I raised my brows in pleasant surprise.

"Hahaha! You like that, huhn?" she asked in a boastful manner. "I didn't want to get you *Patron Silver* after you've had brandy. I'm not trying to get you sick and take advantage of you," she teased.

As I brushed my hands in my lap I replied, "Oh, no, don't do that."

We both laughed. I could see her breasts shake through her halter top.

"So, what have you been up to during our hiatus?" she asked in an attempt to start a conversation.

"You know me: work, work, and more work. Same shit new day. How about yourself?" I wanted to get into her head. I was still off kilter with this *date* we were on.

"Ummmm...I've been dancing, working, helping Michelle out with Erin." She took a swig of her drink, and I took note of her slanted eyes gazing upon me.

"Yeah, I've noticed you helping Michelle out a lot. Is everything okay?" Michelle didn't look too well at my birthday party.

"Well, yes and no," she replied before taking another sip of her Cosmo. "Michelle has breast cancer that has advanced to stage three. She's been undergoing a much more aggressive form of chemotherapy. It's depleting her energy which is no competition for a toddler. So, she needs all the help she can get," Rayna shared.

"Oh, wow. I'm sorry to hear this. It's fucked up...pardon my

French. I didn't know you had so much on your plate." I was short of words and didn't know where to go from there.

Rayna chimed in with, "There's a lot you don't know about me, Azmir. Much of this is because I am not an open book. I have... major trust issues and it's been a huge handicap for me over the years. But I've been able to skate passed it until now," she disclosed.

I kept quiet to hear what she was trying to get out. It seemed a little painful for her, but she was trying to get something off her chest, and I was all ears. I stapled my eyes to hers agreeing to listen to whatever she was prepared to share.

"Virtually, the only person I've been able to open up to is Michelle and I'm sure it's come with some headaches for her. Being so guarded provides me protection and allows me to...to cruise beneath the radar with minimal damage. But it also comes with a great deal of loneliness. I mean, I can take on a physical relationship without involving my heart with the best of them...but encountering you has...has illuminated my problems," she paused with that.

As she spoke, she avoided eye contact with me. Rayna was incredibly uncomfortable, but I couldn't hold her hand on this; she had to muster the courage to express herself. The one thing terrifying me concerning Rayna was her inability to open up to me and freely convey her feelings, I needed this. I took a sip of my drink, never leaving her eyes.

She continued with, "I am, by no means, asking you to take me in like a lost puppy. But I am telling you...this...this thing between us..." she paused again. This time she chuckled to herself and craned her neck further showing her unease of this conversation. I waited.

She looked at me and I maintained my fixated gaze on hers, showing she had my undivided attention. She jerked her chin in the air trying to regain composure. She even took a sip of her drink. At this point, humor had overtaken both of us, and together we laughed. Hell, I was even a little nervous at what was coming.

She finally forged ahead, "This thing between us *is good*. I like it and would like to see where it goes."

At that, I nodded my head and broke my silence with, "So would I."

"Would you?" she asked and sighed in relief.

We laughed again. It was a bit awkward.

"Sure, I would. Why wouldn't I?" I admitted as the waiter came with our first course.

I picked up my fork, ready to dig in when she called out, "Azmir."

I looked up at her. "I really do apologize for my behavior. I hope to one day erase that image of me out of your memory." She had the most sincere and docile look in her eyes. I was taken.

"It's all good, little lady. Don't sweat it," I tried to assure her.

"No, it is and was not. I am truly sorry." Rayna looked away as she was contemplating her next set of words before returning her gaze upon me. "I'm not comfortable with the money thing. I hope you can understand that and honor it." Her words were soft and earnest.

"What about *the money thing*, Ms. Brimm?" I needed to be clear. I am a wealthy man and didn't like to be criticized for how I courted a woman, particularly one I was very interested in. After this moment of candor, I knew Ms. Brimm was that woman. She was what I wanted to acquire, and I wanted to employ every resource available to me to gain her, to mark and brand her mine. *Shit – this feels crazy!*

There was a shifting going on during this meal on this vineyard changing my world forever. This force had a name.

Rayna Brimm.

"I just don't need it. The car was a huge help and I really appreciate it...a lot. But you've shared a sneak peek of your mind with me, and I am in awe of your brilliance and tenacity." *The tenacity I am planning to exercise to win your heart.* I thought as she paused. "...that's all I can bear right now; all I want and need."

I nodded for the sole purpose of making Rayna feel secure. I knew the only way I could possess her was to garner her trust. She was delicate and I should move accordingly. I was resigned to making her mine from that moment on. I would try on her terms.

We enjoyed a delicious dinner and once we were done, the waiter came with a box of *Padron Family Reserve #44 Maduro* and *La Aroma de Cuba Mi Amor Magnifico* among other stogies. I had to indulge. Rayna and I engaged in meaningful conversation while there basking in the picturesque scenery. She tried explaining her perspective on me paying off the Sebastian dude and tried to the best of her ability to describe her insecurities with trust. I felt her.

We walked the ranch and were back to our normal speed with laughing and light banter exchange. I could admit we had chemistry—sexually and mentally. It was just the emotional aspect we had to reel in.

We talked so much when I finally glanced at the time I jumped. "Oh my goodness! It's late. We have to head back to the airport."

"Damn, I'd forgotten our means of transportation." Azmir noted lowly. I could tell I'd accomplished something very few could say they had. I had managed to relax Azmir so, that time was completely forgotten about.

On the plane we didn't say much. After buckling in, he turned and looked over to me. *This man is heavenly handsome.* I briefly drank him in, his eyes were piercing under his long lashes and his lips were moist and inviting. *I remember those lips all over me.*

He looked exhausted and sexy as all hell. "Ms. Brimm, this was a nice surprise...*in more ways than one.*"

My heart fluttered as I smiled sheepishly. "You're sexy even when you're tired, you know that?" I declared.

His eyes shot up to mine. "Oh, do I look tired?" he scoffed.

"Yeah," I answered with a giggle.

Azmir paused with his eyes squinted and looking forward, "Among other things, I feel like I've been on a physical and emotional journey with you this evening." Then his gaze returned to my eyes causing scorching blood to course through my veins, but I was unsure of his sentiment.

It must have worn on my face because he snorted as he tapped my knee, "This is a very good thing, Ms. Brimm. Now I feel like we're getting somewhere," as he continued searching my eyes. His tone soothed with promise.

I parted my lips in hopes of his comment being a prelude to a kiss. But he turned forward and rested his eyes.

I wanted him and bad. This made the forty-five-minute plane ride back to L.A. seem like an eternity. I wrestled with potential reasons why he hadn't kissed me or shown any affection. *If he said we're getting somewhere, wouldn't that mean together? Did I divulge too much? Did I give him the impression I was saying goodbye?*

I pulled up to his car to drop him off. He turned over to me and my breath hitched in anticipation of what was to come.

He only asked, "What are you about to get into?"

I figured he was making small talk to end the night comfortably. Much to my dismay, I obliged with, "I'm not sure. I may stop and check on Michelle and Erin before turning in. I don't know if they're home though. I'll call as soon as I pull off."

"Okay." And then there was a brief pause. "Thanks again... though I'm feeling like I've just been pimped," he joked regarding our time together. We both laughed at that one. *Men are so egotistical.* He left and as the car door slammed shut, simultaneously lightning struck through my heart.

What the fuck have I done? This did not end the way I had intended it to.

I called Michelle, but to no avail, so I headed straight home. By the time I got in, she called me. I began my vomiting of the mouth, giving her the full rundown of my romantic evening as I threw my purse down. I retreated to my bedroom, turned on the shower and peeled off my jewelry.

"Shelly, I fucked up. Why do you think he didn't ask to hang out?" Closing the summary of my evening, I was desperate for clues.

"Well, you didn't exactly ask him either. Why didn't you ask him if he wanted to extend the evening?" she asked out of pure innocence. I knew deep down inside she hurt for me.

I was so emotional I couldn't process my thoughts.

"The bottom line is he didn't ask and we're not together right here and right now," I whined into the phone trying to fight back my tears. That's when I heard the doorbell sound.

"Is that your doorbell?" Michelle asked in shock. Unless it's her, I never have guests. And at this ungodly hour it was unheard of. I was so wrapped up in my thoughts I didn't think to ask who was there before opening the door. I just swung it open.

"Azmir?" I murmured. I couldn't believe he stood before me...all six feet and four inches. He didn't wear his usual panty snatching smirk or coochie creaming smile. Instead, he had his heart-wrenching, sexy ass, passionate deep glower.

Michelle was speaking in the phone, but I couldn't make out a word because I was enraptured by his presence. The sight of Azmir was so divine it hurt. He swooped down on me, pulling me into him at the small of my back. His mouth swung open as he reached down in target of mine. All the while he backed me into the wall as he closed the door behind us. His kiss was hard and purposeful. His tongue was agile in search of every portion of me as he devoured my mouth and fragmented me into pieces. I groaned involuntarily. That's when he came out of his trance and looked me in the eyes. His gaze immediately diverted to the phone.

"Tell them you have to go," he demanded under no uncertain terms.

I looked at the phone before pulling it back up to my ear and muttered like a child, "Shelly?"

"Is that Azmir?" she quizzed as he stood erect there before me and I looked up into his eyes.

"*Un–huhn!*" I answered, not moving from his sensuous gaze.

"*Girl, bye! Call me in the morning!*" Michelle shouted. She probably really wanted to say I should have hung up in her ear long before then.

Azmir gently removed the phone from my hand. Not taking his eyes off me, he walked it back to the end table near the couch and then returned to me. He wrapped me in his embrace again, this time by grabbing my lower back and thrusting my body into his. His other hand gripped my face taking me into his. His tongue ran silky through my mouth, and I felt sedated by his aggressive passion.

"You think you were going to leave me once again?" he growled somewhat angrily.

I didn't know what to say. Before I could think of anything, he lifted his chin up towards the back of the house, scowl still in tow.

"Is your shower running?"

"*Ummm...* Yeah," I had to come back down to earth to process the question.

"So, you left me to shower, aye?"

He effortlessly lifted me, at least a foot off the floor with my feet dangling, charging to my bedroom and then into my master bathroom where the water was running.

Letting me down, he kept his eyes glued to me as he stepped out of his shoes and placed his mobile phones on the vanity. Then he lifted me and had me straddle him at his waist. He continued to kiss me long and passionately as he walked me into the shower.

Crap! Is he really this bold of a lover?

Not sparing my hair, he let the water sprinkle onto me as his lips left my face and trailed down my neck. I began to moan. He placed one hand on my ass and his grip made my body jerk as his tongue descended down my cleavage. With his alternate hand, he undid the top of my halter.

Damn. How does he know how to unman my dress?

The halter pieces collapsed, and my breasts tumbled out of their restraints. There were so many sensations taking over my body. Drips of water began hitting my nipples and as in an automatic response, my hips started gyrating. I wanted...no—*needed*—Azmir inside of me. He raised me up effortlessly so my breasts were level with his mouth and began licking my nipples. Licking turned into sucking and sucking turned into pulling. I swear I could climax from that alone.

"Oh. My. God. Azmir!" I panted as he continued to give equal attention to my nipples.

"What made you think you could just leave me..." He licked my nipple and greedily kneaded my backside. "...hanging twice in a row?" He stopped. "You must not know Azmir Jacobs, Ms. Brimm. Allow me to acquaint you."

He took my dress and drew it up until it was entirely at my waist and ordered me to take it off by pulling it over my head. He didn't want to let me down. With a little time and hassle I removed the dress over my head and tossed it to the floor. While doing so I could feel him tussling beneath me. He then hooked my thong with his thumb, seeming to assess it with his fingers all while his tongue was buried deep in my mouth. The next thing I heard was a rip...and then another as I felt my panties being pulled from beneath me. He was an animal, and I loved every minute of it. He took his thumb and found my pearl massaging it as he sucked on my neck.

"Azmir!" I cried out.

Azmir didn't answer, but he eventually removed his hands from in front of me and then lowered my body down toward his pelvic area where I felt him enter me. I reclined my body until my head touched the shower wall. Coincidentally, it thrust my sex into him. I somehow opened my eyes and caught him gaping at me with such raw intensity. I could not control my sounds. I became aware of my mouth being opened when I had to spit out water. I held on to him by his shoulders and eventually his neck.

His face was unreadable, in a scowl as he plunged into me, forcing my walls to make room for him. I kept clapping my sex into him. I couldn't help myself. Azmir felt good as fuck inside of me. As he pounded me and I him, you could hear the sounds of our skin meeting and that of my breasts flapping. Every time I looked into his sexy gaze, I could swear the sex deepened. I became lost in him, willing my body over to his command and pleasure, submitting again to his carnal needs and desire to possess my body. My entire pelvic area began to go numb, and I could only feel what was happening internally. I knew it was coming.

As my orgasm began its first wave, I couldn't help but shout his name. My rhythmic thrusts had turned into wild gyrations on his lap. In that moment, I felt so libidinous...so erotic. I bit my lip to stifle my cries. His eyes loosened as he watched me come all over him; hard and forceful. And through my drunken haze I could see, suddenly he didn't appear as angry. It was as if all his fury had washed away while a violent orgasm wrecked my body.

He backed us out of the shower and rested himself against the counter of the vanity where he pulled me closer to him and shifted his arms, one-by-one, underneath each of my legs while I straddled him. Eventually both his hands were hooked onto the back of my shoulders, and he drew my lower body closer to him. I reached up to kiss him with little effort as he held me so close. I left his lips and traveled to his ears as he continued to bury himself in me. His mouth was on my left shoulder. I felt his teeth grip me intensely yet deliciously as he pounded away at my core. I felt a sensation traveling down to my vagina.

Azmir pumped and thrust and pounded into me. He was aggressive and domineering in his pulling down on my shoulders, forcing himself deeper and deeper. I loved this, his possession and greedy need of my body, *of me*. I could feel him growing even larger inside of me as if his length could become more immense. Oddly, I knew he was about to explode. Within seconds he roared with passion, releasing himself inside of me. No words. No names. No pleas. Just explosion. I was caught up in blissful realms with Azmir.

He let me down. My legs wobbled so I had to hold on to him until I was able to gather my bearings. He was muted. While I was there resting my face against his hard bubbled chest. I realized he was drenched from the shower.

Crap. He has to get out of these clothes.

I pushed up off him and began to pull his shirt up. He assisted by pulling it off. His T-shirt followed. Next, I pulled down his denims. As I knelt down to pull them from his legs his remaining erection startled me, it was sheathed in rubber. Azmir snickered as he pulled it off. *When did he put on a condom? Shit! I didn't think to protect myself! This never happens. What the hell has come over me?* I pulled off his pants, boxer briefs, and socks.

"You can *now* go shower." We both laughed. "I'll go grab a towel set," I shared as he stepped back into the shower.

When I returned, I noticed he had begun lathering up his hands. I jumped in with him, poured shower gel into my scrub and began washing him from neck to toe. I admired his body at every discovery. Azmir was handsomely chiseled. His carvings were a masterpiece. His shoulders were broad and hard. His back was smooth and incised. His six-pack was calling my name. And the trail of hair from his navel to his manhood was so inviting to my tongue. I had to remember I was a guest to his body; not the co-owner so I kept my composure the best I could.

His legs were well toned. And his toes were surprisingly beautiful. I could scrub him for hours but what I really wanted was him inside of me again. As he rinsed off, his phone began to sound from the vanity, where he'd laid it before discarding his wet clothing. That damn phone was my rival at times. It reminded me I was on borrowed time with Azmir because he was in high demand.

He looked at me as to ask if I minded him attending to it.

"Oh, go. I'll just finish up and be right out."

As he stepped out, I rolled my eyes.

After my shower, I walked out into my bedroom and found Azmir sitting on the side of my bed with a towel wrapped around his tapered waist. He was viewing the contents of his pant pockets on my nightstand.

"I took the liberty of running your clothes through the washer. I'll put them in the dryer once they're done," I explained.

He smiled, very contented. *Whew!* I was fluttered with relief.

"I guess this means Mr. Jacobs is stuck with me for a little while longer," I teased still uneasy about his desire to stay. I didn't know if he wanted to run out and tend to whatever his call was about. I chose to be more aggressive about my wanting to be in his presence a little while longer.

He gave me a squint as if to say he was confused. That was followed by a smile. That smile was my cue. I looked down at my toes to cure my nerves before dropping my towel. When it hit the floor, I looked up at him to gauge his reaction. He looked pleasantly shocked. I walked over to him and straddled him while standing. I lifted his head and buried my tongue in his mouth. My inner walls throbbed. It was as if I was not satisfied just minutes ago. I wanted more. He grabbed the back of my thighs and began to caress them while I sucked on his bottom lip.

"Can I have more?" I asked. This time I was surer of myself and my ability to keep him there with me. My confidence had returned.

His hands ascended to my backside. He exhaled hard and ardently. "Ms. Brimm, at this moment you can have anything you ask. I am so caught up, control of my body has fuckin' fleeted," he admitted while directing my attention to his soldier fighting for attention underneath the towel. When I looked back up, his eyes were drunken with desire.

I loosened his towel and grabbed him in my hands and began stroking from base to tip. I couldn't believe how much it extended beyond what I originally saw. He was ready. I stood him up, reached underneath the decorative pillows and pulled the blanket back. I nudged him to lie down. He did. I grabbed another condom off the nightstand where all of his personal belongings lay. I was in control and held all of my faculties this round.

As I guided the condom on, I provocatively licked my lips. He gave me his panty snatching smirk and I scooted up to make myself comfortable in my new seat. One thing about being on top of Azmir is taking in all of him. And there was certainly a lot to take in. But he was so satisfying, I loved obliging his size. I began plunging into him as I stared deeply into his eyes. He did the same. Azmir loved watching me as our bodies fused.

"What are you thinking about?" I couldn't help but ask as I grinded.

"If you're making love to me." I stilled. I couldn't believe my ears. Thinking a frog must have jumped into my throat, I couldn't speak. He kept a steady expression on his face but still had an intoxicated look in his eyes telling me he was enjoying me.

"What do you think?"

He swallowed as he closed his eyes and smoothly pushed into my hips urging me to continue my thrusts. "If this is just smashing, I can't imagine how much better making love would be...because I am in a place rarely visited."

I was all in. I went down to kiss him as I continued my ride. He pulled his arms around me and began to rhythmically meet my plunges. He gripped me tightly as if he wanted to be one with me. I tried to remain in control but every time his sweet breath hit my face and his grip intensified, I lost more and more of myself. I was floating further and further away from my center of gravity. My body was afloat and my mind drifted after it. I didn't like the escape of lucidity.

"Azmir, what are you...doing to me?" I cried out passionately, my face buried in his neck. I tried raising my body to see his face. I could hardly lift my torso from his fierce grip but was able to move my head a little. His eyes were closed shut as if he were fixated on something internally.

Damn! Could this man make an ugly face? He is so fucking sexy.

My body started to tremble against Azmir's forceful thrusts.

Wait! This isn't supposed to be happening so soon.

Just that abruptly, I erupted, melted all around Azmir. I felt it all the way down in my heated toes. Azmir must have too because all I heard was the sweetest, most gentle, ever-manly calling of my name, "Oooooh, Rayna!"

It made me gyrate like no other time in my life, which prolonged our orgasms.

The next morning, as my body was awakening from a hard sleep, I began getting flashbacks of my most recent memories. Azmir. His scent. His touch. The sound of his harsh breathing. I could smell him. That's when reality hit me, and I remembered *he was here last night.* I reached over to caress him. His back. His chest...*hell*—anywhere. I didn't feel him. I opened my eyes to search and no Azmir. I jumped up.

No! Did he leave while I was asleep?

"Ms. Brimm, good morning," he greeted with his coochie creaming smile. It was a morning *must have* a girl could get used to.

He was sitting in the chaise Michelle had given me, making the damn thing look good. He looked refreshed in his jeans exposing the band of his boxer briefs while holding his *Blackberry*. I looked at the time on the nightstand and discovered it was eight seventeen a.m. I didn't know what time I had finally gone to bed last night. I remembered getting Azmir's clothes out of the dryer and ironing his jeans and shirt. I didn't know what time he would be ready to leave so I wanted his things ready for him. Then I washed and blow-dried my hair in the powder room so the noise wouldn't wake him. After, I was beyond exhausted and climbed into bed with him. In his sleep, he pulled me closer and buried his face in my neck. I rested peacefully.

I see he found his clothes.

"I had an epiphany while you were asleep," Azmir spoke soft and evenly. "Judging by your reaction moments ago when you thought I'd left, I can deduce you felt similar to how I did last night when you dropped me off."

I squinted my eyes. I was lost. Seriously confused.

"I've fallen for you. I haven't fallen for a woman in years...but I'm man enough to admit it. The question is what do we do about it."

He looked at me in search of an answer. I was short of one. I was also puzzled as to where this was going. He waited. I nervously combed my hair back with my fingers while I searched for an answer and began to get self-conscious about my appearance.

"Please don't try to fix your hair on my account. I find it very...organically appealing," he growled lowly.

Organic? It was all over my head in a huge muffin I imagined.

He put his phone down and walked over to the bed. With my arms, I cupped my naked breasts hidden underneath the sheet. He sat next to me. *Crap.* He was asking for an answer. *I don't have one!*

"I'm a little out of my league here, Mr. Jacobs," I offered cowardly.

Loser!

"Hmmmmmm..." he followed.

Did I disappoint him? Shiiiiiiiit, Rayna!

"Why don't we start by spending more time together. Last night was good," he murmured as he played with my ruffled mane. "Not the sex...*well, that was...phenomenal*," he smirked shyly.

I coyly snorted as well. He started planting small and soft kisses from my neck down my arms.

"Why don't we try to sync schedules? You send yours to my assistant and I'll have him send you mine weekly. That way we can plug each other in regularly," he offered with the most sincere look in his eyes.

I was still a little out of it. "I don't think I have a formal schedule the way you do, Azmir," I admitted. I was distracted by his lips embracing my upper torso.

"Oh, you do," he uttered matter-of-factly. "Between work, dance and your activities with Michelle, you're a very busy woman."

Hmmmmmm... I guess he's right.

Michelle and Erin's activities alone consumed me, and they were all scheduled in advance.

Perhaps this could work.

"Okay, I think we can make that happen."

My thoughts must have been weighing on my face again because he asked, "What's wrong?"

I lacked the articulation to explain I didn't know how that would help or where he wanted it to get us. Hell—it was too early for such a heavy conversation. I didn't even know what I'd be doing *this* morning.

All I could come up with was, "What's next?" as I searched his face for an answer.

His face twisted up in a smile, amused by my statement.

"Well, it's still morning, so breakfast." His look of amusement shifted into a panty snatching smirk. "And there's nothing I'd enjoy more than eating *you*. I love the taste..." He kissed my shoulder. "...and the feel of you pulsating against my tongue." He then released the sheet from my arms' grip. My breathing caught and my insides clenched.

"Lay back and watch me enjoy my meal," he commanded.

And with that, I rested back on the pillow and allowed Mr. Jacobs to have his way with me.

CHAPTER 2

Rayna

It had been nearly a week since our makeup and Azmir had just returned from Massachusetts late the night before. My strong-willed stubbornness would not allow me to invite myself over to his place for a fix, *a taste of A.D.* when he landed the evening before.

When I finished up with my last patient, I picked up the telephone and called out to the reception area to ask Sharon about the rest of my appointments. I was plotting, gauging if I could creep next door to see Azmir. I wasn't quite sure about what I would do if he were there but decided to figure that out later. Sharon informed me of two patients that had yet to arrive. That was all I needed.

In desperate haste, I asked her to hurry and reschedule the two appointments. The flower vase filled with a beautiful arrangement Azmir had sent over almost hit the floor when my handbag swept it as I sprinted out of my office. On a mission, I was flying next door to the rec. In no time I reached the waiting area and heard Sharon say in quick speed, "Oh, and Mr. Jacobs called a few times while you were with patients. He asked that you call next door when you were available." I don't think I let Sharon finish her sentence as I jetted out the door.

Minutes later, I was seated in the waiting area of Azmir's office. My stomach was filled with jittery butterflies. I had been fantasizing about him for days. It had been a grueling four days since the last time he was inside of me, I was starved for his touch.

It was about three thirty p.m. and Peg wasn't as cold as our first encounter, but she still made it known she was in control. I tried to crack a smile at her as a sign of waving the white flag; I needed her as an ally not an adversary. She managed to squeeze out a nod as if to tell me it was the only semblance of friendliness, I was going to get from her.

Azmir's office door opened and out came about a dozen of his rec staff members, from what I could tell by their emblemed polo shirts. It didn't appear to be a happy meeting, no one was wearing a smile on their face but that of gloom. After they filed out, I saw Azmir. He rubbed his forehead while straining his eyelids as if he were stressed and tired. When his eyes had finally landed on mine, he smiled appreciatively. I felt a clench in my valley and my legs tightened, as if I needed to add any more lecherous torture than I'd already had in the past few hours just thinking about him.

"Ms. Brimm," he greeted professionally, but with the widest smile. He motioned, welcoming me into his office. "...have a seat," he continued as he roved past me to Peg's desk.

"Peg, what time did you request to leave early?" he asked.

I couldn't quite hear the rest of their dialogue once in his office.

When Azmir returned to the office, he strode past me towards his desk where he placed a file and asked, "Have you eaten?"

I looked down at the floor thinking about the answer to that question. I had met with Michelle at eleven under the guise of a business meeting and because I had so much to fill her in on, I'd only had an iced cappuccino.

"Now that I think about it, I've only had a small bowl of fruit and an iced cappuccino since breakfast."

He cocked his head to the side pushing his tongue into his molars, turning me the hell on per usual, as he processed my answer. I didn't know if that was a good thing or bad, but I wouldn't ask.

"I was trying to catch you for lunch. When I spoke to Sharon, she said you'd left for a meeting before lunch, so I tried to be squeezed into your schedule. I ordered Italian."

I really didn't hear what he said because I was too busy daydreaming about slaying him right on his office chair. I sat there drinking in his irresistible presence. Today he was dressed less formal than his usual business attire. His lengthy frame stood tall in gray tailored suit pants and a well-fitted black dress shirt with black oxfords. His rectangular belt buckle was visible, though the Prada banner was vaguely printed on the bottom right corner of the face. Azmir oozed class and elegant taste. I had visions of him strapping my arms together with it just as he had during our last time together while on the back of his cabin cruiser when he fucked me into oblivion against the backdrop of the sun setting on the Pacific while we were on our way back from dinner on Coronado Island.

That night was magical. We made love under hues of red, orange, brown and gray—the best night light I'd ever seen in my life. Azmir seemed to have come alive as rain drizzled over us. I asked that we go inside the cabin, and he adamantly declined, offering to pay to have my hair done the following day.

Damn. I recalled vividly how his strong hip thrusts rivaled that of the ocean against the boat while tiny drops from the sky fell upon my tauten nipples, intensifying the experience. I came with a thunder nature couldn't match. I screamed so loud and riotously as I melted around Azmir who, as he whispered commendations of my outburst in my ear saying no one could hear but him *and he wanted to hear it all*, plunged deeply into me relentlessly. Every last orgasm he graciously conferred bruised my vocal cords. *An amazing experience.*

I was stunned to learn he owned a boat and knew how to operate it. He said he bought it when he purchased the Marina Del Rey apartment from an associate desperate to dump everything and move. He figured he'd get a boating license and enjoy the experience. *Thank goodness for the boat, the license, and the man.*

Breaking my reverie was a knock at the door. Azmir announced it was okay to come in. Peg rolled in a silver cart with white linen. The cart was loaded with food from fried calamari, spaghetti, penne in vodka sauce, lasagna to chicken Caesar salad and rolls. I was floored. *I had been on this man's mind just as much as he was on mine today...well, maybe for different reasons.* It was extremely thoughtful.

"What would you like to drink?" Peg asked.

Azmir eyes traveled over to me.

I guess I looked dumbfounded because Azmir answered for me, "A few bottles of water, lemonade and a bottle of Pinot Noir, please."

"Yes, Mr. Jacobs," she acknowledged before exiting.

I then thought to wash my hands, so I headed to the en suite bathroom. He got up to move over to his desk at the same time and my backside brushed against his pelvic area. I peered back at him as if to say excuse me when I noticed his gaze on me with heavy lecherously slit eyes. After leaving the bathroom, I saw Peg had returned with the beverages.

"Is that all, Mr. Jacobs?" she asked.

He glanced at me to see if I needed anything else. He never took his eyes off me when he answered, "That'll be all, Peg. Let me know when you're leaving for the day."

I could tell he wanted me. At this point it was written across his damn forehead. I had to indulge myself or I would have burst. I walked over to him slowly, I wanted to be sure I was really picking up those vibes so I wouldn't make a fool of myself at his place of business.

Once I reached him, I stood on the tips of my toes and kissed him just with my lips. I figured I'd see how receptive he was to that before I went any further. To my surprise, he grabbed me at the small of my back, reached down and threw his tongue into my mouth. It was over at that point.

I began unbuckling his belt, then I unzipped his pants. I was on a mad hunt for his tool that had haunted my every thought that day. When I found it, it told me I was thought of as well and I began to stroke it from base to tip. It was so long and its skin—soft and smooth, *velvety*. The muscle...*the muscle* was nice and hard. With each stroke I threw my tongue further in his mouth and Azmir growled with pleasure. When he could no longer take it, he turned me around, awarding chaste kisses down my neck while leading me to his desk. Once there, his strong arms reached up my pencil skirt in search of my panties. *Oops!* I didn't have any on. I'd taken them off in anticipation of this.

His intoxicated eyes fell upon me, and I whispered, "I've been craving this all day. I didn't want to waste any time."

My heart raced as I awaited a reaction. Azmir didn't speak, but I saw the twitching of his jaw muscles as he processed the invitation. He moved papers and folders out of the way and sat me on his desk after pulling my skirt up to my waist. Azmir got on his knees taking a trip down to my private parts. His skilled tongue was firm and quick this time, and after only a few seconds of this I couldn't control myself. My legs were jerking along with my back spasms, but my orgasm wasn't close enough for me to have felt the sensations I was experiencing. I didn't like the intensity of the pleasure I was feeling because just as with all of my previous experiences with Azmir, I had no control. *Damn Azmir and his oral skills!*

"Let it go, baby. I need to be inside of you," he urged breathing against me.

That sent me over the edge. When the time arrived for me to climax, I had to muzzle my cries. *This* is what I had been fantasizing about all day. *This* is where I wanted to be with Azmir...in sheer bliss. For those few seconds in paradise, I was in love with this man. He *was* Divine!

When I was done, he lifted me off the desk and bent me over. I wondered what took him so long to enter me until I heard the unwrapping of the condom. *Damn!* The thought of a condom had escaped me once again.

He took me from behind. As I felt the wide crest of his penis at my entrance, I had to keep from screaming as he entered me so forcefully. I had to get used to his enormous size.

Once fully inside he asked, "You okay?"

"*Mmmhmm,*" was all I could give.

He started off slow. Azmir was long, wide, and heavy, filling me to the hilt. I bore every inch of him; he wanted me to. Spread across his desk I felt bare. Vulnerable. Something he always pushed for without words. And I had no choice but to adjoin with him on a level far more than physical, although how intimate I didn't quite know.

After a while, I could tell he was ready for his release because of the speed he had embarked on and the tight grip he had on my hips. I moved his one hand up my back to release the unbearable impassioned clench. His other hand followed suit. I had begun to flex my walls and enjoy his strokes. I felt him pull out almost fully and then back in. He was long stroking me deliciously.

"Damn, Brimm," he cried out desperately in a low and labored tone, making me cream even more. I even had the inclination to start throwing it back at him.

"What are you trying..." he attempted. He started grinding faster.

The phone beeped. "I'm done now, Mr. Jacobs. Is there anything you need before I leave?" Peg paged.

Damn her for interrupting my lovemaking session!

Azmir's strokes came to a halt. I turned to look back at him to see what he was going to do. He hit the speaker button. "You're good, Peg. Enjoy your evening," trying not to let her hear he was out of breath.

She tried to return the well wishes, but he immediately disconnected the call. Azmir waited about three seconds more before resuming. Again, his strokes sped up. I started thrusting back at him again. I couldn't believe the feeling engulfing me. I was about to come. *Again.* All I could do was push my face into his desk calendar to keep from screaming as I felt his hard thighs smack into the back of my legs. I was too embarrassed to let him know I was climaxing again. I'd yet to reveal he was the first to deliver me a vaginal orgasm. I was certainly not prepared to express it today. But my body began to convulse, which had to give it away. Azmir was fucking me with potent horsepower. There was no other way to describe his gusto. And I enjoyed every frantic insertion.

Azmir followed me into oblivion minutes later, making sure I was done, pumping himself into me obstinately. He collapsed on my back when he was through.

"Damn, Brimm," he mumbled trying to catch his breath and we snickered together.

This could never get old to me. Azmir's sex and body could never become mundane to me. I couldn't understand the spell he had over my body to cause me to respond to him like this. *I could get used to this.* I already had.

We remained splayed until our heart rates slowed, and our relaxed breathing returned. It was such an intimate position and proximity. Odd. I wasn't in pain or uncomfortable by his weight—inside or out, just a little curious about the linger. My eyes danced in their sockets as my face rested against his desk calendar. Azmir's face was buried in the back of my neck, and I felt every breath he took against my skin.

Before I could assemble the words to ask why he was still there he murmured, "Rayna?"

Wrinkling my forehead, I screeched. "Yes..."

"I don't share," he whispered after a pregnant pause.

"I-I don't understand." *What in the hell is he talking about?*

Azmir abruptly plunged into me, causing my entire delicate body to spasm.

"I don't share," he repeated in more of a growl.

"Okay," I trilled to a new octave, trying to control my hormonally heightened body.

I was borderline paranoid about the state I was in. My body betrayed me without fail for Azmir. I couldn't believe how needy I was for him. I was panicking and would agree to anything to get out of this precarious position on his desk to collect myself.

Within seconds, Azmir rose and retracted from me, earning another body tremor. I hoped like hell he didn't catch it until I turned and saw his knowing grin.

After taking turns washing up in his bathroom, we ate lunch. My hunger pangs developed after my sexual appetite had been satisfied. He fixed me a plate like a gentleman. We eventually found ourselves eating out of every dish communal style. Time got away from us until one of his cell phones rang. The other had been ringing practically the entire time I was there, but he'd completely ignored it, so I didn't understand why this one was any different. He answered it.

"Damn, Ock! I lost track of time. Give me about twenty minutes and I'll be downstairs," Azmir informed apologetically.

He then turned back to me. "Brimm, I forgot about a meeting I had an hour ago."

"Oh, that's fine."

I wasn't ready to leave him but understood Azmir was a busy man. I had actually considered myself lucky to have had such a satisfying afternoon with him. We cleaned up our feast and left out together.

That man is one intriguing creature.

Our relationship had taken a new course. Though nothing was simplified, things got a little less complicated. I'd become entrenched with desire for Azmir, against my indurate nature.

There were many demons I battled where my heart was concerned but there was a shifting in me, something undeniable and horrifically uncontrollable. I seemed to somehow make room for him in my world—or perhaps he made room for himself there. We spent voluminous time together fine dining, going to concerts, on romantic boat rides, simple dinners, even extravagant mini getaways. We were hot and heavy, but we never took on any titles to help define roles in one another's lives. B.A.J., *Before Azmir Jacobs*, this would have been perfectly fine for me—in fact, preferred. But unfamiliar emotions were conjuring I had little control over and that didn't sit well with me.

I attended the charity event with him and got a glimpse of his reputation *and benevolence* on a community level, gauged his prestige and experienced more of his variants. The more exposure to him the deeper I fell. The sex remained skilled, raucous at times, bruising, impassioned, combustive, and the best I'd likely ever experience. I'd become addicted to it, dependent on it, and quickly epiphanized it was something consuming my every awakened moment and even my subconscious when I'd dreamt about him.

I was able to be free with Azmir and trust his sexual guidance and passion. He never talked about committing to me exclusively for anything more than sex—and neither did I for that matter, but when we sexed, we were *total*. Complete. Satisfied in every way. There was no room for another lover because he depleted all curiosities when he touched me. I wasn't ready though. I wasn't prepared to let him in. Azmir was a lot of man to take in; I couldn't fight the fear of having bitten off more than I could chew with him. His self-placed pedigree, his lifestyle, his remarkable journey, and promising destiny scared the shit out of me. It left little space for me to plant my feet in his universe. He was a tall order, *a satisfying feast. An improbable possibility.*

The prospect of him did no good to oppose my self-loathing and fears of inferiority. But I was caught up with him, had relented in his chase to a new level of me.

love

belvin

Azmir

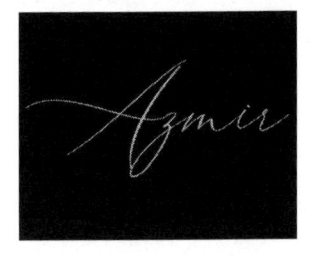

As I sat in the diner sipping on tea, I gazed lazily outside where the rain was coming down and the clouds were gray. I glanced down at my *Breitling* to see it was about two thirty p.m. I'd only been there about ten minutes, but I was eager for my party to arrive.

Soon, through the glass window, I saw Petey running in front of the diner with his jacket partially covering his head, trying to keep from getting wet. He was a baldy so I'm sure he felt every drop hitting him. When he entered, he looked around in search of me. I waved my hand to reveal my whereabouts and he immediately noticed me.

He briskly walked over and while sitting down he mumbled, "Yeah, man, it was a set up," very calmly.

"Damn." I bawled. I knew it.

I'd spoken to my mother several times since my birthday. She explained her drug charge sentencing and told me the *FED*s arranged for the early release under the condition that she assisted in an investigation targeting Big D. Apparently, they were sniffing around my trunk, but she was adamant about not taking part in my investigation.

Long story short: Big D and my pops were beat cops, or uniformed officers, who allowed their greed to take over back in the eighties, which incidentally was the height of the dope game era. My pops had the connects but Big D had the heart to knock mid-level hustlers for fairly large amounts of their dope. It wasn't until my dad took notice of me sniffing around, trying to get in the game by peddling weed when he grew a conscious and told D he wanted to end their arrangement. D didn't like it and tried to convince my father otherwise, unsuccessfully, so he set him up. No one really knows the details behind who D worked with, but my mother surmised from a comment D made one drunken night a few days after my dad's funeral.

"Life must go on, Yazzy, or you'll get run over just like your old man. Follow me and you'll stay alive for that little boy of yours." Before you knew it, D had my mom set up in Chi-Town transporting out there. The amounts were so large the *FED*s took notice and eventually hit her with twenty-six years.

"*They came and raided Denise apartment one day when you was in school. I begged 'dem to let me make a few calls to get you some help. The only person I got was D who said it wasn't shit he could do for us.*" Yazmine paused in her story to collect her emotions. "*They tried to strip me as soon as I rolled up in that bitch. I had to damn near kill dis dyke that was coming for me. I was in solitude for the first four months in 'dat bitch. By 'da time I could write, you musta' done left cause I ain't hear shit back from you. Nobody knew where you was. I was sick as hell in there over that shit. Then every once in a while, Denise people said they saw you coming through but none a 'dem had da' sense to tell you to holla at me. I was fucked up knowing Daryl had his nasty paws on you,*" my mother continued to explain during one of our recent conversations.

It didn't take long before she shared with me her hunch of Big D setting up my father's murder. I've never tolerated conjecture, so I reached out to some of my BX compadres. It took a few days before someone confirmed they were paid to put a bullet in my dad's head.

"This mufucka," I spit just above a whisper. I immediately sensed the need for pillory.

"Don't sweat it, my nigga. You ain't slip. I'm just glad you thought to run this inquiry, ya know." I understood he was trying to provide a little encouragement. Then there was silence for a few seconds.

"What's the plan now, Duke?" Petey asked for his marching orders.

"I have a few things in mind." Immediately, David came to mind. I needed to reach out to him to assess one of my options. "Let me breathe on it for a minute and get back to you." Petey nodded in concession. "What's the deal with ol' girl?" I asked as I braced myself.

"I'm still working on it. My connect got a bug in North Cacalacky..." He was referring to North Carolina. "But he's coming up with a dead end there. She ain't discuss no names of family or friends wit' nobody there. Homey came up wit' a old boyfriend she used to fuck wit'. He should be touching down wit' him tonight. Then he gonna holla at me about it," Petey ended.

"Indeed, Crack." I dismissed him.

I stayed at the diner for about an hour after he left. I tried to think why the *FED*s would be on my back and how did my mother tie into all of this. *Did I have a snitch in my camp?* My mind raced with question after question. Damn near everybody felt suspect to me.

Then my thoughts went to Rayna. Although the longer we were together the more she trusted to tell me about her past, I still felt she was keeping something from me. She had no family she kept in touch with? Was Michelle the only person in her circle? It couldn't be. She would occasionally disappear for a couple of days, and I had a feeling she was dipping out of town. At this point, I needed to know the skinny on everyone near me. I didn't want to take anything at face value.

Fuck. I had fallen for Rayna. A lot. So much so I had to assess logic over emotion. I'd stepped out of character and treaded unchartered waters so to speak.

Love uncharted.

Hmmmmm...

The waiter came over for the third time asking if I wanted to order food instead of re-upping on tea. I left soon after leaving a one hundred dollar bill.

I was meeting with Big D when my phone went off. It was my personal line but an unfamiliar number, so I chose to ignore it. Afterwards I checked the voicemail and learned it was Michelle giving me a call about Rayna's birthday. Apparently, it was approaching, and she wanted to be sure she wasn't stepping on my toes with the plans she and the girls had brewing.

They were planning a weekend reunion back in North Carolina at their alma mater. Rayna never talked about her birthday other than it was in July. And, if I understood Rayna correctly, she wasn't exactly that tight with her fellow alums. None but Michelle, of course. She said she indulged in hanging out mostly on the strength of Michelle. I could tell she tolerated them more than she let on, but the fact of the matter was Rayna maintained she had no friends other than Michelle. She also recently shared North Carolina never felt like home. I wasn't convinced she would enjoy what they had planned. It wasn't my place to offer my opinion, so I thought to do it indirectly. I called Michelle back.

After all the greeting pleasantries and broaching the topic she asked, "Azmir, did Rayna even mention her birthday to you?" in such a parental tone.

I couldn't lie. "Not at all."

"Damn it, Rayna!" Michelle bit out.

"I do recall, months ago, her mentioning it was in July. When exactly in July?" I asked.

"The twenty-first," she answered."

"Well in the spirit of secrecy, I have a plan," I shared just before filling Michelle in.

Rayna

It was a scorching afternoon in July, and I'd just stepped out of the spa and was feeling great. I was grateful to Azmir for his urging me to go at his expense, of course. As I received my massage, I reflected on my life and how stable it was. I was keeping up with Akeem's commissary and lawyer's fees. My greatest hopes were for a soon release date. I had thought of going home for Thanksgiving to visit Chyna and my grandparents. The last time I'd called my grandfather had taken ill. Michelle's health was fair, and Erin was developing quite nicely. Life was stable.

My relationship with Azmir had started taking shape. We indeed began spending more time with each other. And while it was new for me, I must admit I enjoyed getting to know him better as well as his inner circle. Our intimacy expanded far beyond what I thought my heart could ever handle. Azmir was different from what I'd dreamed of in a companion, *if I'd ever dreamed*. He studied me, taking cues from my inclinations, my routines, and tested out every theory. If I orgasmed from behind or with one leg up over his shoulder, he tried it again and timed it to precision so when he returned to test his theory, he could anticipate the outcome.

Just like when he made my body quake on a boat in the waters of Cabo San Lucas during the setting of the sun. He laid me, limb by limb across the intimate cabin cruiser we traveled on for our brief weekend excursion and tortured my hungered body relentlessly with his deft tongue and then repeating a similar process when he stroked me with famine and virile possession of my body. That experience changed my existence.

Azmir contemplated my body, measuring it at every touch. Even when I was out of commission, tending to business with mother nature, he seemed to have trained himself to respond to my physiological needs without prompting, keening himself to those of my emotions. His care was gauging and contemplative. His touches were deliberate and well strategized and though he never spoke about it, I'd picked it up. It was something I'd never had.

The more he stripped me physically and demanded my body to submit to his needs the more I was made aware of my inner blemishes. These things developed a debilitating panic inside of me, causing me to fear he'd one day soon be awakened to my darkest secrets and most threatening deficiencies. I didn't want to expose the imperfections in me, didn't want to acquaint him with my scars. And at every turn of his discovery, I fought with desperation of self-preservation.

As I waited for the valet to bring my car around, my phone rang snapping me out of my trance, it was Michelle.

"What are you doing, girl?"

"Just getting out of *Serenity*. What's up with you?"

"Oh, nothing at all. I just e-mailed you our itinerary for next week. Our flight leaves out of LAX at eleven twenty, babe. Okay?" she informed.

"No problem, Shelly. I'll be there with bells. Are you guys sure I can't at least pay for my flight?" I sighed. I mean, it was generous enough that we were going to The Bahamas and staying at the *Atlantis* resort.

"No, Rayna. Don't worry about anything but having a good time. We are all excited about going to the Caribbean, girl!" Michelle was filled to the brim with glee. Secretly I was happy about vacationing as well, even if it was with her friends.

"What plans does Azmir have for you?" she asked.

"He's been so apologetic about being out of town the entire week of my birthday. We're going to dinner next week. I guess that will be our time of celebration."

"Oh? Where?"

"Not sure."

"You know, Rayna, I can't believe you didn't tell your boyfriend about your birthday. That's off this planet!"

Michelle was annoyed. As much as she tried to conceal her disappointment, she couldn't resist feeling the need to bring it up again.

"He's not my boyfriend, first off. And for the hundredth time it just never came up, Shelly! I'm not used to having anyone in my life special enough to share small details like that with," I defended.

"That detail isn't small when *you* spend his birthday with him, dance for him and his friends and hit him with the coochie to top it off! I keep telling you to let loose with this one. It's okay to be vulnerable and..." she stumbled.

"And what?" I asked with a snappy attitude.

"And in love. There. I said it!"

"Damn, now you hit me with the L word. It's only been—"

"Five months since your first date," Michelle interjected.

Five months wasn't long in my book. But Michelle was right, I needed to rethink this relationship. The time had flown by so quickly that what was five months felt like five weeks. Azmir and I spent endless nights together when he wasn't traveling. We were in a great place, we talked freely with a comfortable flow of exchange and our sex was mind-blowing. I wanted him to enjoy me, whatever good I presented. And I sure as hell didn't want to disrupt that with talks of falling in love. I didn't want to scare him off.

"Yeah...whatever. My point is love takes time and more time for me to get in it. We're taking things slow," I continued with my pushback.

"Okay, but remember life can be a lonely journey without someone to love. And I won't be around much longer to be the only person to take the journey with you!"

"Shelly, why in the hell do you always have to talk that bereavement shit? Please!" I screamed exasperated. She always got me with that. I hated to even think about life without Michelle, let alone her dying. With that, I ended the conversation as I drove off. I had crazy errands to run to get ready for my date with Azmir.

At dinner the following week and the night before I was due to leave for the Bahamas, Azmir and I enjoyed a wonderful meal at *Crustaceans*. I loved their crab puffs and garlic noodles. The wine was superb, the conversation flowed well, and the ambiance was ever so present. The restaurant is known for its French-Colonial décor, floor-level pond and aquarium leading from the cocktail area into the main dining area.

Azmir had let hair grow on his face just the way I liked—*no*, actually loved! Tonight, his goatee was ferine, I loved seeing his dark facial hair against his smooth chocolate skin. *Damn!* This man knew what he was doing. He donned a simple black *YSL* T-shirt with black denim jeans and his black classic Jordan's. *Delectable*. But our conversation took a left turn for deep this particular evening.

"You're so intense. It intimidates me," I blurted out.

His eyes flew up and met mine, widened in wonder. I could even see his spine level and his head straighten. I can't say from where the nerve derived, but it spilled out. My heartbeat tripled after the words flowed from my mouth. But it was my truth, something I'd been suppressing for months now. He was always reserved and perched with an eagle eye. I wanted to know what he was thinking at times, though I could never muster the balls to ask.

"I never endeavor to intimidate you." There was a slight pause. "I mean, I know I have the tendency, but it isn't a tactic I employ with you," Azmir muttered.

My mouth dried and my eyes danced around the room to avoid his searing gaze. I wanted to say so much but was afraid to fully express myself.

"So, you are aware of doing it to others?"

"Yes. I've been made aware in senior staff development trainings. It's where my subordinates can be totally honest about my governing in hopes of strengthening our team. In all honesty, I was aware of my aggressiveness prior to the trainings. It's a mechanism needed in my management days way before I entered the corporate arena. But here with you, it's not something I want. It would be counterintuitive."

To what? There was an uncomfortable pause. One he knew he had to fill. And he did.

"Look, Brimm. I may not be the easiest to gauge but I'm certainly not aiming to be an anomaly with you. If you feel uneasy or question something where we're concerned, I need you to address it." His eyebrows knitted as he gathered his thoughts. "Relationships aren't my thing. I'm no good at them. People may be surprised considering my last one, but that one functioned with so many complexities, when it ended it came with no regrets on my part."

His head went down to his plate playing with his food. I could tell he was mentally constrained, something I was all too familiar with. It surprised the hell out of me how I'd felt the sudden urge to throw him a bone. Who in the hell was I to give him a hand expressing his feelings when I sure as hell didn't have a grip on mine? But I wanted to assist.

"Azmir, you've confided in me how you've been unable to open up to women completely because the one woman you truly loved and trusted abandoned you. Now, I know you've said that, logically, you get how your mom is different from women you date but we both know she's representative of all women for you. The way you perceive her will fashion how you receive women. Many people are faced with the same problem...men and women alike," I declared with confidence.

"Does that apply to your view on men?" Azmir asked with such sincerity in his eyes.

You have to appreciate he was a "cool" guy, who wasn't led by emotion but instead business and logic. We'd yet to cross the bridge of emotionally themed conversations, but this inevitable and dreadful exchange was going to get even deeper. I had been caught extremely off guard, my therapist cap had been knocked clear off my head and I guess it showed because as he took a sip of his brandy he chuckled.

"What do you mean?"

"I mean...in all the time I've known you—you have never uttered a word about your father other than he left your family when you were coming up. I can't help but wonder what effects his actions have had on you because even if there's no more to the story, him leaving is enough. I can tell you are extremely guarded and self-sufficient as hell. All is derivative, which means that determination and hard-assness comes from somewhere...some place," he analyzed.

I stilled with an empty expression for a minute before saying, "Wow. I don't know what to say. I know I can be stubborn as hell, but I thought I had gotten better...*with you*." I noticed my voice trembling down at *"with you."* That could only mean he was right.

"I'm just saying..." he spoke as he shifted positions in his seat, "...it should be obvious our relationship has budded into something meaningful. But I've been a little hesitant—*hell*—shook to even touch on the subject. I don't want you to feel I'm trying to box you into something you haven't signed up for, so I've been letting shit breathe," he expressed before a pause. "I guess what I'm saying is help a brother out, Brimm," he continued.

"What do you mean? I haven't given you any reason to believe I'm not in this thing with you, have I?"

"No. Not that you aren't here but...you're holding back."

"Azmir, this is coming from a man who dates other women..." I attempted.

His eyebrows rose and his body went rigid. He looked me square in the eyes, "Hold up. I am unequivocally not dating anyone else—"

I interrupted. "Please don't sit here and tell me you don't have other affairs, Azmir. *Please* don't insult me." My delivery was soft, yet stern as my voice trembled and I rounded my neck to try to stretch out the sudden knots forming. It was one thing for him to qualify the various relationships he has with other women, but it's something completely different to deny them all together.

"Allow me to finish, Rayna." His hands were raised defensively. "I said, I'm not dating any woman but you. I may have residual relationships, but they are all meaningless and pale in comparison to what..." he hesitated.

"To what, Azmir? I mean...I would like to know where you're going with this," I demanded in the softest tone appropriate for our surroundings. My emotions were curling up, self-preservation mode was threatening. *Please no!*

Suddenly his head cocked to the side and his tongue pushed against his molars. "You're not sleeping with anybody else, are you?" His tone was laced with pure speculation.

I was shocked. This man had to be sleeping with at least one other chick but was trying to lock me down? The truth of the matter was I wouldn't dare have slept with anyone else. Not only was the sex superb, but I was mentally locked on this man. I wasn't so confident he felt the same way. Hell—he practically just admitted to sleeping with other women.

"No, Azmir, absolutely not. Why would you go there?"

He paused for a brief moment before sighing, "A man just needs to know he's not sharing his woman."

"So, now I'm your woman?"

He never responded, didn't even lift his head from his plate as he cut into his food.

This conversation was getting way too deep for me. Plus, I had to relieve my bladder, so I excused myself and headed for the restroom. As I stood, Azmir rose from the table to see me off. I loved when he did that, very chivalric. When I headed off, I made sure I sashayed my ass in my new mini, *Betsey Johnson,* dress and sexy pumps, inside snickering at his insecurities about me being with other men.

While freshening up in the ladies' room, I made sure my makeup was still tight. I was really feeling myself and couldn't wait to get Azmir's fine ass in my bed—or wherever he'd have me.

As I walked back to my table and spotted Azmir, I noticed a huge ribbon at my place at the table. The closer I got the better the view I got. It was a small brown gift box on top of a pink envelope both tied together with pink and brown ribbons. It was cute. The minute Azmir noticed I was back at the table his eyes were glued to me. He had been giving me that intense gaze all evening. Either he was horny as hell or Azmir was catching feelings for me.

I took my seat.

"May I...?" I asked, referring to the gifts awaiting my return.

"Please..."

He was in his usually imperturbable posture with his typical piercing gaze.

First, I opened the envelope, which was a greeting card. Among its contents it read, *"In a complicated world where nothing seems to come together, one thing is simple and those are my feelings for you. I'm happy you're in my crazy world."*

I looked up at him and I saw deep into his eyes. There was fire behind his dark orbs. They expressed so much. My heart warmed, and all those dry feelings developed earlier withered instantly.

Nothing could escape my mouth. Even if he wasn't exactly saying he was in love with me, he was definitely saying he was damn near there. I could tell he was a little uncomfortable with my gaping.

"You're not done." He pointed to the gift box.

"Oh!"

I had gotten so caught up in the moment, I totally forgot about the actual gift. The card was a gift within itself.

I slowly unwrapped the bow on the box and opened it with shaky hands. I was still unaccustomed to receiving gifts from a man. Inside the box were the most breath-taking diamond drop earrings. I couldn't believe he had been so generous and thoughtful. They had to be at least three carats.

"Azmir, I don't know what to say. These are so beautiful. I can't believe you did this."

He nodded his head in acceptance. He was such a man's man, minimizing emotions.

I felt like I had to reassure him after receiving such a lavish gift. I had to try harder.

"Listen...I know you were trying to address my emotional deficiencies earlier. I want you to know I know they're there and I'm going to try and work on them. I realize now how I have major trust issues—with everyone, but men in particular. Just please be patient with me as I work through them. Can you do that?" I vulnerably asked.

"If you need me to."

His voice was raw and assuring, speaking to the arctic cages of my heart. I followed up by gesturing for a kiss and he obliged.

My phone rang and I knew it was Michelle. Not many people had my personal cell number and even fewer called.

"Hey," I tried keeping my voice appropriately low.

"Na-Na, that blue sarong you let me borrow last month, are you planning on wearing that while away?" I'd totally forgotten about it.

"No."

"Good because I want to pack it to wear. You don't mind, do you?"

"Of course not. Knock yourself out."

I affectionately glanced over to Azmir who was quietly finishing his meal. He was so easy to ogle. What was even more appealing was his insouciance of his superior features. There were times where he seemed to be aware and other times just oblivious. But everyone else took notice of his beauty whenever I was with him. There was always an eye constantly stealing a long appreciative gape, particularly of the female persuasion.

"Awesome! Hey, you still out?"

"Yes." *Like, really, Michelle?* She was practically yelling on the phone. I could tell she'd been a little buzzed. I'd just hoped she had timed it well against her prescription schedule.

"Have you sucked that big black cock yet?" I gasped and my eyes flew up to Azmir who appeared unalarmed, and I silently prayed he hadn't heard her over the soft music of the restaurant. After my assessment I went back to her.

"Shelly, you know I can't do that now. We've talked about this before." I tried sounding admonitory, I really didn't want to discuss this with him mere inches away.

"Suck his cock, Na-Na! That's an order! He'll love it, and you will, too!" I heard the humor in her voice. She was out of control, and I'd planned to rip into her in the morning.

"We are *so* not discussing this right now. I have to go. Please don't overdo it tonight. We have an early morning, Shelly," I heeded, ending the call.

Letting out a deep exhale, I slipped the phone back into my clutch and before I could fully pick up my fork—

"She's right, you would," Azmir spoke evenly and sotto voce.

Could he be referring to...? He ignored my quizzical gaze, keeping his eyes down to his food as he cut into his chicken.

"I...I would what?"

"You would enjoy pleasuring me orally." Slowly, his eyes

ascended to mine. "Why can't you do it?" Azmir seemed to have sung those words—directly to my sex. I felt it leap.

My face heated up in sheer embarrassment. I was really going to harm Michelle the following morning when I got my hands on her size four ass.

"I can show you how to please me if that's what you're concerned about. I would enjoy it." *How could he keep a straight posture and equable tone when taking on a topic like this?*

"*It*—It's just that... I—"

"You don't have to discuss it if it makes you uncomfortable. I just thought I'd give clarity to the subject." He went back to his food as he continued, "It's not like you haven't given it some thought."

I was frozen in my seat, not knowing where to go after a heady exchange.

"Finish your meal, Brimm. We'll work around it," he commanded as he maintained his attention on his plate.

After dessert, we left the restaurant. I was ready to get him alone, it was almost torturing. As we stood outside waiting for the Bentley, I was admiring Azmir's beauty. He was tall, beautifully dark with striking features, just extremely handsome. *Damn is that goatee working for him!* His urban look was casual but definitely stylish and appealing.

As I gave him a once over, I fantasized about what I was going to do to him once we got back to my place. I reached over to grab him and when I did, I gently pulled his face down to mine. He came to me, and I kissed him softly. When he pulled back, he gave me a look of passion. I had to go for it again whether we were in public or not. I moved into him again for another gentle pat on the lips only after, I didn't withdraw, I went back in with my tongue. He reciprocated and I could tell by the speed of his tongue and breathing he wanted me as badly as I wanted him. My panties grew moist. I stroked the visible muscle in his jaw, running my pads against the soft quills of his facial hair. His tongue was so cool and agile. He took his left hand and placed it on the small of my back. I got so lost in the moment; I forgot where I was.

Out of nowhere, there was the sound of a horn snapping us out of our tryst.

"Come on. That's our ride."

We continued our foreplay in the backseat of his Bentley while on our way to my place when his cell rang. He ignored the first phone as he lifted my dress and pulled me closer to him so he could ruffle my panties until he eventually found his way to my private valley. His adroit fingers played amazing tricks with my clitoris as his tongue paralleled its movements in my mouth. I tried to keep up with his kiss. It was heavy, telling. Communicatory of his needs. After a while I couldn't keep up because I had to catch my breath. He had developed a strategy with his long fingers. He'd start on my pearl with the tip of his fingers and then insert them into my passage. Taking in that feeling along with his luscious scent and his pressing weight on top of me made me wild.

I eventually relented to the pleasurable torture by whispering, "Stop...you're going to make me come all over your backseat."

"It's my backseat and my pussy. You're good," he growled into my neck before nibbling.

I didn't know how much longer I could hold out. I tried to be discreet as possible, knowing we were not the only two in the car. He was making this so difficult. I wanted more of him—all of him.

"What about Ray?" I panted.

"He can't hear or see. Trust me."

Azmir was so tall. I could only imagine how his lengthy body was positioned in the rear cabin of the car. While it was spacious inside, it wasn't a bedroom. When he advised we had no ear or eye hustlers I decided to play ball.

I pushed up to ask for him to let me up. When he did, he gave me a deep gaze, further turning me on. He took the fingers he used to pleasure me and stuck them in his mouth. Without words I knew he was saying he wanted me *badly*. And Azmir always got what he wanted, even me.

I situated myself on the floor of the car while kissing him, tasting traces of myself on his lips. Situated between his legs, I removed his jacket then began pulling his shirt and T-shirt out of his pants. I made sure to continue with our tongue mingle. At one point I removed my tongue enough to whisper, "Azmir."

"Hmmm?" he responded.

"It's too bad you're not my man," I continued as I looked into his eyes seductively.

"Why do you say that?" His voice was a mere low baritone pitch. By this time, I was pushing his shirts up to his hard chest.

"Because if you were, I could do what I've wanted to do for some time now," I informed. I'd begun licking his chest and making my way down to his stomach.

In an aroused state, he let out a sharp breath and chuckled as if *he* was then being tortured. Then he murmured, "Oh, yeah? And what's that?" Although he knew damn well where I was going.

At this point the conversation was done. I was headed south of the border as I licked his abdomen and was unbuckling his belt and jeans.

When the second telephone call came in with another ring tone, he mumbled a string of profanities while reaching for the phone to answer it.

Damn that phone!

I stopped to let him take the call.

"Peace...Peace," he answered his cell in a thick Brooklyn accent. I could hear a wispy voice on the other end but couldn't make out any words. Azmir asked, "...anybody hurt?" as I lifted myself off my knees, again, the voice from the phone came through. Azmir's face tightened as he listened intently. "Alright. I'll be right there. Lay low!" he ordered.

"Ray, after we take Ms. Brimm home, I need to go over to the spot off of Crenshaw," Azmir called out.

"Yes, sir," Ray replied in acknowledgement.

"Is everything okay?" I asked, disturbed by the abrupt change in plans. Although we didn't exactly plan to go back to my place together, it was understood we would.

"I'm sorry," he muttered before burying his face in his hands. Instantly, he shuddered in his seat and screamed, "*Fuck!*"

I paused as I didn't know what to say. I'd never seen him up in arms like this. There was silence for a few seconds before he offered, "I'm sorry. That was my peoples telling me my barbershop in the *"C"* is on fire right now and it doesn't look good."

"I'm sorry to hear that, Azmir," I replied in a low sympathetic tone.

He sat back in his seat massaging the bridge of his nose between his eyes. He looked so perplexed. I didn't know what to do. After a few more seconds of awkwardness, while looking out the window, he placed his right hand on my left thigh. I took it as a sign of him being ready to let me back in. Although it was a huge risk, I moved closer to him and lay on his chest. He followed up, folding his arm over me. We rode this way all the way to my house. Once there, he got out to walk me to the door.

After I opened the door, I turned to him, "I really do hope everything turns out okay."

As soon as those words left my mouth, I felt reduced to a teenager who couldn't find the appropriate words for the occasion. He kissed me on my forehead, said he'd call, and promenaded back to the car.

I didn't hear back from Azmir all night. I had gotten a text from him the next morning while at the airport. It read:

ENJOY THE ISLAND, SWEETHEART. HAPPIEST OF BIRTHDAYS!

I smiled but couldn't help but still feel disappointed by not seeing or speaking to him since he dropped me off the night before. I was ready to take our intimacy to another level. What I didn't want him to know was something I hadn't quite shared with Michelle; I'd never really gone down on a guy. I'd licked and maybe even engulfed once, pulling out immediately but that was just a method of foreplay when I was drunk fucking Tyquan. I'd never inhaled or sucked with the means to an end in mind. With Azmir I wanted to, I wanted to make him lose control while melting into my mouth. I wanted to match his sexual dominance and skill, even if it was damn near impossible. I wanted to try. How could I go wrong? If I couldn't pleasure Azmir orally it wouldn't be for the lack of trying. But it never happened.

The flight out was cool. I took out my *iPhone*, went into the music app, threw on my sunglasses and slept practically the entire flight. The girls chatted it up in anticipation of our vacation. I knew I was being rude but didn't care. They were used to my reclusive propensities. They made do as if I wasn't there.

Michelle hated this trait I had but I explained to her a while ago the girls were not exactly my friends. They were just long-term associates. They put up with me out of respect for Michelle and I did the same. We had good times together, but for the most part that was it. A part of me thought to try to be a part of the group seeing we were vacationing in celebration of my birthday, but I was in a funk thinking about Azmir.

Our limo pulled up to the *Atlantis* resort. I didn't think much of it until we arrived at our rooms, or I should say my room. It was a huge suite. We stayed at *The Cove*. I didn't pay attention during check-in as I didn't make the accommodations. The bellman took us up to our rooms and mine was the first stop.

As we ascended on the elevator he shared, "We are going to the club-level suites. Should you have any needs, please feel free to contact the concierge."

Damn, they went all out for my birthday, huhn?

"Here's the first suite." The bellman unlocked and opened the door.

The suite was immaculately oversized. Because it was a corner suite, there was a wall-to-wall ocean view. Everywhere you looked you saw blue. *Simply amazing.* The bathroom had shiny marble floors and an all-glass shower. It was like something in a brochure only better. The bedroom had a huge king-sized bed with a sitting area and the same beautiful view of the ocean. While I was admiring the room it dawned on me how there was only one bedroom and one bed. I wondered where in the hell were these broads sleeping because I wasn't sharing a bed!

"Where are the other beds?" I asked as politely as I could.

"Oh, this is the birthday girl's suite. We have our own," Britni informed. "Damn, I'm ready to see our suite now. Let's go, little man!" she continued.

"Hell, yeah!" April concurred.

"You stay here and unwind. We'll have lunch and hang out by the pool in a couple of hours. I'll call you with our room number," Michelle spoke up as she was the last to leave the room.

"Wait. All of you are sharing a suite and I'm in this massive one by myself?" I quizzed.

"You're the birthday girl." She wrapped her arms around me. "Just relax and enjoy. If you get lonely, I'll come running, sweetie!"

Shortly after she left the room and then the suite, I went out into the living room and admired the view. The more beauty I saw the lonelier I grew. I didn't think I'd enjoy the next five days no matter how good the girls' intentions were.

After unpacking and then a shower, I threw on a bikini and a sarong and headed down to the restaurant as Michelle instructed. The grounds were breathtaking. I loved hearing the island music and the tranquil energy from the staff and fellow tourists. On my way down, I saw a group of guys admiring me. One even had the nerve to hiss me reminding me of *The Clan*, adding to my pining of Azmir Jacobs. Everything reminded me of A.D. I didn't know if it spoke volumes about my warming to him or if I hated the sentiment altogether. I just kept with my stride until I saw the girls sitting at a table.

I sat at the table in awe, "Damn! Ladies, this place is fly! I have to give you all props on this one!"

"Okay. Can we let her in on the surprise now?" April asked.

"No. Let's hold off a little," Michelle gently advised.

"What surprise? Shelly, you know I don't like surprises," I scolded.

"Don't sweat it, Na-Na. Take it all in," she advised just before giving April a nasty look. The waiter coming to the table interrupted my line of questioning.

After lunch we walked around the resort to make ourselves acquainted. We ended up in a club. The music was a little too pop for my taste, but the energy was definitely nice. After about an hour, I was ready to leave but could see the girls were all enjoying themselves. April found herself a local with friends. She came over to us with a brown skinned, muscular framed guy with locks. He had the brightest teeth I had ever seen. She was grinning from ear to ear.

"L-a-d-i-e-s! This is Bobby. He and his friends are going to another club off the resort and are inviting us to tag along. Are we interested?" she screamed over the music.

"That depends," Michelle responded. "Are they buying drinks?" she flirted.

"If that's what you want," Bobby agreed with a thick West Indian accent.

"You down, Na-Na? It is your birthday after all," Michelle asked being politically correct.

"By all means, you guys go and enjoy. I haven't been able to get that hot tub out of my head. I'll catch up with you later," I offered.

If Michelle didn't know me as well as she did, she'd decline on my behalf, not wanting to be rude. But she knew better.

"Okay...if you insist. Just as long as you're doing something *you* want," she advised, and they walked off. I was two seconds behind them trying to finish my drink.

I flew back to my room to see if I had a text or e-mail from Azmir. Nothing. With that, I grabbed my iPhone and headed down to the Jacuzzi. I knew my girl, Mary J, would comfort me with her *"Share My World"* album. I had a buzz from my drinks at the club. Now it was time for me to stretch out in the hot tub and zone out.

I began to think of my relationship with Azmir. I didn't understand how he could give me such a touching card and beautiful *and expensive* jewelry all to leave that abruptly and not call. I couldn't help but doubt everything he said at the restaurant. As I was doing a little introspective thinking, I started going over what this relationship meant to me. Did I want to give it my all? Had I fallen in love with Azmir? Did I still have too many guards up with him?

Could I let him in?

The one thing clear was it damn sure felt good being with him. He made me feel so protected and well kept. I knew I had gotten on him in the past about doing extravagant things for me financially, but I just didn't like it as much as other women would. *Was I pushing him away? Did my father's departure leave me fucked up and unable to thrive in a relationship?*

Damn! I knew I wasn't getting any younger and needed to find someone to share a little happiness with. At least, that's what Michelle had kept preaching to me.

I had to have been in there for over an hour when a bellman asked how I could stay in such hot water for so long. I didn't realize it had been that long. I ended my train of thoughts with remembering Azmir hadn't attempted to contact me since we parted ways, so it really wasn't all that necessary to wreck my brain trying to readjust who I was.

I left the hot tub and decided to tour the resort some more. This place was ridiculous! I couldn't help but to wonder how much the ladies spent on this trip. There was so much life and high energy given off here. The music...and the people who seemed to have left their troubles far behind was so much to take in. I walked through the casinos listening to the slot machines go off one after another. There was a comedy club and a theater. The décor was fascinating.

I moseyed my way back to *The Cove* and allowed my curiosity to get the best of me. There was one guy alone at the desk. I guess in this late hour there was no need for anymore. I asked the gentleman the price of my room per night. He asked for my room number and began typing away. This was taking longer than I had anticipated. I would've hated for the girls to have walked up on me. I could tell by the look on his face there was a problem.

"Our system is frozen. It could be daily maintenance," he murmured as he pressed keys and then looked up to me and informed, "But I can tell you the *Sapphire* suite runs between nine and fifteen hundred dollars a night." The phone rang in the middle of his answer. "I'm sorry. I have to take this," he murmured before answering the phone.

I walked off as soon as he took the call. I was floored. I couldn't believe they shelled out that much money for my birthday. Did they each take out a loan? Or did they max out their credit cards? I knew they were all professionals, but they didn't have bank like that! We were due to stay for five nights. That means they paid up to fifteen grand for our hotel stay alone.

What the hell?

I went back up to my suite to call Michelle's room to see if they'd gotten back from the club. I got no answer. I decided to hit the sack. Between the day's travel, stressing over Azmir, exploring the resort and then finding out the astronomical cost of this vacation, I was hella exhausted.

The next morning, I was awakened by the sound of the telephone ringing. As I sat up to gather my bearings and remember where I was, I reached for the telephone. It was the concierge. Evidently, Michelle requested I be awakened and notified of our spa appointment.

"What time is the appointment?" I asked.

"It is at nine a.m., ma'am," the concierge answered.

After hanging up I looked over at the clock on the nightstand. It was a minute after seven. I lay in bed for a few minutes to gather my thoughts. Azmir was leading them. I told myself in that moment I needed to let my feelings about what had happened the night before I left go until I returned home. In the meantime, I was at a luxury hotel on a beautiful island, apparently costing the girls a wad of cash.

I jumped up, washed my face, brushed my teeth, threw on leggings, a T-shirt, and sneakers and ran over to the fitness club. I spent an hour in there between the elliptical and working on my abs. After I was done, I returned to my suite to shower and then met the girls at the spa there in the resort.

We had most of our services done on the beach while the soothing breeze flowed over our bodies. The soft music played low as to not interfere with the natural sounds of the ocean waves. This was such a serene experience, adding to my concerns about the cost of this vacation. While we were receiving manicures and pedicures, I broached the subject.

"Wow! First the lavish suite now spa treatments on the beach. This feels like the lifestyle hip-hop artists rap about. What did I do to deserve generous friends like you guys?" I teased.

"Well damn! Can we tell her the secret and get it over with already?" April asked while her petite pale fleshed frame relaxed in the spa chair. Her straight blonde extensions were blowing in the wind. Though I never shared it, April's traditional European features were flawless.

"Why should we not after that outburst, April!" Michelle barked.

"You can't keep a damn secret to save your life, girl. Lisa was right!" Britni hissed.

"What in the hell do you mean, Lisa was right?" April responded and an argument ensued from there.

As they went back and forth, I asked Michelle about the surprise. "Well, Na-Na, this trip was sponsored by a true admirer of yours," Michelle shared with a huge smile on her face.

"Admirer...Azmir?" spilled from my mouth as it hung open. Apparently, I yelled because the other girls began giving their two cents.

"Yeah girl, everything! The flight, the suites, the spa treatments, food—you name it!" April contributed.

"He was very generous, Na-Na," Michelle attempted to inject a little grace.

"Why would he do this?" I asked, looking at Michelle yet speaking rhetorically.

"Why the hell would he do this? I hope it's because of that sweet trap you're throwing on his ass. Shit, that's what I would chalk it up to. You know, girl!" Britni high-fived April.

"I know that's right, girl!" April followed up. "You are fucking him right, aren't you, Rayna?" April asked as she and Britni looked to me for a response.

I ignored their gold-digging, no-man-having asses. I looked at Michelle. "Shelly, my room alone is at least a grand a night. If you do the math and add up all our rooms that's damn near twenty grand!" I exclaimed as April and Britni listened absorbedly.

"Oh, no Na-Na. We're all sharing a suite. He was insistent on you having your own. You know, for privacy. Even he knows how introverted you are," she informed as she made gestures with her eyes to make reference to Britni and April. That was code for he knew I didn't get down with them like that. But my question then was why would he pay for them?

"We originally planned to take you back to North Carolina and hang out there for the weekend but when I called Azmir to be sure we weren't interfering with any plans you two already had he told me you hadn't even mentioned your birthday. Although he didn't exactly say it, I think he felt a little slighted. He thought this would be a good way to get back at you for being so undisclosed."

She gave a contrived laugh to lighten the moment. A laugh I was sure wouldn't have been provided had we been alone. Michelle stayed on my back about giving Azmir a chance.

"Ummmmm...Rayna, you never answered my question. What's that chocolate like in bed? Does he melt in your mouth?" April asked while laughing with Britni. I could tell Michelle's patience was running low.

"I think that's three too many mimosas for you, April!" Michelle warned.

"Why would you wanna know? I thought all you tricked were old, rich Italian men on their death beds," I reciprocated.

Britni and Michelle belted out huge laughs. Even the masseuse chuckled. April, though upset, kept her chicken-head ass mouth shut at that one. I put my sunglasses back on and lay back in my chair trying to process what I had just learned.

After our spa treatments we had brunch at a deli there on the resort. As an act of peace, Michelle convinced us to participate in water sport activities. But just before, she pulled me aside and gave me a maternal verbal lashing. She suggested I suspend my mixed feelings about Azmir funding this trip because it was done out of benevolence. I reluctantly agreed and immediately began working on my disposition so I could enjoy the luxury vacation. Besides, a part of me was relieved Britni and April didn't pay for this, so I didn't have to reciprocate.

We parasailed, snorkeled, and took a boat around the island. We even had time for a bus tour around the island, viewing other resorts and the impoverished areas. It was sad to see the clear contrast of beauty and poverty in one small vicinity. That truly amazed me. Michelle had a slight emotional breakdown experiencing it. I tried to console her as she silently wept right there on the tour bus. It was slightly embarrassing, but I understood how my dear friend was extremely sensitive. In all, we had quite an adventurous day. We took lots of pictures and even videoed some of our excursions.

We arrived back to our rooms at around seven in evening. I threw off my clothes for a much needed shower and washed and blow-dried my hair. I sprayed my body down with lightly scented body oil and slipped on a racer back dress falling well above my knees. I was headed to the phone to call the girls and suggest we check out the comedy club before I heard a knock at the door.

"Ya'll must have read my mind," I muttered underneath my breath headed towards the door. I grabbed the knob, swung the door open, and was extremely surprised *and baffled*. He stood there in all of his six feet and four inches of chocolate grandeur. His head was tilted toward the floor, plastered with an enormous boyish smile.

"Happy Birthday," Azmir uttered in his silky baritone pitch.

"What are you doing here?" I breathed while eyeing him from head to toe.

"...coming to be with you." His Brooklyn tongue was so strong.

Out of nowhere, emotions flooded the forefront of my brain in spades. I didn't understand it. My face started to spasm, my bottom lip quivered, and I began to cry. For once I didn't care if I was exposed. I pushed my inhibitions to the side and ran to him. I jumped into his arms like a child, only I gave him the biggest and wettest kiss ever. His smile remained as he held me and managed to grab his luggage to bring inside the suite. I melted emotionally in his strong arms.

"Why are you crying, sweetheart?" he murmured while staring adoringly into my eyes.

"I'm so angry with you!" My voice shaking. I was experiencing a barrage of emotions.

"Why?" His brows knitted together, and eyes squinted.

"Because I think I've fallen in love with you." *There.* I sheepishly admitted.

"Shit. It's about damn time. Is that what it took...a trip to the Caribbean to finally get you open?" He attempted humor. But he was very much sober when he snorted just above a whisper, "There's no need to cry about that. It's a good thing. I got you, girl."

While I was clutched to him in a straddling position, he took his right hand and wiped my face to remove as many as he could without a cloth. I took his hand, lowered it from my face and kissed him madly. I slipped my tongue as far down his throat as it could go. He didn't seem to mind as he shared his tongue with me generously as well. I fell back into the same trance I was in the night after *Crustaceans*. His right hand found its way to my ass and gripped it gently. I had one hand on his face and the other on the back of his head while our lips and tongues made love.

"Damn!" someone shouted. I looked toward the voice to see we'd left the door open. It was the girls. And of course, April had to be the mood buster. Michelle looked shamefaced, and Britni, as if she was salivating.

"Our bads! We didn't know you had company. We'll come back later," Michelle explained as she physically pushed the other two out of the doorway.

"Oh, nah. Please come back. I'm not here to ruin the girl-bonding taking place. You ladies enjoy yourselves. I'll have my time when you're done," Azmir offered gazing into my eyes.

"Who's here with you? Petey and Kid? Mark and Eric?" I asked, finally coming to my wits.

Amir shook his head. "I'm dolo."

"Noooo. You came all the way out here to wait in a room for me? That's not cool." I turned to the girls. "Where are you guys going?"

"We were going to try out that *Nobu* restaurant," Britni answered.

"Are you hungry? We can have dinner and catch up after," I offered to Azmir. Michelle extended the offer by insisting he come along.

"It's a bet. I need a minute to freshen up," he agreed.

About a half an hour later, we were in the restaurant eating

Japanese cuisine. The restaurant was delightful in ambiance. We had plenty of food and drinks. At first, I was concerned about mixing April with alcohol in Azmir's presence, but it went over well. We had great conversations about the economy, religion, and the state of the black culture. April, surprisingly, had stimulating commentary to add to the last topic. But the most popular topic was celebrities. The girls had loads of questions about people in the industry. It was very interesting to say the least.

After dinner we took a walk on the beach. There was a fire show going on and a few feet away there was a beach party. The ladies parted from us and went on the prowl. Azmir and I watched the fire exhibit in amazement. We moved on to the party and enjoyed the natives taking center stage dancing exotically. I was on my third drink of the night when Azmir, who was standing behind me, whispered in my ear, "That's a little excessive for you isn't it, little lady?" I smiled and continued to watch all the festivities. He was right, but I was overcome with contentment like no other time in my life, so I used little discretion. One of the dancers came over to us and tried to pull me back into the middle of the circle with him. I bashfully pulled my arm back and waved no with a smile.

I motioned to Azmir for us to leave. We held hands the entire walk back to the suite. While we were waiting for the elevator Azmir kept staring at me. I asked what it was all about, but he said nothing. The elevator doors opened, and I walked inside. Before I could turn around, Azmir had pushed me into the corner, pushed the button for our floor, and began kissing me breathlessly. It was a welcomed gesture. We were all over each other. He stopped for a second, gazed deeply into my eyes and murmured, "You are so beautiful," before continuing his assault on my mouth. I couldn't believe we were starting our foreplay in the elevator.

Azmir

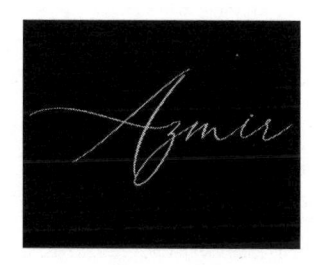

When we were in the lobby waiting for the elevator. I was checking Rayna out. The Caribbean sun and air worked well with her. She was a caramel complexion naturally, but the sun had given her a hint of bronze. She was glowing—fine as hell. My dick got hard just looking at her. She had my head speeding, but I'd finally had her where I wanted, emotionally. The trip was worth it. I wasn't even supposed to be there. I canceled a potentially lucrative partnership meeting with a housing developer just to be with her. I can't lie; now that I wasn't getting ass from anywhere else it was time for a dose of Brimm. But I needed more than that. I needed to be *with* her. She was like home base. *We all gotta go home from time-to-time.*

As we waited for the elevator, I took notice of her hourglass shape. I couldn't tell if she was wearing any panties under her short dress. Her ass wiggled a little at every step she took, turning me the fuck on. When she turned to face me, her cleavage looked bountiful and delicious as hell. Her eyes were chinked from being tipsy. I tried to warn her of overindulging, but figured it was her birthday, so she was allowed. She was rocking her natural hair. It was pretty long and fluffy. She still had lip-gloss on from before dinner although it had dulled. I wanted to devour it until it was completely off. She looked sexy as hell in her natural state.

When we stepped into the elevator I could no longer hold back, I started going at her. I could tell she was taken by surprise, but she caught on quickly. As I deepened the kiss her breathing quickened and I could tell she was really enjoying it, enjoying me. Shit—I was too. I couldn't help but admire the fragrance she was wearing. All of my senses were heightened in that moment. When I nibbled on her neck, I caught a glimpse of her facial expression and had to stop to take a closer look. She made the sexiest expression, almost as if she was being delightfully tortured. I had to tell her how beautiful she was.

I slid my fingers in between her legs in search for her cave. She was wearing a G-string. I played with her clit—*my clit*—as I licked her breast. *Damn!* She was so fucking responsive, always ready for me. When the bell rang for our floor, I peeled myself off her and let her walk off. But she pulled me right back onto her once we were off. I picked her up and she wrapped her legs around me. She licked my ear and then moved down to my neck. I almost lost my balance. Her little tongue was wild. We finally made it to the door of the suite, and she pulled out the key to open it.

Once inside, she hopped down and pushed me out of the doorway. She unbuttoned my shirt and then untied the drawstring on my linen pants. Rayna started licking my neck and worked her way down. She detoured at my chest and licked east and west then south, continuing her descent to my naval. My dick throbbed bordering pain. Her tongue was warm and wet. I noticed myself breathing out of my mouth instead of my nose while she traveled down my pubic hair. Abruptly, she rose from her knees in search of my eyes.

With her eyes towards her nose, she whispered, "I want you to teach me."

"Teach you what?" I knew exactly where she was going but needed to hear it from her. It turned me the fuck on when she verbalized her desire for me sexually.

"How to please you with my mouth."

My chest rose and I let out a long chain of air.

"Are you sure?"

She nodded her head emphatically. Eager to please me. Sexually studious. I was happy out of my ass.

I studied her body's stance. She stood before me with her

hands clasped in her pelvis. Her head slightly bowed, and her shoulders relaxed, such a submissive posture. My dick lurched in my pants. I took her by the hand and traveled over to the living room, moving the center table. She stood where I left her and moved when I invited her into the center of the room.

I could see her heart beating frantically in her chest and I could also hear her pussy pulsating. She was ready. I kissed her softly nipping at her bottom lip then brought my hands to her back and lifted her dress over her head. I dropped it onto the floor, exposing her peach bra and matching satin panties. I prefer lace but Rayna looked good in them all.

She removed her bra releasing her swollen breasts. I took them into my mouth one at a time tasting them and pulling at her rock-hard nipples. I loved her breasts, they're so sensitive and supple. As I stood there devouring them, she moaned until I stopped. Her eyes were soft and fervent awaiting my lead.

Needing to taste her lips, I kissed her again to prep her mouth for what was to come. I placed my hand on her shoulder nudging her down, to which she caught on quickly and dropped to her knees. The visual of her kneeling down before me, waiting for my command, was intoxicating.

"Remove my pants," I ordered and Rayna, with jittery hands, grabbed the top of my pants and pulled them down along with my briefs. I kicked them to the side and peered down at my strong man against Rayna's nose. She eyed it with a heaving chest. The visual, *goddamn*! I took myself into my hands and stroked from tip to base. Rayna's eyes were stapled to my hand actions, and I watched her lick her lips and not out of seduction, but I could tell she was salivating at the show.

"Put your hands over mine to gauge the pressure," I commanded.

She brought her heavy arms up and her soft hands laid over mine. She mimicked my movements after adjusting the pressure. In no time, I slipped my right hand from beneath hers and felt her tighten her grasp on me. My spine shivered at her touch. We worked together over the beat of my speeding heart and then I removed my left hand. She balanced the pressure in her hands and mastered the coordination. Rayna was determined and it showed. I placed my finger in her mouth, and she began sucking immediately. I could tell she was ready for me, she moaned at the combination.

"Add small bites into your sucks. Not too hard, just faint enough for me to feel a sensation."

She attempted it.

"Easy," I cautioned.

She lightened up on the nibbling.

"Eh...eh...A little more pressure."

She adjusted appropriately.

"Ahhhh...right there. Now this is what you will do intermittently. But if you want to drive me wild..." I started to withdraw my finger from her busy mouth, trying not to give in to the wonderful hand job she was giving me. I stopped pulling my finger when only the tip was left inside. "...you scissor softly on the head for warming appraisals. But that's only at the beginning when you're warming me up. Okay?"

She nodded her head with my finger still in her mouth, I slowly pulled back and she scraped her teeth gently over it. *Fuck! This is going to be good!*

Without instruction, Rayna moaned and quickly lunged forward. She flickered her tongue on the head with athirst, causing my belly to lurch. She started off with the soft scissoring of my head. *Goddamn.* In little time, she took me into her warm, soft, and well secreted mouth, sucking me—working her way to the base temporarily removing her hands. She wanted to taste me, all of me. I gave her the time to acquaint herself and accurately use the soft head chomp method skillfully. She looked up to me for evaluation and through slanted eyes I gave her a nod. She did it several times before I released a throaty groan.

Rayna started to work her hands back in gripping me firmly, gulping me with need. I watched, drenched in eroticism as she hollowed her cheeks sucking me in. Heat spiked my groin, and I didn't know how long I'd be able to hold out. I watched her suck me so deep into the recesses of her throat and moan in satiation. She felt so good, sending warm sensation all throughout my body emanating from the core of me. Rayna employed the small scraping as she pushed me in and out and back in again. I was about to lose my fucking mind as I felt the convex of my cock down her throat and her handle on me. Each time her tongue rolled over my head my abs jumped. I started to lose my balance but caught myself. As her pace in strokes increased so did my jolting.

"Look at me," I demanded and when those round brown eyes shot up at me I could tell she was just as entranced as I was. I felt my knees buckling and my balls trembling, I knew I was about blast the fuck off. I couldn't do it in her mouth, she wasn't ready for that yet. I could never disrespect my lady by shooting in her mouth without notice. I'd lost myself entirely in the short time we'd been indulging but I had fucking sense.

"Ray, baby, I'm about to come. When I tilt your head, I want you to pull back, so I don't come in your mouth."

Rayna worked harder in earnest anticipation. She pushed and pulled with hunger and randy. Her breasts clapped in the air and her full mouth bulged from my erection. My orgasm tipped and that was my indicator. I tilted the top of her head, but she wouldn't budge. Tingles zipped up my chest and down to my feet and my stomach jerked. With both hands I tugged at her head. But she wouldn't stop. She shook her head no and started moaning and I felt the humming vibrations as my head hit her chords.

"Fuck, Rayna!" I bit out as I pumped into her head and mine spun off its axis. Rayna enthusiastically vacuumed every seed shooting from me. I nearly lost my mind. *Shit!*

When I was done and just before my breathing slowed, I lifted her from her knees into my chest and she straddled me as I kissed her wildly.

"Damn! That was so fucking good." She giggled as she snuggled into my neck, somewhat bashful. "You did very well, had me moaning like a bitch. You must have some experience."

I don't know what made me open that can of worms. I didn't want the answer—didn't need *that* truth.

She shook her head in my neck.

"None?"

"None that involved sucking on a penis and certainly nothing resulting in an orgasm. I liked that. I wanna do it again."

She's never given head? Even better for me. I couldn't envision someone else having her mouth.

"Good. Let's keep it that way—all of it," I muttered.

"Now I wanna scream like a bitch," she whispered in my ear, it garnered a hefty chuckle as I gripped her ass tighter walking her into the bedroom. She had me going.

When we reached the bed, she rearranged the pillows as she does when she's ready to mount. After, she guided me to lie down. There was something new in her disposition, she wanted to take the lead. I didn't mind, in fact I liked it.

She then went to her *iPhone*, started tapping on it and then inserted it in the dock on the nightstand. She put on a track, which was seductive at best. I didn't know the song, but it sounded a lot like Jay's girl continuously singing, "*Yes!*" I figured it was a female thing, but it definitely contributed to the mood.

She backed up to be sure to provide me full view of her slowly removing her panties to each beat of the song. Not that I needed any more of a reason, but I was aroused like a motherfucker. My tongue tingled at the sight of her exposed breasts and the hair in her pelvic area. I wanted to taste it so badly. She teasingly did a little belly dancing number while taking off her G-string. I was ready as hell as she slowly climbed aboard, and I noticed her eyes softening.

"Let me make love to you, baby."

"You've never made love to me before?" My eyebrows rose in anticipation of her answer.

"Have you to me?" She didn't pose it as if she was looking for an answer as she panted deliciously in my face.

She pressed her lips up to mine and inserted her tongue shortly after. She started grinding methodically on my lap. I stopped, abruptly halted in my lecherous state.

"Damn! I don't have a rubber."

Her heavy eyes shot up to mine, piercing me. There was an abbreviated pause before she finally spoke.

"It's okay. I need you so badly right now," she whispered, desperate and ready to go.

Rayna was always bolder and more unpredictable when she was in heat. But I didn't want to take advantage of her. I knew the game and why the rules were so important. I didn't want to complicate shit between us.

"Are you sure? There are several ways I can pleasure you outside of penetration." I was giving her an out. As much as I prayed she wouldn't take it, I wouldn't be able to live with myself if things went awry and she expressed regret.

"Azmir, I don't want anything between us tonight. I want you to feel all of me. Is that okay?"

"What's so different about tonight and why does it have to be just for tonight?"

"*Shhhhhhh...*" she hushed me while using her hand to guide me inside of her.

As she enclosed around me, she gave a sharp intake while her eyes rolled to the back of her head. I knew at this very moment if Rayna were to become pregnant, I'd take care of her for life. What I would do for my child went without saying. No matter what, I'd care for her, do anything to keep her within arm's length of me.

She took her time fitting me in, making sure she was comfortable. I thought I was going to explode prematurely when she eyed me with intensity as she glided down. *Fuck! I'm never going in sheathed again.* The sensations I felt from her warm walls sliding down my cock could start a war.

Before long she slowly whispered in my ear with labored breathing, "You feel so good. It's like my insides are carved for you."

Her pace was moderate. She was trying to take me all in as she stared me square in my eyes. She was really making love to me. As she grinded her breasts danced. Her taut nipples bouncing in my face had me out of control. She would slow down and then speed up. The inconsistency delayed my explosion.

I could feel her tightening and relaxing her internal muscles. I grabbed her ass. *Damn!* She felt incredible.

"I don't wanna be with anyone else. *This...all of this...is all yours.*" She exploded all over me, melting onto me. Her pussy constricting deliciously over my stick.

The thought of what I was in...what I was feeling being all mine made me lose control. I tried to hold back as much as I could but between what she was putting on me, her words and her sensual tone, I was in bad shape.

"*Oooo! You're scratching...my...asssssssss. Go ahead. It's...alright. Let it...go. Don't...worry about me...baby. Let....it...go!*" she sputtered as her soft breasts clapped my face.

And with that, I had no choice but to let it blow.

CHAPTER 3

Rayna

Life began to move so fast after my birthday excursion. One debacle I was faced with just two weeks after our return was the recurrence of Michelle's cancer. It happened *so* all of a sudden. She was in and out of the hospital and it was all consuming.

I'd practically moved into her place. I had to in order to help out with Erin. She needed to be taken to all her appointments including the doctor, acting classes, and soccer. In addition, I made sure Michelle was transported back and forth to chemo and radiation therapy as well as doctor visits. She had others helping out when I couldn't, but I assumed the responsibility of primary caregiver.

The responsibility grew so great that with the permission of the higher ups of the firm, I brought in consultants to take appointments for me when I needed to be with Michelle. The only reason the idea was entertained was because it was Michelle who was being cared for; the niece of one of the partners. If such wasn't the case, I'd be in a heap of trouble. I could tell they preferred per diem consultants rather than stretching the therapists on staff.

One Saturday Azmir and I decided to hit *The Grove*. I had a few things to pick up and so did he. I'd been putting going to the mall off with my crazy schedule, but this particular day Michelle insisted I get out and be with Azmir. It was a beautiful day in sunny California, so I was happy to obliged. After doing a little shopping, we decided to have a bite to eat. We spent our entire lunch debating the top five best rappers. We agreed on the best but couldn't sync the order of our lists otherwise. The conversation spilled over into our post-lunch stroll and found its way into a store or two.

"You think LL's one of the best because of his ability to stay relevant after over twenty years in the game, but I'm basing my rankings on lyrical style and content," Azmir argued.

"And you allow being a Brooklyn-native to factor into your ranking. You cannot have three Brooklynites in your top five, MirMir!" I pleaded.

Not too long after those words left my lips I heard, "MirMir? *Hmmmmm*... Based upon that pet name, I can tell you're fucking her, and she likes it. You must be into it as well because you do have her in the mall, a place where it can be assumed you've spent money on her. It must be the newness of the pussy because you *are* carrying bags, which means she's got you spending a little cash. Oh, and judging by the names on the bags, you're not making it rain on this hoe." That was followed by a chorus of laughter.

I turned abruptly to find this beautiful light complexioned woman with long silky hair parted down the middle. She wore bold orange-red lipstick and donned a cute, off-white maternity blouse exposing her cleavage, white capri pants and white stiletto slide-in heels. She had handsomely sized diamond stud earrings, a beautifully decorated diamond brooch above her left breast and wrists full of shopping bags. I could tell she was a diva. My question was how recent a lover was she of Azmir's with her belly bulging the way it was.

My heart raced, mouth dried and eyes immediately flew to

Azmir to find his reaction to this bitch calling me a hoe. Azmir didn't appear ruffled at all. His demeanor was calm and very well anchored, *per usual*. Azmir always possessed the ability to remain placid during less than favorable events. I guess it was a characteristic required for a man of his caliber. He took a cursory glance at her and turned his head back to what he was doing as if her being the donor of such callous jargon didn't surprise him at all.

"Tara..." he uttered extremely deadpan as he placed the item he was eyeing back on the shelf.

I could tell he was very familiar with her, but I was still waiting to judge where he was going with this so I could decide on my follow up. Secretly I was panicking. This couldn't be happening to me. Not now. Not after I allowed my feelings to run wild for this man. The suspense kept me on edge.

"Is that how you introduce yourself to the *next* woman?" Azmir continued, still browsing the shelf. "And are you expecting me to top that indecorous rant with an insult? Because if you are, I'll pass."

I think I saw a hint of a mocking grin on his perfectly sculpted face. Even in the midst of my anger I couldn't deny Azmir's impeccable features.

Tara wore this addling expression, and I could tell she was ready for a verbal war but wasn't provided a cue.

And that's when I came in feigning a puzzled look on my face, "*Tara...Tara?* Ohhh, Tara!" as if to say I finally realized who she was from a previous conversation with Azmir about her.

I wanted her to know I wasn't a garden variety chick on his belt, but that we had informative conversations about our previous relationships. Azmir mentioned the *"next"* woman. He's not the one to consider just *any* woman his, which led me to believe she was his most recent ex—an ex he'd never informed me of being pregnant, but that was neither here nor there. I had to verbally jab this bitch right back for her unprovoked and cruel outburst.

After a thorough once-over of her—*complete from head to toe*—I noticed Tara was beautiful and well suited. That intensified the sting. Fuck that! I felt a burning sensation course through my chest. Immediately, I felt out of place, as if this moment of her and Azmir sharing air somehow made me the intruder. I don't know the last time I'd felt a twinge of jealousy. And I was damned pissed about feeling it here with her.

I followed with, "You're right, sweetheart. She *is* narcissistic," with a giggle in my tone. I then took his hand and strode off. She and her two cheerleaders looked like asses! I could tell she was caught completely off guard.

After we were a few feet away she screamed, "Bitch, you think you got him!"

No response was necessary on my behalf. Had she not been pregnant that story would have had a different ending. My violent tendencies still laid dormant waiting for the right opportunity. But for now, I had to collect myself. I felt the walls of self-preservation elevating all around me. *Survival.*

As we waited for the valet to bring the car around, I seethed in silence. Azmir had a whole other world I wasn't privy to until now. Pain seared through my chest, and it took every bit of strength I could muster not to break down.

He broke the ice once in the car. "Okay. Go."

Azmir didn't even look me in the face, he just braced himself, cowardly thinking I would discuss this casually in his car after having discovered a pregnant ex. *Is he out of his mind?*

"I'm sorry...?" I asked with an even breath, baffled by his direction.

"I know you have questions about her. I'm prepared to answer them," he clarified in his CEO mien.

This doesn't work that way, Jacobs!

"I just don't like surprises or feeling like the third party out...I have no clue as to what just took place in there and I'm not comfortable with that." I tried being cognizant of my tone, I didn't want to bring too much emotion to the situation. I was in control!

"You handled yourself well in there," he tried to assure me. "Tara *is* egotistical. It's funny how you hit that one right on the head," Azmir continued with a chuckle.

When I didn't join in, he relented, "Tara is an ex. We were together for quite some time and the breakup came as a surprise to her, although a blind man could see the shit coming."

He glanced my way while driving and I kept my eyes glued to the pavement ahead, so he knew I was not satisfied with his answer.

"I've talked a little about her to you. Not every detail because she doesn't matter, not to mention the complexity of the situation. I have an extensive and extremely sensitive business relationship with her father. It's a fragile relationship but as you can see, we're both aware of the termination," he included.

I choked down my pending tears. He was skirting around the big issue.

"What about her belly? Make me *aware* of the details concerning that, Azmir," I demanded still facing forward.

"That's not my baby, sweetheart." His voice very firm, just above a whisper.

I wasn't impressed, neither was I convinced. My heart twisted in pain and my throat restricted preventing the bile rising from my belly. I felt sick.

"Oh, yeah? And are you *both* aware of that?" I could no longer conceal my anger.

Needless to say, we parted on bad terms that day.

I didn't see Azmir for weeks. He called and left messages, but I never returned them. We did, however, correspond a little through text when I asked him for some time. I tried to explain how the pregnancy was a deal breaker. I didn't think I could wait for the birth of the baby to learn of its paternity.

The way I viewed it was she had a few months to go and in that time my feelings for this man could have increased tenfold. I was not so desperate I would take on a man with a child, a child conceived just months before we became involved no less. And my brief encounter with the Tara chick told me she would play the hell out of the baby momma role. I could see myself choking the hell out of her ass and catching troubles I didn't need in my life.

My heart wouldn't endure the aftermath of a breakup if he were to decide to be with her because she was, in fact, carrying his child. Where would that leave me? No. Right now I would manage the sting of disappointment. I was undoubtedly in pain. The disappointment played similar to the countless encounters with all the men who I took on over the years. Azmir was good and damn intriguing, but he wasn't worth me taking on baggage of that nature. It was difficult to stay away. Difficult to survive the lonely nights, but I managed. Because that's how I mastered getting from day to day in my life; I managed. Through pain, betrayal and mistrust. I managed. *Alone.*

Within that time, I decided to begin my Azmir detoxification.

Nearly three weeks later, I went out to a trendy nightspot with Michelle and her girls. Michelle had started to even out with her sickness and demanded to get out to feel some level of normalcy. Britni was always going to the latest and hottest clubs in L.A. and this one was on her list. The energy was crazy inside, and the music was exhilarating. I had a ball on the dance floor and had to keep reminding myself to take it easy because I had on a very short off the shoulder, taupe, sequin dress. It fit like a large T-shirt. I loved it, but quickly learned it truly wasn't the best thing to dance in.

One of the things I loved most about L.A. was how at the trendier clubs, there was a great mixture of people blending ethnicities and ages. I threw my ass from one side of the room to the next. I was wild and thrilled to be out again. I made dance floor friends with a gay guy. He had olive skin with groomed facial hairs and a neon pink Mohawk. We jammed to the music like nobody's business. There were times he emulated me and I him out of pure fun. It was a blast, so much fun I needed a break after a while.

As I walked off the dance floor, I threaded over to our table where Michelle and Britni were sitting to get money from my purse. The table was close to the dance floor, so we had a good vantage point and quick access to our things. We agreed someone would be at the table at all times to watch our things, so we alternated.

April so happened to just walk up as well and yelled over the music, "Damn, I'm thirsty as fuck! All this dancing has my ass sweating like a fucking farmer. I'm going to the bar to get a soda or something. Does anybody want something?" That damn April had the filthiest mouth of the bunch.

"Hold up. I'll go with you. I want another drink," I shouted.

We made our way over to the bar together and ordered our drinks. April's drink came first but mine, which was a peach martini, seemed to have been delayed. After waiting a few minutes, I grew impatient not understanding what the hell was taking the barmaid so long. I used the metal pole at the bottom of the bar as a stepping stool to look over on the other side, hoping to see what the dilemma was. I could tell she was held up doing something back there. My irritation forced me to fix my attention back there to learn of the issue delaying her. As I was doing this, April tapped me on the arm and shouted something inaudible over the music, but I couldn't hear her. I got down off the bar and asked her to repeat herself. I noticed her face had brightened and sea blue irises were glued to something fascinating across the room. I leaned in closer to her.

"Oh, my god! Your boo is here, girl. Look!" she squealed animatedly.

"What?" I asked almost at the same time as she shouted, "Over...at our table!"

Without thought, I turned to see what she was referring to.

I glanced over towards our table to find Azmir bent over exchanging words with Michelle. My body froze in place, and I could no longer hear anything but the beat of my heart as blood rushed through my veins quickening my pulse. How crazy was it that he was at this place tonight!

Azmir's presence was always commanding no matter where he went. His tall lean frame stuck out over his entourage's. Before I knew it, Michelle had pointed him toward my direction. My first instinct was to make a volte-face to the bar, but it was too late. He had seen me. I couldn't help it; I completely turned my body around back to the bar.

Of course, in true April fashion, her blue orbs and attention stayed fastened across the room. She used her straw to twirl in her glass while she lusted over Azmir.

She even had the nerve to go as far as to say, "Mmmm...mmm...mmm! If you don't want that man, Rayna, I got something for that ass. I knew I should have snatched his ass up before you started fucking him." She continued after a short pause with, "Who am I fooling? I could give a rat's ass that you've fucked him. I'll take him anyway."

Her neck twirled swinging her silky bleach blonde hair with perfect golden highlights, her pointed nose protruded, and narrowed lips pouted salaciously. If she and Michelle were not distant relatives, I would have strangled her ass years ago.

I wouldn't even dignify her comment with a response. Though, I must admit I was surprised she would be so bold to even admit that. April knew I would break that ass off in a heartbeat. I guess I was too preoccupied with being jarred by Azmir's unexpected presence to even give light to what she'd said.

Trying to steal another glimpse, I did a double take when I saw the woman standing next to Azmir, taking in the atmosphere as he bent over to talk to Michelle. She was relatively short and wore black leggings and a black halter-top as she gripped a martini glass. Was he really going out with someone else that quickly? That thought killed my buzz. My initial thought was to leave. I thought it would be too weird to stay there knowing Azmir and I were in such a strange place. I mean, I'd practically shut him out of my life for weeks.

Now, I really needed a drink. After a few seconds of deliberating, I decided to stay and play. If he could easily move on with someone else, so could I. *Alone*.

A half hour later found me on the dance floor again with my gay, neon-pink-haired dance partner. I shimmied with my drink in my hand. He motioned to me saying he had to leave. I waved goodbye while still getting down when I noticed my martini was done. It was a bold move on my part but when I saw the broad Azmir brought whispering in his ear while they eyed the dance floor from a distance, I decided to go for my third drink and find a new partner. This time one of the heterosexual nature.

That didn't take long because immediately after leaving the bar, a short and bulky dark-haired guy tapped me on the arm gesturing he wanted to dance. *Perfect!* I obliged and we strolled into the crowd and created a space to bust a few moves.

I could see Azmir from where I was dancing. He kept looking at me with no break in his gaze. I took a sip of my drink seductively and moved closer to dude who was all into it. I don't know where the nerve came from, but I decided to start ticking. Ticking is when you methodically switch your hips in conjunction with your arms and/or shoulders to the beat of the bass. The best tickers incorporate seductive gestures with their movements to enhance the performance. I knew my behavior was borderline chicken-head but simply didn't give a damn. I did that for a few seconds before switching up moves. When I turned my back to him, he came closer to grind on me. I didn't particularly care for that but couldn't resist him because I was on a mission to put on a show.

While into my groove, the dark-haired dude kissed my bare shoulder. I couldn't stand for that, so I scooted up, so he was no longer touching me.

He whispered in my ear, "Where are you going, Miss?" as if that would turn me on. I turned to face him and began to shake my head *no* in a polite manner and with a smile while still dancing.

Before I knew it, I felt someone tapping my shoulder and turned to see Azmir's tall and lean frame.

I don't know why but I tried, "Excuse me?" over the loud music as if he could hear me.

He began pulling me by the hand. I yanked back to let him know I was not going with him. It happened so quickly I lost the grip on my drink and the glass fell.

It wasn't long before the dark-haired guy I was dancing with noticed the commotion and yelled, "Hold up, man! What the fuck are you doing?" so loud Azmir was able to hear him.

The last time I'd seen Azmir seething and ready to attack like this we were in Puerto Vallarta. It was terrifying to see him near that point again.

"What?" Azmir howled as he turned around with frightening fury in his eyes and started walking towards him.

At the same time, I noticed two big burly men were coming our way. I knew right away they were Azmir's security team, and I began to get nervous. Azmir got close to the guy with his hand still gripped on my wrist and bellowed, "Fuck you say?"

"I *said—*" was all he got out before Azmir hauled off and punched the shit out of him.

He didn't have any win. The poor guy never saw it coming. He fell to the floor unconscious. I saw two other guys rushing in our direction. I assumed they were friends of my dearly departed dance partner. They didn't look very happy. I couldn't believe I was caught in the middle of these super charged men.

One of the guy's, who was laid out on the floor, friends went to throw a punch at Azmir that was effortlessly caught mid-air by one of Azmir's security team. The interception was so seamless it appeared choreographed, only I knew it wasn't. My dance partner was out like a light. Azmir continued to whisk me off the floor. I had no idea where he planned to take me, but knew he had no right.

"Wait, Azmir! You have some fucking nerve to bum-rush me like this! Where is your girlfriend you brought here?" I protested while being pulled behind him.

He never responded. He just kept his stride toward the back of the club. I was now perplexed. *Where in the hell were we going?* We moved so fast my body flapped against the speed. It didn't help that I was drunk off my ass.

I noticed another big brawny figure screaming at the crowd to move out of the way. He flew past us and cleared a path.

"What the hell, Azmir!" I yelled. As we passed other patrons, their attention turned to us. I couldn't believe this was happening to me.

Finally, we headed towards a back door. The big guy swung the door open for us and once out Azmir ordered, "I'm good here, Ock. Give me room. Just watch the door."

I was still asking him what nerve he had trying to manhandle me after bringing a girl to the club that night. He didn't utter a word. He carried me into the back parking lot behind two large garbage dumpsters before letting me down. Once my feet were on the ground, we stood face to face. My heart raced as I seethed, embarrassed by his outburst, confused at his confrontation, surprised by his presence. He smelled so good in his proximity and memories of good times—extended periods of elation pooled the front of my mind. I didn't want to think of *happy* underneath the heat of his gaze. I didn't want to be so close to the very thing that was no good for me.

He was angry.

Sexy.

And here, right here before me.

The craziest thing happened. There was a magnetic shift.

When I looked into his eyes a torrent of emotions, one of which being lust, overcame me. Azmir's smooth skin glistened under the moonlight. He wore a black collared shirt rolled up at the sleeves with black denim jeans and black designer sneakers.

His beauty was scorched and had suddenly overtaken me. I felt the heat radiating between us, something I'd never experienced with any other man. But then again, this wasn't just any man. It was Azmir Divine Jacobs, the man who somehow had stolen my frozen heart from the steely chambers of my dark desolate chest and was trying to thaw it for his benefit. *Or for mine?*

As I gazed at the well-trimmed goatee on his jaws and chin, I also took note of the scowl he wore. *Is he jealous? Is this his reaction to me dancing with a random man?* We were doing a stare down.

I lost.

His grimace was searing. Without words, he told me I had crossed the line. *But how?* We were no longer together. *But his scent is provokingly familiar and his scowl deliciously tantalizing.*

Then another weird thing happened.

We kissed.

I don't know who went first but I knew it was something we both wanted. Our embrace was wild. Hard. Possessive. Feral. We were like possessed animals. The kiss was so jagged and fast. I never thought I'd participate in, or even like rough embracing. But to my surprise, I loved it. I pulled him down into me to deepen the kiss and wrapped my arms around his neck as I brought his body down into mine. He lifted me from my thighs and saddled me onto his waist. He began sucking on my lips and licking my chin, madly. When the sucking traveled down to my neck, I lost it.

"Come on," I demanded with little breath to spare.

He knew what I was saying. I wanted Azmir right then and there. My body ached for him, and I could give a damn about where we were or who was watching. I needed him inside of me.

With me clasped onto his upper torso, he began unleashing his wanting cock from his pants. He wasn't moving fast enough for me. I licked his left ear before going to his right. I could tell he enjoyed it. I could hear the long and hard coursed breathing he tried to manage. He shifted my thong to the left as he searched for my canal.

Finally!

He was entering me. I don't know if it was the alcohol or my body simply missed his touch, but he just glided inside of me with little effort. This has never happened with Azmir. I was so wet as he gripped my cheeks and began pounding me. I clawed to him tightly, focusing on my walls welcoming him in. After just a few thrusts, I was ready to join him, and I began to forcefully grind. He felt so good. I felt so enlivened, so awakened as he held me like a feather.

The more my body yielded to him the higher I ascended. I positioned myself so my upper body was arm-length to his. I just held on to his shoulders as I threw my sex to him. Our force was so hard, and he was so deep. The moment was so impassioned and organic, we communicated our frustrations with our bodies and not our mouths. We both felt anger, desire, longing—and the desperate need to release it all.

What I suddenly realized was Azmir was marking his territory with this act. He felt threatened and needed to make it known I belonged to him as if I was property. I, un-regrettably, didn't mind.

He pounded and heaved, pushed and pulled. It didn't take long at all for me to feel that quickening in my belly, and I clenched my vaginal walls to milk him just as my orgasm started to build. And violently I came, helplessly witnessing my body shudder uncontrollably sending my jerking spine to and fro ferociously. I buried my face in his shirt to stifle my yelps of pleasure. Just before I was done, he did the same by concealing his groans in my neck, pulling me forcefully into his hard chest, involuntarily letting out a snivel.

When our jolts slowed, we maintained our firm hold, further communicating in silence. I felt the zapping of energies between us. We were starved of each other, robbed of one another for weeks. *Inopportunely in love was I.*

He eventually let me down. My legs wobbled. He must have picked up on it because as he fixed his clothes he gave me a look of concern, one I tried desperately to ignore. It was cold of me to do but I wasn't quite ready. I took a minute to collect myself before attempting my amble back inside. I led the walk of shame to the club with Azmir just a few steps behind me.

Once inside, I noticed Michelle talking to one of Azmir's handlers, more than likely inquiring of our whereabouts. After that episode I'm sure she was afraid out of her mind. I walked up to her and grabbed my jacket from her hand, "Come on. Let's go," I murmured.

She didn't exactly look relieved, more like a fuming mother with her errant cub. She wanted answers. The other girls stood next to her, all wearing quizzical expressions just the same.

"What in the hell was that? Where were you for over twenty minutes? The cops and ambulance were here, and I had no idea if you were one of those who left on the stretcher!" she howled, alternating her focus between me and behind me at Azmir, inviting him to answer.

Nervously, I turned back and saw Azmir listening in as one of his handlers whispered something to him, all the while his eyes were glued to me with the same scowl and intensity, he wore from the moment he snatched me off the dance floor.

"Are we leaving, Divine?" the girl, who came to the club with him, screamed over the music.

Hearing her reminded me of my frustrations with him. Had he really played me by moving on so quickly *even if he didn't know I'd be there?* I didn't know whether to feel cheap and used or that the joke was on her, because he had just fucked the shit out of me behind the club she was *in* during their date. Or, again, was I the trash dumpster whore who didn't care he was there on a date? I was so confused and unsure of myself. Not to mention slightly still buzzed.

Azmir never answered her, at least verbally because I never heard a word from him. Michelle's gape stayed on him. She didn't know if he had hurt me or not but knew something definitely had happened because we were both behaving conspicuously by wanting to leave.

I grabbed Michelle by the arm, "Let's go, Shelly."

Reluctantly, she followed but not without paying Azmir a few more nasty looks before turning on her heels.

As we walked off, I heard, "Yo, where are you going?" It was Azmir.

Michelle jumped and turned around in an alarmed manner. I knew she was frustrated by our bizarre and fragmented interaction.

Along with my feelings of self-debased obscurities were specifically those of insecurity and embarrassment. Right away, I thought if he was asking where I was going, he was putting himself out there to ol' girl. There *was* something between us. I rubbed the back of my neck and gave a reversed nod in Michelle's direction as if to say I was going to her place.

"I'll send the car," Azmir informed loudly.

Michelle immediately turned to me for my response in hopes of getting some answers as to what happened. I fought the smile begging to eclipse my face. Oh, it was a wrap! If his *"date"* didn't know I was someone special in his life she knew then.

The ride back to Michelle's where everyone had met earlier to leave for the club was weird. The other girls were cackling and carrying on almost as if nothing had happened, and to my delight. Michelle would only speak when spoken to and I was completely silent. I knew she was going to rip me a new one once at her place. I felt so dirty and needed to wash the sex I'd just had in the parking lot minutes before off me. I was wearing Azmir in between my thighs.

When at her house, Michelle practically kicked the drunken girls out in anticipation of reprimanding me. Once she closed the door on them, she turned and set her dangerous gaze on me as I sat on the couch like a child waiting to be scolded.

"Spill it, bitch!"

Ouch! She'd primarily call me out of my name when she was absolutely angry.

"I know...I know! I just don't know how to explain it. It was all so weird," I attempted, rubbing my temples.

"No! Fuck that! Start with the dance floor fiasco. Was he crazy or what?" she demanded in her valley girl trill.

"I thought he was for a moment," I murmured trying to gather my thoughts. My buzz was wearing off and the details of that night began settling in.

"Rayna Brimm, if you don't start talking, I'm going to kick your ass!" she screamed trying to intimidate me. And it worked.

I forced my pleading eyes up to her and opened my mouth hoping something would come out, but nothing.

Frustrated, she shouted, "Okay. Let me try to help you out. The biggest question I have is what the fuck happened after the dance floor? Did you guys go to the bathroom?"

I shook my head no.

"Okay now we're getting somewhere. Did he take you outside?"

I nodded my head yes.

"Well...what the fuck happened then?" Already she was getting tired of the guessing game. I tried to use my hand to motion an explanation but that didn't work either. Exhausted from defeat, I took both my hands and buried my face in them.

She walked up to me with wide eyes and a collapsed mouth and calmly surmised, "You fucked him, didn't you?"

I nodded my head in shame. I felt so low.

We discussed the girl he had there with him. Neither one of us could answer whether or not they were romantically involved. We went back and forth about the potential for a real relationship between Azmir and me. Of course, Michelle was a proponent, even after she said how she'd overheard a conversation at the nail salon about the radio personality, Lady Spin, being linked to him. My head continued to spin. I didn't know what to say to that. I told her I needed to shower. I felt nasty wearing sex *from behind a garbage dumpster.*

While in the shower, Michelle yelled to me, "Na-Na, Azmir's driver is here to pick you up."

Damn!

It had been a long day and I didn't know if I was up to seeing him.

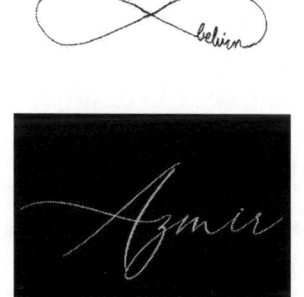

My phone rang and I answered to find it was Ray, my driver. He had arrived at Michelle's pad and was informing me he was waiting on Rayna.

"Indeed," I replied.

After I hung up the phone, I looked down at my left hand. I had it wrapped in an ice pack to help with the swelling. I hit dude with the left instead of my usual right because I didn't think. I was fucking mad as hell! If he saw me snatching shorty up off the dance floor like that, he should have known something was up between the two of us and just walked off. What random dude is going to just yank up a woman like that without a connection to her?

I couldn't stop thinking about the number she was doing with him trying to show her ass. After I saw him kissing on her, I told Marcus to watch my back because I was going in to get her. I didn't think it would get ugly but had him on the lookout just in case. I can't front, I was to ready to shut that shit down if I had to. *What the fuck was running through her mind dancing like that?* When I first stepped on the scene, she was with an obviously gay man, but when the other dude asked her to dance and tried to kiss and feel all up on her ass, it was over.

I didn't really know what I was going to do with her once I snatched her ass up. I just knew I wasn't going to stand there and watch her play herself.

What really fucked my head up was what took place in the back of the joint. I knew Rayna was a little freak but didn't know she got down like that. I was fucked up in the head! If she didn't know, she was soon to find out she was mine. I mean, I wasn't about to sweat her ass, but we needed to make some serious decisions—and tonight. Shit needed to be solidified.

An hour or so later the doorman called to inform me of my guest having just arrived. Minutes later, she was ringing the doorbell to my apartment. I opened the door to find her wearing a figure fitting white sweat suit with the hood covering her head and her *LV Keepall* hanging from her shoulder. Rayna looked distressed.

She gave me little eye contact. I took it to mean we were both in awkward places behind this shit. She dropped her duffle bag on the floor and stood there as if she was waiting for further instructions from me. I was at a loss. I tried to play it cool.

"What's this all about?" I asked to break the ice.

"You tell me. You summoned me," she muttered dryly.

"Quite frankly, I don't know what to say—" I began until she interrupted.

"I can't do this, Azmir! I'm not property. What is this game we're playing? Where are we?"

"That's what I wanted to discuss—"

"If we're going to be friends then let's do it with minimal conflicts. If you just want to be fuck buddies, then tell me. But anything outside of those two things I can't promise because of your situation," she continued firing off, referring to the pregnancy issue.

"Rayna, that is not my baby," I tried to assure once again.

"Can you prove it?"

"I will be able to prove it soon. Believe that."

"That just isn't acceptable." Rayna's voice crackled into a whisper.

"What can I do to get back into your good graces? Do you want me to have the paternity test done in utero? I can push for it if it'll satisfy your inquiry."

"Are you using condoms when you fuck other women?" she spat out of nowhere.

Whoa! That hit me like a ton of bricks. *What is she insinuating? That I am some type of gigolo going from woman to woman?*

"Where is all of this coming from?"

"Just answer the question. Let me know what I'm up against. And don't forget the Spin girl...the deejay I met a few months back. Oh, and the one from the club earlier, either!" she hissed.

I was fucking offended. "Ray, I will swear on a stack of Qurans that before tonight I ain't touch no pussy since yours in The Bahamas! I told you then I wasn't fucking anybody else. Where is this going?"

"Ummmmm...I think it's fair for me to ask since you've gotten in the habit of fucking me raw!" she continued with venom until I decided I needed to correct her.

"Hold up! You initiated sex without protection, Ms. *"I don't want anything in between us"* in the Caribbean! And if I recall, you were the one demanding sex earlier...not me! Where are you going with all of this, Brimm? I'm not going to sit here and allow you to make me out to be a womanizer one minute and some damn perv the next! I've never pressured or manipulated you into shit." I was about spazz.

She got quiet. The silence remained for seconds. She backed herself onto the wall near the door and fell on her haunches.

"I am so confused! I hate this place we're in! What the hell is this? I'm really having a difficult time figuring out your feelings for me. And don't claim to have been open with me all this time because if you were, I would have known about this Tara girl and her pregnancy! This is the very reason why I've been avoiding relationships—they're too damn complicated. Do you know right now I'm feeling like a whore after that episode earlier? I mean...what decent woman allows a man she's only been dating, *before taking a hiatus for nearly a month*, to fuck her behind garbage dumpsters in a parking lot in the back of a club? I've been trying to answer this ever since it happened. And did I mention the guy was there with another woman? This is all too much for me. I can't do this!" She collapsed her head into the palms of her hands.

Once again, she involuntarily exposed her vulnerable side. I couldn't believe she had all of those insecurities. I didn't have the words to answer those questions. The young broad, RinRin, with me was an aspiring rapper. I'm acquaintances with her manager and he wanted her to hang out with me to develop her image. She was dope, but ain't have shit for me.

I saw Rayna was absolutely clueless about my feelings for her. Shit, I counted twenty-two days since we last saw each other. I had a few of my people tail her a couple of times while we weren't speaking just to keep an eye on her. I hadn't resolved to just walking away from her.

It's funny that she brought Spin up. Rayna would be shocked to know I almost smashed her again recently, but just before going in I got turned off because ol' girl wasn't fitting the "Rayna bill." I remembered how well things *didn't* go that night after I rejected

Spin. Our relationship plummeted after that experience. Even though I couldn't get Rayna out of my system, I wasn't going to chase her. My pride wouldn't allow me to do it. She had to let the Tara being pregnant, shit ride. It was a moot issue. I was done with it.

I was still a little confused about where I wanted my relationship to go with Rayna. The one thing I had been clear on was my strong feelings for her. I didn't know if it was my age catching up to me or what, but I had never felt this way about a woman before. I felt like I was addicted to her. She had concerns of me being with other women when little did she know, I was too wrapped up in her to notice anybody else. Again, I was fucked up in the head.

I saw her there squatting on the floor. She wore no makeup, only lip-gloss. Her hair was up in a ponytail. She looked sexy even in sweats and Ugg boots. I extended my arm to help her up. She obliged and rose to her feet. People would be surprised to know I'm not a man of many words when it comes to love. I wanted to express my feelings to her as well as my desire of her physically. It had been almost a month since I'd had that ass. I needed my fix and what transpired earlier was just a tease.

I took Rayna back to my bedroom and lit the decorative candles around the room which had never been used. I didn't know how well this would go over; she didn't seem to be in the best state of mind. But I had decided to try my luck. I needed to have her. Again.

After removing every piece of garment she wore, I asked her to lie on the bed and wait until I returned. I went to the kitchen to put a few cubes of ice in a bowl. Then I went into my medicine cabinet to retrieve a piece of *Halls* from the pack I had stored in there. When I returned, she was lying on her side using her left arm to hold her head up. I put the bowl and cough drop down so I could remove my shirt. I stood at the side of the bed examining her curvy body. My erection arrived. I chewed a piece of ice then popped the Halls drop in my mouth. I was ready to go in. I did some things with Rayna I'd never done with anyone before.

I had her lay face up with her back flat on the bed and her head at my pelvic area. When she did, I bent over, grabbed her by the waist and lifted her in the air until her sweetness was square in my face and thighs on my shoulders as I began to taste her peach. She was a little heavier than usual but still a lightweight, which made it easy for me to hold her while I explored her valley from a new view. I could tell she was new to this and didn't know what to do. She fiddled around while she hung upside down. I gave her a minute to adjust her head to a comfortable angle. I made sure she felt the coolness of the cough drop as I gripped her soft ass. I could tell she felt the sensation because her body tensed up. I enjoyed tasting her. She was always so fresh; her internal fragrance turned me out each time. I heard her moans and didn't want her to climax, so after a while I gently let her down on the bed.

She was ready for me. She undid my pants, laid me down and took me into her mouth. I maneuvered her body into a six-nine position. She challenged me not to climax before her. I was down. As she had my toes curling like a little bitch, I was on a lovemaking high. I grabbed her ass cheeks and pulled them to my face. She couldn't take it and stopped pleasuring me because she could no longer focus. She sat up and began riding my face. She made sounds new to me. She went wild. Not before long, she began to break in her rhythm and her body jerked. I could tell she was preparing to climax. I wasn't ready to end this, so I stopped.

I then stood her on the floor facing the bed and had her bend over as I entered her from behind. Once settled in, I grabbed her waist and shifted her weight onto my lap until we established a balance. I eventually worked us into the Titanic position where her upper torso was at a forty-five-degree angle in the air, and I held her arms down behind her back. This position drove me nuts. I penetrated her so deep; I thought I was going to lose my mind.

Something about her canal felt different, she was creamier and more swollen than usual. I pushed the possibilities of why to the back of my head. It was a bumpy ride and the mere sight of her limp body being controlled by me made me feel superior and took me to another level. I noticed her ponytail going in each direction. I pulled out the scrunchie and her hair fell into her face. I could no longer see her eyes but imagined how sexy her expressions were. There was something about her willingness to me exploring her body turning me on. I heard her moan and knew it was incredible for her, too. I knew this was an awkward position, so I didn't stay in it for long. I felt awesome and like I could go all night long, but I had to switch it up.

After I let her down, she turned to face me. Her mane was tousled in her face. With heavy dark eyes she squinted. "Is that all you have for me?"

Rayna was telling me she was enjoying me by way of challenging me. I grabbed her by the face and devoured her mouth. I was enamored by her. She straddled me as I walked her back onto the bed and laid her down. I stood on my knees over her, lifted her legs, folding one over the other in a cross formation, and pushed into her chest before entering her. She was so damn flexible. This was another position allowing me to go deep. I was in a spell. I had to regain my steadiness, especially after her challenge.

Eventually, I switched it up by placing my feet on the floor, standing over her and pulling her toward me before going back in. This was a big mistake because I now had more agility. The sound of my cock going in and out of her added to the experience, which is why I didn't put on any music. The sounds I heard throughout our lovemaking session took me to ecstasy. Her extending her legs straight into the air woke me out if my trance but didn't break my pace. I found myself pounding her. I began hearing our skin collide in slaps. Her moans started and gradually turned into screams. I knew she was climaxing.

She cried my name, "*Di*—vine...*Div*—ine!" Rayna's orgasm did it for me. I felt her vice grip on me. I couldn't hold it any longer. As I exploded around her, I found it difficult to hold my balance, I didn't want to fall on top of her.

Goddamn.

Rayna

Life's complicated. Isn't that the memo constantly being hammered into our psyches?

Life's not fair. Isn't that what the humble hearted use to get from day to day?

All is fair in love and war. Now that, that's bullshit!

Nothing about love is fair. The shit is painful and overrated. My life had been consistently complicated, and it was unfair I was relentlessly at war with myself when trying to make sense of love. Azmir tried waving the white flag the night after that god-awful club episode. He made sweet love to me and practically begged me to advise him of how to repair us. There was so much going on in my head, so much strife in my heart. He assured me if given the chance we could fix anything obstructing our way. *What way?* We weren't even an official couple. Azmir spoke fruitless optimism.

What he didn't know was what I had been in denial about for weeks. I was pregnant. Azmir and I went without birth control since The Bahamas. I don't know what I was thinking or if I'd been thinking at all. This is the only man I felt close enough to—*to* trust without a condom. Tyquan, I didn't trust—I was just stupid. This Azmir made me forget to put one foot in front of the other to walk each time I was in his intoxicating presence. I was caught up in such impulsive realms with him I didn't think.

It was August, my breasts were enlarged, and mornings were filled with vomiting and queasiness. I spent very little nights with Azmir because Michelle's condition had become so shaky. I hadn't taken a pregnancy test because of all the things going on in my life at such an accelerated speed. I didn't have time for another inconvenient truth. My period was weeks late and I wouldn't stress Michelle with this, she was sick herself. It tore me to pieces when I reflected on how polar her health was to just a month ago. And I couldn't handle turning Azmir off with this. Things were too calm between us. He had been so helpful and understanding with Michelle. He paid for her home healthcare when I needed time away for professional travel.

My hips had begun to spread so quickly. Sex with Azmir had slowed down tremendously because I couldn't bear him finding out. He was so underneath me, demanding to spend so much time together, making me wonder if he had sensed it. But I didn't want to be Tara. I wrestled with the question, *would he try to deny mine, too?*

Your heart senses things your mind cannot comprehend. I felt in my heart he wouldn't, we were so connected. He was so attentive and consistent. But I still had those looming fears of him coming up short. I dealt with it as I do all other things I can't deal with—I distanced myself from him. I ran.

Weeks after the club incident, I had taken Michelle to see her oncologist. After he entered the exam room, he grabbed the rolling stool, sat on it and scooted close to Michelle. A chill traveled my spine.

He grabbed her hand, "Michelle...dear, according to your biopsy not only has the cancer returned but the bastard has metastasized amok. Sweetheart, there's nothing more we can do. As you can see, in your current condition, another round of chemotherapy could wipe you out. Your body cannot withstand that."

You could tell he spoke regrettably, but it still was a terrible blow. My knees buckled. A tear fled my dear friend's eye and her bottom lip quivered as she forced a smile to her face. I could tell the news hit her hard, but she was still in fight mode. She was such an optimist. I jumped up and abruptly left the room. I couldn't let her see me cry, she didn't need that.

From that moment on, Michelle began preparing paperwork for a will. One day I walked in the house with groceries and saw what I initially thought was an elderly woman at the dining room table writing. My senses quickly came to me, and I realized Michelle's physical condition. She went from weighing one hundred-twenty pounds to a mere eighty-two. She was literally all skin and bones...a skeleton. She walked with a cane and couldn't stand upright. She had no facial hair or that of her head. She wore turbine-like wraps to keep her head warm. Her skin took on a yellowish tone with the exception of the deep shade of brown half circles underneath her eyes. Her teeth protruded through her lips as the fat ebbed away.

She had succumbed to her disease.

Fucking cancer.

"What are you doing out of bed?" I reprimanded.

She slowly turned to face me as I was trekking past her heading to the kitchen. When she turned, she *really* resembled an old woman as she slowly lifted her arm to wipe her running nose. She managed a smile and murmured, "I needed a change of scenery." Her words were labored.

"When is Britni coming to pick up her makeup bag? It's been three days. Can she really go that long without it?" I asked, trying to break my bleak thoughts of Michelle's condition.

Britni and April were dedicated to Michelle's care, which surprised me. I didn't believe they could stop thinking of themselves long enough to care for someone else. They pleasantly proved me wrong.

"Oh, I'm sure she has backups in her car and at work," Michelle replied with mirth.

As I was unpacking the groceries in the kitchen, Michelle slowly sauntered in and rested against the counter. I glanced over at her, "You need to be laying down, Shelly, with your feet up. We don't want your legs to give out on you like before."

"Yeah...yeah...yeah!" she retorted. "I need to talk to you, Rayna." I knew when I heard my full name I wasn't going to like the context of the conversation ahead.

"I know this is a difficult time for you having to see me slip away like this—" Michelle started.

But I interrupted with, "It's not about me right now. Please don't think about me for a change—"

"Rayna, let me finish." She raised her hand in protest.

"I can appreciate what you're going through, even in my current condition. You're familiar with the term *Rest in Peace*." It wasn't exactly presented as a question. I allowed her to continue. "That's what I want to do, Rayna. I want to leave here knowing my loved ones will be okay. Erin is young with so much life ahead of her. It's too soon to have any concerns about her not faring well in life. She has so much passion and hope in those little hazel eyes. She's loved and supported by people who will help get her off to a good start in life; people like you, Amber, and other relatives."

Michelle paused to catch her breath before continuing and I held on to mine. "But I am concerned about you. Who's going to be with you...to love you unconditionally, comfort you when you hurt, call you on your bullshit when you want to go into the elusive corners of your mind, feeling the need to protect yourself, to make you laugh when it rains and to hold your hand when days are cold?" Another pause for oxygen. Another moment I went without it as I adjusted to my impending reality.

"Na-Na, I've been in full support of your relationship with Azmir and that's because you sparkle in his eyes. I saw it the first night we ran into him at *Cobalt*. When he laid eyes on you, they did a dance any girl would die to experience. He's romanced you beyond your imagination, paid off your debt to Sebastian's weak ass, given you a luxury car at no expense of your own, made love to you with wild passion and flew you and your associates—*not friends*—to the Caribbean with all expenses paid. Although you don't make the man feel needed, he's still in your life after months of chasing you." She took another pregnant pause to gather herself. My heart clenched and my body trembled as I fought back the tears. I was so tired of crying, so I fought like hell to keep them at bay.

Michelle doesn't need my weakness. Just assurance.

"All of this from a man of Azmir's elite status...he could have just about any woman he wants. Hell—he could have those associates he flew with you to The Bahamas if he wanted! You *have* to give love a try, honey. Your wellbeing depends on it. You cannot go through life alone. If you're planning to, you're taking a detour to an early grave. You deserve to be loved. Yes, *even Rayna Brimm!* I need to know you get this before I go. Please tell me you get me." With her cold skeleton hand resting on my forearm, she pleaded through tearful eyes.

She was practically begging me to take heed, showing dire concern. I felt sick to my stomach. I didn't believe I was capable of meeting her request. She didn't even know about the pregnancy I'd been keeping from him, *from her*. There was no way I could even begin to encompass the crux of her pleas. I didn't have the capacity to take on my shit. I was too preoccupied with championing for Michelle and Erin. They were easier, a lighter burden than my own. But I was unable to articulate this to her in that moment. So, I managed the moment, did what I did best in life. I managed.

I lied to my best friend that day by nodding my head in comprehensive accession. I didn't have faith in myself. She was the only person who did.

Michelle died less than two weeks after our conversation. She put up a hell of a fight with that cancer, but it gave her little time. I felt depression like no other time in my life. I felt emptiness, a phenomenon I'd never battled before. Days blended together and nights triumphed with extensions stretching into the subsequent bleak days. I became a shell, impermeable on the outside to protect what was delicate and fucked up on the inside. I'd forget to eat and sleep. I made sure her final wishes were made known to her family. She was cremated and dispersed in the Pacific Ocean.

I was so numb throughout the ceremony. I felt so alone in a room full of people during her repast. I'd never acquainted myself with her family. Many of them knew of me though I had no knowledge of them. I'd guessed they'd heard about the girl Michelle virtually returned from college with. The one she took in and helped get a job. A life.

I just sat and went in and out of consciousness as I watched Erin run around with her distant cousins while others ate and socialized. I had hurt for her. She would no longer experience the wonder of her mother's love and devotion. She'd never know how great and selfless of an individual her mother was. If Michelle gave me such a generous portion of herself, I could only imagine what she would have given her own child.

Life's complicated. Life's unfair. *All isn't fair in love and war.*

CHAPTER 4

Rayna

I was in my bed, engaged in restless sleep when I felt a sharp pain in my abdomen bringing me to a blustering awakening. I pulled myself up and grabbed my hardening belly. Another wave of pain struck through my body again. As I rose in bed, I noticed blood where I sat in my sheets.

Shit!

I panicked. My first thought was to call Michelle.

Fuck!

My best friend was no longer an option. The pain hit again. I couldn't think of anyone else I could call. I grabbed my purse, keys and towels and tottered my way to the car. I drove myself to the hospital in unbearable pain. I was bleeding and growing weak by the minute. Bringing the car to an abrupt halt, I illegally parked and floundered out of the car making my way into the emergency room and was seen immediately.

I stayed overnight for two days. I'd miscarried my fetus. I felt so numb. It wasn't because I was connected to and bonded with a six-week-old fetus, but because I had disconnected from my own body so much I didn't feel a loss.

I felt *lost*.

Michelle was gone. And consequently, so was Erin. Life lacked rhythm. I had no purpose to my days. Azmir had been in my corner as much as I would allow. Once again, we were in a weird space. I'd never informed him of Michelle's passing or my miscarriage. He tried contacting me, but I wouldn't take his calls or texts. I had no one to call but work to inform them of my need for sick days.

I was under observation because of the blood loss, major dehydration and having a DNC performed to cleanse my uterus of what was once life inside of me. The nurses thought it was odd how I had no visitors and made no calls. Azmir had been calling frantically all week. He sent texts and emails.

On the second day, he left a message saying he came over to my house only to find I wasn't there. For all I knew, he tried looking for me at work, but I hadn't been there in nearly a week since Michelle's passing. I lay there in my hospital bed and cried on and off until I was discharged.

The nurses asked how I would get home and explained how for liability reasons, I could not drive myself. They placed me in a cab to go home when I was discharged only for me to catch a cab back to the hospital to pick up my car. I went to work the very next day as if nothing had happened. I was a zombie.

A week later found me at *Katsuya* having lunch with Britni and April. They asked to meet to—I'd guessed—grieve together. I wasn't interested in group bereavement but would do anything to honor Michelle's life, and if that meant putting up with her friends for a couple of hours, I would do just that.

"I just can't believe she's gone. This has been a fucked up week. Who's going to replace her?" Britni moaned; her face was pale bringing full attention to her red nose. She looked to have been crying for days.

She annoyed the hell out of me the most. *Why would you think of replacing a friend?* I know people don't always know the right thing to say when death occurs *but come on!* I just played with the straw in my glass of unsweetened raspberry tea while staring down at the table.

"That's just it, Brit. No one could ever replace her. We just need to find a way to move on. She would want that." That was provided by April. She seemed to have a little more sense than her bestie. I was being tortured during this tête-à-tête between them.

We sat quietly for a few minutes. I had nothing to offer and wasn't in the mood to improvise. April broke the ice by saying, "Rayna, I know this comes at a loss for us, but I know you will be greatly affected by this. You two were like sisters."

After taking a few seconds to process her words, I knew my time of silence had expired. I needed to contribute or be considered rude and insensitive to Michelle's friend.

I offered, "Ladies, it's definitely going to be a rough period ahead, but we have to muster the strength to get through it. Michelle was a mighty force who left an imprint on all of our lives. We have memories of her that will last a lifetime. As long as those memories last, she will live on. I find peace in knowing that." Yeah, a mouthful considering I didn't have shit to offer.

Britni's eyes began to swell up and April went to console her with a hug. Britni struggled to say, "There are so many questions like who's going to care for Erin and what's going to happen to her house..." before her voice teetered off due to the enormity of emotions rushing in.

After a pause I attempted, "There are many things that we don't know as of yet—" but I was interrupted.

"Yes! There are lots of things we don't know about the man we're fucking. Like, let's see. *Ahhhh...* Yeah! Like he's a damn thug in *Burberry* business suits. Did you know that, sweetie? *Or* that everything you benefit from being with him is a result of *my* hard work and training!"

It was the bitch, Tara. By the time she paused, several of her girlfriends had appeared, frantically trying to pull her away from our table. This made her get even louder. Seeing her was the last thing I needed. I'd been hanging on by a thread.

"You may be into ballers, so you probably don't give a damn about any of that. But just in case you have a shred of decency in you, I thought you should know so you can run the other way," Tara continued in her tyranny.

As she spewed this directly in my face, I just sat there looking at her in complete stoicism with incredulity. It was obvious Tara didn't know how to read my reaction and it pissed her off.

She continued, "Oh, I get it! Dumb bimbos like you can't even comprehend the help I'm giving *to make* the right decision. Pitiful! All you broads know how to do is swing those legs up in the air and fall to your knees!"

Although Tara disgorged street jargon, you could tell by her delivery she was a valley girl. Her words weren't threatening, but she was bold. Really audacious—*each time I saw her.*

Her one associate yelled, "Tara, that's enough! She doesn't want any trouble. You're acting very ghetto in here."

And another followed with, "Tara, you're pregnant. He's not worth it!"

Simultaneously, April looked at me and asked, in the state of incredulity herself, "She called *you* a dumb bimbo?"

I guess she, too, was caught off guard by the accusation. Clearly, Tara had no idea of my credentials. *Shit.* Who was I to rain on her parade by explaining how the man she had obviously been obsessed with wasn't with a hood-rat? That narrative wouldn't make her feel superior.

I had to get out of there. Though mad as hell, I decided to play along.

I pulled out my wallet, dropped a crisp one-hundred-dollar bill on the table, stood to get square in Tara's face—as close as her swollen belly would allow.

"Ladies, that's for the bill, courtesy of Divine. As for you, if it wasn't for this belly, I would mop this bitch with your fucking face.

Do ya'self a favor, check my record before confronting me like this. I thought *you* should know *that*."

Just before I turned to walk away, I noticed staff members of the restaurant as well as other well-dressed women charging towards our table.

Tara sputtered, "She called him Divine! I knew she was a hood-rat!"

I purposely referred to him by his street moniker to further her assumption of who I was. I could deduce she was having a baby shower because from my peripheral view I could see balloons and a few other women still sitting in an area adjacent to ours.

That bitch had a good view of me, and I had no idea she was in the room.

I felt like it was all too much hitting me at once. I couldn't take the extra drama. It was then I subconsciously questioned my decision to work things out with Azmir. I'd planned on telling him about Michelle's passing later on. Those plans got derailed after my run in with Tara's ass.

After leaving the restaurant, I returned to my office. I had patients to see. Because of my absence for Michelle's death and funeral and then my hospital stint we were backed up. Many of my patients declined to see my proxy while I was out and therefore, I had extended my hours to catch up. *I had nothing better to do.*

I felt like a huge part of me had gone with Michelle's death and Erin's departure from my life. Amber told me after the funeral in so many words to not call her about visiting Erin, she'd call me. I knew that meant I was locked out of her life. I feared this during Michelle's last days but was too afraid to stress her out with putting something together ensuring I'd stay an intrinsic part of Erin's life. I knew if I stood any chance at seeing Erin, I'd have to hire an attorney. I'd just hoped it would work.

All is fair in love and war, right? *Right.*

I had become so depressed. It was such a contradicting cocktail of emotions. I wanted to be alone to deal with my loss yet at the same time the deceased would never approve of the method of my grieving. I eventually realized how in our final conversation, Michelle was pleading with me to open my heart to trust another individual other than her so she could rest in peace. The enormity of my emotional handicap must have been extremely stressful for her. As much as I wanted to honor Michelle's final wishes, the situation with Tara was weighing on me. I was in so much pain.

In a rare act, I called back home to check on Chyna only to learn my father had succumbed to a long bout with prostate cancer. I didn't feel compelled to pay my last respects, only to be there to support my sister. Chyna sounded so choked up. She said she'd been trying to contact me for weeks to let me know he had taken a turn for the worse. I suddenly recalled how I'd been virtually living with Michelle since my birthday. I'd only shared my home number with my family. *Was that really the last time I'd checked in with her?* I told her I'd be right out there.

Two days later, I was checking into the *Embassy Suites* not too far from the airport. I called to track down Chyna but got my grandmother instead.

"Yeah, chawl, Chyna been runnin' these streets like life ain't got no limits!" my grandmother moaned. "I'm getting too old to be chasing afta' her. Your grandfather been down since his stroke and I ain't got no help."

"Okay, I'll talk to her when I get there," I offered.

Chyna was a wild child because her parents abandoned her. I was no help because I no longer sent for her. For some reason, even calling home depressed me. I wanted no memories of home. Outside of Keeme, I disconnected myself from everything Jersey. I'd send her Christmas and birthday gifts and even paid a visit when she graduated elementary school. But until recently, she was too young for me to relate to. I know it sounds cold, but I couldn't bring myself to take her on. I think until this trip I had no conscience of it. Maybe Michelle's death opened my eyes to the fact of me having isolated my real family. I depended on her for so much I'd substituted those relationships.

These thoughts caused me to cry. I hated crying but those blue feelings overcame me so quickly. The mere thought of Michelle jolted my stomach. I felt that emptiness again.

My phone ringing caused me to judder as it startled me while I sat on the hotel bed. I immediately thought it was Chyna, but when I grabbed the phone Azmir's name popped up. I pushed the button on the top of the phone to ignore the call. I realized I hadn't spoken to Azmir in nearly three weeks. Again, life began to happen so quickly. I had to admit it would be great to have someone by my side and Azmir would more than qualify. He had been so supportive in the past, but I felt like he'd been adding to my stress as of recently. It was almost as if he had another life and I felt like I couldn't trust him. I'd rather nurse myself back to a better state of mind alone than deal with the unknown.

After showering that rainy afternoon, I headed to my grandparents' home. When Chyna opened the door, she ran to me and jumped into my arms.

"Oh my fucking gawd...Rayna! I can't believe you really came!" she cried.

To say I was taken aback by her reaction to my presence would be an understatement. I felt her petite frame descending off me and quickly thought reciprocating her embrace would prevent the fall. Chyna had grown into a gorgeous young lady. She was a lot skinnier than I was at her age and she'd always been lighter in skin tone than Akeem and me. She had red kinky twists in her hair and was making a fashion statement with it. I noticed her gold heart shaped bamboo earrings with her name scripted on a plate running through them. She broke our embrace by stepping back and taking inventory of my being with the biggest and most enthused smile, "Damn, you pretty as hell!"

Before I could thank her, she screamed, "Grandma, look! She beautiful!" very hood'esque.

My grandmother and grandfather came to the front portion of the three-family home to greet me. My grandmother was just as round and plump as a snow-lady and Grandpa was tall and quite frail. I noticed his maimed arm and the left side of his face drooping from the stroke, I had assumed. It was pretty sad seeing him in this condition. The house smelled as it did when I was coming up. Many pictures on the wall were the same. The ones new to me were those of Chyna coming up. I was once again reminded of my neglect of her. It was crazy seeing her at various stages of her life. Stages I'd missed.

My grandmother offered me food to which I declined. I didn't have much of an appetite as of late. Chyna brought me into her bedroom where she had Chris Brown, Soulja Boy, and Waka Flocka posters plastered on her walls. I saw pictures of her and some young guy who I had assumed was her boyfriend. There were poses of them kissing and embracing and some of him alone. Her music was blasting so loud even she knew it was difficult to engage in a two-way conversation with it at that volume. Instead of turning it completely off, she turned it down to a moderate level.

We sat on her bed and initially just stared at one another. Chyna was a cutie. She had features of both our mother and father. She had gotten one of those piercings between her cheek and top lip, marring her beauty. I'd guessed that was the fad for the kids of her cohort. It took away from her natural splendor in my opinion, but who was I to say?

I broke the ice by saying, "Chyna, you've blossomed into quite a beauty. Then again, you've always been gorgeous."

She giggled like a schoolgirl before saying, "Thanks," in the shyest of tones.

"I'm sure the boys are just loving you," I continued my genuine doting.

She continued to laugh nervously. I was immediately reminded of what a teenager was like. I have a few as patients but so far removed from entertaining one I forgotten the awkwardness involved. I tried a different way of starting up a conversation.

"So, what's going on with you?" I asked hoping it would get her to talk.

"Ummmmm...nothing, I guess. Just school," she answered, taking the bait. *Whew!*

"Well, how is school? You should be preparing to graduate soon, right?"

"Yeah...I'm a junior. I think I wanna go ta' college. I don't know. I might do hair."

"Okay. Well, give it some thought and I'm sure you'll make the best decision for yourself." I decided that quickly to end the torture.

"You went ta' college, right?"

I nodded in agreement.

"Did you like it?" Chyna was finally trying to engage me in conversation.

"I went and I think it was one of the best things I could have done. I hope you can find what you like to do and make it happen, too. If it's not college, it's okay, but do something that will help you become independent. Grandma and Grandpa won't always be around, you know," I softly admonished, keeping in mind my grandmother's woes with Chyna.

"Ummmm...okay. I will." Chyna then followed up with, "Mommy be asking 'bout you a lot."

That comment hit me like a ton of bricks. I couldn't recall the last time I'd even thought about my mother. I hadn't seen her since I left for college. My grandmother would mention her when I called back home, but she generally never shared much other than what related to Chyna.

All I could muster was, "Oh, yeah?" which was not a question although it sounded as such.

"Yeah. They transferred her from *Straight & Narrow* to *St. Joe's*. She still on dialysis. I told her 'bout smoking 'dat shit knowing she sick, but she don't be hearing nobody. She gone' end up just like my daddy...watch." Chyna started to tear up.

I didn't know what to say. This news was all foreign to me. My mother was on dialysis? *For what?*

"I'm sorry to hear that." I didn't have anything else.

We chatted for about a half hour more before I rose to leave. Exhaustion hovered over me. I hadn't been sleeping for weeks, and the flight out here probably pushed me over the edge. Chyna's lack of maturity and etiquette didn't allow her to offer to walk me out.

I stood in the kitchen and spoke briefly to my grandmother who sat at her kitchen table with the Bible out to her right, clipped coupons to her left and knitting a blanket in her lap. The conversation was short-lived, likely because whenever I do call and check in, it's her that I speak with. I gave half-hearted promises to stop by before I left the following day to return home. That was me, in and out. I'd seen all my soul could bear. I kissed her and headed out.

On my way to the door, I heard my grandfather wheeze, "You look just like yo' momma when she was yo' age...just as beautiful as the sunrise. Heehee!"

Startled, I stopped to give him my full attention. "Only difference is you selfish like nobody's business. Yo' momma was the most generous and selfless woman I knew. That's how the drugs caught up ta' her, you know. She was a people pleaser. So much that she forgot about herself. I don't know what she saw in my son. Heehee!" He tapped his chair in mirth. "He was like you; when some'in ain't go his way or life wasn't rosy, he hit the road runnin'. That's why he left you girls, your brother and yo' momma, you know. He never even looked back. Heehee!" He paused looking off into the distance as he faced the stained wall that boasted pictures of smiling faces from decades ago.

He continued, "Yo' baby sister ended up here because nobody wanted her. Akeem. We all know his story: them streets swallowed him up. Yo' momma runnin' 'round here after a crack pipe with a dead kidney from that new disease—*heap*...hepa...tites or something."

That's why she's on dialysis! My mother has hepatitis.

Damn.

"She still down there in them projects even though she 'pose to be in rehab. She was there one day and ran off. And you...well, let's just say maybe you had half a mind to leave this ugly life of yours behind ya for greener pastures, but you left even the people who did you no harm. You know what dat tells me?" My grandfather now shifted his gaze to meet mine. "Dat right there tells me you ain't no better off where you at because you ain't yet make sense of the trouble inside ya. The pain is all inside ya. Not here wit' me or yo' grandmother or Chyna...the people who ain't hurt ya. It's within you, honey. Until you free ya'self of them troubles you gone' keep running like that daddy of yours. May even die a lonely death." He paused for a few seconds.

My breathing hitched and my eyes blinked, fighting back the stinging tears from the blow he'd just dealt. Those last words rang familiar. Some of the loudest I'd last heard from Michelle.

He continued, "I bet you ain't even married...are ya? And dat's because you can't let nobody near ya. Pretty educated girl like ya'self ain't spoken fo' 'cause ya damaged. I'm sure it ain't because the boys don't want ya'. You got 'dat college degree so I know you got ya'self a good job. You just ain't right in here." He touched his chest referring to the heart.

He ended there, mercifully, because I didn't know how much more of his analysis of my pathetic existence I could take. I didn't know whether to be offended or look for an epiphany in the message. But I couldn't deny the gravity in it.

I made it to the car before breaking down. His words wounded me. His description of my mother brought me back to the woman I knew as Mommy when I was a kid. I then realized all of the anger and resentment I held for her in my heart as a teen because of the bullshit she took from my father caused me to mentally block out her very existence.

When was the last time I've even spoken to her? Has she even tried to reach out to me over the years? I was still in shock. Total disbelief of recent revelations. *She has hepatitis? She needs dialysis? Had her addiction progressed that much?*

Suddenly, I felt the need to see her. I had to just lay eyes on her. My heart began to take on a new ache as I shivered in pain. This was much different than the emptiness I felt when I thought of Michelle. This was guilt. I felt so many ill-emotions all at once.

I found myself going towards the west side of the city. The closer I got to the projects I once called home the more knots formed in my belly. *I have to see her.* As I pulled up in the parking lot of the building where we used to live, it resembled a ghost town. There were no trees or grass, there was no beauty within the vicinity. The night fell upon the city with light rain as I parked my car.

Before exiting, I paused to gather myself. I was about to walk the same soil a young girl was murdered on because of some bullshit concerning me. I took a deep breath and grabbed my umbrella to get out of the car. I saw two people coming out of the building I was approaching, neither of which I recognized.

I didn't want to go in. Memories of my childhood began pouring in. I didn't know what to do. I swore I'd never return to these projects and here I am. I still felt the need to reach out to my mother. I would at least give her my sincere concern for her health. I began to look around for someone I knew. But very few were out in this rain. As I set about walking to the entrance of the building, my stomach became flooded with butterflies. Just before I went to grab the door handle, it swung open. I had to jump back to prevent getting hit. It was Ms. Regina from the fourteenth floor.

"Girl, is dat you?" she screamed, immediately recognizing me. She looked as if she just learned she was on candid camera. I nodded.

"Where yo' momma at? I was just coming here to look for her," she continued screaming. Years of hard living had caught up to her. Her skin had darkened and blotted spots had developed around her face.

"I was just coming to see her. When was the last time you've seen her?"

"Bobbi just told me she went to da chicken pit up the block. She should be on her way back. She got my money, she said she needed ta' get change. Dat was like a hour ago," Ms. Regina informed. "Girl, you know you is pretty as hell! I know yo man is taking care of dat ass. You look good! Let me hold a lil' something. And don't tell me you ain't got it 'cause you looking real clean...too clean to say you ain't!" She hit me with the crackhead hustle.

I wasn't beat for it, so I replied, "Ms. Regina, I don't mean no disrespect, I just need to see my mother. It's a family emergency. If you see her, tell her I'm out here looking for her." I didn't wait for a response. I walked off.

I drove to the chicken pit. It was your typical, around the way take-out restaurant with the word "chicken" in the name. They sold everything from fried chicken, to burgers, to sodas, to blunts. It was a hole in the wall, but artery-clogging food was always delicious and eagerly available in the hood.

I walked into the restaurant and saw just a few people. It was dark out and a weekday so there weren't many people out. A tall, slender guy with the nappiest mounting afro was at the counter ordering his food. He kept eyeing the pictures on the menu that were displayed above the register.

"*Ummm... Ummm... Ummm...* Let me get a... *Ummm... Ummm... Ummm...* Let me get a... *Ummm... Ummm... Ummm...* Let me get a..." he mumbled repeatedly as if he had no clue what he wanted. Or as if the menu ever changed.

Then there was a chubby—*no*. A plain ol' fat woman whose skin tone was so dark she looked blue. She wore white leggings and her skin color pervaded through them. Not to mention the rolls in her belly and her thighs were so big her feet were like five feet apart when she stood. She had a little girl with her that could be no more than three years old. The little girl ran around the restaurant doing imaginary play with her pretty bows and barrettes. Her hair was braided masterfully.

I then noticed an old, gray haired, soiled, and indigent man sitting on the ledge of the window. He was dosing in and out of consciousness. I wondered how was it that he hadn't hit the floor with all the tilting he was doing.

I was back at home. *Blah!* What a dose of reality.

The last character to catch my eye was a frail woman who donned a long denim skirt and running shoes. She wore a bold colored windbreaker jacket which was hot back in the eighties, not so much in present day. She kept bobbing her head to music playing exclusively in her mind because I damn sure didn't hear a melody of it.

There was something familiar about her voice. I knew this subconsciously, which caused me to move up closer from behind her to catch a glance of her face. I rounded her from the left and after studying her stance for seconds, I realized it was my mother. My heart began racing and my eyes shot up causing acute pain in the back of my head. She didn't immediately catch on to my gaze although I was well within the inner realms of her peripheral. She had dark rings around her once radiant eyes and cracks in her former plump lips. She looked horrid. My mother appeared extremely ill. I don't know how long it was before she turned to acknowledge me but when she did, she did a double take. It was relieving to know she recognized me.

"Oh, shit," she shrieked as she stopped bopping. "Rayna, my baby?"

She shunned her face by burying it in the crease of her arm. She was ashamed. I was embarrassed for her. She began to weep aloud, and I nervously looked around, uneasy about this emotional encounter. I went to touch her arm in a comforting manner, I hadn't come to scorn her.

"Ma don't cry. Don't cry. It's okay. Come over here and sit down," I whispered, guiding her to a nearby booth.

We sat at opposite ends as she continued to weep forcefully. The snot began to fall from her nose and drool from her mouth. She was a mess. I rose to get her napkins I had to ask for through a Plexiglas. I felt like I'd opened Pandora's Box by searching for her. I wasn't prepared for this. It took nearly five minutes for her to calm down.

"I'm sorry, baby. I swear to my Heavenly Father, I'm sorry!" she pleaded.

"What are you apologizing for? Just calm down."

"I knew you was gonna come back one day. I wanted to be ready when you did. I just been tryna' get myself together for so long so I could just call you. I know I just left you hangin', baby. But mommy's been sick...for a very long time. This demon gotta hold ta me and I can't shake it. I just can't!" she cried.

She was referring to her addiction. The last time I saw her she was a closet addict, now she's a full-blown crackhead and it was heart-wrenching to experience. I had up and left Jersey as a kid and virtually never returned. I abandoned my family. Hell, I hadn't seen my mother since I was eighteen years old. It had been damn near ten years! Well—not quite, but when you round up the number, it's an astounding revelation.

"Have you tried getting cleaned? Is there anything I can do to help?" I asked but with private reservations. I didn't want to fall for the proverbial okey-doke. But if she was really sincere I couldn't in clear conscious desert her.

"I been tryna' get into *Sobriety House* for like three weeks now. They keep telling me to call tomorrow because they beds is full. And that's hard on me. These streets is dangerous. That's why I keep to myself. Regina 'n them hanging out right now and I told them I'll holla at them lata. I can't mess around like that no more," she explained before breaking down again.

She continued with, "Rayna, I got this blood disease now. It ain't the A.I.D.S. or nothing like that. It's called...ummmmmm..." she mulled over the answer while tapping her forehead with her fingers. "*Ummmm*... Hepatitis. There's different kinds and mines is the B. I gotta take this medicine that makes me sick. I be all tired and depressed. Rayna, I need help."

Her openness and courage to share threw me. I was familiar with crackhead characteristics from coming up in the projects. They'll do and say anything for their next high. I guess DNA is powerful because I wanted desperately to help her *if* she wanted to kick this shit. But I suddenly had the urge to get up out of dodge. Being there gave me the creeps.

"Where are you staying? Maybe I could stop by and see you before I go home." I attempted to end our encounter as I stood to leave.

She had the longest face when she realized I was preparing for my departure. "Rayna, you so pretty, girl! I can't believe you here. You have any kids...you married, ain't you? I wanna know what's up with my baby girl." She beamed from ear to ear.

I felt horrible. She wanted to catch up when I wanted to leave. *To run like hell.* I kept looking at people coming into the restaurant each time the door would open, breaking my attention. I didn't know what to say. I was at a crossroads with yielding to my human nature to help her get clean and healthy and maintaining my "*fuck you all*" attitude and returning to my new life. I thought of Michelle and felt a coat of warmth come over me. I had to at least try.

So I offered, "Listen, Ma, if you really want help, I don't mind supporting you. I'll be leaving tomorrow afternoon. I'm staying at the *Embassy Suites* in Secaucus. If you want help, find your way there and I'll see what I can do."

I got up to walk out. Before I could touch the door, she called out to me. "Hey, Rayna..."

Here was the okey-doke. The ultimate crackhead move. I knew she was preparing to ask for money.

"God told me you was coming home soon. That's why I needed

to be ready!" she declared excitedly, then shadows of darkness fell upon her eyes. I guess she felt she had failed me again.

Acute pain zapped my chest; I didn't have a response. I cracked an apologetic smile, turned and headed out. On my way to my car, I thought about numbing the pain. *Alcohol sounds like the method!* I knew not to mix alcohol with depression, but it was divine for anxiety. I needed to take the load off and had a collection of weeks to escape, even if but for a night.

Coincidentally, next to the restaurant was a liquor store. As much as I was in a hurry to leave the morose area of my humble beginnings, I wanted to be stowed away in a bed sooner. My exhaustion was cresting upon me. Quickly, I decided to stop in the LQ to pick up a bottle of Henny. *I hate Hennessy.*

After deciding on the size and brand, I grabbed a bottle and made my way to the counter to pay. The place was damn near empty and smelled of cigarettes and ammonia. My nerves were shot, and my body was coiled so tightly I was shivering. As I was searching my purse for change, I heard my name.

"Rayna...*Brimm?*"

I turned counterclockwise to the sound, and I couldn't believe my eyes. It took a minute to gather my faculties and respond with words falling out in a whisper.

"Theresa?"

In that instance, my attention was snatched by the sight of a stroller in my periphery and small children running around it. Something inside me was unsettled with seeing babies in a liquor store. Theresa must have followed my eyes and abruptly turned to the tots.

"Knock it the fuck off! Don't you see grown folks talking!" That last one wasn't a question.

Theresa's exultant glaze made its way back to me as the store clerk was asking for my payment. I handed it to him and turned back to my childhood friend.

"Girl, where the hell you been?"

"Ummm...you know...here—there. How are you?" I asked, attempting diversion.

"I been here. I see your mother all the time around here." Visions of a frail Samantha whom I'd just left suddenly came to mind. "She keep saying she don't hear from you. What you been up to?"

Theresa's smile was so bright and enchanted. I could tell she was genuinely happy to see me. I wished I could return the sentiment. I was in the middle of an anxiety attack growing more imminent with each discovery of the day.

I swallowed hard, begging my wits to return when I coughed out, "School...you know, trying to get myself together. What about you?"

My eyes swung to the children who were once again engaged in tag play. Theresa followed my gaze.

"Who me? Ain't shit going on wit' me but these bad ass kids." She went to offer the smallest baby in the umbrella stroller the pacifier that had fallen into her lap.

"Are these your babies?" I asked quizzically as I observed the wonderment in the kids' eyes as they played. I remember being that young and carefree, able to shut the world out and enjoy each moment even if the environment wasn't conducive to play.

With ease Theresa informed, "Some of them mine. These two..." she went for two little boys to grab them at the top of their heads to show me. Both had aged cornrows plaited down to their necks as they continued teasing each other. "...and these three is Keysha's." She pointed to the remaining two children, one boy and the other a girl, who were now playing hide and go seek around us and the little girl in the stroller.

"Oh." Hearing Keysha's name made my heart sputter. I hadn't thought of her since my last nightmare about J-Boog about a month ago. That was the only time I recalled her, when those lurid dreams occurred. "I didn't know you had kids," I murmured.

"Yeah, girl. My oldest is by Luck-Star from the South-side.

Remember him, right? His ass locked the fuck up like the rest of them. Shit, my youngest's daddy is locked the fuck up, too. Same shit, different times," she breathed out. "You heard about Keysha, right?"

I shook my head.

"Girl, her ass be up to no good, too. She in rehab now and the state done forced me to take these kids again. I keep telling Keysha she gone' lose these kids for good. Who else gone' take 'em—they daddies? Shit, one strung out on dope, the other one dead and the other one just as much as a drunk as her ass is. I be stressed the hell out. That's why I'm up in here. Now I can't wait to put these bastards to bed and lay up with my drink." Theresa gave a lungful exhale.

Wariness wore on her face. Her golden glowing skin had dimmed since the last time I saw her at our high school graduation. Age had tumbled upon her prematurely. She had been living life hard. My heart bled. I needed to go, and now before I imploded.

"So, what's up wit' you...got any kids—"

We heard a thud on the floor and simultaneously turned our attention to find the kids picking up a bottle that must have fallen during their play.

Theresa bellowed, "What the fuck y'all doing! Get y'all asses over here before I beat the shit outta yous!"

Just then, the store clerk started firing off profanities, partially in his native tongue and the other half in English telling Theresa to get the kids out of the store and that she would be paying for any damaged products.

That was my perfect cue.

Amidst the barrage of angry and threatening words between the clerk and Theresa, I whisked out, "Theresa, I have to go. I have someone waiting on me—"

She cut me off with a cry, "But wait...give me your number—"

"My mother can give it to you. Ask her for it the next time you run into her. I have to go!" I shouted as I loped out of the store, damn near tripping over one of the kids. I was desperate to get a hundred miles between me and home.

On my way back to the hotel, I recounted the events of my day. I don't know which encounter disturbed me the most: that with my mother or grandfather or learning Keysha had become an alcoholic. She was too young for an addiction. *Right?* My grandfather's words haunted my every thought on the drive back to my hotel and my dreams for weeks to come.

As I walked into the hotel lobby, I noticed the desk was unoccupied as I continued to the elevator and up to my room. When I approached the door, I pulled out my key card to slide it through. I opened the door and as I walked in, I saw three tall and brawny men in the sitting area of my room. My chest rose in fear. I couldn't feel my feet to run.

God no!

I jumped and simultaneously felt someone grab me from behind covering my mouth. I began screaming through my nose. I was going to die in Jersey!

"Rayna, it's me!" he spoke firmly as he turned my body to face him. It was Azmir. I was scared shitless! I don't think I'd ever been so terrified in my life.

I screamed, "*What the fuck!*"

"A'ight, god, you good from here?" The one big guy with a petite voice mumbled as he and the others moved towards the door to exit the small suite. Suddenly, they appeared far less harmful than they did when I opened the door. My heart still hadn't found its relaxed rate. I was still in shock, trying to process what had happened. It all had happened so quickly. Azmir gave a firm nod dismissing them.

Once the door was shut, with adrenaline still running on high levels in my body, I looked to him for answers. He didn't quickly offer them. He kept gazing at me as if *I* was the one in the wrong. We had a stare down for a while before I broke the ice with, "You can start with what the hell you are doing here."

"I could ask you the same. I don't hear from you in damn near three weeks. I call, text, e-mail, and show up to your office. What the hell is this all about? And what I really need to know is *how the fuck did Michelle pass away, and you do not tell me?*" Azmir was seething, he had never taken that tone with me before.

I shot him a look that could kill for the outburst. He didn't react.

"What is wrong with you? Why do you keep running? At first, the shit presented a romantic challenge but now it's straight fucking neurotic!"

His beautiful nose had flared, and I saw his brows knit with deep concern. In a nano-second I appraised his handsome features, *even when he was outraged*. Feelings of familiarity started rushing in.

I didn't have a response. There was so much going on in the moment. Just minutes ago, I thought I was being violated and now Azmir is yelling angrily in my face. *Did I mention I had no idea how he was able to get into my room? Speaking of which,* "How the hell did you get in here?"

He scoffed, "After day nineteen of trying to contact you, I got the memo about you were avoiding me. I eventually contacted your job. So, yeah, once Sharon told me where you were, I decided I would have to be forceful. And I used my fucking spare key!" He tossed his right arm toward the door; I'd supposed referring to the big brutes who'd just left. I was still speechless.

"Rayna, I don't know what to do. You said you have a problem trusting people, so I try and make myself more available to you emotionally. Before the bullshit with Tara, I thought we were finally in a good space. You have no damn idea what I've done in terms of extending myself to you. What more do you want from me?"

His baritone voice was calm and unnervingly even over controlled breaths as he stood feet away from me with his hands resting on his hips.

For the first time since my dear friend's death, I lost it. I exploded. "What more do I want from *you*?" I broke into a fit of giggles. They vanished almost as soon as they'd arrived. "I don't need a goddamn thing! Not from you or anybody else! I've been at this thing by myself long enough! I'm not asking you for shit! The only person who ever gave a damn about me is gone! Could I at least get some room to grieve? I just need my space!" I screamed at the top of my lungs. The tears gushed after each word. I had lost all sense of control.

With that, Azmir grabbed his jacket and charged toward the door. He was leaving. I didn't know how I expected him to respond to my meltdown or even if I wanted him to respond at all. But I didn't expect him to turn his back and leave. His brisk actions snapped me back into reality. His pending departure represented loneliness to me. If Michelle was gone, who would I have to call on?

"*You cannot go through life alone. If you're planning to, you're taking a detour to an early grave.*" Michelle's haunting words whispered into the deepest of my psyche.

"*You gone' keep running like that daddy of yours. May even die a lonely death.*" My grandfather's wheezing laugh rang in my ear.

I have no fucking clue where the urge came from, all I felt was the need for him not to abandon me in my lowest state, in my darkest hour. I didn't know how I would sift through this pain I was feeling and needed help. I felt like I *would* somehow die if I didn't sort through the barrage of emotions I was experiencing. In that very moment, Azmir represented Michelle's image for me. A light. I had to cling to what little I had of her left.

I shrieked in a desperate cry, "Azmir, please don't leave me." My world had collapsed. I swear, all of my hope and energy was depleted, vanished from my being. I had nothing left. Barely above a whimper I forced out, "I'm hurting so bad." I choked out the words over my hard sobs. "I swear to fucking god, I'm gonna die in this shit. I swear!" I didn't have enough oxygen to make all of my words audible.

But he heard my despairing appeal.

Azmir turned around and watched me buckle to the floor in the deepest sob. With eyes widened in regret, he grabbed me in a deep clinch and calmly whispered, "Let me take care of you. Hey...hey...hey! I'm not going anywhere."

I bowed in his arms, paralyzed with pain, crushed in defeat. He held me for a while before carrying me over to the sofa. He allowed me a moment to let it all out. I'd wondered if he could sense how it had been pending for weeks. I cried until my body emptied of tears.

After a long space of silence he muttered, "What brought you here?"

I noticed him looking around the room. I had no guards up, I told him everything about my trip out there from my dad's passing to my grandfather's heeding and my mom's condition. He sat and listened to it all in silence. In any other instance, his silence would have bit at me but in this moment, I was so low and in need to release it all. All those things haunting me, had consumed me.

He remained quiet on me, expression ran stoic. Insecurity had finally peaked. I didn't know what to make of it. He sat in the chair across from me with his elbows on each armrest and his fingers tented, fiddling with his beautiful and well-groomed mouth. His eyes faced the floor.

All of a sudden, he rose from the chair and commanded, "Let's go," as he reached for my hand. Befuddled, I reached back.

As I stood bewildered, I asked, "Where are we going?"

"I got us the presidential suite upstairs."

"But wait. What about my room and my things? I've paid for this." I was so confused at this point.

He ambled toward the door and without looking at me he replied, "I had your things taken up to the suite. I'll reimburse you for the room."

Up in the presidential suite Azmir ran me a bath. He was still disconcertingly quiet, and I couldn't get a take on why. I mean, I knew I'd just unloaded on him, but it felt like there was more going on. As I sat on the bed in the bedroom, he tossed the hotel's menu on the bed.

"After your bath we can order you something to eat." He went back into the bathroom to check on the water.

Seconds later, he called out to me, saying the bath was ready. Right after, he came back out into the room and gave me a tentative glare.

"What?" I whispered. *He's too distant right now. What the hell is wrong with him?*

He shook his head answering there was nothing wrong.

"Are you going to disrobe for your bath?" he asked *too* composed. *Why is he rushing me to bathe?*

"Is it just for me?" I was so thrown by his behavior. Where was he going with this?

"Do you want me to join you?" he asked with raised eyebrows, voice still calm.

Ummmmmm...

"Sure," I shrugged.

I rose from the bed and headed into the bathroom. He followed on my heels. Once there, he watched me intently as I removed my blouse. He peeled off his shirt, leaving his chest bare, revealing his wiry upper torso, the one I could never tire from ogling. He stared at my upper body attentively, but his gaze never met my eyes; just kept fixated on my body. If his eyes read sensualism I'd understand at least what was going on in his head. But this—*this*—focus was something entirely different.

"Are you okay?" I softly asked before going any further.

I looked him square in his face. His eyes never met mine. He jerked his chin in the air telling me to continue. I didn't know what else to do so I complied.

I unzipped my cropped jeans and pulled them down. I next

unhooked my bra. Azmir maintained his fixated gape. I let the bra fall to the floor. Next, I went for my underwear. They weren't my usual low cut cheekies, thongs or boy shorts. They were high briefs I normally wouldn't wear. As I rose up from pulling them down, Azmir turned at a one hundred-eighty-degree angle and let out the most frightening bellow I'd ever heard from him.

"*Fuuuuuuuuck!*"

His hands squeezed into fists as he buckled into the vanity.

I jumped, "What is it? What's wrong?"

I was met with silence for a few seconds.

"What happened to the baby?"

He was now turned facing the mirror as if it was painful to look at me. All the muscles in his back and arms flexed at a striking semblance of strain.

I was frozen.

"You couldn't fucking tell me, Rayna? Goddamit!" Azmir spewed.

I took a deep swallow trying to maintain my placid expression. I didn't know how long I'd be able to without breaking down.

"Azmir, what are you talking about?" My voice was barely audible, but my body began to tremble.

He remained with his back facing me. I grew uncomfortable standing in the middle of this bathroom ass naked.

He dropped his head between his shoulders and found the fortitude from deep within to continue, this time in a calm tone, "Your line...from your naval to your pubic hairs, Rayna...you were pregnant. What happened to the baby..." He paused before saying, "...our baby?" His words were labored through his distressed breathing.

My body tremors intensified.

Holy shit! How does he know?

The events of the past few weeks were too much of an emotional ride for me and the tears began to stream down my face as I asked, "*Ha*—how did you know about the pregnancy?" barely above a whisper.

With an exasperated pitch and absolute proclamation, he informed, "Rayna, I am your lover. You think I don't know your cycle? You don't know I am so in tune with your body that I know you are easily aroused and in heat the two days before your period begins and how you have debilitating cramps the first day you start to bleed? That on the last two days, you have mild head and backaches? That you fuck like a champ the first five days after your last spotting? That the days following are your most pleasant in terms of your disposition?"

He finally turned to me in search of an answer. His scowl was new to me. Where was the loving, compassionate and placid Azmir?

How does this man know so much I've never told him?

I didn't think I could quite articulate my cycle the way he'd just done accurately expressed.

He must have read my mind because he answered, "I fuckin' depend on your body to tell me shit your mouth won't."

In that moment, a blanket of guilt covered my body. I felt like my actions somehow robbed Azmir. Over the last few weeks, I never thought much about Azmir and how my life was intertwined with his. How my misfortune was shared by him. I was so used to getting by alone. The tears wouldn't stop. I wasn't familiar with these feelings of guilt and regret for my actions and them affecting someone else. Suddenly I felt cold and heartless. I am a lot of things, but cold and heartless were not my ambition.

"*I*—I'm sorry, Azmir. I really am," I attempted. "It's just... So much was going on...with Michelle...you and Tara's ba*by*—" He cut me off.

"Oh, no! You will not use an *accusation* as an excuse to do this to me...to make long-term decisions concerning me without me. That is not acceptable, Rayna!" he scolded while looking me dead in the eyes and towering over me. He maintained his distance. Seconds later, he turned back toward the vanity.

Things got quiet, but I had to know. I had to ask because I was so confused.

"How could you be so certain my child was yours and be so adamant Tara's isn't?" I don't know where the nerve came from, but I had to know.

He shot back a look that could kill. "What the *hell* are you implying?"

My eyes shot down to my toes. My thoughts were scattered, but I reached up and grabbed one.

"My fear was I would further complicate you...us...if I brought this to you. I didn't want to bother you with my issues," I tried to explain.

"Honey..." he addressed me in a trenchant tone...*derogate even*. "...what you fail to absorb in your pretty little incommunicado mind is you being pregnant is not just *your* issue. It was of *my* doing. It's *my* responsibility, even more so than yours. I am damn near ten years your senior. I should have been more responsible. I knew the ramifications of...of making love to you without protection," he hissed with a swing of his hand, exhausted himself.

There was a brief pause. He needed to breathe.

"I had my suspicions behind the club," he admitted all the while slouched over the sink. "When you came over later and we had sex you felt *different*. I thought I'd give you time to tell me. But when you began to withdraw, I didn't know what to do. Yesterday I couldn't take it anymore. I had to see you...to see if I could convince you to not...do anything irrational." Another painful pause. "Fuck! I see I'm too late."

I understood from that statement he was under the impression I'd aborted the pregnancy. While it was in the deep recesses of my mind, I was so caught up in life I hadn't decided on anything. But I had to clear the air of this misconception.

"Azmir, I didn't terminate the pregnancy," I murmured with my eyes locked down on my mingling fingers.

He stilled and I could see him narrowing his eyebrows through the mirror. He was confused.

I continued, "I miscarried almost two weeks ago."

His head shot up and he gave me a long faltering gaze through the mirror before turning to me to read my body language.

"Oh, shit. Rayna, I'm so sorry," Azmir whispered softly and slowly, which was a far cry from his earlier outbursts. He engulfed me as his long arms folded around me. He kissed my head.

"Why didn't you call me? I would've come."

"*I*—I don't know," I answered at a loss for words.

"Who was there to comfort you?" he asked with pain in his words, still gripping me in his arms.

"No one."

He withdrew his embrace but kept his hands on my shoulders as he peered down into my weary eyes. "How did you get to the doctor...the hospital?" he interrogated.

"I drove myself," I murmured suddenly feeling vulnerable as the images of my ride to the hospital flashed before my eyes. I hadn't recalled the experience until this moment, causing all feelings of lowliness and incredulity to come crashing upon me.

He closed his eyes to find relief from the thoughts in his head and rested his forehead against mine. His arms around my naked body once again providing much needed warmth. We stood there for what seemed like an eternity.

"Rayna, I'm here. No more secrets. No more guards. All truths. Cards up. All trust...from here on out," he proposed as he looked deep into my eyes. He was in search of my soul. His body was positioned so that his head was leveled down, matching my height. His hands were gripped on to my shoulders.

My eyes were heavy, trying to make sense of what Azmir was asking of me. I don't think I'm capable of being much to anyone. I'm not even sure I want anyone to trust me completely. But once again, I didn't want to disappoint the only person willing to take a chance on me. I'd lost my best friend. My sister.

"Deal?" Azmir implored again, only this time with more power behind his question. My throat constricted.

I nodded in agreement and succeeded in holding back the gallons of tears begging to fall. I didn't know what was being asked of me but for the first time in my life I was willing to do what I had to do to meet a man's needs.

Could I be all he needed? Was I enough with all of my deficiencies?

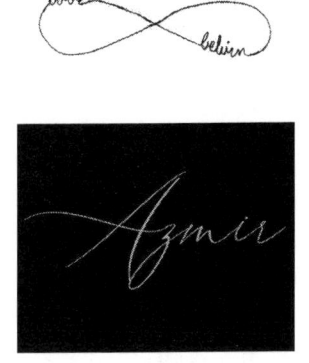

I took in every word Rayna spoke to try to understand her. I figured she must be a sane case of bipolar because she definitely had her highs and lows. But once again, I saw the little insecure girl through her eyes. We spent the night there in the suite. The next morning, I rose early to make arrangements for us to have a mini getaway in Atlantic City.

Rayna had a rental car needing to be returned near the airport. I had my people ride with me to turn it in while she stayed back at the hotel. When I returned, I encountered a frail woman in the lobby. I only took notice of her because of her constant twitching. I slowed down to get a better look at her. She looked lost there in the atrium of the hotel. She eventually turned toward my direction. She had a look of confusion in her eyes.

"Pardon me. Are you looking for someone?"

"*Umm... Umm...* My daughter here somewhere but I can't find nobody who work here to help me get at her," she protested as she kept trying to adjust her jacket.

"Is your daughter, Rayna?"

This had to be her mother. I saw so many similarities in her features. She had Rayna's beautiful chestnut eyes and full lips. You could tell, at some point, she had the same caramel complexion before her dope habit.

She gave me a look of distrust. "Who you?" Samantha demanded with an angry expression.

I offered, "I'm a friend of hers." But her facial muscles didn't relax. I reassured, "Rayna Brimm?"

After a long pause and deep gaze into my eyes she asked, "You her ol' man?"

I had to think about my answer. "I can take you to her so you can talk to her," I offered as a friendly gesture to gain her trust.

Her eyes widened. "*Umm... Umm...* See, she said she gonna help me get this shit off my back. And I swear to god I was gonna do it!" Samantha exclaimed, so embattled. "But I ain't even gonna waste her time. I don't want her to get mad at me. I ain't seen her in so long. I ain't wanna play her." She was getting ready to tear up. I can tell she was earnest in not wanting to blow her opportunity.

"Just tell her I came through to say sorry and if she could come see me next time she come home. I'll be ready then," she continued with big and hopeful eyes.

I couldn't let her just disappear like that. Not considering my situation with my own mother, and the fact of Rayna needing family, she needed support. I chatted with her for a few. She was very forthcoming, but adamant about not bothering Rayna. I gave her a few dollars and my card so she could contact Rayna when she was ready and got her a cab back home. I didn't know what to make of our encounter, so I decided not to tell Rayna about it.

When I got back up to the room Rayna was just getting out of the shower. I had coffee for her and asked was she hungry.

"Nah," she sang. "I'm just drained. I feel weak and...just blue. I don't think I'm ready to return to my reality either. I know people do it every day, so I need to just man up and face the music," she brooded pensively.

"What exactly are you feeling?" Rayna gave me an expression of confusion, or I was dumb as hell for asking.

I chuckled before explaining. "No," I declared while shaking my head. "We're going to start something new. It's called communication. To the best of your articulation, tell me what you're feeling," I requested, sounding like a damn therapist.

She looked to the wall directly in front of her to collect her thoughts. Then she belted, "I'm physically tired...confused... mentally exhausted. My neck is in knots from the stress. My joints are tight, too. I'm uneasy about what you must be thinking, although you're still here. I'm wondering for how long before..." she paused.

Her eyes zoomed into the floor. I hated seeing this confident and fiery woman so insecure and vulnerable. This must be what Michelle knew of Rayna.

"Don't think too hard. We're here...together...this moment." I grabbed her hands and put them to my face, trying to capture her eyes. They eventually met mine. *Ahhh...there she is.* "If it makes you feel any better, I'm not in the know of what's down the line for us either," I pleaded in her eyes as I kissed her soft hands.

"Come on. Let's take a long ride," I offered, rising from the chair.

"Where are we going? My flight leaves at one."

"Oh, then you'll be missing your flight, Ms. Brimm." My eyebrows met my forehead.

She shook her head in contest of my itinerary. "Azmir, I have to get back to work. I've missed so many days over the past three weeks. I may not have a job."

I was confused. "Are you telling me you flew out here for just twenty-four hours? Rayna, that five-hour flight is exhausting alone. If you think you're bleary now, just wait 'til you encounter your first patient tomorrow. You'll be fatigued. You need reprieve."

Her eyes left mine as if she were processing my words. She exhaled before her rebuttal, "Azmir, I have to return. Now that Michelle isn't here, neither is my job security."

"Do you fear you'll lose your job? Do they have legitimate reasons to terminate you?" I was in search of answers.

Rayna

I didn't know where he was going with all of this. "Again, Azmir, my life has changed so much with losing her. She meant so much. She's the reason those bastards didn't clip me for walking in on a blow job," I sighed, winded from the memory of that dilemma.

Not withdrawing his gaze from me, he pulled his phone from his waist, pushed a few buttons and held the phone to his ear. A few seconds later, "Ed, Azmir Jacobs here. Yeah...I have a prospective client who's in need of your aggressive services. She's an employee of *Smith, Katz & Adams Physical Therapy* there in SoCal. Yup. She will need preemptive counsel to ensure they understand any unlawful or faulty termination will not be tolerated from her crafty superiors. Yeah. Uh-huhn. Her retainer will be at your disposal expeditiously. Indeed." He ended the call with his coochie creaming smile.

He returned the phone back to its holster, "Done. Now, contact Sharon and inform her you will return on Wednesday. We need to go. A car is waiting downstairs."

"Azmir, I don't have enough clothes, or toiletries..." I pleaded.

"Rayna, last I checked A.C. has shops and boutiques where you can get whatever you need for an enjoyable stay," he spoke in a manner telling me his decision was final.

Wearily, I relented.

It was eight in the morning on a Wednesday, and I was sitting at my desk sorting through the mountain of mail that had been collecting. While still dealing with the odd sensation in the pit of my stomach I'd had since losing Michelle, I felt rested and refueled. I smiled as I acknowledged how Azmir had had a hand in it.

Atlantic City was nice. We stayed in a beautiful and most spacious suite at the *Borgata*. The suite was exclusive with a breathtaking view of the Atlantic Ocean. We ate very well and were able to catch a few shows on short notice. We also shopped out there. There were countless designer boutiques Azmir insisted we indulge in. The shopping was primarily for me as I learned Mr. Jacobs had a personal stylist who did all of his shopping. To say I was thrown was an understatement. How much did this man earn that he didn't buy his own groceries or clothes he donned oh so well?

And about his appealing nature: days and nights alone with Azmir were equally torturing because of my orders to abstain from sex until the end of my next cycle. I still had some time to go. Azmir never attempted anything with me, it was my feverish ass who seduced him. We were able to resolve several six-nine episodes to provide much needed release. That man loved my private areas; *he tended to them so well.* He worked on them as if he were starved. And I enjoyed every bit of it. The man was an extremely passionate lover.

Today would be long, they'd be this way for weeks to come. I had so much catching up to do with patients, records, and housekeeping details. But I was prepared for it. I could use all the distractions available to help me cope.

I was tending to Mr. Saunders' injured rotator cuff when my phone alerted me of a text. It was Azmir.

How's your day treating you?

Busy. I didn't realize the time. I haven't lifted my head since I clocked in. How are you?

Merging and acquiring. What time do you think you'll be done?

I finished up with Mr. Saunders' prescription before returning to his text.

Perhaps 8:30PM. Errrrrrrrrrrr... I replied frustrated by the prospect.

Hit me up when you're walking out. I have someone I'd like you to meet.

Hmmmmm...

Mr. Jacobs, I regret to inform you that I'll be in no mood to exchange pleasantries with a stranger. Can we arrange another time? I hit send as I walk into my next appointment.

I greeted Mrs. Henson and sat at the workstation to view her chart when my phone went off again.

No. I don't think my pal wants to wait. We'll meet you at your place. Peace.

My place! Why is he bringing a "pal" to my house? What the hell?

"Ms. Brimm?" Mrs. Henson called out.

"Ummmmm... Yes?" I snapped back into our conversation.

"Your figure. You seem to have lost weight. What are you trying new?" Mrs. Henson beamed with wonder in her eyes.

Azmir had commented on my weight as well. My clothes were less fitted as of late. He didn't like it, neither did I. But I didn't think Mrs. Henson was being malicious with her inquiry, just curious.

"I've been so busy lately I haven't been completing the six basic food groups as I should, you know?" I offered as an answer.

She gave a warm smile, "Well, you're still a lovely looking woman, Ms. Brimm. Take care of your youth. It will dissipate before you know it," she admonished. I gave her a full smile and nodded in agreement.

It was eight fifty-five p.m. when I was turning off my office lights. My stomach had been grumbling, which oddly reminded me to text Azmir while en route home.

As I unloaded the tacos out of the bag, I heard the doorbell. I knew it was Azmir and opened the door. He stood there in all of his six-feet and four-inch magnificence towering me. He wore black denims, a black T-shirt, *Gucci* belt, and black high top *Lavins*. And there was that coochie creaming smile.

He is sexy as hell. No... No... No! I couldn't succumb to the sexual energy between us. *I have to abstain until the end of my cycle I'm still awaiting.*

"You're beautiful...and hungry," he observed. I wore a pencil skirt, silk sleeveless blouse and was still in my panty hose. But what he was referring to was the taco I was chumping down on as I answered the door. I blushed in embarrassment. I was starved.

With a mouth full of taco I explained, "I missed lunch."

He furrowed his eyebrows sexily and pointed to the side of my mouth. I raised my hand to my face to inspect my mouth and found a gulp of guacamole there. I tried licking the rest off.

He squinted his eyes in passion and commented, "Interesting how I forgot your tongue is so swift," with a lecherous smirk.

Focus, Rayna...focus!

To change the subject I quickly blurted, "Where's your friend?" He looked confused.

"Oh, yes! Your new pal as well. He's waiting in the car. I just wanted to make sure you were prepared before bringing him in." And with that he does a beeline back out of the door.

Weird. He asked me to be prepared but he wanted to make sure I was prepared? I went back in the kitchen to fetch another taco. God, I was famished.

When I turned to go back into the living room, I saw Azmir standing tall in the thruway. He startled me. But the brown fury dog he cradled in his arm caught my attention as well.

"Oh, wow! What is this?"

Azmir wore the biggest smile, "He's a Pomeranian. Eight weeks old." He beamed with excitement.

I placed my taco back on the table, wiped my hands and walked over to him and the pooch.

"He's beautiful, Azmir. I didn't know you were fond of animals." I went to pet the dog.

"I've been told they make great companions. I got him for you." He gave me the deepest gaze.

Oh, this man knows how to appeal to my libido without effort. Back to the pooch, Rayna!

"For me?" I repeated in hopes of gaining understanding.

"Yeah. You're here by yourself and I don't want you alone. I thought our pal here could serve as the man of the house." There was his deep gaze again.

I played with the dog as I tried collecting my thoughts. Azmir was so thoughtful. It was something I hadn't learned to get used to.

"Man of the house?" I asked before leveling with his eyes again.

I grabbed the Pomeranian and retreated to the living room placing him on the floor so I could further inspect him. Azmir's intense stare was burning a hole in the back of my blouse. I could tell he was up to something. Seconds later, I focused on the beautiful *Gucci* collar with a case on the pooch. It was conspicuously too large to be on a dog no more than five pounds.

With narrowed eyebrows I asked Azmir, "May I?"

He nodded, granting permission.

I opened it and a large gold skeleton key fell out. I caught it and examined it. I didn't get it. My head shot up to Azmir who wore a stoic expression when he muttered, "Come move in with me."

I lost my breath.

"Move in...with you?" I whispered.

I couldn't wrap my brain around the concept. It was too huge of a request. His head leaned to the side exposing his long eyelashes. He was expressing vulnerability. *Shit!* I didn't want to find myself in a position of disappointing Azmir. He'd been such a rock to me over the past few days. I needed time to process this.

"Azmir," I started while looking around my humble home. "I just bought this place. I'm just getting comfortable here. I can't just up and leave as if I were renting."

"You don't have to up and sell it," he gently informed while squatting on the floor next to me and the Pom. "You can rent it out or use it as a second home to get away from me when I drive you crazy...though I don't endeavor to ever do such a thing." He scrunched his eyebrows, nose and lips gesturing he was at a loss with the idea of him driving me crazy.

I took a deep breath. "Azmir, you can't just pop this on me with no rhyme or reason. I..." I was at a loss of words. He lifted me onto his lap after he sat flat on the floor.

"We can easily be two ships passing in the night. We work next door to each other a few days a week, but it's not enough. Now that you won't be as busy as you once were considering your former obligations to Michelle, I find myself wanting to be with you more and more. I hate the thought of you being here alone." He paused.

My heart constricted. I wasn't ready to respond.

"Just think about it."

I pouted my lips like a child. "Okay."

There was silence.

"So, what are you going to name him?" Azmir quizzed, breaking the awkward place we had somehow found ourselves in.

Hmmmmmm...

"I don't know yet." I sat and quickly pondered.

He kissed me gently on the forehead before lifting me back onto the floor and rising.

"I have to skate, Ms. Brimm."

I frowned. "You're not staying? But I bought you tacos." I was disappointed.

"Nah. Ray's out waiting for me," he murmured while drawing me into him, interrupting my view of the pooch as he pawed at the key to Azmir's apartment.

I had to ask, "Do you want your key back while I think about it?"

He shook his head no as he looked down at me. I hope I hadn't screwed up again. I just needed to take things slow and figure myself out after recent events.

"I wish you could stay," I admitted.

"I have a few things to tend to. Besides, if I stay, you're going to have to come up with a convincing explanation to your doctor as to why you didn't keep her orders," he warned clenching his jaws.

Damn!

He lowered his lips to mine and gave me the warmest oral embrace. He was so passionate and tender I honestly lost my balance. Per usual. Good thing he had his arms wrapped around me.

Azmir

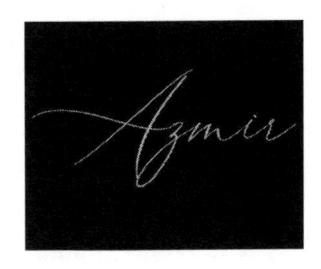

As I'm pulling away from Rayna's home, I'm pensive. I bought her the dog for companionship, but truth be told I'd rather have her staying with me. Considering the letter Michelle wrote, it seemed befitting. I mean, what in the hell was she doing there alone anyway? If she shot me down, she would, at least, have some form of life there. She didn't seem too keen on the idea, but I could be persuasive in my pursuit.

I was at a business dinner when my phone went off alerting me of a text. It was Rayna.

Is this pity for the miscarriage? Azmir, I'm really okay. It's life and unfortunately my reality.

The hell?

Why would she assume I pitied her? I asked her to move in with me, not offer her free gynecological services.

My dearest Ms. Brimm, if it were about the loss of OUR unborn child who would be pitied, you or me? I responded, in a riddling mode.

I just don't want to jump into anything for the wrong reasons. You just got out of a relationship. I don't want to be the cause of your obligation to getting into another.

That would be plausible if I lived with my ex. This is something entirely different. I want to share a life with you. Is that too hard a concept? Where was she going with this? Why was she making it so difficult?

Azna.

My forehead wrinkled. *What in the hell is an Azna?*

? Was my reply. I was totally lost.

I named the pooch Azna. Azmir+Rayna=Azna. Alpha and Omega. she replied.

Hmmmmm... Beginning and the end.

Was this some subliminal message? I didn't ask...just buoyantly believed there was.

"Mr. Jacobs...?" I heard someone trying to regain my attention. My head rose in attention.

"Are you amenable to the terms we've agreed upon?"

A slight smirk broke on my face as I realize I'd just bought yet another company. This one was small...only three hundred and sixty employees, but larger than the one we acquired last week. My partner, Richard Roberson, is unrivaled at the game of business mergers, acquisition, and liquidation. He'd been on the radar for nearly six years, and we've been partnering for three. He has a slight understanding of the history of my rise and was willing to take a risk with me. He'd been mentoring me and poising me for my next level of success. I've been easing my way out of the drug game. It hadn't been the most simplistic of tasks, but this new venture has fueled my motivation.

Things were about to speed up. My travel will increase along with my paper. This is one of the reasons I was adamant about Rayna moving in. I needed her closer. I wasn't trying to leave her available for another man. I was trying to brand her. Only if she'd trust me.

After that meeting I had another with Petey about a detective who apparently had been going around inquiring about my affairs in the streets. Word got back to Petey that the detective was looking for anyone with indictable information. I'd heard for a few months how this same detective had been talking to local officers in my street territories where I conducted my businesses, but they assured me they remained tight-lipped. I could have a little more faith in them because they had to lose their careers *and* places on my payroll for betraying me. But street niggas had less to lose. So, we needed to strategize ways to contain this problem. In the meantime, I had my attorneys working on a way to fire warning shots in order to protect my brand.

The sooner I exited the game, the easier I could sleep at night. The quicker I got Rayna to consent to sharing my bed, the more my life would be complete.

CHAPTER 5

Rayna

It had been a long day. Hell, it had been a long two weeks at work. I'd been putting in twelve hours a day, minimally, ever since my return from Atlantic City with Azmir.

I'd arrived at Azmir's place at the marina with Azna.

"Good evening, Ms. Brimm," the concierge nodded.

I didn't know why he'd been so insistent on me spending more nights at his place. The previous evenings hadn't been good because I'd been dog-tired. But I relented on tonight after forcing myself to start work two hours later in order to get more sleep the night before. I didn't want to show up at his doorstep yawning. Coincidentally, today was the first day of my birth control pill, something I'd have to remember to take daily.

Ugh! The thought of being a slave to a pill is exasperating.

But I remembered. And here I was at Azmir's, still tired but not fatigued, which I considered a huge improvement to just the day before.

"Penthouse suite, Ms. Brimm!" Roberto sang as the elevator doors were opening.

"Thanks, Roberto," I returned.

I stepped out of the elevator with my pooch clutched in my arm and my briefcase clasped in my hand. I advanced toward the door while in search of the key. The golden key...the big golden skeleton key to Azmir's apartment. He insisted I use it since giving it to me.

As I approached the door, I heard the bass from a familiar tune streaming from the apartment. It was immediately joined by a horn. I turned the key and opened the door to find Azmir and all of his lengthy grandeur singing to me...without shoes. He was wearing a dress shirt with the first few buttons undone and was pulled from his dress pants as he lip synched to the tune using a spatula as his microphone.

I'm done.

I'd never experienced him so relaxed and larky. His long legs swayed to the rhythm and his arms emulated the words flowing from his mouth. It was a jazzy tune. Very romantic. Though I perceived this to be out of Azmir's element, he seemed so comfortable with his performance. You couldn't ignore the words flowing from the speakers with how Azmir gestured them. *This man is damn fine even when he's taking grave risks with his masculinity.* His flow was sexy as hell.

He continued his prance towards me, and I let a squirming Azna down to the floor. He reached for me, pulled me into him and continued to whisper the lyrics into my ear. When the male's verse was up, he softly muttered, "Dance with me, Ms. Brimm,' as he removed my purse, keys, and briefcase from my arms. He began foxtrotting with me.

Damn, he's...good!

He rested his mouth on my ear as he held me close and twirled me around before dipping me towards the floor. Who knew Azmir Jacobs could ballroom dance?

I was aroused. The stressors from work had dissipated, instantly withered away. I was now in a cocoon with this man who had *turned me into his slave*—per the lyrics of the tune—with his swag. He smelled so good. I got lost in a trance. *Does he mean what he's relaying to me by way of the lyrics of this song?* In all honesty, it didn't matter. I was caught up. I didn't want to come out of this web he'd ensnared.

Exhausted? *Who's exhausted?*

While James Moody blew his horn Azmir had me suspended in the air, dipped to the floor, staring into the depths of my eyes. My lips were ajar, wanting his. He eventually broke the seductive gaze with a panty snatching smirk and then letting me up.

"Happy you're home. Hungry?" he muttered as he ambled toward the kitchen.

Not for food.

"Ummmmm... Yeah," I responded while gathering my bearings. Seconds later, he brought out a glass of red wine. The place smelled delicious.

"Mmmmm...what's Boyd whipped up tonight?" I asked as I slipped off my *Monolos*, courtesy of Mr. Jacobs.

"I gave him the night off," Azmir informed as I took a huge swig of my wine.

Oh.

"Smells good," I complimented.

"My specialty," he shared as he approached me. "Can I get you anything before dinner? Would you like to freshen up or unwind?"

I lied. "No. I'm ready to eat," my delivery noncommittal. I would've much preferred jumping on him as an appetizer.

"Good. The salads are on the table." He extended his hand to me. I took it and felt a current run through my body.

At the dining room table, he pulled my chair out. I moved to the table just before he scooted my chair underneath me. He kissed the top of my head before taking his seat across from me.

"So, how was your day, Ms. Brimm?"

I took a forkful of my Caesar salad.

Mmmmmmm... Tasty!

"Long," I managed a smile.

Azmir took a sip of his wine. "So, are you still considering Saturday hours as you mentioned a few days ago?"

I took a long gulp of my wine. *Ooooh.* My buzz was setting in. Drinking on an empty stomach will do that. Azmir chuckled. There's no doubt I was the subject of his humor. The alcohol settled in by the second; I couldn't give a damn. I took notice of his teeth. They were so well aligned with his supple lips. I wondered what they tasted like with traces of wine on them. *Have I ever tasted them that way?* Suddenly I couldn't recall.

"Ms. Brimm, you don't want dinner right now. Do you?" he asked in his CEO mien, though his eyes sparkled with deep desire.

Shit! Am I panting out loud? How does he know? Oh, well.

I gave him an unequivocal "No!"

I batted my eyes feeling bashful for the first time when it comes to sex with Azmir. Who was I fooling? I was in heat. I hadn't had intercourse in over a month. I obeyed the doctor and today was the day I was cleared for sex. And I hadn't been intimate with Azmir since our return due to our conflicting schedules.

He rose from his seat and traveled to my side of the table. "Follow me. I have something to show you," he commanded.

I followed on his heels. Clearly this man could lead my hot ass straight into the pits of hell and I'd fit right in with the heat.

We headed to the master suite and then into the bathroom where I saw a warm and soft glow of lighting. He had the whirlpool drawn with dozens of candles burning all around the tub, down the steps and into a walkway leading up just a few feet from the door. His eyes stayed fixated on me as I admired the luminosity of the fiery ambiance.

Oh, my! He went the full mile to create a romantic landscape. This could have only meant he was looking forward to tonight. To me. To be anticipated is an enchanting marvel. Overwhelmed, I turned to Azmir. He was wearing the most innocent, purely impassioned and prurient expression.

"More wine?" he asked, extending his arm to retrieve my glass.

I lunged toward him knocking him into the wall. I reached up and threw my tongue in the back of his mouth without giving him a moment to prepare. He grabbed my ass pulling me into him and let out a mild groan. My kisses trailed down to his jaw then down to his neck. I sucked his Adam's apple as my hand explored his chiseled chest and abdomen. My libido was on overdrive.

"Ms. Brimm...let me refill your glass and go to put our dinner on hold. I wanna take my time with you." He spoke over my wild panting. "I've gone without your loving for about a month. I need to savor every second," he whispered, eyes squinted with a hint of a smile.

I snickered in embarrassment as I let off him. He quickly regained himself and made his way out of the room. Azmir returned in no time with a fresh glass of wine for me. I took the glass and sipped from it. Seeing he went so far as to refresh it, I figured the least I could do was make use of it. He watched me. I wondered what he was thinking.

He eventually walked toward me removing the glass from my hand. With his mouth, he licked the crease in my lips neatly before sucking on my bottom lip.

"Pinot Noir tastes better on your lips," Azmir murmured against my mouth. I couldn't breathe. This man had me enraptured yet once again.

He unbuttoned my blouse until he could fully open it, exposing my breasts through my black lace bra. Azmir's mouth dropped when he saw it was mid-coverage. My breasts looked like they were spilling from the half cups. His mouth hung open as he ran his thumb across the brim of the bra. He brought his face down and inhaled my breasts. My panties soaked up my natural juices generously flowing from his action. He didn't touch them with his mouth, which was painfully torturous.

As I rested against the vanity, he slowly lifted the hem of my skirt until it was at my waist. He observed my matching lace panties. Azmir looked up to me and whispered, "I like this, Brimm. I definitely approve. You should wear lace every day."

I flashed him a lecherous smile.

He lifted me by my legs and rested them on his shoulders as he lowered himself. I balanced myself on my arms using the counter of the vanity as he buried his head between my legs and gave a sharp inhale. My eyes shot open at his bold act.

"There's no better fragrance than that's between your legs, Rayna. Damn. I even crave this in my sleep."

He swatted his tongue over my sex with such force I felt it through the lace. I gasped and wondered if he felt my vagina pulsating.

"*Vicky Secrets* or *LePerla*?" he asked.

"*VS*," I answered surprised he didn't know. He'd bought me somewhere in the neighborhood of fifty bra and panty sets since our return from the East Coast.

In an instant, he ripped them off and began tasting my love in such an act of feral. I moaned loudly. I needed this. My body needed the relief. He worked me over licking me from top to bottom. Going in and out of my canal, doing his signature butterflying of the tongue inside me.

"Ooooh!" I moaned.

I had to constantly remind myself to breathe. As I threw my pelvis at him, he groaned. Then he worked his way to my pearl and nibbled on it ferociously. I knew it was a wrap. My orgasm had arrived, and quicker than I expected as I gyrated and screamed like I was descending on a roller coaster. There was a time where I was conscious of my orgasmic sounds, but with Azmir I never seemed to have control to even care.

Azmir peered up as he wore that panty snatching smirk. "Did you enjoy that? I sure did," he muttered just before letting me down.

My legs wobbled and it took me a few seconds to gather my bearings. He began to undress me while staring deep into my eyes.

"I love pleasing you, Ms. Brimm. I can't get enough of you."

I couldn't believe he was speaking these words to me. Once naked, he assisted me into the monstrous tub. The water was extremely warm, borderline spicy. It took some time for me to submerge my entire body, but once I did it was a heavenly sensation against my skin.

I watched as Azmir undressed. It was a sight to behold. It was amazing how with clothes he appeared slender and mildly fit, but when he took his shirt off you could see how deliciously well his body was sculpted. He was truly a work of art. And when his penis sprang out heavily, I squirmed in the tub as I salivated. He caught on to my enjoyment as he jumped in across from me.

"Ahhhh! Still warm," he mumbled before gathering a pool of water in his hands and splashing it in his face.

Sitting opposite of him, I extended my legs and rubbed my feet on the outside of his thighs before going inside. My feet eventually made their way to his tall erection, and I tried to the best of my ability to stroke it with my toes. His eyes darted down to his lap to watch. In no time, Azmir was all over me again, consuming with fierce hunger. He lifted me from the water while I straddled him and traced kisses from my neck down to my breasts shattering me into a million pieces. With his mouth, hands, and appendage, he showed me how much he'd thirsted for me while my body had been out of commission.

I woke up in search of Azmir. I reached over to touch him and found a cool groove on his side of the bed. I glanced over to the clock on his nightstand, and it read two thirty-eight a.m. I got up and sauntered into the hallway and down the corridor looking in his office, the living room, and kitchen.

What the hell...did he leave?

Then I noticed right off the living area, the flow of the patio curtains from the wind blowing through them. I made my way over to the door and called, "Azmir?" as I stepped out onto the balcony. The view of the water always blew me away. I looked down to the left and he's there enjoying the ambiance of the marina.

"Hey, Jacobs, it's late," I muttered as I approached him.

"Or early," he replied with a snort.

I lowered myself onto his lap and he embraced me willingly.

"You can't do what you did to me earlier and then abandon me after. It makes me feel used," I teased.

He smirked, "You can't put on me what you put on me earlier after not putting it on me in so long and expect me not to be transfixed. It's hard to sleep after that."

His eyes never met mine. Something was wrong.

"Azmir, what is it? Something isn't right."

He shook his head as he widened his eyes in a flutter. It was as if he was trying to shake something off.

Did I do something wrong in there?

"Is it me?" I let slip involuntarily.

"No, baby, it's not you at all," he denounced the thought immediately. He pulled my chin to his lips and kissed me softly. I was convinced. I'd also felt the current flashing inside when he touched me. He gazed deeply into my eyes before relenting. His eyes diverted back to the view of the water, "All right," he expelled a lungful sigh.

"A few months back...on my birthday in fact, I got a call from my mother."

What?

"I thought you haven't heard from her in years," I mention with incredulity, more in terms of a statement than a question.

His right hand shot up gesturing a defeated concept, "I haven't."

"Well, what did she say? Did she give any explanation for her absence?" I felt more maternal and protective than romantic. *What gives?*

He gave a sexy chuckle. *Damn! Azmir, I'm trying to get out of aphrodisia here and you're not helping.*

"She's been incarcerated. All these years she's been incarcerated." He paused with his gaze fixated onto the marina. "Funny thing is she's been out for nearly a year and she's just calling. She said she's been looking for me...but I don't know..." his voice trailed off.

"You have questions," I discerned.

His eyebrows shot up. "Hell yeah," he affirmed in a casual tone.

"Well, you won't get them answered if you don't ask. *Ask.* Ask her all the questions your heart needs to be at peace with this. Ask."

His eyes were still in the distance. There was another pause before he snapped out of his trance, "Those decisions can be made at another time," as he drew me closer to him. "Right now, I'd like to decide how I subdue the burning desire I have to be inside of you again."

Damn. I'm done.

Azmir lowered my legs on either side of his as we both faced the water and took the tips of his fingers, dancing them up my thighs. I sharply drew in a breath.

"What are you wearing?" he teasingly asked while traveling to my pelvic area. "A thong, aye?" he commented at his discovery. I reclined into him, planting my head against his clavicle bone. I wanted to squirm because his hands felt so good and intrusive, but I decided to fight the urge and just close my eyes.

"*Hmmmm...*" he groaned as his first two fingers found their way to my pearl. He played with it, massaging it over and over and over again. Simultaneously, his right hand came up to reach my right breast and he gently stroked it. I tried to fight the urge to jolt. But his soft breathing in my hair increased my aroused state and there was now too much going on to keep me calm. His two fingers slid their way down into my canal.

"I thought you'd had enough," he whispered referring to my natural lubrication, no doubt. Then the low whistle of his teeth goes off. "You just may have been missing me as much as I've been missing you. Let's see," he droned, pulling my camisole down under my right breast...then left. I felt free. He pinched and pulled my nipple. I could no longer keep still. His fingers went in and out and I gyrated along with them causing friction. I felt his erection throbbing beneath my ass, down to the back of my right thigh. My senses were on overload.

"Ahhhh...Azmir," I cried out. I heard him snort in my ear.

"Too bad I don't have a condom handy out here...or else I can have something else inside you," he seductively taunted.

My arms moved up and behind me to his head. It kept my hands busy as my body was being worked over.

"Oh, I forgot—no barriers are needed," he low key demanded in a teasing tone.

He scooted me forward on his lap as he pulled down his shorts and underwear just enough to release his indisputably erect and wide penis. He grabbed my near-limp body and lifted it slightly in the air to slowly lower it onto him.

"Ahhhh!" I cried out in tantalizing pleasure. My back arched as he pushed my hips back and forth to control my movements. It gave me a moment to gain my stride. And once I did my strokes were savage and uncoordinated because my sex was that sensitive to his every move. My breasts clapped against each other adding to the erotica. He tried to help me out by flexing his hips, but that just further spun me out of control and caused my upper body to incline in his lap. I grabbed hold of his knees to steady myself.

Fuck! Why do I feel like a teenager having sex for the third time? My control abandoned me. He grabbed me by the shoulders to pull me back.

"Let me put you out of your misery," he muttered.

I didn't quite grasp that until moments later when he grabbed both breasts in his hands and began flickering my nipples. His strokes were intense and well met, causing me to feel his thick cock rubbing against a new wall. Up and down, I moved. In and out he went. My muscles tightened and my stomach seemed to have disappeared. An orgasm tore through me and was so intense that tears filled my eyes. Azmir's tantalizing whimpers from his own orgasm caused them to overflow and fall down into my face as I plunged on his lap. More tears.

I couldn't explain the tears. I just felt emotions and I'm never good at managing them. It seemed every time I connected with Azmir it stirred up something in me; I could not explain. He was so passionate and purposeful when we made love. It was as if he was trying to become one with me...fuse our spirits. Only, I didn't think mine was available. I felt so empty inside until moments like this. And when I came down from our intimate phenomenon, reality set back in, and I was left empty once again.

"Hey. Are you crying? Did I hurt you? What's wrong?" Panic rose in Azmir at each word.

I winced of pleasure as he lifted me from his containment and turned me around in his lap. He ignored the mess made by his translucent specimens escaping me. I couldn't hold back the tears. I wasn't sure how hard I tried.

"No. Don't cry. This isn't a reason to cry. Are you okay?"

After a few seconds I murmured, "I don't know if I can be what you need. You've been so good to me...so patient and kind. And I've been moving at a pace making me wonder if I'm fooling you...*or me*. I don't want to hurt you," I whimpered through my tears.

He was silent and I didn't know what that meant.

"I'm depleted. I don't know how to pursue, let alone, maintain a relationship—intimate or platonic. You deserve someone who can. You deserve so much more." My cry went from weeping to all out bawling as I realized I'd betrayed myself. I told Azmir what my biggest fear was concerning him.

"Hold on...wait...wait," he comforted as he rose from the seat taking me with him. He gently let me onto my feet then wiggled out of his shorts, lifted me in his arms again and walked me back into the apartment leaving the gorgeous view of the marina and the whispering bliss of our lovemaking back on the patio.

He ushered me into the master bathroom, letting me down on the floor. Azmir stepped in the shower to turn it on. After that, he began removing my lingerie. He pulled his black T-shirt over his head before leading me into the shower. I stood in front of him as the water sprinkled down onto my body. I then felt the soft scraping of the body scrubber being applied to my back. Then to my shoulders. He worked his way down to my feet before cleaning the front of my body. He let me wash my private areas while he washed himself. When I glanced over my shoulder to look at him, his eyes fell down to the floor.

What in the hell does that mean? Once again, I'm lost for perception.

Once we were done, he reached over me with his long arms, turned the water off and went out to retrieve a towel he wrapped around me then led me out. Azmir grabbed another towel to quickly dry himself and then wrapped it around his waist. He took the towel from around me and dried me from neck to toe.

When he was done and had wrapped the towel around my shoulders, he muttered, "When I spent time in juvie, I told myself I would not be violated. I came up against a few brutal contenders, but always triumphed, even if it were by the skin of my teeth. I also told myself I would never return. I'm still a free man. About a week after my release, I told myself I would never be poor again and I'd work so hard I would have multiple businesses, giving me an empire. I think I'm at sixteen now...and steadily increasing. I told myself if I found the right woman, I'd pursue her endlessly and give her the world I've abound. Weeks later, you showed up in my boardroom requesting space on my property. I don't make promises to myself I can't keep, Ms.

Brimm." He kissed me on the side of my head. I was at a loss for words.

"I'm not a very patient man. I do apologize for that. I've applied pressure you're not comfortable with. I'll slow down but will not stop until you're mine. However, it must be your choice," Azmir spoke with conviction as we both gazed at each other through the massive vanity mirror.

"What irony, that the one thing I desperately want and am vigorously pursuing doesn't think she's enough. I've amassed four-hundred-thirty-nine million in three years, all on gut intuition and knowing my opponents. I make no mistakes in acquisitions. I seriously doubt if that'll start here." His glaring through the mirror into my eyes said so much that ears couldn't hear.

It was in this moment I knew indisputably I had to work on me. I had to repair my broken spirit. I had to learn to be emotionally sound and independent. I had to learn how to trust people and be loved. I couldn't receive what this man was offering because I knew none of it.

"Come. Let's go to bed. It's late," he ordered.

We retreated to his bedroom, and I asked, "Can I borrow a T-shirt? Since I've soiled my only lingerie here..."

He squinted his eyes then let out a hint of a smirk. "In the third drawer from the top of the first set to the left."

I trotted over into the enormous walk-in closet and located the drawer. As I pulled it out, attractive feminine colors popped out. I saw purples, pinks, soft blues, and ivories, all in different fabrics. There was lace and silk. I couldn't believe he'd brought these for me and stored them at his place, further illustrating his desire for me to move in.

Hmmmmm... I went to the next drawer to find his underwear neatly folded and arranged by color. His cleaning lady does a hell of a job organizing. I opened the next drawer and found crisp white crew neck T-shirts. I quickly grabbed one.

When I returned to the bedroom I stood at my side of the bed as Azmir took inventory of my attire. "This is perfect!" I exclaimed like a goofy schoolgirl and jumped into bed not giving him a chance to respond. He turned off the only light that was on then immediately scooted over to me draping his long and warm arm around me, buried his face into the back of my neck and exhaled.

There's that current. Damn. I hope he didn't feel my body jolt.

"Azmir, what was the name of that song you sang to me earlier?" I had to know.

"*Mmmmmm...*" he hummed trying to regain consciousness from the sleep that was falling upon him. "'*Moody's Mood for Love.*' Quincy Jones," he murmured into my neck.

Damn current!

Hmmmmmm...

"That wasn't Quincy singing on it..." I quizzed.

"Nah. That was Brian McKnight, Take 6 and Rachelle Ferrell."

"It was beautiful," I whispered. "What made you select that song?" Again, I had to know. I'd never seen him so relaxed and spirited as I did during his performance.

He backed his head from my neck.

Shit. Did I screw this up again?

"Because it exemplifies how I feel about you. My pops would sing it almost every night to my mom when I was a kid. Frankie Crocker used to sign off to the original version every night on a New York City radio station. My dad said one day I'd sing it to a woman who captured my heart like my mom did his. I like Quincy's rendition. I've liked it for years. Finally, I can sing it with conviction...because I get it."

I couldn't cry any more tears in front of this man, though they were impending. Although the words easily flowed from his tongue, I had no doubt that they were sincere. I envied that. I wanted the ability to express my convictions so boldly and with such ease.

"Azmir...?" I called out to him, though I knew he was listening.

"I want the courage to sing Rachelle's lines to you. I don't want to be afraid anymore."

There! Not so bad. Butterflies were still invading my belly, but I fought through it.

"I know, baby. And I can't wait," he whispered in my neck and wiggled until he was well nestled.

I heard the sound of an alarm. It played and played and played before I lifted my head.

Damn.

It was my phone, which meant it was time for me to get up and start my day. I hated leaving Azmir's bed, it was so contenting, generous in space, warm and inviting. I reached over and silenced my phone then turned to peek over at Azmir who, miraculously, was sound asleep after the thunderous sound going off. So was Azna, who'd managed to get into the bed at some point during the night. Azmir's bed was a few feet from the floor. *Azmir must have put him up here.* Azna looked like a ball of fur.

I turned back to the fine specimen of a man just inches away from me. He appeared beautiful and alluring, even in his sleep. I rested my head on the fluffy pillow once more and counted to ten, something I often did to help wake up. I then crawled out of bed and tiptoed into the bathroom where I brushed my teeth and washed my face. I searched for all of my belongings from the night before like my underwear, camisole, and jewelry. *We were primal in here just a few hours ago and it's evident.* If I were a mistress and his wife unexpectedly showed up to find this morning disarray, we'd be busted.

As I headed back into the bedroom Azmir was sitting up in bed, nude from the neck to the waist, petting Azna. "Why are you up so early? It's not even six," he spoke in his extra-baritone morning voice. His voice was sexy even first thing in the morning.

Focus, Rayna!

"I have to get to work, Mr. Jacobs," I reminded him.

"Not until eight."

I furrowed my eyebrows in jest. "I have things to do before work."

"Such as...?"

He's being nosey. "I work out...if you must know."

"Stay with me. Boyd should be here any minute. We can have breakfast first then head to the rec to work out before work. You can shower there."

"Mr. Jacobs, I can't. I don't have clothes here."

"Ah-ha! Therein lies the problem. Here's a solution: move in. It's a simple issue of geography." He ended with the panty snatching smirk. *He is so sexy! Oh my...!* "Stay and I'll start my breakfast *in here* and then we can burn off the first few hundred calories...*in here*." He patted the bed.

I smiled shyly as I processed his proposal. "As tempting as that sounds, I can't. I'm going home to workout. I'll take Azna with me. He has a vet appointment on my lunch."

He rose from the bed and strolled over to me oozing sex. When he reached out to touch me, I flinched as I held my arm out.

"Don't," I pleaded harsher than I intended. He paused with a slight look of hurt and disappointment on his face. "Azmir, if you touch me, we both know that I'll succumb to your sexual prowess. Starting today, I am on a new path. Amongst many things, I'm trying to learn how to communicate with my mouth, remember that?"

There. Nice start to this journey, Rayna!

Azmir formed a seductive growler expression with his mouth. *Does he do this to me on purpose?*

"But you *can* use your mouth to communicate this morning."

I gave him a maternal glare to let him know that I was adamant.

I grabbed Azna and headed for the bedroom door. Out of nowhere, the music from the night before started to play in my head halting my stride. I did an about-face back towards him, putting my bag on the floor but keeping Azna in my left arm. I reached up to grab Azmir's face, pulled it down towards mine and gave him the most passionate kiss I'm sure I've ever given a man. I moved with inspiration and hope...hope for us...hope for me. His mouth was warm, tasting so promising and innocent. He was delicious even before brushing his teeth. I was in love with this man and had plans to show him. I finally withdrew my tongue, then lips knowing that at any second I could end up back in his bed.

Taking a step back, I read his expression. He was lost, but he enjoyed it. I exhaled deeply and murmured, "Good day, Mr. Jacobs."

He said nothing, just continued to search my eyes.

On the way out I saw the cleaning lady bringing Azmir's clothes in from the balcony. *Shit! Does she know that they're soiled... with me?* I shook my head at the thought. I had another long day to face. I couldn't waste my time worrying about that. And I was off to start my day. A new day.

While working out I fell into introspective thinking.

I'd meant every word I'd said to Azmir. I needed to work on me. Since my return from Jersey, I couldn't help but be haunted by my issues of trust and feeling of being unworthy of love. I didn't want to do to Azmir what I'd done to Michelle. I didn't want to fail his faith in me. I didn't want to live or die alone. I felt empty and confused. Worst of all, I didn't know where to turn to repair myself. Azmir was great but he was not a solution. I didn't want to seek refuge or healing from a human being. I also didn't want to put too much into one person. I needed help to accept Azmir, not make him some focal point or a sole reason to better myself.

One of my patients, Mary, would always come in talking about her church and the love of Christ, all of the typical and annoying banter of a holy roller who felt that Jesus was the answer for everything. Mary would always boast of her church, and of course, give the proverbial invitation time and time again. Suddenly, I recalled those *patients* that would come to the church as though it was a hospital when I was a child. I had become one of those sick people. No, I didn't have substance abuse issues, neither had I been in prison. But my heart had been imprisoned by fear. I so desperately wanted to free myself of the strongholds that were on me. I decided before leaving my place for work that I would call Mary and finally accept her invitation to church.

It was that simple for me. I had to start somewhere.

I was at *Smith, Katz & Adams* headquarters for a breakfast staff meeting. I always got nervous during them, and I thought it was because subconsciously, I knew I was not necessarily there based on my own merits but that of Michelle's...and most recently Azmir's unleashing of his voracious attorney. Ever since his involvement, I'd been rolled out the red carpet by the practice. I couldn't lie, the feeling was extraordinary.

"Morning, folks," Dan Smith opened the agenda as everyone hurried off the food line and back into their seats to start the meeting. I was too nervous to eat—waiting for the other shoe to fall.

"Well, gang, it's my personal misfortune to have to inform you that we lost John Ephart two days ago. He succumbed to a heart attack while away in Palm Springs." There were countless gasps and mutters in the room.

Okay, so everyone is just as shocked as I am.

I withdrew for a minute, reflecting on my encounters with John Ephart. He was always a pleasant man when the leasing deal in

Long Beach was underway. He didn't interfere much; only when asked. I recalled him patting me on the shoulders afterwards in the parking lot. He didn't say much other than "Great work, kiddo!" but it meant a lot to my raw nerves that were still settling.

Not another passing. Naturally, my thoughts ventured to Michelle. No death would ever compare to that loss. *Snap out of it. Not here. Not now.*

"We have a new law practice in place," Dan continued. "They're eager to get started. The lead lawyer and his team need to meet with all the therapists...including you, Rayna, there in Long Beach. In fact, I recommended that he start with you as you're most familiar with all the locations and system considering your tenure with us. His name is Brian Thompson..." blah...blah was all I heard after that. *Why would he start with me?* The meeting was uneventful after that announcement. I couldn't wait to get out of there.

Work was busy per usual after the full staff meeting. That was the great thing about my job, I enjoyed it so much that I easily became engulfed and before I knew it, it was my lunch hour or time to leave for the day. But along with time would go my energy. I'd brought Azna into work with me so that I could conveniently get him to the vet for an evaluation and shots. I felt like this was a test run at parenting. *Ewwwwww...I don't like the idea of that. I could never be a mom. I don't think I'm built for it. Besides I don't think it's in the cards for me anyway.* I quickly thought to myself considering my loss of fetus recently.

My fearful thoughts were interrupted by an alert from a text.

Your departure left me wounded...and hanging. I don't want to get used to that. I'll buy your house. Just give me a fair price.

He is so sweet. The thought of his generous offer warmed me. *Oh, Azmir, only if things were that simple.*

Don't you have bigger acquisitions to take on, Mr. Jacobs? Sidebar: when's the next time I'll see you? I'd like to

make up for leaving you hanging. I can even lick your wound(s) if it would make you feel better.

I can make myself available in 5 mins but that would be indecorous. If you shared my bed this wouldn't be an issue. Sidebar: Tonight?

Damn. **Tonight wouldn't work. I have - don't laugh - church.**

CHURCH? When did the halo appear? I missed it amongst the whips and chains. He teased.

I know. It's me trying something new to help cure my... issues.

Indeed. Just don't let them convince you that my bed isn't undefiled. Azmir quipped.

Oh, they'd probably submerge me in the baptism pool if they had privy to what you do to me in your bed and out. I couldn't resist my twisted humor. I had to snicker to myself.

Until the next time you're in my bed (where I just might chain you to keep you there)... He replied. My breathing hitched.

Until then... (you wouldn't dare!) I ended our exchange.

Church wasn't too bad. We learned about purpose. We were even assigned *"A Purpose Driven Life,"* something I'd started reading immediately and found myself engulfed in during the first sit down. It was the perfect start to my journey, my self-discovery. It reminded me that my world was bigger than just *me*. That there was a Guider, a Being bigger and stronger than myself Who wanted to be depended on to fill me. The one thing that struck me is how Warren said God didn't intend for us to live like the Monks in isolation. He wants us to commune together because somehow, we helped each other grow and develop.

That was my biggest fear: depending on *people*. I'd come to depend on my solitude. It was a protective barrier. But I also knew that it was no longer working for me. For so many years that barrier only included virtually one person. That person is no longer with me, had left me bereft. That loss demonstrated that I couldn't put my all into one person. I needed to put more substance into myself. I also needed something bigger than *me* to lean on. I couldn't wait until the following week's Bible study to explore the principles of the book.

In the meantime, I'd learned that the pastor of the church was a licensed therapist. I found it odd how I immediately felt drawn to his teaching persona. He was gentle and full of hope, solutions, and encouragement. Pastor Edmondson was a middle-aged Caucasian man who was enthralled by his beautiful wife, who so happened to be African American. They worked as a team that night and I was captivated by how they gelled. I wanted *that* with another human being. I'd suddenly felt overwhelmed by the concept of the journey to get to a point in a relationship where I could flow seamlessly with a man that way. I made note of the church's website and decided to explore it for more information. Perhaps counseling would be a great assist for me during this period of evolution. I sure was desperate for change.

It was a late Saturday morning, and I was in my spare bedroom that I'd managed to turn into a makeshift dance room. I had mini-speakers spread throughout the room and nailed to the walls. I even threw up a few mirrors to give me reflection. I'd been dancing on Saturdays to keep my mind. It wasn't like I had the demanding life that I used to.

I started a piece to Tamia's *"Can't Get Enough."* Our assignment was to create and develop as a choreographer. So in doing so, we had to begin by selecting a song. Jimmy helped me out with the basics, but because it was an assignment, I had to head the choreography. I liked the cut, and specifically chose this because it was relative. The theme of the song was clear. It's seductive, bold and wanting. And that's how I felt. Tamia seemed to climax at the end and *that's* what I seemed to do with Azmir. Time and time again.

I couldn't get enough of Azmir. The things he did to my body sexually confused me as to who it belonged to. He commanded it. I'd had reasonably enjoyable sex in the past, but never did my body respond to a man the way that it had to him. Yes, he was skilled and clearly knew his way around a woman's anatomy, but it seemed as if it were more. Our connection was electrifying. I was addicted to his lovemaking. It haunted my many thoughts. It had me touching and exploring my body to learn more about it. Of course, I didn't possess the courage to tell him any of this. My fortitude was reduced to that of a child's when in his presence. I couldn't discern if that was my self-esteem or simply the result of our energies meeting.

Boom-boom-bap. And one-two-three. Dip - swing - jump. I sang in my head trying to keep my counts. *Oh, I like that. Let me extend that dip to the floor. 1-2-3-4...* "I can't get enough of yooooooou!"

Shit!

My heart plunged from my chest cavity, my pulse rang in my ears and my limbs went numb at the sight of an intruder. I jumped to find Azmir standing behind me. He stood in the doorway holding Azna. How long had he been there? *What the hell!* I flipped the music off with the remote.

"When did you get here?" I asked, startled and out of breath. He looked cleaned and sexy per usual. He wore a white T-shirt, seersucker type of striped denims and white sneakers. He was delectable. But that gave him no right to sneak up on me like this.

With his eyes locked on me, he shrugged his shoulders. He wore an inscrutable expression on his face. My heart was racing, and my mouth went dry. The next thing I noticed was my trembling frame. He scared the shit out of me and had yet to provide an explanation for his visit. He placed Azna on the floor and strolled over to me.

Okay. I think I know the look. He wants me.

He walked up behind me, bent down and while staring at me through the mirror whispered in my ear, "Interesting selection of music."

There's the current.

He then kissed my left earlobe, moved his head to my right side and murmured, "Interesting display of art. I didn't know you were so lithe," and kissed that earlobe. "I'd like to see more," he continued his seduction effortlessly.

"Azmir, I'm not fresh. I'm sweating all over." I tried to ward him off.

I'm panting out of control for crying out loud.

"Bend over and show me that move again...where your hands touch the floor." I wanted to say no but once again my authority over my own body had egressed.

"You're thinking too long. Show me," Azmir whispered.

Slowly, I extended my arms forward and lowered them to the floor. Naturally, my upper torso followed until the palms of my hands were touching the floor.

With his index finger, Azmir drew a line from my neck to the small of my back. Then he cupped my behind with both of his hands. He pulled me up by my right shoulder and as I stood, he removed my tank top, tights, and panties slowly. My heart never returned to its resting rate. He walked me inches over, so we stood directly in front of one of my full body mirrors then reached down and began massaging my breasts. My head fell to the right as my eyes closed simultaneously. He pulled my nipples through my bra. My chest ascended involuntarily to help me to breathe.

"Show me that move once again?" It sounded like a question but really an order. I again raised my arms and descended them towards the floor taking my entire upper body. This time Azmir gripped my ass tightly. He then, with his two index fingers, found my clitoris and rubbed it around and around. Before I knew it, those fingers slipped inside my canal. I moaned. Coincidentally so did Azmir.

"You're always so damn wet, Brimm."

My groans started to deepen. The next thing I felt was his adroit fingers exiting my body and seconds later, he entered me. It was slow and steady, making sure his ample size was welcomed. Azmir was so nestled inside I could feel his cock pulse. I tried maintaining my balance, it was difficult with him inside distracting me. He was grinding at a steady pace. I couldn't control my moans over his thrusts in and out.

"Rayna, I'm going to lift your legs in the air, one by one. You're going to have to show me how limber you are to enjoy this. Let me know the minute you're unstable or uncomfortable. Okay?" Azmir asked in an authoritative tone that actually turned me on.

He expected an answer.

"Yes," I panted, trying to contain the salacious pleasure taking over my body.

He gave me an abrupt thrust as he asked once again, "Okay?" That was borderline painful but very much pleasurable.

"Yes!" I screamed, writhing beneath him.

As he grinded into me he lifted my legs one at a time, taking himself deeper in me. When both legs were totally up in the air, I had to spread my arms further apart to balance myself. My body was extended plank style in the middle of the floor. The deeper he went the more pressure I felt. The more pressure I felt the more lubricated I became. I didn't hear much but the sounds of our lovemaking. He was slapping into my flesh. His penis was swishing with my juices, and it drove me wild by the second. This...*this* is what Azmir meant when he said the best thing about making love was taking in all the senses, in this position we were both forced to. He watched from the mirror hanging in front of us. The sounds were clamorous and erotic.

Once I began taking it all in my insides started quickening. *Shit.* I was about to explode. I couldn't survive an orgasm in this position. I'd fall and embarrass myself.

This feels so good...I can't hold on!

"Azmir! Oh, shit! Oh, shit!" I cried out loud.

There was movement. He swiftly grabbed my belly and released my knees to the floor as he began to pound into me like his life depended on it. I was in the post apex phase of my orgasm, the pounding prolonged it. I groaned several renditions of his name. I felt him swell even larger inside of me and immediately I knew what that meant. He sang mine blissfully as he exploded inside of me, grabbing my cheeks for dear life. His hard body went limp on top of mine as I slowly lay us down on the floor making sure our landing was smooth.

Damn, I love this man.

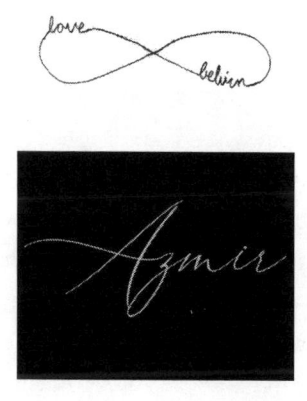

I rolled off Rayna. *Goddamn!* She is as lissome as a motherfucker. That was impressive. I knew she could do it, watching her movements while dancing gave away her nimble abilities. I couldn't believe she didn't give me any pushback. Little Ms. Brimm just may be my type of freak. No matter how demanding I was sexually, she never turned me away. My soldier.

She had her face turned away from me. I playfully tapped her on her shoulder.

"Hey...you okay? Did you enjoy that half as much as I did?" I asked lightheartedly.

She turned her head over towards me and snorted, "I'm not sure I had a choice in the matter."

"What does that mean?" I sincerely asked as I pulled up my pants.

She shrugged and murmured, "I don't know. But I really enjoyed it," with an undeniable bashful smile.

That smile relieved me. I didn't want to hurt her, just to have a little fun with her. As I pulled her up in my arms and onto my lap, she managed to put on her underwear first.

"You never answered my question," she pointed out as I watched her pull up her cotton printed panties. I thought I had replaced *all* of her cottons with lace and silk. She could reserve those for that time of the month. She wasn't comfortable with me gifting her. But I'd take my time rebuilding her wardrobe.

"What question is that sweetheart?" I returned from my introspect.

"What are you doing here? And how did you get in?"

"Oh. I kept calling this morning and wondered where you were. I got a little concerned, so I decided to drop by. I saw your car out there and rang the doorbell. You never answered. I heard the music blasting and called your cell several times. I got anxious, so I came around back with my spare key." I explained.

"Azmir, I'm going to have to notify the authorities of your spare key. You do know that's unlawful," she retorted rolling her eyes with a slight grin on her face. I grabbed her waist tightly and bit her ear playfully. She giggled. "I went to get my hair done at seven this morning. I left my cell here. When I got back, I noticed my battery was dead, so it's been on the charger. I've been in here for a while." She murmured, quickly lost in thought and narrowed her eyebrows, "What time is it?"

I glanced at my *Rolex*. "Almost noon. What time did you start in here?" It was obvious she had lost track of time.

"About nine thirty. Why were you looking for me? And don't

tell me it was for this," she questioned, referring to recent randy events.

"I wanted to know if you had room in your schedule to hang out with me today. And why are you wearing this head wrap?" I asked as I touched it to see how tight it was. She did say she'd just return from the salon.

"My hair is wrapped. Where are you going?" She swatted my hands from her head wrap.

"An associate of mine is having a "*soirée*" at his home in Palm Springs. I thought it would be a nice Saturday outing."

"You tell me the day of? What time is it? I don't have anything to wear. I know your kind. *Express* attire won't work." She sighed in panic.

"Ah-ha!" I exclaimed while letting her off my lap so I could stand. She was right, which led me to my next move. I led her into the living room and her eyes immediately lit up at the bags.

"*Neiman Marcus*, Mr. Jacobs? What is this all about?" she mumbled solemnly. I wasn't sure if she was asking in shock or disapproval.

"I didn't want to take no for an answer so I took the liberty of picking out some things you can wear," I spoke with trepidation, trying to remind myself she'd been okay with what I'd picked out in Phoenix back in June. "Besides, Ray will be back soon. I don't want to leave here alone."

I honestly couldn't wait for her to get over this issue with me doing things for her.

She gave me an austere gaze as she walked over to the bags. She began by opening the suit bag where she discovered the *Emilio Pucci* kaleidoscopic printed fitted dress. I picked it because I knew her ass would puff in that cut. I saw beyond the mannequin.

She shot me a scowl before opening the next bag containing a chunky necklace with earrings and bracelets to match the ensemble. She kept darting her eyes to me, giving me the look of death. It was kind of working. I didn't know what she was thinking.

Finally, she squatted and went to the small shopping bag with an off-white clutch and two shoeboxes. Rayna decided to open the tan *Christian Louboutin* box with the double platform suede tangerine sling backs. She went to the next bag where she removed the Daffodile crystal-embellished suede *Christian Louboutin* pumps. Those went hard. I'd just hoped like hell I'd accurately measured her fashion sense and was correct when I assumed she wouldn't be familiar with the cost of them. She really needed to get over this spending on her thing. For the first time in my life, I wanted to spoil a woman.

Rayna wore a look of confusion while holding the crystallized shoes. She picked up the tangerine pumps and glanced over to me for an answer, to which I quickly replied, "Oh, the tangerine *Louboutin's* are for the dress. The crystals...you'll fuck me in those and those alone—hopefully soon."

She gave me an inscrutable expression. I didn't think it was good.

"Rayna, you could wear whatever's in your closet. What's most important is you coming...and exude all that sexiness that enamors me." I tried ending it with a bit of charm, though it was indicative of how I truly felt. I was crazy about her, just afraid to let it all hang. She fucking made me nervous!

After a few seconds, she rose from the floor, "I need to get your semen off me, it's created a puddle in my panties." And she continued with lowered eyes, "I'll let you dress me up today, Mr. Jacobs...seems you have exclusionary taste." She batted her eyes to soften her statement and retreated to her bedroom.

When she returned about thirty minutes later, I was floored. Her beauty was embroidered. The dress fit far better than what I had imagined. And she moved gracefully in the five-inch *Louboutin's*. Her make-up was soft, but her eyes were well defined. Her tangerine lipstick was the icing on the cake. I couldn't wait to fuck it up. I couldn't piece that together, makeup was out of my lane, but she seemed to have had a grip on it. Her hair was long and flowing against her shoulders and draping her upper back. *How did she go from do-rag to this?* was what begged for an answer.

"You look elegant. I love your hair. What did you do with it?" I asked while standing in front of her admiring her beauty.

Rayna let out a chuckle. "I had it highlighted this morning. Thank you, Mr. Jacobs," she muttered bashfully.

"You look delectable, which is why we need to hurry up and hit the road before I have to cancel on Rick," I growled in her ear, flirting with her. Ray had been waiting outside.

She blushed, beaming gracefully. I grabbed her hand and we left.

Rick's property was stupendously massive. He had been *pseudo* inviting me down for a couple of years now, but I haven't been interested. I recently discovered we have a few business friends in common, so I relented this time. His home had to be eleven thousand square feet. We walked in through the foyer where we were greeted by a waiter with champagne. I took two and handed one to Rayna. I can tell she was just as amazed as I was about the spacious rooms and exquisite decor from our trip from the front door out into the back of the house. A few people were in the house, but most were out back. The closer we got to the French doors leading to the patio the louder and clearer the music became.

I immediately saw people I knew from various circles. His yard was enormous. The patio area was at least five yards long and three wide adorned with cobblestone before you hit the grass. There were two in-ground pools, both of which were being occupied by guests. This was exclusive. I noticed Rayna was quiet.

We found a table and I asked, "You okay?"

"Yeah. I'm just in awe of this estate. I guess the shoes were a good idea," she teased about the things I'd bought her earlier. I had hope she wasn't feeling intimidated. This was nice but these were the most pretentious people this side of the Mississippi.

"Impressive, yeah but too grand for my taste." She gave my comment a silly laugh.

"What's that all about?" I asked.

"I think I'm officially tipsy."

"How is that? You're not even done with your glass." I looked at the glass seeing it was three quarters empty.

"I guess that was all it took," she shared in a more serious manner.

"When was the last time you've eaten?"

"Try around eight this morning," she murmured sheepishly.

"Ms. Brimm, that's very irresponsible of you," I admonished. I didn't want her getting sick.

"Well, I had an intruder this afternoon. One who was after my goodies. So, my bad for forgetting to ask him to pause while I ate."

"Let me go grab you something to eat. Stay put." I ignored her cute jab but left her with a soft kiss on her forehead before walking off.

I went to the various food tables and grabbed her a couple of pieces of finger foods. Anything to absorb the alcohol.

"Hey...*Azmeer*," I heard from a distance over the music. I knew who it was immediately. I always hated the way Rick pronounced my name but tolerated it. I turned around and he was approaching me with his arms wide open. You have to appreciate the visual of a man well over six feet embracing one who's barely over five feet.

"Rick. My dude! How are you?" I greeted.

"Azmeer, it's great to see you out. Actually, I'm happy as fuck to see you. I thought you'd stand me up."

"No. This time I chose to oblige. I even brought a lady friend." *One I need to get back to with some food.*

"A lady friend? This I've got to see, my friend," Rick shouted.

"She's over here."

We walk over to Rayna who's soaking up the atmosphere. Rick talked a mile a minute en route.

"Ahhhhh...here she is. And you left out how fucking gorgeous she is, aye!" Rick teased as he nudged me in the ribs with his elbow.

"Ms. Brimm, this is a longtime associate of mine, Rick Adelstien. Rick, this is a very special acquaintance of mine, Ms. Rayna Brimm."

Rick, being the cock-sucking suck up that he was, reached for Rayna's hand and kissed it before saying, "Now, you, I had to meet. Azmeer here never comes out to play and you must be his inspiration. An extreme pleasure to meet you, Ms. Brimm. Is that Brim as in hat?"

"Actually, two M's—" Rayna replied with a graceful smile.

But before she could complete her sentence Rick blurts out, "Are you being taken care of here?"

A waiter so happened to be walking past us and he ordered, "Hey, you! You make sure this special couple gets V.I.P. treatment, do you understand? I want you to anticipate their every need, understand?" Rick spoke condescendingly.

The waiter left us glasses of champagne and promised to return with food.

"Rick, that was very gracious of you. You shouldn't have," I snorted though I really wanted to say, *Don't belittle the staff to impress me. You're doing yourself a disservice.*

"Nothing is too much for a friend like you, Azmeer! Now, I'll have to go. I see a guy who owes me money. It was great meeting you, Ms. Brimm. Anything you need, you let me know..." he offered to Rayna then looked at me before giving me the all too familiar slap on the arm before walking away.

Rayna laughed heartily. I was annoyed to say the least. Kiss ups are disingenuous people, I detest them.

"And what is your relationship with him?" Rayna asked in amusement.

"Money. He's been asking for years for me to invest in his indie films. I haven't been interested until recently. I'm still on the fence."

"Well, he drives a hard bargain. Be ready to be sold," she warned, still laughing.

"Rayna, I thought you should know I'll be out of town next week," I informed her while twirling my champagne flute.

With wide eyes she asked, "Where?"

"Paris. My partner has a few things lined up over there...potential associates who are in markets we'd like to engage. If I'm lucky, I'll return a man with many connections and more enterprises," I simplified.

"Paris. For how long?" She seemed disappointed.

"I'll leave out on Monday and due to return on Friday. It's a relatively short trip and is extremely hopeful. Will you miss me?"

"Probably more than I can stand." She pouted softly while looking into the distance.

I knew this was bad timing considering we'd been locked at the hip for about a week now. She'd still been grieving and wouldn't have anyone while I was away. Her nightmares she had no idea I'd been aware of were still frightening for her. But this was an opportunity I could not turn away. Things were drastically turning around for me in the land of merging and acquisitions, and I had to strike while the iron was hot.

"You can always come. I'm sure you can request the time off," I offered knowing I'd be more than agreeable to it.

"Don't be silly, Azmir. I could never impose on you like that. I'm a big girl. I'll be fine," she tried to assure unconvincingly. "But I am excited about this opportunity and what it means for your career. I can say I smashed you when," she joked, and we both fell into laughter.

Moments later, as we were chatting, another familiar voice spoke from behind me.

"Oh, wow! I didn't know you'd be here." I turned to find Lady Spin. I wasn't expecting to see her either.

"Lady S," I acknowledged dryly. Right away she locked eyes

with Rayna who stood next to the table. She reached up and air kissed me on the cheek. Not a good move but I allowed it.

"It's a surprise seeing you, too," I attempted, feeling indifferent.

"Did you come alone?" she asked, looking Rayna square in the face.

"No. This is Ms. Rayna Brimm. Ms. Brimm, I'm not sure if you are familiar with Lady Spin from the radio?" I pose as a question knowing damn well, they met at an event a couple of months back.

"Why, of course. It's a pleasure to see you again," Rayna offered with grace.

Spin gave a spurious smile and cut her eyes to me. She was getting the message. She may not have liked the painting, but she understood the picture. Now, I'd always liked Spin because she was easy to get along with and fun to hang out with. She didn't press me for much. She was very direct with wanting a sexual relationship with no strings attached. And I knew her heart was with a guy from a popular R&B group from the early nineteen-nineties. She was nearly forty and knew how to separate her feelings from her pussy or so I thought until today.

"So, how's everything? How's Petey? I have to get back to him about your party pictures. He told me they're ready," she shared, trying to illustrate intimacy between us and name drop. Women can be so conniving.

Rayna just stood there heedfully and coolly watching. The look in Lady S' eyes told me this wouldn't go over easy, which I didn't understand because she was pliant to our arrangement in the past.

To my surprise we were interrupted by Rayna's girl, Britni.

"Rayna! Heeeeeeey, girl!" Britni shrieked.

Rayna turned and gave a huge smile and returned warmly, "Hey Britni. How are you? What are you doing here?"

Britni announced, "I'm here with Spin."

Rayna narrowed her eyebrows in confusion. "Oh, wow. Small world."

Britni had a slick look in her eye. "Yeah, she's my cousin."

"Oh, I didn't know that," Rayna muttered, trying to mask her disappointment.

"Well, it's not like you ever hung out with us outside of Michelle. But Michelle met her a while back," Britni announced.

This was some bullshit brewing. I wasn't looking forward to the outcome at all. Rayna was visibly uncomfortable.

"Oh, cuz! This is a good friend of mine, Azmir—" Spin was cut off my Britni.

"Azmir Jacobs. Yes, he was the sole sponsor of my Bahamian vacation I told you about. And what a pleasure that was," she announced with the most scheming and seductive smile.

"I'm glad you were able to take part in Rayna's birthday excursion...?"

"Britni," she answered my purposely posed question of her name. She was insignificant. I understood what she was trying to do to Rayna.

"Britni. That's right." My tone was wry.

Britni looked Rayna up and down. "Wow, Rayna, you're really gettin' it," as she cut her eyes at me. Was she really insinuating Rayna was pimping me? I had to chuckle!

Women can be really shady.

"Getting it, huhn?" Rayna replied calmly, wearing a smirk while intently reading Britni's eyes. I could tell she was infuriated.

"Yeah, those *Loubou's* are from the spring line. They're on every diva's wish-list and here you are rocking the hell out of them," Britni antagonized.

"Flattery gets you everywhere, B. Glad to have inspired you," Rayna replied mirthlessly.

I had to stop this. I saw a flame shoot up in Rayna's eyes. I didn't want her flexing.

Spin looked at me directly. "I need to speak with you—privately," a little demanding even. I didn't like it. She was trying to enter into an estrogen war and these two were tag-teaming Rayna. If I had to choose, Spin will be picking her bruised ego off the ground. I don't do shows.

But before I could answer Rayna issued, "Mr. Jacobs, you better go, she sounds desperate. Besides, I need a moment with my... estranged...*buddy* here," while her eyes were burning a hole in Britni's face.

"Desperate?" Spin shot back.

Rayna's eyes darted to Spin, "Yes," she smiled ruefully. "See, when you see your former bed-buddy out with a new woman and immodestly ask to speak with him in private, that has a scent of desperation to it. Go, have your moment. I'm generous." She maintained a smile that didn't extend to her eyes, the same she wore when speaking to Britni a few moments ago.

I don't think Spin was expecting that. Shit, I wasn't expecting it. Spin was at a loss for words. And honestly, I was grateful. I would not have Rayna out here doing a showdown with another woman. I respected Spin and wouldn't even want that for her. I think Rayna wanted a moment to settle up with Britni.

Spin bowed out gracefully and I asked Rayna with my eyes if it was cool. She gave me a soft nod and warm smiled. I looked at Britni with pity. *She's about to get her ass handed to her.*

I followed Spin around the bar and to the side of the house to a wooden bench. She stopped with her hands wrapped around her waist and rhythmically patted her feet. It was clear she was in a defensive posture. I offered her a seat to which she declined. I then sat.

"Azmir, what's going on with you and this...young lady? This seems different," she hissed.

I creased my brows. "Spin, I'm lost. Are you asking me for my dating status with Rayna Brimm?"

"Yes!" she answered emphatically.

"I don't think that's owed. Aren't you back with Dalvin?"

She looked affronted. "Yes and no. We're still working out the kinks." She appeared flushed.

"Okay, but during our last conversation you told me you were going back to him, ergo the termination of our arrangement." She wasn't going to make me out to be a lothario. I didn't owe her shit.

"So, I guess what I'm asking here is will she be an issue for us if I want to continue with our arrangement?" she asked with overt sarcasm.

"Indeed."

"Wow. That's really fucked up, Azmir," she murmured, looking out into the distance.

"Spin, you've always been good peoples—with or without sex. I don't want that to change, but right now I have my hands into something. And besides, I was really under the impression that you and Dalvin were back tight again. I don't want to play the in between role. Go and work that out with him or close the chapter so you can move on with someone who deserves you," I advised her genuinely. I really did like Spin, but our time had expired.

She stood there shell-shocked staring into midair. I could swear I saw her fighting back tears. I didn't understand where all of this emotion was coming from. Spin and I were never a couple and had always been honest about not wanting to be. Hell, even if I were single without Tara or Rayna, I seriously doubt if I'd go for Spin. She was too much of a public figure. She was at every party, award show, and fundraising event. She'd dated heavily in the industry as well. I'm a low-key type of man and don't want to ever bargain that.

During our moment of silence at the memorial of our affair, her assistant ran over to her, "Lady Spin, we have to go! You're on soon and we have to mic you!"

"Okay," she returned to the awkward looking fellow wearing oversized yellow framed glasses.

She gave me a glance seeming to want to say more. I nodded in concession, and she walked off.

On my way back to Rayna, I decided to stop at the bar and

refresh her drink. I hoped her pow-wow with ol' girl wasn't too bad.

When I returned to our cocktail table, I noticed Rayna wasn't there. I looked up and saw Rick.

"That Ms. Brimm is hot, bro! She's over there on the dance floor making us all swoon. Are you serious about her, Azmeer?" Rick asked in all sincerity.

"Indeed," I chortled. "Let me go swoon, too," I muttered as I strode toward the music.

I walked up on Rayna who was nearly center stage dancing to Latin music. Her moves were smooth and acute. There were nearly twenty people following the lead of an instructor, but she was getting special attention from him. The short guy was animated and loud. He couldn't keep his eyes off of Rayna who stayed focused on her feet looking over to him occasionally to take cues. Most of the women following on the dance floor were bare foot. But even they couldn't hold a candle to Ms. Brimm in five-inch stilettos. It didn't even seem as if she was trying very hard.

Raptly, I watched them go from one song to another. At that point I was so intrigued I grabbed a seat to get comfortable. I noticed Britni staring and could've sworn she even pointed to me while talking to someone else. Then Rayna looked over at me and gave me a warm smile and wink. I thought the gesture was nice. I stayed and watched for a while. I was glad to see she was enjoying herself independent of me. It was clear the instructor was enjoying her, too. I wasn't moving too far just in case I had to check his chin.

A few people came over to speak, including Rick. He introduced me to Brad, the actor, who has apparently signed on to star in the film Rick is asking me to help fund. He was taking toadying to a new level. Throughout all the chatting I kept Brimm in my peripheral. Eventually, she sashayed over to me slightly of breath, but exuding excitement. I was happy to see her roused and light-hearted. This mourning period had been rough on her. I grabbed her by the waist, drawing her to my hip, kissed her on the head and introduced her to Brad.

"It's a pleasure to meet you!"

"I see you like to move!" Brad emulated a two-step, which was corny as hell.

"I do! I was coming to see if Mr. Jacobs here will join me. I'd like to see his moves," she shared flirtatiously. I was flattered.

"No...no...no. I don't dance. Besides you were looking so good out there, I can assure you the last thing you need is me stepping on your toes at every turn," I replied.

She gave me a petulant pout. She was really in a great mood, and I was tired of sharing my time with her, I wanted to get her alone.

"I think we should get ready to go," I announced gazing at her for her take as I had my arm wrapped around her shoulder.

"Oh, sure." Her smile so soft. "Brad, it was great meeting you. I'm a huge fan." Rayna caressed my hand hanging from her shoulder. I didn't know if I was over-thinking it, but maybe that was her way of inviting me in while she was paying another man a compliment. I liked that.

"Why, thank you, Ms. Brimm. I appreciate that," Brad returned unperturbed. He's used to this type of attention.

Rayna lifted her head to me for direction. I gave Brad some dap and we made our way to the front of the property where Ray was waiting. But before we could make it to the back doors of the house, I could feel eyes burning the back of my head. I turned to see Spin and Britni gawking our every move. I just ignored them and kept it moving. That Britni chick seemed like trouble.

"Thanks for dressing me up and dragging me out of the house, Azmeer!" she jeered, mocking Rick. *Cute.*

"Are you so wealthy that you could help fund a movie with star power like Brad?" Rayna asked intrigued.

I squinted my eyes surprised by the question. "So they say."

We both laughed.

I wasn't accustomed to speaking about my money with anyone because it was so complicated. I'd done extremely well legitimately; it had been noted by the *IRS*. But then I had an equally impressive stash of dirty money *under the table*. I'd keep my dark life away from Rayna for as long as I possibly could. That life was ending and the new one had been promising and rewarding thus far. She was a part of this new life. *Out with the old and in with the new.*

As soon as we were in the car, Rayna scooted over and snuggled underneath me.

"Tired?" I asked.

"It's been a long day." She lifted her head to meet my eyes and clarified, "And it was eventful and exciting thanks to you, Mr. Jacobs." She searched my eyes.

I nodded in acknowledgement.

The ride home was long but smooth. Rayna and I talked some and rode in silence toward the end of our journey. I thought about my exchange with Spin. She was flummoxing. I attempted to be as clear and honest with her as possible, but the look in her eyes was weird for me. She seemed hurt and I didn't understand why.

CHAPTER 6

Rayna

It was a Tuesday evening and time for me to clock out of work. I couldn't help but to feel blue. While Azna is a fury ball of joy, his nuzzling wasn't enough to distract me from my pining of Azmir. I missed him and it had only been twenty-four hours. Normally, I'd be consumed with Michelle and Erin so it wouldn't be much of an issue.

It saddened me to realize I couldn't even call to share my feelings of loneliness with Michelle. I suddenly realized since our return from the East Coast, I'd been with Azmir nearly every day—and I couldn't but guess it had been by his design. Now that he had been halfway across the world, I was lonesome.

Oh, well. I'll get through this day-by-day. I always do.

When I got into the bed, I was alerted of an email.

It's Azmir!

Good evening. You should be in bed by now. Shit - you had better be in bed by now. I'm all too sorry that I'm not there with you. How's our pet child?

Holy shit! He referred to the dog as our pet child! *We share some-*

thing? My belly filled with butterflies. My goodness! Does this man really have this much of an effect on me?

As predicted I am in bed. A very lonely bed. A very cold, lonely bed. Azna is here relaxing with me but he's not 6 feet 4 inches of unadulterated pleasure. However, he's my only connection to you so I'll deal. What are you up to?

Good. I'm taking a bathroom break from a meeting. My body is still on PST. In other words: I gotta love jones. Missing you. Gotta go...

And with that, he was off.

The following day was easier but still dry. I had dance class in the evening. I gave my number to Tamia's tune a test drive and everyone went wild. Jimmy was so elated, he announced how he'd been planning a showcase for our choreographed numbers in a couple of months. He said he'd planned on making the announcement in a few weeks or so but seeing how much work people were putting into them his excitement wouldn't allow him to hold onto it. I was immediately thrilled at the thought of Azmir being there to see me perform the song we'd christened there in my makeshift dance room at my place. Then reality slapped me in the face, reminding me he was out of town, and it would be days before I saw him.

As I reflected on "*A Purpose Driven Life*," I had a revelation. *Why am I holding back on the one person who is asking me to love them? Why do I think I have to mourn alone and be alone on everything? Would it be a foreign thought to believe Azmir's presence in my life is a gift? That his love is in my destiny?* I wanted to shake this shell towering around me, that I somehow convinced myself was for my protection. *Could I just lift it a little to receive love as God intended?* I knew he didn't exactly have in mind for love to be this unofficial, but I felt like I needed to start somewhere and with the only person willing to take a risk with me.

At home while letting Azna out to do his thing out in my tiny yard it hit me: *I'm moving into Azmir's place!* It was that quick. That spurred. That simple. Why succumb to long days and lonely nights when a wonderful man—and one of Azmir's status—is practically begging me to join lives with him?

What's the worst that can happen?

If it didn't work out, I knew I'd always have a home to return to. In the back of my mind, I had haunted reservations of whether or not I was doing this to avoid loneliness. But I immediately heard Michelle's voice admonishing me.

"*You alone are worthy of love!*"

Once Azna was done handling his business, I scooped him up. "We're moving, dude! Let's pack!"

It was late on a Wednesday, about ten thirty at night when I hauled a duffle bag and Azna's crate and other belongings into Azmir's high-rise.

I had a car full of my immediate needs but took up what I could bare. While I schlepped my things from the elevator, down the corridor and into the apartment door, butterflies started to evade my belly. When I pulled out *the* golden key, turned the knob and pushed the door in, nervousness overcame me.

The lights were off except for the ceiling bulbs aligned down the corridor and overhead of the stove in the kitchen. I turned on the foyer light and let Azna out of his cage.

"This is home...for now. Let's get comfy."

About an hour later, after showering, I went about exploring. I started with Azmir's home office. I flipped the switch and watched the room illume. His work room was fairly large and was centered by a huge wooden desk. I sauntered in, observing the artwork on the long walls and countless books on the shelves. Azna followed behind me exploring the floors. I sat in the oversized desk chair and exhaled. I wondered how much work Azmir actually did here. I touched the mouse and the computer lit up. It must have been in sleep mode. The last thing he had up was his itinerary for the business trip he was on.

"Okay, well he wasn't dishonest." Reservations were made for him alone. "No mistress?" I laughed to myself.

"You're technically not his girlfriend!" was the voice of pessimism that had always haunted my subconscious. Not today. Not anymore. I was determined to step out of my shell.

Another page up on his computer was a spreadsheet displayed quarterly earnings for one of his businesses. My inquisition traveled to the desk calendar, and I saw he did engage it as I observed how he had things scribbled on it. There were events, meetings and other cryptic entries.

But what specifically caught my attention was the "RayBs" recorded on various days throughout the month. I'm sure it was the variation of the letters in my name capturing my attention. I went back in previous months and saw them noted on several dates. The earliest I saw it marked was on his birthday.

Hmmmmm...

Shit! *Does he make record of our sexual encounters?* As I sat there reflecting on the dates, I figured it was the only thing it could have been.

What the hell? Should I feel special or weirded out?

Are there other names? None of the other recordings resembled names.

Hmmmm...

I then figured I should leave the office before I found myself doing more snooping. I made my way back to the master suite.

Ahhhhhh...

The plush, supersized, well-firm, and inviting bed of Azmir. The beddings were freshly laundered because I couldn't smell *him*. I didn't like it, but boy, was the comfort of this bed supreme! I twisted and turned playfully between the sheets. I felt like a kid in a hotel room for the first time. My childlike behavior was interrupted by a trill from my phone alerting me of an e-mail. I knew right away it was Azmir.

All tucked in? he asked.

Oh, yeah! And very well, thank you! I decided quickly about not giving away my secret.

That's good. How was your day?

It was mediocre until recently! Rocking! Yours? I couldn't help it. I was exclamation point happy.

We're making progress so I won't complain. Have you any plans for the weekend?

Yup! I plan on staying in *allllllll* weekend long! I was enjoying my private joke at his expense.

Well, hopefully I can get a moment of your time. I've been hoping to extinguish you of your hermit ways. I see I have more work to do. I don't mind. Hit you up later...they're waiting on me to start a luncheon meeting.

Ughhhhh!

The two-minute conversation thing was killing me. After taking a few moments to huff about being separated from this man —*my man?* I remembered where I was, which was snuggled in *his* sheets, in *his* bed, in *his* bedroom, of *his* home. And that would have to do. I had two more days of missing him. After a few more thoughts I dosed off.

The following day, around mid-morning, I got a page from Sharon up front saying I had a delivery.

"I'll be up in a few minutes. I'm finishing up with Mr. Bronson."

"No problem, Ms. Brimm," Sharon agreed.

A few minutes later, I was up at the front desk and the huge bouquet of fruit caught my eyes immediately. I saw Sharon speaking with people, so I remained quiet as I retrieved the small envelope attached to the deliciously decorated edible arrangement and opened it.

I hope these are just as juicy and sweet as you are. Missing you terribly.

Clear your weekend itinerary. Now!

Forever on the Chase,

A.D. JACOBS

Did he really? All the way from Europe! *Well, Rayna, he DOES have several assistants he could have easily e-mailed the request to.* But it was such a sweet gesture.

"Well, well, well! The awkward moment when I see we're interrupting a private moment."

I looked up to see where the outburst had come from. My irises landed on a handsome, light skinned and well-groomed man in an elegant three-piece suit. *But who is he and where does he get the nerve to intrude on my privacy?* He stood next to two other men I assumed were with him.

My eyes darted to Sharon. But before she could speak, he informed, "Thompson...Brian Thompson of *Thompson's Justice Law* firm. It's a pleasure to make your acquaintance, Ms. Brimm.

Judging by the arrangement, it must have been something said in the card causing the glow. Care to share?"

Thompson wore a cunning smirk, one I didn't register as trustworthy. I didn't know if he was being charming or condescending and trying to embarrass me. Either way, I wasn't interested.

"Sharon, I wasn't aware Mr. Thompson was visiting today. How did it get past me?"

"I'm sorry, Ms. Brimm, we've been so busy around here. It must have been an oversight on my part," Sharon admitted apologetically.

I wasn't totally convinced it was her fault. She was right. We'd been swamped for weeks.

"Have these taken into the kitchen for everyone to share and you can start collecting lunch orders from the staff. It's on me again today. Okay?" I flashed a warm smile. I liked Sharon and belittling staff is a no-no in my book.

Purposely putting Mr. Thompson on hold for a minute, I was now prepared to address him, "Now, Mr. Thompson, how can we be of service to you…" I conspicuously peeked behind him, "and your team today?"

That took the spark out of his cocky ass eyes.

"Mr. Smith recommended I begin my file merging of the firm at the Long Beach branch," Mr. Thompson informed more reserved—still with much confidence, but with less of a smug look on his face.

"I'm sorry, but why is it necessary for you to make visits?" I quizzed. The way he gazed into my eyes alarmed me. Was he attracted to me? *Oh, no!*

"Well, my firm's practice is to have all of our clients' records on file. Initially we make copies of all of your files here. Then we add a program to your software, which will automatically merge new and updated files from here on out."

"Well, fine." I tried to maintain my dignified persona, though his presence further annoyed me by the minute. "Sharon, please grant the Thompson firm whatever access they need." I turned to address her directly, I didn't like staring into his face for too long. "Also, out of hospitality, make sure they know where the restroom and breakrooms are."

"Yes, Ms. Brimm. Natalie should be here any moment to escort them back." Just as she ended her sentence Natalie, a studying therapist, who had been interning with us appeared, introduced herself and led the gentlemen back towards the offices.

I turned to Sharon who was eager to speak. Her eyes were stories high and miles apart. "Ms. Brimm, I am really sorry. I should have gone over your schedule with you last evening before closing." I put my hands in the air asking her to halt.

"I meant what I said." I sighed. "It was an oversight on both our parts. Things have been really busy around here. You're extremely efficient at keeping me on task. No harm. No foul. Are we almost caught up with our backed logged appointments?" I asked.

"I do believe yesterday was the last long day. Things should most definitely be at a slower rate starting Monday." As she spoke, Sharon clicked and navigated the mouse of her desktop glancing over the upcoming schedule I presumed.

I gave a dramatic exhale. It must have lowered her guards.

"I see you have an admirer in that gentleman," Sharon whispered with batted eyelashes. She knew she was toeing the line, but I didn't mind. Again, I really liked Sharon.

"Who? That guy? Pssssssst!" I scoffed. "He'd just better stay in his lane. He was very bold seeing it was our first *professional* encounter," I hissed.

"Yes, he was a bit crass. But I don't think he'll be as *well-acquainted* in the near future," Sharon joked referring to my cold shoulder to him. It was well intended.

"Speaking of admirers. I'll have to tell mine," I shared while raising the small note card accompanying the bouquet. "...he needs to practice a little more discretion at my workplace." I let out a long exhale.

"Please don't," Sharon absentmindedly blurted. I was taken aback by her candor. I gave her a look, which requested an explanation. She hesitated before relenting.

"Ms. Brimm, if I can be briefly audacious, I like it. I like to know you're being courted, and quite frankly, doted on. It makes you glow. Not that you're ever unpleasant to the staff but you're certainly more pleasant to be around. Most importantly, you're such a private woman and the only friend I could assume you had is no longer with us. I thought we'd lost you." She gave me a deep fortifying gaze to prepare for the next thing she was about to say. "That is why I gave Mr. Jacobs information on your whereabouts a few weeks ago. I took a risk in hopes of you not jumping off the cliff, so to speak." She hit me with another pause. "Now, I've heard the "tea" on Mr. Jacobs—" I interrupted her.

"The other therapists talk about us?" I was devastated at the thought of it.

"No, ma'am. I'm lunch buddies with a few of Mr. Jacobs' staff. And while they drool over him, they've made me aware of him being beyond professional. There are no rumors or knowledge of him being inappropriate with his subordinates or dating them. So, for me to see him esteem you with these thoughtful gestures makes him official in my book. Plus, you're young, bright and would make a lovely life partner." Overly enthused, she was at a loss for words. "Well, it's just nice is all I'm saying. You deserve nice."

It was my turn to be at a loss for words. I'd never seen her so introspective before. Her words reminded me of Michelle's sentiments. I actually think I needed that.

"Thank you, Sharon. And your thoughts are duly noted—all of them." My words sincere and delivery professional.

"I will send around the lunch menu momentarily," she proposed, reverting back to her normal self. I walked off with her words still ringing in my head.

About an hour later, while I was in my office catching up on my notes, there was a knock at my door. I looked up and it was Brian Thompson. He was really quite handsome. But I braced myself.

"Yes?" I greeted with a mild smile not reaching my eyes.

"Is there another place you store patients' files, Ms. Brimm?"

I thought for a moment. "Ummm...yeah. At home." *Well, my old home or my other home...oh, whatever!* I fought with myself.

"Okay. Well, we'll need access to that computer as well."

"Okay," I agreed with my eyebrows narrowed, somehow finding the thought of him or his team being in my home strange.

He cracked a boyish smile, "I'll contact you at a later date to make the arrangements."

"Okay."

I was once again feeling awkward because I had nothing more to say to him. I hadn't quite decided if I liked him or not. I took back to my notes and eventually looked up feeling eyes burning into my head.

He's still here?

"*Ummmm*... My guys will be here for a couple more hours and have decided to work through lunch. I'm claustrophobic and need air. Is there any place in particular you would recommend...or would you like to join me?" He sounded defeated with is offer, as he should. *I'm not interested.*

I mustered a smile, "We have been back logged for a while now, which is why I've ordered in for my staff. My lunch is already here. But next door...or a few doors over at the Rec center, they have superb culinary. Other than that, Sharon up front can share the menus for the locals."

"Oh, okay. Maybe another time. Thanks for the recommendations." I nodded and then he left.

Good! Ugh!

Little did he know, I had a manicure and pedicure appointment in twenty-five minutes, and he was disturbing me from finishing up my work before I left.

That evening after work, I had gone to my house to pick up

more things to move into Azmir's apartment. I felt I had the last of everything I needed in order to feel at home there. After packing the last bundle in the car, I went to lock up my house. As I walked out, I stood in the doorway and experienced a barrage of emotions. I had only been there a short time, but it was my first home and held an affinity in my heart.

"*Azmir, you had better be worth it,*" I murmured underneath my breath before closing the door to leave. I shot straight up Lincoln Blvd towards Marina Del Rey.

The next day I decided to be trifling and get my hair done on my lunch hour. What I was getting done wouldn't take long. Adrian took me as soon as I walked through the door. As I was under the dryer, I began to experience anxiety about Azmir's reaction to my moving in while he was away.

What if I would've waited for him to return home before moving in? What if he returns in a bad mood? What if his trip allowed him time to reevaluate his feelings for me?

It took every fiber of my being to suppress those fears. This man has asked me to move in with him several times. That will just have to be my focus.

Adrian blew my hair out very nice and bountifully. Azmir had always seemed more impressed with my natural hair. I'm like any other woman who loves the convenience of a weave, wig, or occasional braids, but I loved the way he responded to my natural hair. It *was* quite long and thick. Adrian maintained it well. It fell just at my breasts and below my scapula bone in the back. It had a slight curl and was full of volume. I was in and out in a little over an hour and my tip reflected my gratitude.

As I was leaving and headed back to the office, I got those damn butterflies in my stomach again. This time it was pleasant anxiety and anticipation. The hours flew by and before I knew it, I was back at the high rise preparing for the man of the hour to return home.

love ∞ belvin

Azmir

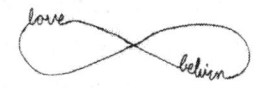

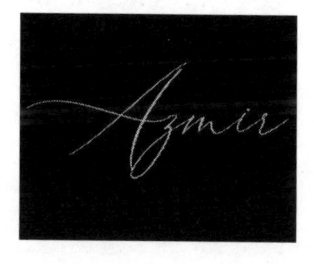

What a long and exhausting flight. I was so happy to be back on U.S. soil. Sauntering into my apartment building, I encountered Manny.

"My man, Manny. How's everything?" I greeted the concierge as he ran over to me and retrieved my luggage.

"Mr. Jacobs! Nice to see you're back. How was your business trip?" Manny asked with the widest smile.

"It was long, but successful just the same."

"Ah, so business is good, I see?"

He ushered me in when the elevator door swung open. I sauntered in with him on my heels.

"Business is sweet. But I'm damn sure happy to be back home. A man can't stay away from his throne too long, you know." I let out a long sigh and rubbed my eyes.

"Ahahahahahahahaha!" Manny belted out an energetic laugh. I didn't find what I said particularly funny but apparently, he did.

He brought my luggage to my front door. I heard music coming from my apartment. This was very unexpected.

With a huge frat boy smile Manny bode, "The best of evenings, Mr. Jacobs!" and scurried back to the elevator.

I opened the door looking for my guest, but to no avail. So, I quickly took my bags into my office and then shut the door. When I returned to the foyer, I saw her standing off towards the living room wearing my dress shirt, her wide-waisted belt and the crystallized *Christian Louboutin's* I got her last week and instructed her to fuck me in. Her hair—natural hair—was pulled up to the top of her head into a loose ponytail. She had on red lipstick and dark eyes. I was immediately turned on.

She appeared solicitous, but after a hard swallow she murmured, "You're early!"

Okay maybe I frightened her.

I gestured with raised eyebrows and pouted lips I was here.

"Well, I'm happy to see you're home. I hope you don't mind me being so...*au fait* with your space." This time she spoke more confidently.

I shook my head giving her an emphatic "no." Her apparent sensual manner had me enchanted.

"Do you like chicken piccata? I've taken the liberty..."

I nodded my head.

"I bet you're tired. I'll pour you a glass of wine. Red or white? Though they say Chardonnay, Pinot Grigio and Sauvignon Blanc all go well with it."

"I want what you're having." I was hoping not to divulge how much I wanted her right now.

"One glass of Sauvignon coming up." Rayna's telling smile confirmed she knew.

At the dinner table, we ate and chatted a bit. Dryly she asked, "So, how long will it be before you travel like this again?"

"In a couple of weeks. We're traveling to South Africa... investing in a company that provides plumbing and water supply to impoverished villages."

"Oh...nice."

I could tell she wasn't all that keen on the idea of me going away, so I decided to change the subject.

"This is pretty good, Ms. Brimm. How many men have you baited with this recipe?" I teased.

She squinted her eyes and smirked. "I'll answer that question as soon as you tell me how often you beguile women by leaving them for nearly a week in order to have them so eager and deliberate to please you?" Her tone was seductive.

Word? I let out a chuckle as I took her in trying to contain myself. I cleaned my plate. I guess my stomach was on "E."

She looked at my empty plate, "Belly full? That's how I need you." We both laughed. "I have a surprise for you."

"And I, you. Me first. Let's go." I grabbed my glass and her hand as I led her out into the living room, guiding her to the couch. "Have a seat here. I'll be right back."

I went into my office and grabbed the shopping bags I'd bought back. When I returned to the living area, I found her sitting relaxed and sipping on her wine. As soon as her eyes met the bags she gasped.

"What is all of this?" she whispered.

"You were thought of while I was away." Again, I found myself a little uneasy because she always has trouble accepting things from me.

"Are you going to open them?" I tried helping her with protocol.

With a stoic expression, she paused for a second before placing her drink on the center table and slowly approached the *Hermés* bag first, much to my dismay. I didn't want her to become overwhelmed right away. Inside was a *Birkin Bleu De Prusse Togo* bag, a scarf, and dog leash. In the next bag was a *Fendi* clutch with matching stilettos. She never closed her mouth and my anxiety piqued. She went into the third bag to find a black, Classic, quilted *Chanel* bag and an embroidered *Chanel* blazer. There were more shoes. Some by *Alexander McQueen*, *Christian Louboutin*, and *Jean-Michael Cazabat*—six in all. I watched cautiously as she opened each bag.

She sat back up on the sofa and looked up at me with a forced smile. I could take that.

"Mr. Jacobs, this is all...extraordinary, I'm sure you know.

And..." she exhaled, "and I appreciate it." She burst out in laughter. I had to follow her.

"That seem quite contrived, Ms. Brimm." I tried containing my laughter.

"You know this is all new to me...the gifts...having someone think of me in my absence. But I'm taking it all in." She hit me with a smile. This one was authentic...confident even.

"Well, you're very welcome. And I hope your graciousness extends itself to what I'm about to say," I gave my disclaimer as she gazed at me pensively.

"I took the liberty of selecting a few pieces of...apparel for you. I couldn't bring them all back so I'm having them shipped to your place. They should arrive early next week." Her expression changed and I could tell she was struggling with something internally. "What is it?" I sighed with my brows narrowed.

Suddenly, a nervous smile stretched across her heavenly face.

"You've just reminded me I have a surprise for you. Though I'm feeling a little outdone with all of this." She gestured to all of the empty bags, their contents, and discarded tissue paper.

Okay.

"Okay. Don't keep me in suspense." I sighed once again.

She goes into the back and reappears momentarily carrying a rather large board of some sort, covered in decorated wrapping paper with an embellished red ribbon tied into a bow around it. She seemed to struggle with it.

"Can I help you?" I offered, jumping to my feet.

"No. No. No!" She hushed me away as she walked around to the opposite side of the center table from me and away from the bags. "Come. Open it!" Her voice was laced with excitement. As I went to grab it in order to open it, I could deduce it was a frame—a heavy one at that. But what kind of painting or portrait is it? *Art?*

I began ripping the paper as she waited anxiously. Once I was done, I walked around to the front and discovered it was a poster size portrait of me watching Rayna perform for me at my birthday party. *Wow!* It really captured my amazement. I'm sure all of my expressions were priceless as hell that night. I let out a laugh.

"Petey sent me the pictures electronically and I had a girl from dance class give it to her husband to enlarge it. Then I had it framed. I wanted to give it to you, so you'll remember to never underestimate me," she gleamed proudly. I remembered that line from our first date.

I placed the portrait against the center table and took her into my arms. She smelled just how I remembered and was just as soft. I reached down and touched her lips with mine, but I didn't kiss her. I just took her all in from up close. She looked confused and wanting at the same time. That's how I wanted her.

"So, where are we going to hang it?" I asked, breaking our reverie.

"Huhn? Oh? I've been wondering where you'd choose."

"*Hmmmm*... It may be indecorous of me to hang it in my office at the rec. Perhaps at *Cobalt*, but I'm hardly there now a days. I want to see it daily...so I won't underestimate you again," I teased.

She giggled and eventually narrowed her gaze upon me, "May I offer a suggestion?"

"Please do."

She gestured to the portrait, "Pick it up and follow me."

I did as I was told. She led me to the master suite and over to the bed. I lay the frame against the footboard. She pointed to the wall over the headboard and murmured shyly, "I was hoping we can put it there."

"Oh, yeah?" I pondered.

"This way we can look at it every night..." her voice trailed off.

Did she just say we?

She must have seen the bemusement on my face because she then took my hand, pulled me over to the walk-in closet and showed me she'd rearranged it to include her clothes. She began opening a few drawers to display her personal items.

She then straightened and whispered, "*If* you'll have me...?"

I walked over to her, lifted her at the waist and she automatically straddled me. I tasted her lips and saw her eyes were heavy, drunken with deep desire and her mouth was ajar and inviting. I placed my hand underneath her shirt—my shirt—and felt her lace cheekies.

Mmmmm... My favorite.

I carried her over to one of the center dresser cabinetries and rested her on there. Her ragged breathing told me she wanted me just as much as I wanted her. I pulled her collar back more to nibble her neck. She let out a moan that was hard to ignore. She reclined her body on the countertop inviting me to her breasts. I had no problem obliging her. As I deliciously found my way in her cleavage with my tongue, I unhooked her belt and tossed it aside. I then unbuttoned her shirt with ease. She couldn't control her moans. I was totally aroused and in a trance. I guessed it started with her vulnerability and willingness to give living together a try. But whatever it was it had me in a zone and I desperately wanted her.

She gripped my neck and shoulders with her soft hands. I then pulled her shirt open to finally release her bra. Her breasts look delightful. Once freed, I began licking them softly and massaging them thoroughly. It drove Rayna wild as she began thrusting her hips into my abdomen. I didn't know how much longer she would last.

Damn, I loved Rayna's body; it yielded to me so liberally. I wanted to take my time. I hadn't had her in days. All I had to hang on to were mere memories. I tugged at her nipples one at a time, making sure they were nice and damp before I stretched them out. Her nipples were a beautiful length and supple.

"Azmir," she panted.

I raised my head, "Yes, dear?" I teased.

"Don't hurt me," she breathed.

"Do I ever hurt you?"

"No..." She tried to control her breathing unsuccessfully.

"...when we do this thing together; don't hurt me." Rayna was fighting back tears. I could tell from her constant blinking as her glassy eyes stayed focused to the ceiling.

I decided to show her how serious I was about this, about her as I continued gliding my tongue down her belly and descended into her sweet peach. She was so wet and ready, I had to pace myself. I licked every inch of it from labia to labia to top to bottom. I went inside of her swollen feminine cave and her body jerked. She held on to my shoulders as my tongue explored beneath her pussy. I tasted that passage, too. I felt her *Louboutin's* on my upper back as she sang my name in so many octaves. When I returned to her clitoris, she began thrusting my face.

"Ooh, baby!" she squeaked.

I grabbed her breasts, let my one thumb dance with her hardened nipple and inserted two fingers in her canal. Rayna made noises I'd never heard from her. I pulled her entire clit between my lips and over my tongue as far as it would go and sucked.

"Divine! Divine! Oh...Divine!" she cried slowly as she lost her rhythm and began convulsing and shooting juices into my face. When her body calmed, she began squirming, forcing me to release her from my sucking grip. Her orgasm had eclipsed.

I gave her a minute to come down and before I knew it, she lunged up, grabbed me by the face, threw her tongue in my mouth and engulfed my shoulders. I wasn't expecting this, but her eagerness pushed me over. Her tongue twirled and twirled in my mouth. She was communicating with me. She reached from behind to pull my shirt and T-shirt over my head. Suddenly, she stared me straight in the eyes with a look of pleasant desperation and hunger as she unbuckled my belt and pants. They fell to the floor, and I quickly stepped out of them as she pushed down my boxers in search of my throbbing dick. She grabbed it, closed her eyes, and deeply exhaled as she stroked me. Her mouth was ajar as she appeared relieved and wanting at the same time.

"Please, Azmir," she softly appealed.

"Please what, Brimm?"

"Please put it inside me. I need to feel you now. Please," she implored.

I scooted her pelvic area toward mine forcing her to lean back. She slowly licked her lips turning me on like a motherfucker. Rayna was doing all the right things to affirm my masculinity. I stepped out of my boxers and opened her legs wide before entering her. She inhaled deeply at every inch I pushed inside her. She was pleasingly tight. I took my time to make room for myself. Midway in I pulled back and her eyes opened wide telling me to come back. And I did. This time it was smoother as her sweet juices covered me from tip to base. My stride was steady but gentle. Rayna opened her eyes and reached for her breasts. She began to rub them seductively. I saw she wanted more so I pulled out and rammed back into her. Her mouth swung open, but no sounds came. I did it again. And then again. This time she belted out my name over and over like a fucking litany.

Damn! I'd do anything for this woman!

I was dangerously in over my head engrossed with her. I pulled her legs over my shoulder and began digging in, impaling her. She was so warm and ran so deep. I thrust deeply making sure I touched her back walls. I developed a pace as her walls squeezed all around me. Her breasts bounced lusciously all over the place.

"Azmir, baby, I'm about to..." Rayna cried out before being shifted into orbit with another orgasm. There was something about watching her come. I felt ownership of not just her orgasm but her body. With that thought, the game was over. I was melting inside of her.

In the shower I looked down at Rayna washing me.

"You know I'm thoroughly enjoying this. You shouldn't start what you can't finish, Ms. Brimm," I teased.

We both laughed.

I could see her mauling over something internally and her smile slowly fading.

"Will we lose the fiery bliss?" she asked with depths of earnestness in her eyes.

"I don't know. I should hope not." I tried providing some type of answer.

Her eyes widened and she exclaimed, "You don't know? You were just in a long-term relationship! Surely you have some frame of reference."

I shook my head at the thought. "That relationship was far different from what we have. It was dissimilar to your traditional boy meets girl. Boy falls in love with girl. Boy and girl lives happily ever after," I attempted to explain in hopes of it being satisfactory enough an answer to move this conversation to the next topic.

"Oh...how?" *Damn.* Rayna never asked questions. I'd grown accustomed to that.

I guessed it was only fair we'd discuss my past with Tara, a little. I took a deep breath.

Here we go.

"Tara and I just sort of...happened. I'd grown close with her dad for years. He was the only family I knew. I mean...I'd been just about everything of a son to him short of living with him. He's always championed my independence. I would visit his crib every now and then and would see her. I never paid her much attention because she was so much younger than me. As she grew, I noticed her staring more and wanting to be around when I came through or when her dad would come and check me out. She would smile and even wink, but I guess I never took her to be more than a cute little girl."

"She had to be attractive to you because you two did end up together." Rayna chortled.

"Eventually I did start taking notice of her adolescent developments," I admitted, giving us both a laugh.

I continued, "On her eighteenth birthday she just popped up at one of my clubs with her girls and began talking grimy. I'll admit I was turned on. I'd never spoken to or interfaced with her in the absence of her parents, and she came at me aggressively. I was a young man sowing my oats, so to speak. She presented very adventurously, and it attracted me to her. I was game. And that's how it all began." I hoped that would give some insight.

"How did you internally resolve sleeping with your mentor's daughter behind his back? I mean...he didn't know she'd come to your club, I'm sure."

She's really inquisitive tonight, huhn?

I didn't understand the sudden interest. Neither did I like the stroll down memory lane. I looked her square in the eye searching for a motive, but to no avail. She simply wanted to know.

"I didn't. So eventually I told him, man-to-man."

"Was he angry?" she asked.

"No. I believe he suspected it."

She was making figure eights into my abdomen with the suds. Her beautiful chestnut irises were fixed on her project, but her mind was churning.

"Why didn't you two live together?" she asked softly.

Where was all of this going? Okay. I'll play along.

"I didn't want that."

"Did she?"

"Very much."

"Were you in love with her?"

Whoa!

I had to take a minute to think about a smooth way to answer such a delicate question.

"I loved her. But when I sat back to evaluate our situation some time last year, I realized I cared for her in a familial sense—minus the incestuous nature." I gave her a mirthful grin. "But I think our undoing was because I'd evolved, as a man my age should. I needed substance and she wanted the facade of substance but was too young to appreciate the true nature of it."

"How old is she?" Rayna asked now looking at me in the face again.

"Twenty-eight," I answered.

"But I'm twenty-seven. Why would you look for something more substantial with a younger woman?" she asked with bemusement.

I reached down and kissed her on the lips, "Because you are more. You were far more before I came along. And I can only wish caring for you the way I intend to will not give you the impression that I endeavor to reduce your *more* rather than be a part of your more. I just want you to let me take care of you, baby. Nothing more. Nothing less." I gazed into her inquisitive eyes. "Now let's go. I have a few calls to make before we have dessert." I closed our shower pow-wow.

"Oh, shoot! I forgot all about my pound cake! We never got around to dessert!" she announced lost in that thought.

"Yeah, I hope you didn't think I'd forgotten. It's a favorite, so I'm looking forward to it and you resting with me in *our* bed." I reached over her to turn off the water.

"Azmir," she called leaving out the eye contact.

"Yeah, baby."

"Have you ever been with her in your...I mean, *our* bed?" she asked timidly.

I laughed and heartily as I shut the water off and proceeded out of the shower.

"What's so funny?" she demanded as she followed me out of the shower.

I grabbed a towel and held it open for her. As she turned, I wrapped it around her and buried her in my arms, "Tara has never been here and neither has any other woman. In fact, you were my only visitor. And now you're a resident." I kissed her softly on the forehead.

"Wait. *Only* visitor?" Rayna asked still haunted by confusion. Admittedly, I could understand.

"I told you I bought this place last year. But I didn't mention I'd only moved in after meeting you." I stopped drying myself off, suspended in thought. "That's when I became inspired to begin making major changes in my life. All of the pieces had been there for months. But you were the final element." I was surprised by my own revelation.

She gave me a shy smile. That faded suddenly and was eclipsed by doubt. Rayna was always inside her own head. I made it my mission to get in there, too. I just had to be patient.

"What's wrong?"

"It just dawned on me. We haven't discussed logistics. How will things get paid for? What am I responsible for?" Her eyes searched the floor as she chewed on her bottom lip in deep thought. Raising her gaze to me she continued, "I've never lived with a man before. What roles and tasks will we take on to maintain this place? It's pretty big. I'm sure it takes lots of time to clean." She looked flushed.

"*Hmmm...* Well, I don't have a mortgage so there's no divvying up that expense."

"No? You don't have a mortgage?" she whispered forcefully in stark shock as she stood frozen gripping her towel.

I narrowed my eyes, not accustomed to talking money with anyone. I must remember she has no idea of my financial portfolio. I have to get used to this and work her in slowly but surely.

"Rayna, I don't believe I've ever carried a mortgage. I pay for homes in cash...unless my accountant advises otherwise."

She appeared overwhelmed; she hadn't even dried off. I took her towel from around her and committed to drying her.

"Okay, that settles the mortgage. As far as the utilities, my accountant has that worked out as well. I only see those types of bills when I request them from her to check and balance my books. That's taken care of." When I was done drying her, I grabbed her hand to walk over to the vanity. "As far as cleaning, I have a woman—sometimes two—come and clean daily. They're taken care of as well. And you know Boyd is here five days a week. There are several weekend availabilities in his contract to be negotiated as needed. Since we've been dating, I've been out with you most weekends, so I haven't requested additional time."

Rayna clasped onto her towel expressing how uncomfortable she had become suddenly. I didn't think this was anything to draw up over.

"What is it now, Ms. Brimm?" I evened my tone.

She looked every which way except for at me. "I keep forgetting you have money. Azmir, that's a lot to take on for someone who has always been so financially independent. Nothing's for free. Right?" Her eyes rose to mine filled with so much consternation my chest twisted for her.

"Listen, I don't want anything from you but this." I pointed to her heart. "If it makes you feel more secure and comfortable, hold on to your house for a little bit...though I don't think you'll be needing it again. Unless you want to get rid of this place and we move in yours," I offered hoping like hell she wouldn't entertain the idea.

"I like the idea of holding on to my place...just until I find my footing here," she tried to reassure me before turning to brush her teeth. I followed suit and started reaching for my toothbrush.

"Whatever will make you happy, Ms. Brimm. I'll grab some cake and then tuck you in before I get some work done."

We found our way back into the master bedroom where she stepped into the closet and put on an off-white silk slip smoothly falling from her shoulders down to her thighs. *Brimm's body is the truth.* I tossed on a T-shirt, basketball shorts, and socks. When I grabbed my *Blackberry*, I saw I had a missed call and message from "Yaz." I listened to the message after cutting a large slice of cake and before meeting up with Rayna in bed.

"Why the sudden long face?" she inquired.

Damn. Is my face really reflecting my processes?

"Nothing really. My mother wants to meet. Not sure if I'm feeling that though."

"Why not?"

I lay down next to her, but on top of the comforter that she's underneath and reached over to her side of the bed to feed her some of the buttery pound cake she'd baked from scratch. I was impressed.

"So, are we claiming sides now?" I teased.

"This is the side I've always end up on, so it seems natural." With a mouthful, she pouted in jest. It was rather sexy.

"Stop smiling at me like that, Mr. Jacobs! It's distracting in more ways than one. Don't forget you've been away for nearly a week." She swallowed her cake. "Plus, I want to know why you wouldn't be interested in seeing your mother whom you haven't seen in almost twenty years." She sat up straight in the bed with her back resting on her pillows against the headboard. She looked down to me as I lay underneath her demolishing the cake.

"I don't know," I murmured losing the giddiness. "I'm not in the head space to open up a can of worms. I've been undergoing enough changes as is."

"That's very Freudian of you, but I'm sure this long awaited resolve is just as important as adjusting to me being here. You deserve answers. You were abandoned," she spoke very full of compassion. With her eyes locked to her lap she added, "I could only wish my father had provided answers as to why he abandoned us before his passing."

Shit.

"Baby, I'm sorry. I have no desire to make you reflect back to dark days on my account."

She interrupted with, "No...no. Not at all. It's just a fact. If you have the opportunity to gain a resolve, go for it. You're owed that, Azmir. The little boy in you needs it."

It had been a while since I'd seen Rayna so strong and therapeutic. It was refreshing to say the least.

"I've been told every broken adult that has experienced childhood trauma carries the child they used to be in them until they address their demons. I could only wish I had that opportunity," she chuckled ruefully, gazing off into the distance.

"What's so funny?" I asked.

"I can't believe I said that. Just months ago, I wouldn't have cared an ounce about my childhood, but since..." her voice trailed off. There was a brief pause. "...since losing Michelle and now gaining you. It makes me want to love better...love you better, now with having someone new in my corner again. And love me better so I can be better at loving others," she explained introspectively, barely looking at me.

"I'll go if you come with me." Wasn't sure where that came from, but it felt right.

Her eyes widened and her mouth collapsed, "Oh, I wouldn't want to interfere, Azmir."

"You wouldn't be interfering, just supporting me. I don't exactly have anyone else in my corner for this type of support either." She searched my eyes speechless. "We'll go to New York for a couple of days, and you'll get a chance to meet my Earth."

Her eyes danced around as she considered my words, "I'd be honored." Her gaze was intense.

Her agreeing was so "un-Rayna." It was so unusual for her to not hesitate and to go with the natural flow of things. It was honestly arousing. *Shit.* Everything Rayna did aroused me. I reached up to her flawless face to bring it down to mine before engulfing my tongue and emotions into an impassioned kiss. She must have felt it, too, because not long afterwards she started to tug at my T-shirt.

In no time, we'd worked our clothes off and I laid on top of Ms. Brimm and made good ol' fashioned love to her missionary style. It felt appropriate and was clearly something she wanted as she pulled me on top of her. Watching her release during her orgasm was so enlivening, it set mine off as well.

I wanted this woman more than I'd wanted anything in my life before her. I had hoped she was willing to be mine.

CHAPTER 7

Rayna

It was a crappy Tuesday morning—*a nine-thirty in the morning and the only two whirlpools our location owned were malfunctioning* type of crappy Tuesday morning. I was standing in the whirlpool with water to my calf muscles surveying the drainage flow, trying to figure out where exactly the problem was. The manufacturing company wouldn't be able to send out a serviceman until the following day. Much of my frustration was because they'd just been out to repair them the week before.

Wendy, our new PT Assistant, was pacing before me, outside of the pool with the manufacturing company on the phone. I was beyond livid.

"Tell him they must send a different service person out—this time a competent one! There is no way we have the latest model pool, we've only been in operation for what...*ten months,* and we've already had two interruptions in service? And why must we wait until tomorrow? Does he not realize we are a medical business relying heavily on this machinery? This is unacceptable!" I howled in my conniption.

Wendy repeated my rants word for word. I knew I was wasting

my breath. Service wouldn't be available for another day, and I had to deal with it. I had been so wound up over the past week or so and this ordeal didn't help. With my miniature flashlight, I searched the pool reeling of disgust from my pantyhose being wet and trying to prevent water from splashing onto my midi dress.

Sharon came into the room and as soon as I saw her my anxiety rose to the next level in anticipation of her telling me my next patient had arrived.

"Ms. Brimm?"

Frantic, I belted, "Yes, Sharon!" I felt my eyes bulging from my head and my body tense up.

"Mr. Jacobs is on line three. Would you like for me to hand you the cordless seeing Wendy is on the handheld?"

I paused trying to process everything happening in the room. The mention of Azmir's name released a few muscles and loosened tendons. I felt an immediate thawing of my disposition. I'd been living with Azmir for about a month now and to say it had been quite an adjustment wasn't saying much at all. I loved waking up to him and lying next to him at night. He was a gentleman who let me take as long as I needed in the bathroom and allowed me privacy in his massive closet when I needed it. He kept the toilet lid up but the seat down at my preference for easy access, and only required me to cook on the weekends. What a great setup!

The only problem was Azmir was never home. His travel had picked up tremendously, so our time together was limited. He tried to make it home on weekends no matter how short his trips were, and we filled our time together with manic lovemaking sessions and going out to shows and concerts to fulfill the dating portion of our relationship. Every moment with him was impassioned and my feelings for him increased with each interaction we shared—even some we didn't. Any and all forms of communication was needed and welcomed as far as I was concerned. Like today.

"*Uh...* Yeah," I uttered, snapping back into reality.

Sharon left out of the room and returned seconds later handing me the phone. She looked anxious, I'm sure from me being on edge.

"Rayna Brimm speaking. How may I help you?" Although I'd been told it was Azmir, I made it a habit of answering the phone at work the same at all times.

"Hey, you," his unintended sensuous baritone voice flowed so silkily through the receiver.

I could tell he had just awakened. I knew his morning voice. It was my favorite of them all and was often used to summons my libido first thing in the morning when he needed sex. I could never resist it. When I thought about it, much of my irritated mood came from not having had him around. Azmir's presence had become such a balance for me, but his absence due to his demanding work schedule had made him scarce. I'd missed him. I'd missed his comfort and company, which went beyond sex. The red fairy had been visiting and I didn't have the assistance of his miracle hands to combat my symptoms.

Turning away from Wendy who was still pushing on the phone with the whirlpool people, I let out a deep, hard, long and yearning sigh.

"Aww, baby..." he sang into the phone empathically. "...you're having a pissy day." His comforting tone tugged at my tear banks, threatening my pending cry. "I wish I were there to help. You're on what...day three, right? You're just about done," he successfully mollified.

He guessed so accurately. *Or was it a guess?*

"How did you know?"

"Ms. Brimm, it's my job to know everything about you and meet your every need. If I were there, I'd give you an hour long foot rub and then stretch your back muscles out."

Yes! How can I forget his foot and back-rubs? They usually had me hot, bothered and ready to go by the time he was done but relaxed, nonetheless.

There was a pause.

"Azmir, you there?"

"Yeah, I'm here. How has your morning gone so far?" He changed the subject from his overt pause.

Oh, Azmir!

"The whirlpools are out again."

"They were worked on just last week."

"Yes. And because they're the latest model, the company only has a handful of trained servicemen to work on them, so we have to wait until tomorrow for someone to come out."

"I can have Stan, our grounds head, swing over to take a look at them. It's probably the filter. Whatever it is, he'd likely figure it out."

"Thanks, Azmir." I let out another sigh.

"Don't thank me just yet." *Oh, no!* "Not sure if you've heard about the Nor-Easter coming from the Caribbean. It's supposed to hit Florida, bringing strong winds and buckets of rain starting tomorrow morning. Brett just told me this morning my flight has been canceled. This means I won't be back for the ball. I'm so sorry."

Crap!

Azmir had been away for close to two weeks. He started his business trip to South Africa and upon return had affairs in Miami, where he was calling from. The dilemma this presented was *Katz, Smith & Adams* was hosting their annual fundraising ball to raise money for services for underprivileged children in the county in two days. This would have been the first year I had brought a date. I was also excited about seeing Azmir for the first time in nearly two weeks.

"It's okay. I understand you can't control nature."

I really didn't feel as indifferent as I'd let on. I was beyond pissed. I'd missed him and had begun resenting his traveling. It seemed as though at the time when we were growing so close to each other his business took off to a new level, but in the opposite direction of our relationship. I'd grown so close to him over the past month or so. I hated him being away so much. Of course, I didn't have the courage to tell him. I didn't want to make him feel as if he had to choose. I had no right.

"I'll make it up to you, I promise. Oh, that reminds me, your gown is ready. I'll have it delivered to the apartment."

"No. I can pick it up on my way to dance class this evening," I declined.

"Are you sure? Why don't you let Ray drive you while I'm away, especially to the ball. I'm sure you'll be drinking, and I don't want to worry about you getting home safely."

"Azmir, that really isn't necessary. I'm a big girl. I'll be just fine."

"This is more for me. It's for my peace of mind." He was fighting me.

"I'll concede to be driven to the ball, but nothing outside of that. It would be weird being chauffeured to work."

"*Hmmmm...* It isn't for me." Azmir could be really pushy at times. It was a sweet gesture, but I liked my freedom. *And privacy.*

Sharon came back into the room alerting me of a visitor.

"Okay. Gotta go. Call me tonight once you get in from your meeting. No matter how late."

"You got it. Try to take it easy for the remainder of the day."

"I'll try." I fought back my tears.

"Indeed."

I didn't want to let him go. "See ya."

My day couldn't get any worse. It was so bad; I felt those light flutters in my stomach. Empty sensations having nothing to do with hunger. I swung my legs over and out of the pool and drug myself out of the room. When I had gotten to my desk, I changed out of my hosiery and washed my feet as best as I could and as quickly as I could from my bathroom sink there in the office. I paged Sharon asking her to send the visitor back to my office without thinking. Seconds later, I heard a tap at my door.

"Come in," I welcomed with the most pleasant voice I could muster considering my raw temperament.

Brian Thompson peeked his head in with his brows lifted. I was surprised to see him. *What is this all about?*

"It's been a long day *this* early in the morning?" I knew he was making an attempt at breaking the ice. I had assumed he was referring to having to wait to see me.

"I could say the same about your visit." My eyebrows furrowed.

"Oh? How is that?" Now his eyebrows were narrowed.

"Your visit—so early in the morning. And so unannounced," I practically sang with a faux smile.

Thompson was handsome. I'd started admitting that to myself back at our last staff meeting he attended to formally introduce his firm. He was fairly tall...maybe six feet...with flawless ivory skin, a shade lighter than mine. He maintained a low Caesar cut like Azmir. He also had a nicely manicured goatee. I couldn't tell if he was fit but through his tailored suits, I saw no evidence of a bulging belly or a plump booty. I hated seeing men with big booties. It wasn't my thing.

And while Thompson wasn't exactly my type either, I couldn't deny his good-looking features. Unlike Azmir, I could tell he was very much aware of them as well. He exuded arrogance. I could also tell he tried to keep a handle on it in my presence because it was clear it didn't appeal to me. I was glad he quickly got the memo. I wasn't quite sure if he was hitting on me or trying to endear himself to managerial staff for professional reasons. He hadn't made it clear as of yet. Even seeing his approach in my office confirmed his timid nature around me. It was a far cry from our first encounter.

"I had contracts to pick up from Sharon. She didn't tell you?"

"No. But then again why would she?" *Don't you have assistants who could have retrieved them instead?*

He gave a nervous laugh.

Sorry, Thompson, this is just not my morning.

"Well, that explains my visit and...I just thought to drop in to say hello to you."

"That is quite nice of you. Is your firm done compiling the practice's files?" I added trying not to soften my curtness.

"Not quite. We still have the Beverly Hills and Ocean County offices to get to. *Smith, Katz, and Adams Sports Medicine Center* has been in business for a very long time. There is a lot of ground to cover."

I had a hunch Brian was attempting to prolong his visit.

"Well, if the staff here in the *LBC* could be of more assistance just give us a call."

"There's something I wanted to ask you."

"Oh?" *What now?*

It's not that Thompson annoyed me. I just wasn't interested in seeing him on the fly without reason and in case he *was* interested I wasn't game for any play. I didn't know how to go about telling him. The clear cut version would've been that I was living with a man. The only problem with that was Azmir wasn't exactly my boyfriend. Hell, we didn't even have a monogamy agreement, but it was expected. I hated being rude to him, but I wasn't exactly available.

"I'll be at the ball on Thursday. Will I see you there?" Thompson was no smiles but all intense eyes and jaw flexing, which I took as a sign of nervousness.

How cute. But that question also brought back my suspended blues of having just learned Azmir wouldn't be able to make it.

"That's the plan. Yes."

"Will you be escorted by a significant other?"

Was this his way of asking if I was dating? I mean he had to know I wasn't married, right? *Is this your game, Thompson?* I played along.

"No. Will you bring along yours?"

"None to speak of."

I nodded my head and added a simultaneous smile. I didn't

know where to go from there, and quite frankly, I had no interest in going any further.

There was a knock at my now ajar door. It was Sharon.

"Ms. Brimm, Stan from the rec said he was sent over by Mr. Jacobs to take a look at our pools."

My mouth fell open and I looked for the time on my watch. I hadn't been off the phone with Azmir ten minutes and already his maintenance guy was here to see if he could fix our pools.

"Oh, wow! I didn't expect him over this early." I was pleasantly surprised by Azmir's presence—*in his absence.* And so apt considering Thompson was there.

"Mr. Jacobs said you guys would need it for business today and asked that I come right away. It's really no problem at all. I work on pools part time," Stan craned his head in the door behind Sharon.

"Okay. Sharon can show you to them." I felt the first cinch of hope I'd had in days.

They left Thompson and me alone again.

A grin flashed upon his face when he asked, "Can I be forward?"

Feeling far more relaxed thanks to Azmir's gesture of kindness, I consented. "By all means."

"Either you don't find me that appalling or you prefer those of the feminine persuasion because I have been working for that broad smile you just let up off a few seconds ago since I've knocked on your door."

Geesh!

I was not expecting that. My now elated state would not be outdone. I gave a muffled, but obvious, laugh and calmly answered, "No, Mr. Thompson, women do nothing for me."

"*Uhn-huhn.* So, it's me." He was affronted with raised eyebrows.

"Mr. Thompson, we're colleagues—"

"...consenting colleagues. At least I am." He cut me off.

"Conflict. Of. Interest." I attempted to ward him off.

"You just said you weren't gay."

Ha!

"You're witty. I'm impressed."

"Shit. I was just thinking I had no chances."

"Mr. Thompson, while I appreciate the effort, I'm not interested in dating. Right now, it's not...possible." I tried being as polite as feasible.

There was another knock at the door.

"It's open," I sang somewhat sarcastically.

"Ms. Brimm. I took a look at the pools. I had a hunch, so I went straight to the filter, and they were installed wrong. I left notes for the repair guy. Whoever installed them was in a rush because they made a few careless mistakes."

"Really?" Professional incompetence pissed me off!

"Yeah. Those pools are the newest in the game. It can be complicated if you're not properly trained or at least know what you're doing."

"Stan, let me offer you something for your time..." I jumped up to grab my purse.

"Oh, no, Ms. Brimm. Mr. Jacobs has it taken care of. If you need me to shoot over when they come tomorrow just give me a call. I finagled the vent to function temporarily. You should be covered."

I gave a deep exhale. "Thanks, Stan. I really appreciate your time."

"No problem. Have a good one," Stan bodes before leaving my office.

Azmir's arms stretched so far and wide. I didn't know if I should be elated or have my blues confirmed.

That man!

"Oh. So, I have competition!" Thompson's revelation snapped me out of my trance as he his speculative gaze roved over me.

I couldn't help but blush. "Conflict of interest, Mr. Thompson."

"We'll see about that. We. Shall. See," Thompson emphasized his last words before leaving out.

Once he was gone, I took a gulp of my morning java, which was now above room temperature then reached for my phone, smiled and took a picture of myself. I sent it to "*A.D.*," as he was listed in my contacts, with the following caption:

My vastly improved mood courtesy of A.D. Jacobs.

Moments later, I heard a ping. It was Azmir, of course, **It's my job. Get used to it.**

I texted back, *****conspiring naughty ways to repay the favor*****

Ha! Indeed.

The day sped up and when lunch rolled around, I'd gotten another surprise by *one Azmir Jacobs*. He had *DiFillippo's* send over an order of crème brûlée. He knew just what to do. But his generous and thoughtful acts once again reminded me I had to wait an additional day to see him. It pulled at my heart.

That evening I'd stopped by the boutique to pick up the gown Azmir had selected for me. I was trying something new—letting Azmir dress me. I have to admit his selections always impressed me and agreed with my frame. The seamstress urged me to do a final fitting when I told her she could bag it for me to leave. If Azmir wouldn't be there—there was no need to go the extra mile. She fought me on the issue and after reluctantly trying it on, I went straight to dance class and practiced my Tamia routine.

The night of the ball had arrived. My mood was sluggish, but mother nature had nothing to do with it: she had retreated. I was really in need of Azmir's company. *As soon as we get together, he gets busy.* My thoughts were grim and blue during the whole ride over there.

As I sulked inside Azmir's spacious and luxurious limo, I

wondered why he had a limo and how often he used it. I was surprised when I walked out of the lobby and saw Ray waiting with the door open. The lighting inside was mild and the music pouring from the speakers was soothing...smooth, like Mr. Jacobs himself. The *XM* radio panel caught my attention. The station streamed smooth R&B classics—the likes of Blackstreet, Silk, Guy, Jodeci and countless others. It smelled of new car and the ambiance was mellow and relaxing. *So, this is another one of your toys, huhn?* I felt like a kept woman, like I had belonged to Azmir Jacobs.

I eventually allowed my mind to wander to thoughts of what if he were here? *Would we make it to the ball? I think I could slay him right here in his ride. Hmmmmm... Would he be too tall? Would he let me? Could I muster my inner-exhibitionism to do it?*

We pulled up to the venue. I saw folks scurrying inside. I checked the time and discovered I was twenty minutes past the start of the event. *Perfect. Let's get this stodgy experience over with.* Ray opened my door and I gracefully glided out, being sure not to give him an indecent show.

"Okay, Ray, how does this work?"

With a strong guffaw, reminding me of old Saint Nick's, he supplied, "Well, Ms. Brimm, here's my number." He handed me his business card. "Call or shoot me a text and I'll be here in less than five minutes. How long do you think you'll be?"

I sighed, feeling annoyed at the night's events, "Two hours, tops."

"Why the long face on such a beautiful girl?" Ray's compliments comforted like a dad's to his baby girl. It was nice.

"I'm missing him badly, Ray. And he was supposed to be here with me to help circuit the mundane." I felt a knot build in my throat. I didn't recognize the emotion. *Am I about to cry?*

"Young lady, I'm sure wherever Divine is, he's making his way back home to you. I've never seen him so smitten." He gave the belly shaking laugh again.

"That makes two of us, Ray," I muttered sullenly then I ambled toward the steps leading to the entrance of the building.

"See you soon."

I gave myself a pep talk all the way to the ballroom where I saw stiffs loosened up on the dance floor. That was actually something I'd been looking forward to. My thoughts shifted to Michelle and how she would have had me bellowing in laughter at the sight of her uncle and his colleagues dropping it like it's hot on the dance floor.

I didn't know who I'd be seated next to or be forced to chat with. I had no desire to do the *disingenuous banter about things we could chat about during office hours* thing. I had wished Sharon or the other girls from the practice were there to talk to, but they weren't invited. This was a fundraising event, and they didn't fill the tax-bracket requirement. Heck—neither did I, but I was there to boast of *our exemplary services and how they benefited poor children. Blah!*

I was stopped by a couple of familiar faces before finding the bar. While waiting on my drink I took notice of the grand ballroom. It held culture and grace with its oval shaped ceilings in gold trimmings. The live band sealed the deal bringing you the sixties feel. The bartender handed me my drink and I immediately saw Mr. Adams, one third of *Smith, Katz & Adams Sports Medicine*, waving his arm gesturing for me to come over to him. I took a sip of my martini and sauntered over to him near the dance floor. I hadn't worked much with Mr. Adams but what little interfacing we did he had always been pleasant, unlike his god-awful son.

"Rayna! You look quite elegant." He smiled broadly. His wife stood beside him politely nodding in agreement.

"Mr. and Mrs. Adams, always a joy to see you two. I trust all is well."

"They most certainly are. Our Lisa is expecting our first grandchild any day now." Mr. Adams' eyes danced with pride.

"Wow! Such an exciting time for you two. Congratulations! I'm sure you two will be the best grandparents."

"Yes! And we're hoping for more in the not-so-distant future," Mrs. Adams crowed when her eyes excitedly hiked to a young woman standing in the cypher. The woman was plump with a long silk taupe gown hugging her voluptuous figure and complimented her pale skin. Her cinnamon hair was fixed in long Shirley temple curls draping across her shoulders. She wasn't drop-dead gorgeous by any means, but still wasn't the worst on the eyes. Overall, she looked very much un-alluring with her large round and droopy eyes.

"Oh?" was all I could let escape.

"This is Alexandria Wilkerson. She has just agreed to Sebastian's hand in marriage after dating for nearly two years."

I had to have blinked my eyes twice, unable to veil my surprise. *Sebastian had been with someone for two years while scratching my back for dates...and his money?* I caught Mr. Adams' eyes imploring me to greet his soon to be daughter-in-law.

Oh! My manners.

"Congratulations, Alexandria!" *There. That wasn't too contrived.* "You're marrying into a wonderfully supportive family." That was more sincere. The Adams' were good people.

Alexandria didn't speak much. She was all nods and goofy smiles. *What the?* What tickled me was Mrs. Adams' need to mention the engagement. She knew Sebastian and I had gone out on a couple of dates and dropped not so subtle hints of wanting her son married right away. Little did she know, he was the asshole of the century. Thinking about the possibility of marrying him brought the bile from my belly to my throat. I grabbed my chest trying to calm myself when I felt a gentle, yet unfamiliar touch on my elbow.

"Are you okay, Rayna?" I turned to find Brian Thompson. He looked distinguished in his black tux and bow tie. His eyes were squinted with concern.

"Yes. I guess the drink doesn't agree with me," I offered up feeling like it made sense after it left my lips.

"Oh, here's our Sebastian here!" Mrs. Adams cried.

Sebastian approached us with his usual wobbly stalk. It was such a turn off. He pushed his glasses up as he did every six and a half seconds. I was still holding my chest when he approached us. Gawking at me, he was admiring what he saw, that much I could gather.

Ewwww!

Mr. Adams gave another admonishing gape my way, I'd assumed for me to congratulate his son.

Oh, for crying out loud!

"I hear congratulations are in order. The best to you and your impending nuptials, Sebastian."

Sebastian joined sides with Alexandria, oddly drawing her into him, much to his mother's delight. Mrs. Adams was beaming from ear to ear. Sebastian gave an arrogant nod followed by an awkward fall of silence.

"Let's go and freshen up that drink, why don't we?" Thompson saved the day with his keen observation of a failed peace gathering happening between the Adams' and me.

"Enjoy the evening," I bade before turning and walking off.

"You look magnificent. I didn't recognize you at first," Thompson esteemed as we made our way to the bar.

"So, are you trying to say I clean up well, Thompson?" I feigned offended.

"Oh, not at all. It's just a new side of your beauty and style I'm witnessing here," he shared conspicuously appraising my ensemble.

"Tsk-tsk, Thompson. Conflict of interest ring a bell?" I wave my index finger gesturing *no!*

"You're not gay. Neither are you married; therefore, I'm allowed to appreciate what I see."

I chuckled. "Thanks for the compliment, Thompson," I returned wryly.

The emcee of the evening asked us to locate our assigned seats as the program would begin in fifteen minutes. The announcement halted our pace to the bar.

"Can I get you something while you grab your seat?" Thompson offered.

"No thanks. I'll just finish this one." I gave a conspiratorial wink causing his hearty chuckle. "But I'll follow." I figured I had nothing else better to do.

At the bar I stood with Thompson as he ordered his scotch. I suddenly had the urge to pee and thought it best not to try and go once things got underway.

"Will you excuse me for a minute while I go to the ladies' room?"

"Sure. I'll be right here," he informed as I walked off. I could feel him channeling my booty lustfully as I strutted in the direction of the ballroom's exit.

I was able to get in and out of the restroom in no time. When I looked into the vanity while washing my hands, it dawned on me how I must have left my clutch at the bar. I couldn't freshen up my makeup though thankfully, it was all still intact.

Back at the bar, Thompson was still there waiting as agreed. He had one foot up on the medal rod at the bottom of the bar while resting his alternate leg on the floor with his arms folded on the bar top. I spied my clutch.

"I'm glad you stayed in place. Can't lose this," I shared, retrieving it from the bar. Thompson still held his amorous gawk.

"I meant what I said. You are working that gown, very elegant."

I narrowed my brows at him. I thought of how Azmir was so insistent I wore this particular gown. *It must be a man thing.*

"Thanks *again*, Mr. Thompson," I offered sardonically.

"Tell me, what would you be doing if you were not obligated to be at your employer's fundraising ball this evening, Rayna?"

Before I could think to answer, I generously, and very pleasantly, inhaled an intriguingly familiar fragrance summonsing my libido. I'd suddenly become aroused in a way I'd never experienced. I'd sensed him before I heard or saw him.

"Well, I hope with me, where she belongs," a baritone voice, twisting my stomach muscles, spoke so fluidly with hidden snarl.

I felt his arm hook my waist and his hand reached down to my belly causing me to feel claimed and secure. I gasped as I looked up to find Azmir all dapper in his dark blue *Tom Ford* suit. His eyes were glued to Thompson who stood with his mouth fixed in an "O" shape clearly at a loss for words. Azmir didn't smile. In fact, he peered at him with an expression unfit for words. Azmir broke his glower to look down at me and I could see almost instantly his eyes softening as he kissed me on the forehead. Those trustee currents zapped through me causing me to lose my breath.

"Azmir," I breathed trying to steady my lungs. "You made it."

"Of course, I did. I couldn't have missed this for all the tea in China." He couldn't hide the sarcasm.

I was winded. "But I thought—" I muttered before he cut me off.

"You're not drinking that, are you?" I looked over at my hand squeezing the martini glass giving away my edginess. "It can't be fresh. Plus, you've walked away from it. Let's get you something else." He sensually chastened in my ear, but loud enough for Thompson to hear.

"Rayna," Thompson called out, once again allowing his arrogance to rear its ugly head. *Not right now, Brian. You don't want it with A.D...* I begged in my head. "Who's your friend?" he inquired.

I was in the middle of the two sitting on the bar stool as Azmir stood behind me. I could hear Azmir behind me ordering drinks, though I wasn't sure of what. I looked up at Azmir, who winked at me with a flexing jaw, before turning back to Thompson.

"Brian Thompson, this is Mr. Azmir Jacobs. Mr. Jacobs, Thompson is the practice's new attorney."

"Firm," Thompson corrected.

"I'm sorry?"

"Law firm. I have a team of attorneys working for me."

Seriously?

"Duly noted," I returned, feigning rebuked.

The emcee spoke again starting the program. Azmir grabbed our drinks and took my hand leading me away from the bar. I craned my neck back, giving Thompson an apologetic smile. I noted that neither Azmir nor Thompson greeted each other after I'd introduced them. Oddly enough, Azmir led me straight to our assigned seats as if he knew exactly where they were. I saw my place card there on the table, to the right of it was Thompson's and to the left Mr. Katz and his wife were seated. Thankfully, Azmir didn't notice and simply descended into the seat to the right of me.

Dinner was tasty. The program was less exciting. I was only grateful I didn't have to orate. I was stunned when the host announced Azmir's donation of twenty thousand dollars to the event earmarked for the Long Beach City area, *naturally*. They only announced large donations. Apparently, Azmir's was the second largest from a personal donor. I was proud and impressed and turned on. Jim Katz jolted toward Azmir with his creased eyes widened in wonderment, as did everyone else at the table. With grace and class Azmir gave a soft bow of the head along with a most humbled smile. I wanted to throw my arms around him but thought it not appropriate considering the crowd.

As dessert was being served, I realized Azmir hadn't said very much to me since we were seated. I didn't like the vibes I'd been picking up, so I scooted closer to him.

"Hey, you." I batted my eyes, still feeling giddy inside by his surprise attendance.

"Hey, yourself." He took my hand and planted small soft kisses on them causing my chest to rise.

"I've missed you. You've really outdone yourself this evening, Jacobs," I admitted feeling and sounding sappy.

"You're worth it, Ms. Brimm. I don't know whose expression

was more picture worthy, yours or your lawyer boy's." Azmir's tone was soft and even, but his words were acute.

I wrinkled my nose. "Thompson?"

Azmir raised his eyebrows.

"He's not an issue for me. Perhaps his arrogance is, but I avoid conversing with him and that helps in curtailing his conceit."

"You see him regularly?"

"Hardly. He's new to the practice. I've seen him once or twice at the *LBC* office," I whispered in his ear as the program was still going on.

He kissed my hand again, causing those trustee zaps to coarse my now delicate body. "We'll be sure to keep it to a minimum."

We? Azmir's declaration turned me on. It was already that I had to endure smelling his customized fragrance—my favorite aroma—all throughout dinner. I wanted him. Sitting through another course was even more torturous. Once we finished dessert, I couldn't take it anymore. I needed to leave.

I whispered to Azmir I needed the ladies' room and after which we'd be leaving. He rose from the table with me, and I walked toward the restrooms to freshen up.

On my way out of the ladies' room I heard, "Rayna, there you are. Hold up."

I didn't have to turn to confirm his creepy voice. *Great.* In no time he was at the heels of my feet.

"How can I help you, Sebastian?" My faux smile well plastered.

"Don't give me that attitude. I'm willing to play nice."

"Quite honestly, we don't have to play at all." My voice was soft. I only wanted him to disappear—forever.

"Come on, now. I just wanted to tell you how good you look tonight. That's if your benefactor hasn't told you already."

Whoa! Was he serious?

"Speaking of benevolence, did that Mr. Jacobs spend as much on this gown as he did on your debt to me."

"*Hmmmmm...* Now what I consider benevolence is Alexandria

in there taking pity on your less than endowed ass and marrying you. That's charity in its sincerest form." My faux smile had returned.

Although he scoffed, I knew Sebastian was wounded. My lack of interest in him deeply disturbed him.

"You bitch!" he seethed.

"You prick ass bastard," I softly snapped back at him.

We engaged in a stare down I was not backing down from. He no longer had any power *He had his money.*

"You didn't pay me back that ten grand. I'm sure of it."

"Ten grand? Are you talking vigorish poker again, sweetheart?" Azmir's commanding voice chimed as he took me in by the waist pulling me into his hip. I broke eye contact with Sebastian to look up at him and noticed his twinkling eyes doting on me.

"Something like that. We were discussing a check I'd recently sent to Sebastian to repay an old debt."

Azmir's eyebrows furrowed as he peered down at me and then darted his eyes over to Sebastian, then back at me once more. "You repaid him ten grand?"

"No, it was more like fifteen. No big deal." It was my turn to spew arrogance. Azmir role playing scheme worked. Sebastian's eyes were pouncing back and forth between Azmir and me looking for a crack in our story.

"That's a lot of money. Do you know how many things I can do with fifteen grand? We must talk about this in private," Azmir feigned anger.

"Sure." I pretended to straighten Azmir's bowtie. "But right now, I want you to get me out of here," I purred.

"I'll go call the car," Azmir murmured before walking off.

I was right on his heels after supplying, "Goodnight, Sebastian," while smiling ever so sweetly.

I turned on his muddled expression, enjoying every moment of his bemusement.

No sooner than I had gotten to the threshold of the venue's

vestibule, Thompson appeared. He halted almost in my path. His piercing eyes were glued to me with something intense behind them. If I'd ever questioned his attraction to me, it ended in that moment. He confirmed it via his deep gape.

"Rayna, I want a word before you leave."

What? Now?

I opened my mouth to speak but was quieted when I heard, "Ms. Brimm, say goodnight," Azmir, a few feet away, commanded authoritatively, very much calling on his CEO mien. It startled me and made very evident the awkward moment I was in.

Apologetically, I muttered to Thompson, "I have to go. Goodnight." I walked over to take Azmir's proffered hand and we headed out of the banquet hall.

Outside, Ray was waiting with the car door opened and Azmir stood across from him to allow me to get in first. Ray donned a conspirator's smile which told me he was a part of Azmir's surprise visit. *How else did he get here?* I returned a huge smile of gratitude.

When the door closed and we were sitting at a proximity too distant for what my body ached for, I couldn't help but stare at Azmir to try and drop subtle hints with my eyes of what I wanted to do. I needed him desperately, to reconnect with him and requite for him illuminating my world. We pulled off and he didn't return the gaze, so I scooted closer to him causing his eyes to dart over to me. With sharp currents shooting from my breasts to my toes I drank him in. Azmir was beyond good looking. His features were extraordinary even in his pensive state.

"What's up, Brimm?" he murmured.

I leaned into him and kissed him softly on his warm lips. When I pulled back, I noticed his eyes getting heavier and were curious as to my motives. That's when I rolled up my gown slowly, being sure not to disturb the integrity of the fabric and watched as his eyes zeroed in on it. Once it was hiked to a reasonable level, I straddled him, drawing his face into mine and sweeping his mouth with my tongue. Though surprised, I could tell he enjoyed it as he gripped my arms holding me tightly.

"Tell Ray to ride around until you say."

His eyebrows furrowed and he asked, "Pardon me?"

"Tell him. I can't wait 'til we get to the marina. I need you now." I felt his log of an erection beneath me as I begged for him.

With a scowl, he reached up to push a button. "Ray, take the scenic route until I instruct otherwise."

"Yes, sir," Ray's calming voice complied through the intercom speaker.

I went to kiss him again and after seconds of indulging me he pulled back and asked, "You think we should talk about the events at the gala?"

I looked deep into his eyes. *Huhn?* I had thought about what events he could be referring to. Then it hit me.

"About Thompson? *Sebastian?*"

"Sebastian is a fucking ass. I was two minutes from smashing his frames into his cranium."

"Then who...Thompson?"

He said nothing but had answered my question.

Not now. Not with how I'm feeling.

"Azmir, I've told you, Thompson isn't an issue for me. And quite honestly with how I'm feeling right now I resent him for being a topic of discussion while I'm trying to reconnect with someone who means more to me than—"

So I didn't have to go any further, I lunged my face at him again, kissing him ferociously, pleading with him to put me out of my misery. He grabbed me, holding me tightly, eventually working his way down to the nape of my neck. I moaned and with a pull and tug released his bowtie. He reached beneath my gown for my hips to soon learn I was bare underneath. He stopped and regarded me with suspicious eyes.

"Why do you think I went to the restroom?" I offered over panted breaths.

He didn't budge. I fought off my pride because I felt a grave amount of desperation for him. I couldn't force him into the sphere of love and need to share and express the adoration that I was floating in at the moment. It would be pointless for me to even be there myself without his willingness. But I wanted it...I wanted him badly.

"Azmir, please. Indulge with me. Here. In this moment. No one else matters. Just you and me." My plea was primal and desperate.

At the sound of my words his mouth shot open; I thought I'd heard him gasp. He searched my soul through my eyes, and I pleaded once again with mine. Within seconds, his face softened, and his posture relaxed as he embraced me, holding me to his chest.

"Okay," he murmured into my neck.

I reached down taking his face into my hands to meet mine once again in an oral embrace. I released the first few buttons in his shirt taking my tongue down to his neck then clavicle then his upper chest. My desire for this man was heady. I felt his breathing increase and could even hear mine over the soft music flowing from the speakers.

"Azmir," I moaned his name in anticipation of him being inside of me.

My hands traveled down to his waist where I unfastened his pants, and he lifted so I could pull them down just enough to release his heavy and jutting appendage. I stroked him from base to head reeling over how ready for me he was.

I lifted my hips to position myself to take him in. His expression favored mine, ready and in deep need. As I sank down onto him, I felt how tightened I was *and recalled how large he was* but stayed my position, working him into me. Azmir was wide and long, filling me to the hilt. His fullness caused hot flashes to scorch through my body and sweat beads to accumulate above my top lip. I learned this when he brought his thumb up to wipe it off and swept it over my lips before kissing me savagely. He was losing control just as I had.

"Damn. Brimm, you're tight," he spoke intoxicatingly, with heavy eyes and lips ajar.

"I've missed you. My body has missed you," I cried, just above a whisper, working him in, onward and upward, in and out.

The spikes of pain caused by my thrusts were mixed with the pleasant throbbing of my walls and the sensation from my body expelling juices to welcome him in. Before I knew it, my attempts were rewarded by pure unadulterated bliss of my sex moving silky, up and down on his steely cock. Azmir reclined by scooting his lap forward allowing me to take full control and I was more than happy to oblige.

As much as I tried to calm my cries of ecstasy, the divine feel of him inside of me, his alluring scent, the utopian music, and our carnal behavior in the back of his limo with his driver just a few feet away, sent me over the edge and in no time. I felt my orgasm nearing. My strokes started to accelerate, and I jolted forward taking him into my mouth. As my orgasmic spasms quickened, I sucked on his lip. It was the only way I could keep from screaming. My back jerked as I exploded all over him. I needed this...I needed to give this to *him*. To demonstrate what he does to my body. To show him what it's like after going so long without his touch. In this moment, no one else mattered, not Thompson and not Sebastian. It was just this man who had stolen my heart and had claimed my passion. A man who I felt indescribable emotions for. He had meant so much.

I felt his hands travel up to my neck, gently pushing my torso back, anchoring me as he pumped mercilessly into me, and I didn't resist. Azmir opened his mouth to release a silent cry plunging himself into me with mighty flexing of his hips prolonging my outer orbit experience until his orgasm ended its course and he was depleted.

We sat there for close to three minutes until he interrupted our respite. "You're dripping," he whispered causing me to jump up, wincing as he separated from me. He pulled a handkerchief from his pocket and held it out while I ascended from his lap, catching excess fluids.

"Here, use these." He grabbed the cocktail napkins displayed near the stereo panel. Taking a few of them, he gently wiped my inner thighs until what was left of him on them was smeared and dried. As he instructed Ray to proceed to the marina, I cleaned my most private part and I could see Azmir in my peripheral touching his face.

"Do you have a mirror of some sort? You went a little H.A.M. on my lip." His deep, baritone voice sounded all but afflicted. I was too languid to be as embarrassed as I would have typically been.

"I'm sorry." My tone was indifferent as I attempted to straighten my gown. "Look in my purse. I should have a compact in there."

The dress was pretty long and stubborn to my correction. I had only needed space to stand and allow it to fall into place. It didn't help that my body was overcome with exhaustion brought about, no doubt, by the writhing orgasm I'd just reveled in but also from the taxing past few days I'd had. Azmir's oversized firm and plush bed and Mr. Sandman was calling.

"What the fuck is this?" Azmir's voice was even but greatly commanding.

My head snapped over to him, startled by his audacity and begging his pardon.

He was holding a place card from the charity dinner, flipping it back and forward so I could see both sides. The front of it displayed Azmir's name scripted in fancy calligraphy, but it was crossed out by a pen and the back contained Brian Thompson's name and from what I could deduce, his telephone number. I quickly figured out why Azmir's place card wasn't next to mine.

When did he do that? And how in the world did it end up in my purse?

Common sense kicked in bringing my memory back.

"I left my purse at the bar next to Thompson when I went to the restroom earlier." My lungs contracted releasing massive amounts of hot air, taking my exasperation of this Thompson character with it.

"He's not an issue for you but he damn sure wants you." Azmir threw my words back at me.

My eyes were pinned to his as my mouth hung open. I wasn't expecting his fury, he was beside himself with animosity for some insignificant guy who didn't stand a chance with me.

"Do you know how ridiculous this is?"

He scoffed, "Ridiculous? He's bold enough to discard my place card and use it like a napkin in a bar to slide you his number...*and* slip it in your purse? That's ridiculous to you, Rayna?"

I was losing my patience. He was blowing this out of proportion.

"Azmir, you find it difficult to learn a man finds me attractive and tries to make a pass at me? Everyday I'm with you, without fail, there are women gawking in your face, not caring I'm there. I'm fully aware you are...beyond gorgeous so I tolerate it. You know why? Because as long as it doesn't follow you home, I can deal. I expect the same level of flexibility in return. Thompson is an insignificant part of life, just like your legion of admirers. I have *zero* interest in him. End. Of. Story!"

"He's *trying* to follow you home," he hissed, staring aimlessly out the window.

I suddenly realized I was out of breath. I couldn't believe his temerity.

"You didn't introduce me as your man," he muttered like a petulant child, his eyes still fixated on outside passing objects.

"Is that what this is all about? *Is it?* What should I title you? Tell me! Since when has this been so significant? Because I can't recall a time when you've referred to me as anything other than my name!"

"*Since when?*" Azmir shot me a look of incredulity. "When you're living with and fuckin' someone exclusively it counts as significant in my book," he scoffed and in a nanosecond I saw there was something other than anger behind his eyes, I saw fear. But what did he have to be fearful about? We were good. We were together. I'd done everything he asked of me in terms of joining lives.

Was that not enough?

With a hoarse delivery I could barely recognize I admonished him to see things from my perspective. "Not now. Not after...this." I gestured of our recent carnal episode there in the limo. "Azmir, when you're away it's like my life...my happiness is put on hold until you return. It's like I'm forced to hold my breath until I see you, inhale you once again. Baby, if I'm not breathing, I certainly don't have the capacity to give attention to another man. I'm sorry you can't see that, and honestly, I realize there isn't much that I can do to make you understand it."

Defeat engulfed me and I shut down, tuning everything and everybody out to nurse my broken ego. I was wounded. The remainder of the ride home, the elevator ride up to the apartment and even preparing for bed was met in pure silence. That night I slept hard and sound. Although I was beyond hurt by him, his presence back home and nestled next to me in bed brought an undeniable sense of comfort, allowing me to rest for the first time since he'd left almost two weeks earlier.

Azmir

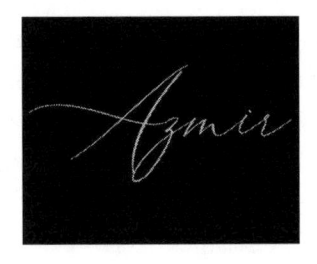

I woke up to a streak of glaring sunlight escaping into the room. My body's internal clock came with an alarm. I didn't need to look at the time to know it was just before six thirty. Just months ago, I'd wake at five twenty-five daily. Perhaps having Ms. Brimm as a new bedfellow had brought about my increasing ability to rest at night.

I rolled over to her and reveled in her beauty. She looked so peaceful and beatific while asleep. I also couldn't deny her fresh-face sex appeal. Her skin was fair and virtually spotless. The burning temptation to touch her bare shoulder was overwhelming, but I thought not to considering our fight. Flashbacks of events from last night's gala began flooding my head.

I tried shaking off Brian Thompson's impudence of pulling a switch-a-roo with my damn place card. *The fuck this prick think I am?* I had to fight off the urge to make a trip to his office because I don't want to be too forward.

And that clown, Sebastian! I had wanted so badly to ask Rayna what incited her to give his ass the time of the day. I hid my detestation for him beneath my false naïveté last night though I had far more revelatory things to say to him, but the last time I used my discretion with him I damn near lost Rayna, and I wouldn't risk that again.

As I showered and had breakfast, I couldn't shake how Rayna made so little of Thompson's offenses. He was way out of line, and I'll be sure to be a little more aggressive the next time I see his ass.

Rayna and I exchanged very few words. I could guess she was still upset from last night and truth be told I was still perturbed my damn self. I was sure Chef Boyd could cut the tension in the kitchen with one of his high-end cutlery pieces.

By the way she was dressed, I could tell Rayna was planning to work out before work. Before parting ways, I gave her a slow and meaningful kiss on her head, grateful she would still allow me to. We said our goodbyes and parted ways.

My day began at eight and started hectic as usual, but today with an unusual turn of events. I wasn't even scheduled to be in town but that didn't lessen my responsibilities. I participated in a conference call from my office at the rec for the first hour. Brett made me aware of a few executive performance evaluations I needed to tend to, but before I was scheduled to, I insisted I go ahead with my cafeteria appreciation act.

We'd purchased gifts for the culinary staff and because of my hectic schedule recently, I hadn't gotten the chance to present them. I went down and hurdled them to bestow words of motivation and encouragement. I caught the batted eyes and giggles from a couple of female admirers. I had become accustomed to this type of behavior but didn't allow it to faze me or cause me to conduct myself as anything less than their professional leader. I didn't care for the horribly hidden attempts at flattery by them but put it aside for the task at hand. They worked hard and were highly recognized by local appraisers. I was proud of their efforts to take my vision of affordable, yet distinguished culinary works and garner accolades.

As I was speaking, I saw Petey burst through the silver double doors of the kitchen leaving them flapping in the air. His face was placid, but his aura was far from calmed. He approached me and leaned in my ear, "Yo, Duke, Tara went into early labor. They say she needed a emergency blood transfusion."

Why hasn't someone called? I went to reach for my phone and immediately realized I'd left it charging in my office. It died on me last night, and I was so fucked up from the events of the gala that I headed straight to bed and forgot to charge it. My thoughts shifted to Rayna, wondering if she'd tried contacting me since I'd been away from my phone.

I wrapped up the pep talk understanding they had to get back to work themselves. After flying upstairs to my office to retrieve my things we headed over to *Cedars* to see about Tara. On my way I viewed my missed calls and texts, relieved none were from Rayna. I'd thought to hit her up but quickly decided against it recalling how distant we were just a few hours before. I did shoot Ray a text telling him where to meet me for pick up. I'm sure Petey had his own packed agenda and I'd need a lift from the hospital. Ray hit me back in receipt.

Then inspiration hit me, and I called Brett asking to have flowers delivered over to Rayna's office only to have him check her calendar and learned she was in a staff meeting at the main branch. Callow thoughts raced through my mind to question if Thompson was in that meeting with her. I managed to fight it off.

I had begun to develop jealous tendencies concerning Rayna and it was so out of character for me. I couldn't place the reasons behind it, and *that* was killing me. The thought of Rayna being with another man caused my blood to rush heatedly through my veins. Prior to last night, those thoughts were distant nightmares but Thompson's presence in the picture made the nightmares my reality. The last thing I needed was a man, who could give her a blemish-free future *without the illegal baggage I carried*, coming in and sweeping her off her feet.

"Yo, Duke, you look nervous back there. You good?" Petey's calling out from the front seat snapped me out of my deep rumination.

I knew he was referring to Tara's baby and the possibility of it being mine. Truth be told, I hadn't given thought to it since Rayna learned about Tara's pregnancy, when she all but left because of the mere possibility of me being a father. That's how confident I was about the paternity. The only thing concerning me previously was Rayna learning about it. And once the cat was out of the bag, my trepidations vanished.

"Nah, Crack." I couldn't fight my introspection as I sat alone in the back of the *750Li* and endured Wop's chancy driving. He kept bobbing in and out of lanes.

I knew the baby wasn't mine. As callous as that sounded it was the truth. I hadn't fucked Tara in nearly a year and the last I checked it took ten months to produce and incubate a baby. She was off my stick about a month and some change before getting knocked up.

We arrived at Labor and Delivery and were directed to the waiting room where we found her cousin, Stephanie, and several other friends and family.

"Oh my god, Azmir! You made it!" Stephanie shrieked with panic in her eyes, running over to hug me.

"How is she?" I asked.

"We don't know much about her yet. They had to take the baby via Caesarian section. Her blood cell count had already been very low, and she lost so much blood the doctor had to give her a transfusion. I'm just so happy you're here." She damn near sobbed in my arm.

That's when I saw Big D appear from behind the doors wearing scrubs. *Did he help deliver the baby?* His eyes were large and red as he sauntered over to the waiting party. His scowling of me was searing. I knew we'd have to address this at some point. I just wondered how soon now that the baby was here.

"How are things with her?" I asked once he arrived over to me.

"We tried calling and texting you. After failed attempts I called Petey. Were you indisposed?" Big D was being coy. He saw me standing there in a suit. It was clear I had been working.

"My phone died last night and was forgotten while charging in my office. I was attending my staff downstairs when I missed the calls." Sufficient enough of an answer without giving him my life story.

He shook his head. "Ready to go back and see them?" His voice was low and calm, revealing his distressful state.

I'd quickly thought about how precarious this situation was. I nodded and glanced over to Petey who regarded me stoically in return but gave a slight nod. I followed Big D back to her room and once we got to the nurses' station of her floor, I had to suit up in scrubs as the baby was in the Neonatal Intensive Care Unit. I didn't ask any questions, though a few bounced through my head.

We entered a room where I saw nearly a dozen tiny newborns resting in incubators, some smaller than others. Many of them could fit in the palm of my hand. I followed D to one with a pink card on it designed for a girl with the name *A. Jacobs* handwritten on it. Naturally, it arrested my attention, almost like a punch to the gut.

Big D's eyes rested on the pint-sized baby who had a tube running into her nose and bore a couple of bruises I was later told happened during delivery. She lay there peacefully, resting on her back with her hands clawed. I observed the knitted pink hat covering her head and her miniature pamper. She looked so helpless and...precious.

So, this is what parents experience while looking at their newborns. My mind jumped to Rayna and if she'd be overwhelmingly protective of our child had we ever been fortunate enough to deliver. *Me a father? I can't wait.* Rayna would make a great mom and could show me how to care for a baby.

"Little miracle, huhn?"

Huhn?

Spun from my thoughts, I looked over to Big D asking with my eyes for him to repeat himself.

"Babies. They're miracles. This little girl came a few weeks early but by miracle, she's with us."

"Tough delivery?" I'd guessed this was a good time to learn the story behind the early delivery.

"Yeah," he sighed softly. "Tara woke up bleeding in the wee hours of the morning. She walked across the house to my bedroom, leaving a trail of blood behind her. She only made it as far as my door before passing out. Seeing her collapse nearly cut my heart out my goddamn chest, man. I got her here and the docs said not a moment too soon," his voice cracked. "She could have lost the baby and slipped into a coma herself. I was supposed to be on duty last night." He expelled another cough to cover the crack in his voice. "She would've been alone."

I didn't know what to say or do. I'd been on D's shit list for months and not just for my estrange relationship with his daughter, but add to that, my announcement of officially leaving the game at the close of the year. Outside of business, he'd have no dealings with me. Ironically, because I'd been so wrapped up in my affairs with work and Rayna, I had been shielded from his resentment towards me. In spite of our troubled relationship, I didn't like seeing him choked up like this.

"Let's go check up on Tara." I grabbed his shoulders giving him a manly clench. He led the way out and to Tara.

When we entered her room I saw her cousin, Danielle, holding a cup of water as Tara sipped through a straw. Danielle turned toward us and formed a scowl once her eyes landed on me. I ignored it and made my way to the side of the bed.

Tara lay there hooked several ways into a machine, appearing weakened and fatigued.

"TaHarry," I jokingly referred to one of my former nicknames for her I'd come up with years ago. It blended her first and last names. I wanted to lighten the somber mood.

"Azmir," she croaked hoarsely. "You came."

"Yeah. I told your dad I'd forgotten my phone in my office charging."

"I thought you were still in Africa, Miami or somewhere Peg said when I called last week. What's in Africa?" Tara sounded so weak, but underneath the docile demeanor she was accusing me of being neglectful. I could tell she was still pushing the paternity issue.

"South Africa. Work."

"Let's leave these two alone. I'm sure they have lots to discuss," Big D ordered to Danielle, and they excused themselves leaving us in Tara's private hospital room.

"What's the doc saying?"

"I'll be feeling back to normal in a week or so, but I need lots of rest." She shifted in her bed trying to sit up. "Azina is fine...fully developed but they need to keep an eye on her to be sure her lungs are working at one hundred precent."

Azina? What the fuck? Is she really taking things this far? I backed up a few inches into a chair to take a seat. *Azina?*

"Azmir, you're going to need to look for my nurse so she can give you the papers to sign the birth certificate."

"Tara, my position hasn't changed. I will not assume responsibility until it's confirmed I am, in fact, her father. With that being said, don't you think it was quite presumptuous for you to give her a name so closely resembling mine?"

"I see you haven't changed." She sighed in disappointment. "Okay. We'll just have to prove it to you; in the meantime, I'm not changing my daughter's name. Your connection will obviously be delayed but our world must go on." Even in such a feeble condition the sarcasm in her voice couldn't be missed.

"I can arrange for the test—"

"No. I don't want you to have to do shit. I'll take care of those details and contact you," Tara cut me off.

"Whatever you're most comfortable with. I don't endeavor to disrupt your new world. She looks very precious in there and deserves all your attention and love. Let's not prolong this cloud hanging over our heads."

"Azmir, the only person predicting rain is you. Tell me," she cleared her raspy voice. "What will happen when she turns out to be yours? Have you given any thought to that?"

"Sure, I have. I'd be the best father I could be with whatever necessary lifestyle adjustments it would take."

"Including your new girl toy, the dancer?" Evidence of my hunch, Tara was still as bold and fiery as ever.

"Who I date isn't up for discussion and has no bearing on my potential role as a father."

"Will she agree with that?" she fired back.

"My personal life is none of your business and that's final." I was losing my patience. Ill or not, Tara was about to get cussed the fuck out in her sick bed.

"It *is* my business when it concerns my child...your child."

"*If* the test result yields such facts, I will handle the affairs of my life while you stay in yours."

Her head jolted as her eyes grew. I knew that was a low blow. Tara still wanted to be together, and I could tell she thought my feelings would change once this baby had arrived. I needed it to be clear they wouldn't right away. I looked at my pocket watch for the time.

"I have to go. Is there anything I can get you or the baby?"

She was still dazed and through her eyes I could see she was processing my question as my previous comments weighed on her mind.

"A car seat." She murmured, lost in her ruminative thoughts. "The one I got from my shower has been recalled. I just sent it off yesterday with the intentions of replacing it, but I had gotten so tired I went home to rest thinking I had plenty of time..." her voice trailed, and her eyes fixated on some distant object.

"Indeed. You'll have it today. Call me if I can be of any help. I'll wait for you two to recover before expecting the test, but I do suggest getting it done not long after."

I rose from my chair and grabbed Tara's hand as a means of being kind. No matter what our differences, she had meant a lot to me over the years. Our time had come to an end but my general respect for her was still present. She was Big D's daughter, giving us a sort of agnatic connection.

She placed her left hand on top of my right. "Why can't we work things out?" Her voice was drenched in desperation and diluted in regret. "Is it because of your new friend?" She referred to Rayna as she frantically searched my eyes. "If that's the case, I can be patient, Azmir. I'll stand back until you work your way out of it with her."

Was she consenting to being a side chick? Tara was far more unhinged than I'd given her.

"You're not accepting responsibility. You're more culpable in this than you're willing to admit, but know this one thing, T; you can fool a lot of people by not disclosing your blunders but when it's just you and me in a room, alone with no outside influences, you cannot withhold them from me. Your indiscretions will never be forgotten, but let's not allow your denial to get us to a place where we can't be cordial. We have too much history not to be. Your dad doesn't deserve a war between us," my voice was low yet steady.

She heard every argument of my message, based upon her reaction. I peered directly into her eyes for seconds before leaving her room.

Big D was in the waiting area, in the corner on the phone when I made it back. I didn't interrupt him because I didn't want the questions, so I left out instead. Ray was waiting outside as arranged.

I hopped in the Bentley. After closing the door, I instructed, "*Katz, Smith and Adams* headquarters," and we peeled off. En route I couldn't shake the experience of seeing those helpless newborns laying there waiting for the clock to tick for their growth and development. Parents going through that must be overwhelmed. I'm sure with the right partner I could get through it.

Tara was playing possum to the consequences of her indiscretions. She wanted people to believe I was the negligent parent, but

I was willing to play at her speed for a little while longer. I didn't give a fuck about what people thought of me anyway. They didn't affect my paper or my livelihood.

When I recalled Big D's testimonial of Tara's pre-term labor, I couldn't escape the dark and horrid thoughts of Rayna's recent miscarriage. She was alone when her body dispelled our baby. Visions of her courage during those lonely hours, days had my head spinning. I would never allow her to experience that again. *I swear.*

I was in the reception area of *Smith, Katz, and Adams Sports Medicine Center,* waiting on the receptionist to locate Rayna. The digital clock hanging over her head read eleven fifty-seven a.m. and my hands were speed typing on my blackberry, firing off instructions to an already busy Brett. I also had a few other business-related e-mails to address. I heard the door to the office area open and turned my attention to find it deploy several people dressed in either business attire or white coats. Most looked famished and overcome with boredom and others, indifferent.

"Mr. Jacobs, the staff meeting has concluded, as you can see, they're filing out now. Ms. Brimm should be making her way out as well. She never stays after," the young receptionist revealed with a snicker.

Not many seconds later, I see Rayna appear from the door looking just as spiritless as her colleagues. When she recognized me, she stopped in her stride.

Her chest visibly rose before she exhaled, "Azmir, is everything alright?"

I nodded but remained silent. Her hair was set in a poof on top of her head with the ponytail in the back. That was one of my favorites of hers. She donned a cranberry blouse falling just to her ass and tied at her waist with a fitted, knee-length ivory skirt with nude shoes matching the skirt to a "T." Her accessories were ruby red and gold. Rayna looked edible.

Now more collected after my response she asks, "How can I help you?" It was clear she was still somewhat alarmed.

"I came to take you out to lunch, if that's allowed."

"I have my first patient at two."

"Then we should hurry, shouldn't we?"

I wanted to reach down to hold her, bury my face in her neck, and inhale her intoxicating tang so badly, but kept my composure. I was frozen in time for a minute drinking her all in. Apparently, my amorous desires didn't go unnoticed.

"Azmir!" Rayna hissed in a lowly tone.

I looked up to find a couple of the reception-area girls giggling at my lack of self-control.

"Let's take this out of here." She softly took me by the arm and pulled me towards the lobby, then out the door.

"Ray can drive us to lunch and drop you back off to your car." I held the car door open for her and she crawled in, greeting Ray as she scooted over leaving me room.

Turning to me she asked, "What's this all about, Mr. Jacobs? It isn't every day I am chauffeured to a spontaneous lunch date by an insanely sexy and irresistible guy. You had the girls at the front desk salivating. I'm sure you'll be the core of water-cooler blather for the next week or so."

"Or until something far more significant happens there in the lobby." I caressed her cheek. "I've missed you," my tone relaxed, my emotions raw.

"You're finally feeling what it's like?" she shook her head. "You saw me just this morning. What's come over you?" She was crisp, but I had probably deserved it.

I immediately knew from where her aggravation had derived. "You didn't seem to take offense to Thompson's brashness," I pleaded.

"You didn't give me a chance to. It was almost as if you were accusing me of doing something wrong," she shot back. During her short pause, she diverted her eyes out the window. With a hard and long exasperated blink of her eyes, she buried her face in her hands and exhaled. "Azmir, Thompson was absolutely wrong…and bold but so help me god, he's just an outside force to me. We have many of them. In my world there's just you…me and you. He's on the outside with everyone else."

Her eyes came to meet mine once again. "I'm not good with being scolded. I've been alone for so long I internalize it more than you intend for me to, and I feel isolated. If there's a problem, you have to address it in a better manner until I give you a reason to do otherwise. Okay?"

Not wanting to fight and contented hearing her express her feelings I conceded with a nod. I was already fucked up in the head from my earlier visit to the hospital.

When we arrived at the restaurant, I held her hand from the car to the door of the eatery and all the way to the table where we were seated. I didn't want to let her go despite the cold vibes emitting from her. We sat side by side and I draped my arm around her.

"How was your day?"

"I was in a meeting all morning. There were a few interesting tidbits of information given but overall, the annual babble from upper management. Layoffs are looming."

"You're going to be okay, aren't you?" I found myself squeezing her hand in concern. Although, I knew no matter what I'd take care of her, if she let me. I'd make her let me.

"Sounds like it, but we'll hear soon which locations will have to start pink-slipping their support staff." She waved her hand in the air, pushing away that conversation, "I don't want to talk about my work. After that meeting I can use some distraction. Tell me about your day."

The waiter came to take our order and we took a minute to make our selections. Rayna and I both passed on alcohol as we were both on the clock. She ordered a salad, and I followed suit.

Once he was out of earshot Rayna turned back to me. "Your day, sir?"

"It's been eventful." I sighed. "I had business to take care of with Robert first thing this morning followed by a staff briefing at the rec." I examined her earrings with my fingers causing her to shift in her seat. I liked that I had an effect on her.

"That didn't sound eventful at all," she softly giggled trying to compose herself.

"Well, that's because I'm not finished." I murmured in a moment of fortitude. "Tara had her baby this morning."

Rayna's mouth dropped. She swung around to face me, scooting back. I could swear to seeing all the blood drain from her face. I braced myself for how this would go down.

"When? How? You were there?" She couldn't hide the restlessness in her voice and I'm not sure she tried.

"Likely around the time I was headed into work. C-section. And obviously I was not there, neither do I think it would've been appropriate for me to have been."

I watched her eyes bounce back and forth aimlessly in anxiety. I knew instantly she needed security and affirmation.

I ran my thumb down her cheek and over her bottom lip and before I could speak, she jerked her head back withdrawing from my embrace.

In a forceful whisper she advised, "Just say it. You don't have to perform any pity rituals to break the bad news."

My eyes widened in total shock; I didn't like seeing her unnecessarily defeated and misled.

"Nothing has changed between Tara and me, and not a damn thing will change between you and me."

"Well, why the long face and sentimental affection? Azmir, something has affected you." She searched my eyes.

I gave a deep swallow. "Rayna, I don't know why but all the time I was there, even in the NIC-U, all I could think of was you and what our lives would be like today if..." My hand somehow appeared at her belly as my words failed me.

She gasped and her body steeled. She looked down at my hand and used hers to cover mine.

"Azmir, you want a baby?" Her eyes were filled with terror when she shifted them back up to me.

The waiter returned with our food, but we remained cemented in the same positions. When he left, her lost eyes were still plastered to my face.

I let out a strong exhale. I didn't know what in the hell I was trying to say I wanted, but whatever it was I wanted it to be with Rayna.

"Not right now, but eventually." I was lost in words and feelings—something happening far more increasingly when it came to Rayna.

She let out a deep exhale and her body visibly relaxed.

"Is a baby with me that horrid of an idea?" I was offended.

She jumped to me, wrapping her arms around my waist. "No. No. That's not it at all. It's just I'm not sure I'm capable of being a mother."

"Are you saying you can't have children? Are you speaking from a medical perspective?" I was confused as hell.

She sat up and faced the table. "No, I don't mean physically—well, nothing I'm aware of. What I mean is with all of my issues. I can't possibly nurture another human being." Her face was empty and her eyes haunted. She picked up her fork to start eating her salad.

She couldn't possibly believe that, could she?

"The more I thought about how reckless I was this summer with going without protection, I had to think about the stupid risks I took with potentially another's life. I've never—*ever* been so irresponsible with sex. I don't know what..." Her thoughts interrupted her speech. "I know how it happened. *You*," she whispered as though it was illegal or immoral. "Motherhood may not be in the cards for me. I can't bring a life into this world knowing my deficiencies. No one deserves a broken mother."

We ate in silence for a few. I measured her words exposing a new level of her self-abhorrence. Why couldn't she see her strengths instead of her weakness? Rayna's package, by far outshined, outweighed, and out measured most of the women I'd encountered in my life. She was unbelievably gorgeous, educated, extremely talented, ambitious, and more independent than my alpha-male ego would prefer at times.

Emotionally, she clearly had deficiencies but what woman didn't struggle with balancing them considering their chemical make-up? Even that she had been working on by way of her religion and counseling. She was wonderfully packaged *and hopefully for me*. I wanted her. I wanted room in her heart and soul—in the world of Rayna Brimm. One could guess I was no better than she was because I couldn't express these things to her. I was too afraid. She was too flighty.

So badly, I wanted to share all of my life—my past and future with her but the details of it were too sensitive. She was too fragile, and I wasn't fully convinced she wouldn't run, leaving me more fucked up in the head than anyone else could possibly have. There had to be a way to work toward her ultimate trust without disclosing the complications of my world.

"I can't believe that," I admitted after swallowing my food and reaching for my drink.

"Hmmm?"

"I can't believe you're incapable of motherhood. You were very dedicated to Erin. You're still fighting to be a part of her world. If you were so selfish and unable to connect to a dependent child, you wouldn't be fighting as hard as you are to be that to Erin. This is your opportunity to make a clean break and yet you're fighting."

Her eyes closed as pain overtook her at the thought of Erin. It was a sensitive topic but a truth needing to be highlighted to prove my point.

"You would be parenting that girl if you had no opposition to it, wouldn't you?" With her head still collapsed she nodded. I knew she would. Though I wasn't sure Rayna would be sharing a place with me had Erin been with her, and the thought didn't sit well with me. I was a selfish man when it came to Rayna. Having Erin in her life would've taken much adjustment on my part. *I'd cross that bridge once we get to it.*

I grabbed her and wrapped my arms around her. I hated seeing her in pain. I didn't intend on this being a somber luncheon, but I guess this is one dynamic of a relationship.

"I'm going to prove to you you're capable of being any and everything that I need you to be and, more importantly, you want to be. If you stick this out with me, I'll prove it. Deal?" Buried in my arms, she nodded her head profusely. I felt her pulling at my shirt balled in her hands.

We stayed this way for a while until she pulled her head up and reached up for mine to engage me in an impassioned kiss, knocking my ass off kilter. She traced my mouth with her tongue, it was deliciously invading. I tasted the ingredients of her salad and I'm sure she sampled my lunch as well, but none of it mattered. Rayna was exposing her raw, bare, and unadulterated soul and I tried sucking it all in. In this moment, I didn't focus on us being in a restaurant and not in a private room, showing affection I was not typically so inclined to do in public. My focus was more on the connection we'd just made, one step in a lifetime journey I wanted to take with her.

The waiter appeared, observably embarrassed. "Sir, I recalled the timing in which your assistant said you had available for lunch. In keeping with that, would you like this wrapped?"

We looked down at our barely touched food and Rayna sheepishly chuckled.

"Wrap the beauty's. I won't have time to finish mine."

Checking her phone, Rayna yelped, "One eleven! I need to be headed back to the office!"

"Okay, we'll get you back there as soon as your food is wrapped."

"This is my treat," Rayna's words were strategically brisk.

"Forget it, Brimm. You know I don't roll like that." My tone purposely sharp.

"Oh, no. Not even your CEO persona rearing its controlling head can keep me from paying. I realize we're in Beverly Hills and can afford it considering the absurd amount of money you've had deposited into my account a few weeks ago. It took a while for me to catch it. I haven't had the need to visit my accounts over the past few weeks because you've been taking care of everything, but I needed cash for church offering the other day and when I read the balance on the receipt from the ATM, I nearly passed out! I called the bank to inform them of their astronomical error only for them to tell me the deposit was legit. That is an insane amount of money, Azmir. Enough to pay my monthly expenses for nearly a year," she scolded.

Shit. Rayna didn't like when I attempted to take care of her.

"I just wanted to make sure you were covered while I was out of the country."

"Covered? Azmir, I don't have to worry about food because your personal chef cooks my breakfast and dinner, *and* you have lunch delivered to my staff several times a week. I no longer have a cleaner's bill courtesy of your very capable housekeeper. I have no need to shop for clothes because you buy everything from my jacket to my underwear. I don't pay a car note because you donated a brand new *S550* fully paid for...and your chauffeur seems to know every time the car goes below a half a tank of gas and refills it without fail. Now that I think about it, the only thing I do pay for is my hair." Rayna was out of breath.

"And your manicures and pedicures," I attempted in humor.

Shaking her head she informed me, "Actually, that's taken care of through my full-service spa treatments I was made aware having a membership to, all courtesy of a Mr. A.D. Jacobs."

I didn't speak but shrugged.

However, she was incorrect. Rayna still paid her mortgage and all other monthly bills generating from her house. I didn't want to bring it up because I didn't want to upset her and have her put a stop to what little I had been able to do. I offered several times to buy her home, but she had yet to relent. I figured her still having it gave her a sense of independence from me and I wanted to respect that. But I must admit, I enjoyed taking care of her.

"My god, Azmir, it makes me want to see your annual expense report." She shook her head and raised her index finger. "No, I don't because that would make curious to how much you earn and I don't want that answer right now, if ever."

I laughed at her bewilderment. She shot me a look as to ask what the joke was.

"I'm meeting with my accountant this afternoon after my session with Tyler. I can have her print you out whatever you need to satisfy your curiosities." I was kidding, of course. My money was too complicated an explanation.

She rolled her eyes with a smirk on her face.

While on our way back to her car, I asked, "What's on your agenda tonight?"

"I have Bible study at six. Why? Do you have something in mind?"

"Nothing I would deem more important than that. How long is the service?"

"An hour."

"Indeed. I'll meet you at home around eight. You mind hanging out?"

"I'll load up on caffeine." She grinned. Reaching inside her purse she pulled out a napkin and wiped my face. "A bit of my lipstick is smeared on you." She dabbed the outer lining of my lips.

"I could think of lots of places on my body where I'd love to have you smear your lipstick."

Rayna gasped. "Don't," she begged in an unintended seductive tone awakening my cock. She darted her eyes to Ray to remind me we weren't alone. I couldn't give a damn.

I kneeled down to kiss her, surprised by the little time it took for her to reciprocate. She pulled my head down into her face and let out a low moan, careful to be heard by me only. I was so turned the fuck on I felt like a bitch. I employed every fiber of discretion I had to not rub her tits or ass. I was hurting so bad I allowed a guttural groan to escape causing her to stop with her eyes wide and weary. She looked over to Ray who was ever the professional, keeping his eyes fixated ahead with no hint of acknowledgement to our backseat near-copulation activities.

He pulled into the parking lot, and I walked Rayna to her car with my erection in tow.

She clicked for the doors to unlock with her remote, and I opened the door for her. After tossing her things in she turned to me looking as disheveled as I felt. Her eyes lowered to my bulged pants, and she licked her lips so seductively. Looking back up to me she attempted to speak, and I knew what about.

"*Ummm... Azmir...*" Her voice was throaty, wanting.

With both my hands I brought her face to mine and embraced her once again. Her moans were longer and harder. I was caught up, in fucking public again, no less.

I withdrew. "Brimm, you have to go, and I do, too. At this rate I'll have your ass pinned in the air out in your job's parking lot."

She smiled. "See you tonight."

"You had better."

On my way back to Long Beach, I e-mailed Brett a list of things to send over to the hospital for Tara and the baby when I received a text from Rayna.

I didn't want to let go. Thanks for lunch, A.D...

And you think I did? I would have enjoyed having you for lunch much more if we didn't have to return to work. Stop texting while driving. I thought of Tara's mother's accident and didn't want Rayna taking any risks.

In your words ***indeed***

My workout with Tyler was exhilarating. We started off with a little cardio and went straight into the ring for some sparring. The two-hour session flew by. After hitting the shower, I headed over to the office of Laura Bower, my ever-efficient accountant. I'd been with Laura for nearly six years when my money grew to amounts I could no longer Rubber band and stash away after paying taxes. With very little questioning, she set me up with various accounts and investments to grow and secure my money. Laura was the only person who had the closest of an accurate estimate of my worth. I still had stacks buried and stashed for any emergencies I *couldn't* think of.

We went through the usual, which is every nook and cranny, each and every crevice of my finances she managed. I once heard the rapper, 50 Cent, say he didn't understand how those who were wealthy at one point and lost it all say they don't know where their money had gone at the hand of its managers because he sat with his accountants regularly to go over his books. Well, we are kindred souls in that respect because I met with Ms. Bower monthly, and in between, if necessary, for an account of my money.

"Well, Jacobs, as you can see there are the same expense activities as last month. However, your income has increased seventeen percent from the closings of these contracts from your latest M&A deals," she pointed out on the projection screen using a laser pointer.

Bower had a team who collectively managed my affairs, but I preferred talking to just one—the boss—because if something went wrong, it was on her head. I liked the software programs she used to create graphs and charts to illustrate my portfolio. It provided a visual.

"And this fluctuating green field? It looks small compared to the other columns." I pointed with my own laser.

"Your regularly occurring monthly expenses such as your household, staff payroll—personal contractors such as your barber and stylist, my salary, etc. The cause of the fluctuation is your quarterly taxes. Obviously they're not paid monthly as are those other expenses, causing a drop and fall depending on which is due." Bower's voice was strong and projected, as though she knew her shit. That's the way I liked her, a pit-bull in a skirt.

"Oh, and speaking of, I know you expressed wanting to keep a minimum in Ms. Brimm's account but as you see here..." She clicked to a new screen, which provided a more detailed view of one of the expenditure columns. "It hasn't moved since the deposit a few weeks back. You haven't given the word to do another transfer. I figured either she doesn't know it's there or doesn't spend immoderately."

Her brilliant blue eyes met mine when she swiftly turned her head toward me for an answer. Blonde bouncy micro curls flew through the air.

Bower was frugal and when I asked her to start moving money into Rayna's account she didn't do so without professional apprehension. I don't know which contractor was most protective over my affairs: her or my attorney, Chesney. I damn near had to pontificate a proposal to have her allocate *my* money. She knew this was something outside of my normal practices.

"She discovered it last week. And let's just say she wasn't *pleasantly* surprised. Let's see what type of spender she is based upon the timing in which she expends it. I'll keep you informed," I muttered.

Bower held her hands out defensively conceding to my will. "I won't fight today. Almost all of my clients who are in the habit of doing this, against my sound advice of course, find themselves replenishing faster than they anticipated. She's known about it for an entire week and hasn't touched it is a bit unusual, but we shall see."

"How are those Swiss accounts coming along. It's been, what... three months? And I'm still nervous. Depending on how they do, I plan on sending more."

Bower went back to her flicker to bring them up. "Jacobs, the wealthy have been doing this for centuries. Your money is protected, foolproof. I'm not sure what more convincing I could possibly do."

"Indeed." I let out a deep breath pulling out my watch. It was getting late, and I had a meeting with *The Clan* about transitioning my empire.

I wrapped up my meeting with Bower and continued on with my day.

The Clan and I met at a warehouse in Glendale and were five deep inside and four out on guard. Our time together was always short, and communication was cut up, which meant we didn't discuss every detail of a transaction in one setting. We never knew if we had flies on the wall. At the close of our meeting Petey went in.

"We gotta have 'dis shit on point before going to the connects tryna' get in they favor." Petey was trying to school Kid and Wop.

I decided to leave my crown to Kid and Petey's to Wop. I tried being diplomatic, sharing the love. I wasn't one hundred percent sure of leaving them in my wake to do business, but they'd always been loyal and deserved a shot. Like young pups they were all eager nods and yeses.

"Divine spoke to Santiago and Paulio a few months ago and they agreed to meet with y'all soon. They'll give us a date when they ready," Petey continued.

I took over. "In the meantime, we gotta shipment coming in a couple of days. Wop, you hit the drop spot. Kid you split it up. You know the package is ten mill and that's six hundred and twenty-five keys. All the leu's get their keys except for Black. He ain't re-up. I got somebody on his ass while y'all get ya tips wet on acquisitions. Don't sleep or fucking yawn cause the streets are watching. They may not know our moves but they're damn sure waiting for somebody to slip the fuck up. Don't let it be you. Shit is realer than ever in those streets. Those kids are dumber but fucking faster." I gave them both deep cutting eye action. They knew what time it was.

"Time is up. In a minute." Petey raised his hand giving them dap before we exited the building.

"Tomorrow," Petey confirmed.

"Tomorrow," I agreed, and we parted ways.

It was close to five and I had a little shopping to do before meeting Rayna back at the marina.

CHAPTER 8

Azmir

The following night I met Big D at the Santa Monica Pier. I had my peoples with me hidden among the crowd. I didn't trust D although I knew I was his muscle and he'd call upon me whenever safety was an issue. This predator was a snake, and one should never underestimate a snake.

He seemed perplexed before I informed him of my issue. He wore a long trench coat with khaki pants and a white polo shirt. He kept scratching his temple as I spoke, which was a sign of deep thought and stress from him.

"So, I'm planning my next move with ol' girl. Big D, I gotta be honest here; I don't know where all of this is going, much less what it's about. I'm kinda fucked up in the head with it," I exclaimed playing a role, awaiting a response.

After a meditated pause he replied, "You're gonna have to cut off all means of contact with her, Young Blood. Don't continue talking to phish for a motive. If they had something, you would be in cuffs by now. If you don't talk, you give them shit. I'll have my guys look into it. I still have a little pull with the *FED*-dy's."

His words were clear and cautious, but I could tell he was

preoccupied with something. So I asked, "You good, Big D? What's eating at you, man?"

He looked at me as if he'd come out of his trance and forced a smile on his face. What he couldn't conceal was what he wasn't telling me. His advice was fair but there was something he was leaving out.

He went first. "Listen. Just don't do anything rash until I look into this. It may be nothing; it may be something. Either way we want to err on the side of caution. Okay?" He ended looking for me to agree.

That was what Big D brought to our partnership: legal eyes. He was well seated in the justice system after spending damn near forty years in law enforcement. He'd been well-connected and versed in the law. He would hold off investigations and advise during legal woes. He'd have officers reassigned at the border when trafficking and troopers recanted their reasons for pulling over dirty drivers. It was a marriage made in heaven. Until recent discoveries.

"D, if there was something I should know, you would tell a nigga, right?" looking him square in his eyes. I could tell when someone was misleading me by doing just that.

"Aww, come on, Young Blood! Would I do that?" he answered.

That was all I needed.

My mentor, the man who had guided my life like a father was lying to me. He had shit all fucked up. My chest tightened at that discovery, and disappointment engulfed me. Years of trust and devotion abruptly vanished. I couldn't believe I'd been so naïve to his deceit. I'd always known Big D had a huge corruptive feature to his persona, but never did I expect to be on that side of it regarding me and my family. This was the end of our path, perhaps the beginning of my fury.

"Indeed," I answered before a lingering pause. "*Ummm*... D," I called out.

"Yeah, son?"

"She's also alleging you had my pops killed."

D's eyes rose to me so quickly and defensively. It was almost as if he'd been jabbed in the gut.

"What the fuck is up with your line of questioning to me, Young Blood?"

I held my hand out trying to deceivingly present as harmless. "I'm just asking about the bullshit she's running, Duke. Easy."

"Divine, you think I would set up your father, a man I endured training academy with? Somebody I had to face those racist pigs with? Do you know what hell they put us through?" he asked, suddenly becoming aware of his heightened tone and muting.

"I owe that man my life. Too many times he talked me down from killing those pigs. That's why it was no sweat off my goddamn balls to take you in." He wiped his forehead while looking out to the water and I continued to study his theatrical antics.

He looked back to me. "What proof does that *bit*—" he caught himself. With a calmer resolve he continued. "what evidence does she have? I'm a subscriber of hardcore evidence, son," he howled, resolute to his story.

I pulled out my *iPhone* and hit play to a recording where a now forty-six-year-old reformed Muslim was telling the story of how a young uniform strolling the beat in Brooklyn in eighty-six had a proposition for him. He described the officer to the "T." His citing of this officer arresting him twice prior to the murder being on his record made his story more influential. He mentioned things only Big D could know like my father's schedule for that day and what he'd be doing at that school—watching his son accept an academic award.

Once the recording was over, Big D stood frozen in his steps, unable to speak. So, I did it for him.

"You don't need to say anything at all because I got it from her. In light of recent discoveries, Daryl Harrison, our business and personal relationship is officially terminated. In the future you do not contact me directly. You will go through commercial channels. Our partners have been notified, only those who are directly affected by our former union. Whatever projected monies you have allotted to you will be rerouted. My reign is eclipsing according to previously said plans, so this cut out should not affect your pockets much at all. I've made you millions. You're good."

I could swear D aged at least fifteen years at the sight of the video, which confirmed Yazmine's story. See, if D had been given time to think of a way to deny his involvement this would have been far more difficult. He's a conniving fuck, and the trait was inherited by his daughter. I'd placed the phone back in my pocket and D was still motionless. I extended my hand to him to add to the sting.

"Detective Harrison, this has been a lucrative yet misleading partnership, but how can I bitch with what I'm sitting on," I meant it as a statement. Purely rhetorical.

"Divine, hold up...now hold up," he begged with a new posture and all.

I gestured with my face to say I was listening, but D had nothing to say.

"D, I'm a busy man. I've got to get up outta dodge." I turned to leave with my snipers in place.

"Divine, I need more time. I wasn't prepared for this," I heard D mumble as I strolled to my ride.

Fuck outta here.

love ∞ belvin

James Lombardi

"Goddamn!" I whispered as my digital camera powered off due to the battery dying. "Fuck me!" I yelped even louder. I had trailed Daryl Harrison to Santa Monica and for the first time I see him with this Azmir Jacobs fellow—*all for my fucking camera to die on me!* I was going to have to wait until I replaced the batteries to see if I got a single shot. I knew that mutherfucker was in bed with Jacobs! The problem was a picture would go a long way compared to my word alone.

I had to quickly decide if I wanted to continue to trail Harrison or follow Jacobs. I'd been following Harrison for over three weeks and today is the first time I'd been able to see him with Jacobs. I eventually decided to follow Jacobs and see where he lived or hung out.

About an hour later, I found myself in Long Beach at a recreation center. I guess the guy wanted to go workout. *So, he's a health conscious thug?* I sat in the car for five minutes before going inside to see where this mutherfucker had gone. I didn't want to blow my trail, so I needed to move.

As I entered the doors of the rather impressive facility, it appeared more of a upscale club than a recreation center. I idly wondered which of the major chains owned this place. Huge plasma screens met me at the door displaying news, health notes and games amping up the energy immediately. The walls were bright with chrome fixtures and the floors were wide and carpeted.

I was eventually met with a well-poised, young kid at the front desk.

"You look lost. Can I help you, sir?"

He seemed to have taken a stab at professionalism, so I entertained him. Plus, I began to notice how large the facility was and knew I couldn't just search around aimlessly for hours looking for Jacobs.

"Umm, yeah. I'm looking for a friend of mine. He came in minutes ago...tall, dark, wearing a gray tracksuit? Oh, and a low cut," I asked knowing I was taking a chance but hoping for the best. I'd seen at least a dozen people enter the building since pulling up.

"*Ahhhh*... No, sir. Don't know who you're talking about. That description would fit countless men in here." He peered at me with blank eyes.

"*Ummmm*... His name is Azmir. Last name Jacobs. He just checked in?" I asked desperately, sounding like a twat.

"Oh, Mr. Jacobs?" The kid's eyes grew in recognition. *Thank fuck!* "I just clocked in. I'm not sure if he's in today. I can call up to the admin offices to check." The young guy went to dial a number on the phone behind the counter. "What time is your appointment with him?"

An appointment? Why in the fuck would I need an appointment with— Then it dawned on me!

"I know him from a mutual friend. We get together and play ball every week. He recommended I come train with him at the place where he works, and I told him I'd swing by to check him out for myself. I tried catching up to him when I saw him walking in, but I guess I took too long to park. If you could just point me to the gym he trains in, I can go pop in on him."

My balls were sweating. I lied with the best of them, but adrenaline was pumping as I felt myself getting closer to Jacobs. I wanted to know more about this low life.

The kid at the front desk wrinkled his eyebrows as he lowered the phone. I didn't immediately know why, but I could easily discern I'd fucked up.

"Sir, you say you're looking for Mr. *Azmir* Jacobs?" his eyes set quizzically.

Fuck me!

"Yes, I can find my way back there if you point me the way," I tried to disarm him, fighting hard as hell to not apply my natural official's tone.

"Sir, you're going to need an appointment to see Mr. Jacobs. And I'm sorry, but I cannot let you past this point without verifying your membership." He stood, buffing out his chest.

The kid could be no more than five-nine. I could squash his little beetle ass if I wanted. He wasn't attempting to appear threatening, just authoritative. I guess that came along with the job. In all honesty, the little shit was polite and apparently witty. He saw the holes in my fucking story. I had to come up with something on the fly.

I'd be damned if I was going to let a petty job as a fitness manager come between me and getting to this worthless twat. I knew what would shake his pathetic ass. I was on the clock with Munick. He granted me an extension after my last deadline. *The stiff!* I knew he wouldn't extend his grace anymore. His retirement was nearing and who knows where that would lead me in terms of an assignment. I had to take my chance and it needed to be now.

"Do me a favor," I asked while pulling out my card and writing on the back of it. "Give this to Jacobs..." I handed him the card. "... along with this message: *'He doesn't want to fuck around with me,'* Got it?" I asked the young lad.

He never looked at the inscription on the back of my card. But damn it if I didn't see the spark in his eye when his suspicion of foul play was confirmed as I turned on my official's tone and scowl. His mouth hung open and he softly nodded his head as I pivoted and made my way out of the building.

It wasn't until I'd slammed the car door shut that it hit me.

Azmir Jacobs was more than a manager at this recreation center. The pisser was the fucking owner. I'd had his financial jacket on file but never familiarized myself with the details of his empire. I blew my opportunity at a face-to-face with Jacobs. I was outsmarted by a kid! Just when I was so close.

Motherfuck me!

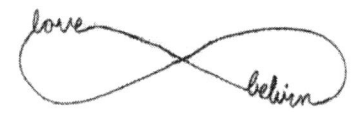

Rayna

We arrived at *JFK Airport* in New York City and immediately the energy changed from West Coast placidity to Empire State bustle. You had to appreciate the antithesis of the two. We claimed our luggage and located our driver from the car service Azmir arranged for us. We had muscle with us, and I had no idea why, but hadn't found the heart to ask. Azmir had been distant during our entire commute, not giving much away. I dismissed it as him coming down from an already long morning seeing we ascended into the friendly skies around noon.

We pulled up to *The Peninsula*. Talk about opulence. I was only familiar with this place because of my days interning for the practice. Mrs. Smith and Mrs. Katz would have me book rooms there for them and their families during Christmastime. This was extravagance at its best.

When we approached the front desk Azmir told the concierge, "Jacobs, A.D., check-in."

The young woman smiled politely and began typing into her computer. She couldn't stop sneaking glances at Azmir. He was tall and very commanding in stature. Even outside of his formal gear his beauty was breathtaking. I could have easily become offended, but I was used to it at this stage in the game.

I looked over to the handful of people who walked through the lavish European style lobby, I was curious about their socioeconomic statuses. Affluence didn't reserve an appearance. Speaking of which, I'd suddenly become conscious of my wardrobe. I wore a pair of blue cropped jeans, a white T-shirt and leopard *Diane Von Furstenberg* wedges courtesy of Azmir who forced me to shop at *The Grove* last week. I had no idea what made me so uncomfortable about him spending money on me, but it really did. I loved clothes, shoes, and accessories just as much as the next, but I didn't want to take from him more than I gave. Heck. I didn't get to buy his clothes. He had a personal shopper to do it.

The concierge's voice snapped me out of my withdrawn thoughts.

"Yes, Mr. Jacobs, I see we have a superior room and a deluxe suite reserved for you for the next three nights and four days."

I gasped—I thought quietly, but apparently too loudly because Azmir turned and gave me the most alarming gaze.

"Is there a problem, Ms. Brimm?"

I felt so reduced. I didn't know what to say. He turned completely around to me giving his back to the concierge.

Okay, there's a little privacy.

"Ummm... No. Ah—I'm just taking notice of the evidentiary superfluity of this place. Azmir, I have an idea of how much a standard room and a standard suite cost at this place. It's a pretty penny. I mean, is this all necessary?" I whispered feeling the confidence of a twelve-year-old.

The sexiest, libido-provoking grin flashed upon his gorgeous face, but it was also accompanied by a twinge of annoyance. I braced myself as he turned to the woman who looked perplexed behind the desk and demanded, "A moment, please," in all of his CEO authority. She quickly backed away from the counter as he turned his attention back to me.

"Ms. Brimm, have you any idea of how hard I work? Do you know how many hours I put into a single day's work?" He looked at me expectantly. If he wanted an answer, I was coming up short today because I had none.

"I work an average of nineteen hours a day. The first few years yielded very little returns but today my time and money work for me. I've been a millionaire since the age of twenty. Very few know, and I like it that way. My point is I'm paid. I like *'superfluity'*—no. I love it. I've earned it and now you'll have to adjust to it as well. I'm a large man and need space. Suites accommodate that. Also, I'm traveling with a woman I'd like to spoil with *'superfluity.'* That isn't a foreign concept."

Stunned and extremely flushed—somewhat turned on, I murmured, "Oh, I can understand but a suite at the local *Marriott* would've impressed me."

I was so uncomfortable with this discussion. And it was clear he was too, but even with all of the frustration in his face he kissed me softly on the forehead, turned back to motion to the concierge and approved the rooms.

A bellhop came to retrieve our luggage as we took the elevator up to our suite after dropping Marcus, our security, off on the floor of his room. The bellhop opened the door to the suite, and I was blown away at first sight. The entire place was immaculately decorated. *Yup.* Our suite with the wonderful Fifth Avenue and Fifty-fifth Street view.

As soon as we were inside Azmir headed straight to the

bedroom. I wasn't too far behind him as I silently appraised the suite. It was obvious he was less intrigued. By the time I entered the bedroom, he'd began emptying his pockets and asked, "Wanna drink? Cocktail?"

He looked so wound up. I knew my questioning him down in the lobby added to his foul mood. He'd been uneasy all day and I didn't understand why, Azmir was far from a moody individual. Around me he was usually so cool and affectionate even. I didn't like seeing him this way. Guilt started kicking me in the butt. I didn't want to ruin this trip for him. It was a big deal, as it should have been.

"*Ummmm...* Sure. Surprise me," I answered warmly and seductively.

I wanted to change the course I felt responsible for us charting. And ironically an amorous mood came upon me. I wanted intimacy to calm him and relax me. But Azmir wasn't on the same page as he quickly picked up the phone and discharged orders to the concierge.

He then turned to me, "Look out for them. Dinner reservation is in an hour."

He sauntered into the en suite bathroom and not before long, I heard the shower running. I exhaled. I didn't, until this moment, realize just how on edge I was about my setting him off. After being dazed for a few seconds staring at the bathroom door, I decided to get up and unpack my things.

I'd showered, brushed my hair up into a bun ponytail on top of my head, applied my makeup, and dressed. As I heard Azmir chewing someone out on the phone from the living room, I gave myself a final look over in the full-length mirror in the dressing area of the closet. *"Not too bad, Rayna,"* I cheered myself on. I had just hoped Azmir liked it. Going out with him was always eventful and I tried to look my best.

I wore a new figure fitting, white, mini dress falling a few inches above my knees with a pair of cheetah print calf hair strap *Givenchy* sandals. Azmir snuck these sandals on the floor of my side of the bed a couple of days before our trip. When I stepped out of bed, I hit the box. There was a note attached saying, *"To the best roommate ever."* Of course, he wasn't around for my reaction. I sent him a text saying thanks. It was really thoughtful. I found myself smiling in the mirror all over again recounting the event.

As I walked out into the living room, Azmir was looking out the window still on the phone. I noticed the fruit and cheese platter on the coffee table, and suddenly realized just how hungry I was and how I hadn't eaten much all day. I swiped a few grapes and blocks of cheese and began to stuff them into my mouth absent-mindedly when I heard him say, "Rob, I'll hit you in the morning. I've got to go," very abruptly.

With one eye raised, I turned to look at him, not immediately realizing I had my right hand to my mouth and my left hand pining my clutch to my pelvis. Azmir appeared jarred, causing my bewilderment. With a mouth full of cheese and grapes I grumbled, "Everything okay?"

He closed his eyes and quickly flashed them open again, only wider and muttered, "Yeah...yeah. You look...amazing, Ms. Brimm." Azmir's forehead wrinkled and then his eyebrows rose. "My words fail me."

I'd totally forgotten about my attire, distracted by the food. My heart was relieved. Why didn't I expect him to react well to my appearance?

"Oh...thanks," I managed as I tried clearing my mouth.

His deep gaze didn't break as he murmured, "Even with a mouth full you're out-of-this-world gorgeous."

Butterflies were released in my stomach and my carnal thoughts returned, but so did timidity. Azmir's compliments never grew old to me.

"Hungry?"

"*Mmmmm-hmmmm*," I replied, swiping the last of food from my palate with my tongue.

"Let's go before I change my mind and take you back to the bedroom for my dinner and dessert instead."

Please do! I begged in my head because I didn't have the heart to bring it out of my mouth.

Dinner was at *Le Bernardin* in Mid-Town Manhattan on West Fifty-First Street. After we were seated, the waiter came over to introduce himself and rearranged our table. He went over the menu and specials. His script was quite lengthy, but I didn't hear a word because out of nowhere, my eyes connected to and locked with Azmir's. It was most bizarre.

We started a gazing contest, and I felt such a stream of energy transmitting from him. He lost the contest when he flashed his panty snatching smirk my way. His teeth were so perfect, and his supple lips were proportioned to them so well.

Man, I could eat this man! He was gorgeous. I giggled nervously like a child.

I didn't realize the waiter was still there until Azmir shared, "I know you have a penchant for fish. This restaurant serves top notch seafood...the freshest."

"Oh," was all I could manage. That was considerate. I'd idly wondered if he'd made the reservation before or after my rude scolding of his hotel choice earlier. "Thanks, Azmir," I crooned giving a warm smile.

He gave a slight nod. "Would you like to start with Noir or Riesling?" Azmir knowing my favorite wines, never failed to warm me. Could this man look so good and be so attentive to my preferences at the same time?

"Pinot will be fine."

"A bottle of your finest Pinot Noir and a Grand Marnier martini," Azmir turned and requested of the waiter before he turned on his heels to fetch our dinks.

"So, when exactly do you meet with Yazmine Jacobs?" I attempted to initiate conversation.

"Sunday." His attention was fixated on the menu.

"Oh, okay." *Why did we arrive here on a Friday?* "Are you prepared?"

With a raised eyebrow he asked, "Prepared?"

"Yeah. Do you know what you want to ask her?"

With his eyebrows furrowed Azmir processed my words in deep thought. "I haven't considered what I'd asked. I just figured I'd let her speak...explain."

I snorted, "Well, what if her explanation doesn't meet your needs? Surely, you have things needing to be addressed to help you move on."

There was a brief pause as Azmir sat with his elbows pressed to the table, resting his chin on his knuckles bringing attention to his perfectly trimmed goatee.

"*Hmmmm...* Good point, Ms. Brimm," he murmured mostly to himself.

The waiter returned with our drinks and as he poured my wine he asked if we were ready to order. My eyes darted to Azmir who was looking at me, though his head was face down toward the menu. I hadn't explored the menu. Moments later his head shot up and he ordered bass for me and steak for himself and for appetizers, shrimp cocktail and mussels in red sauce. Azmir handed the menus back to the waiter and turned his attention back to me.

"If you had the opportunity, what would you ask your father?"

Whoa!

I wasn't expecting that question. "*Ummm...* I don't know. It's been so long since I've visited those thoughts of...my dad...my childhood."

"We have time now. Talk it out. It may inspire my questions for

Yazmine." Azmir bore no emotion before taking a swig of his martini and nodded in approval of it.

"*Hmmmm...* I know a good one. I'd ask if there was ever a time when he was enjoying himself—having a particularly great experience and wished to himself my mom, brother, sister, and I were there to share in that moment with him." My eyes went back to Azmir and saw him nodding his head while taking in my question.

"Okay," he muttered as he stroked his goatee.

He looked so delectable.

Focus, Rayna. Focus! I hissed to myself.

"And what else?" he asked as the waiter brought a large plate of mussels in red sauce and shrimp cocktail in a huge martini glass decorated attractively. I watched as the waiter paced away.

I examined Azmir's face to try to figure out where he was going with this line of questioning. But his eyes were fixated on me telling me he wanted more.

"*Uhhh...* I'd also ask if he ever came to check up on us from afar. What were his daily prayers concerning us if they existed at all." I shrugged.

"Mmm-hmm," he urged me to continue.

Ready to end my time under the spotlight I shot back, "And if he were given the opportunity where would he want to be placed in my life today...and if he'd desired to be in my tomorrow."

Azmir fed himself a mussel as he pondered my responses. "Interesting, Ms. Brimm. All very interesting," he muttered reflectively.

We continued our dinner, taking on lighter conversations. We started too deep. I couldn't gauge if he was still peeved with me or had gotten past it. While waiting for dessert Azmir extended his long arms and stretched out his neck in a big yawn.

"Excuse me," he offered softly. I took note of his heavy eyes. He was extremely handsome even exhausted.

"Tired?"

"Sapped. It's been a long forty-eight hours."

I was reminded how the night before, Azmir didn't get home until after four in the morning and we left for the airport at nine. One thing he was right about in his rebuking me earlier was him being a hardworking man. Azmir worked like a horse even if I didn't have total knowledge of his day-to-day affairs.

After dinner, we returned back to the suite. It was after twelve a.m. Eastern time and even I was being called by the Sandman. Once I came out of the bathroom from showering and removing my makeup, I saw Azmir wasn't in the bed. I walked out to the living room expecting to see him on a mergers call. I thought I'd have to muster the nerve to tell him to disconnect the line because I was in need of him.

The suite was pretty much quiet, only playing extraneous noises from things outside. I reached the living room to find Azmir's lengthy body facing the window, sprawled out on two single sofa chairs. One held his upper torso while the other supported his feet. He laid there with all but his shoes on. He was a beautiful sight to drink in.

Boy! The things I could do to you right now, Mr. Jacobs.

He looked vulnerable and welcoming, but most of all tired so I decided right away I wouldn't try anything with him. Feeling the urge to lay with him, I slowly crawled into his lap and planted my head on his chest. He smelled so good and was comfortably warm.

I exhaled deeply and basked in everything Azmir. I thought of how nice this was, being in the arms of someone who cared for me and wanted me with him. He seemed so peaceful and uncomplicated. If I was not mistaken, I could feel Azmir's bone protruding through his pants, poking my backside. My head shot up at him and stilled when I saw his serenely sleeping face.

If only you were awake. We could make good on that promise.

My thoughts drifted to all things consisting of him.

I woke up the next morning in bed. It took me a minute to realize where I was and how it was obvious Azmir had placed me in here. I opened my eyes to see I was facing the window and turned over to check on Azmir, only he was not there, though his tantalizing scent was. I rose from the bed and set out for the bathroom to find him, but to no avail. I heard him on the phone, business related no doubt. I could always tell by his tone and vernacular. He was in the living room.

"Peg, that's truly unacceptable of the water company. *Deer Park* has been vying for our business for years. You have full autonomy to terminate our relationship with them and move along to *DP*."

His tone was placating, and he looked over to me and rolled his eyes in annoyance of the conversation. Old Lady Peg can be a lot to handle...*I know*. I glanced over at the clock, and it read eleven thirteen. This man never rested.

He tossed me the breakfast menu. *Good*. I was starved. I looked over it...waffles, pancakes, French toast—*ahhhhh*...French toast!

After breakfast, he offered to take me out for a city stroll. How could I resist? I dressed in a white, off the shoulder, tunic kimono-styled dress with floral print and flat silver sandals. I drew my hair into a ponytail against my right shoulder and let my dangling hair rest upon my clavicle bone.

While looking myself over in the mirror my disappointment grew at the realization of Azmir not having touched me since we'd been on NYC soil. I was starved of his touch. Robbed of his fiery affection. Inwardly, I cursed myself for being so attached to this man and so soon—not that I had any frame of reference. But I didn't like the need I'd developed for him. This was so not like him, but I didn't have the nerve to address it and resolved to letting it blow over.

We hurried out of the suite with him barking instructions to someone on his *Blackberry*. He didn't get off until we arrived on Fifth Avenue where I took note of the various high-end stores. We walked past several of them until we got to *Rolex*. Azmir opened the door and held it for me to go inside, which I did.

An associate came over to greet us and Azmir asked about a specific watch. I wondered to myself if he had planned to purchase an icebreaker gift for Yazmine. I stood at an adjourning case admiring watches as they spoke.

"Ms. Brimm?" Azmir called over to me and I joined him.

I immediately noticed the sales associate baring a watch. Its beauty was breathtaking.

"This is...exquisite, Azmir. You sure have singular taste," I mustered, pondering if that was what he was getting her.

"Can you try it on?" he asked, looking at me inscrutably and I was suddenly confused. I looked over to the ever-smiling sales guy and felt embarrassed, so I reached out my arm for him to slide it on my wrist.

"Looks a little oversized but if you give me a moment I can size it for you," the sales associate offered and walked off to do so after Azmir nodded giving permission.

My eyes went back to Azmir who was gazing at me intently. He eventually mentioned casually, "Ms. Brimm, I thought it would be nice if we had matching timepieces. I get lots of compliments on mine and wanted to share the love."

I gasped as my eyes involuntarily widened. "Azmir, you don't have to do that." This was all truly unnecessary.

He exhaled loudly through his nostrils as he flexed his jaw. "It's simply a gesture of intimacy. It's really not that big of a deal."

I didn't mean to upset him. I just didn't get why he liked to spend his money on me. For crying out loud he'd already purchased several things for me last week alone. As much as I was conflicted in thought about this I was not trying to ruin the weekend, not this important one anyway. I'd just have to sit him down about it when we returned home.

He gave me a cold gape, one actually melting my heart.

Ohhhhhh, Azmir! Why must you be so difficult?

The sales guy called out. "Would you like this wrapped or would the lady like to don it today?"

Before Azmir could respond I yelled out, "I'd like to wear it." My forced smile never left Azmir. Azmir didn't return the smile, but his expression softened. We really need to get over this impasse. He paid for it, and we left for more sightseeing. No need to mention, there were no more purchases made.

We returned to the suite to rest and change. Still no touch or mere affection from Mr. Jacobs. I was so tense and emotionally wound up I withdrew from him just to protect myself.

With security in tow, we headed out for the night. After a scrumptious dinner, we attended a listening party in the *Meatpacking District* for an up-and-coming artist signed to one of the bigger record labels. There was a small crowd but lots of energy. We sat cocktail style in the room where there was informal seating and not enough for every guest. I could surmise it was by invite only because Azmir had to give his name, and have it verified by a list when we arrived.

The young male artist was a mix of R&B and country. The songs played and performed featured minimal effects from electronic instruments. His sound consisted mostly of guitar, drums, keyboard, organ, and a couple of live horns. It was eclectic but I enjoyed it. The artist, Ragee, spoke a lot about the sounds of the singles and inspiration behind the lyrics in between tracks. It was like being at an intimate concert.

Ragee sang a cut about being blissfully in love and not knowing why. The lyrics blended so well with the horns accompanying it. It struck a chord. At one point during the performance, I looked up and found Azmir's searing eyes. I didn't know why he was staring at me. Perhaps I swayed a little too hard? I didn't think I did. But then out of nowhere, he shifted closer to me and draped his arms around my waist as I was perched on a barstool. He bent down and softly kissed me behind my ear. That good ol' current flashed through my body. It was so powerful I had to steady myself by using his arm. I'd missed him so much. It was as if I'd been there in the Big Apple with an entirely different man.

It was a good moment. So good my heart had urged me to say

so much, but I lacked the gall to tell him how much I needed his balance and affection.

Perhaps later.

In the middle of my thought, a brown skinned, medium build guy with well-tailored clothing and noted jewelry approached Azmir.

"Divine!" he called out. The song had ended.

"Money Mike. What it do!"

"I'm surprised to see yo ass here. When the event coordinator mentioned your RSVP, I was like this dude ain't coming. He never shows!" Mike shouted in excitement while giving Azmir a manly hug and dap.

"I never RSVP and not show, man. You know that."

"True...true. Where you been? Niggas been tryna touch you for the West Coast love and ain't heard from you in damn near a year." Even with his sheer excitement and pleasant surprise of running into Azmir, Mike was cornering him.

"I've been grinding, man...switching up my shit."

"Yeah! I heard about your born day party a couple months back. I got my invite, but I had to prep my artists and shit for the *BET Awards*. My bad, man! I heard that shit was off the fuckin' chain. I ran into TyTy, and he told me Jay, Ye, Common, Mo, Black and all 'em niggas was there representing!" Mike screeched as he was amped up at the news.

Azmir's tone wasn't as spirited. He had his one arm wrapped around me and eventually slipped his other as well. *Talk about PDA.*

"Yeah, that shit was proper. My right hand, Petey Crack, went all out. Even threw in some surprises that still got me feeling blown away." He ended lowly and squeezed his arms around me as if he were speaking directly to me.

"Oh, Money M, this is a good friend of mine, Rayna Brimm. Ms. Brimm, this is Mike Brown. He's the top A&R from the label. I go back with this dude since grammar school. I remember you following Stacy Bronson home. Had her scared of your pissy ass and now look at you. You the man up in the industry now. Proud of you, duke," Azmir declared sincerely.

A face-splitting smile eclipsed Mike's face. "I appreciate that, Divine. Nice to meet you, lady." He gently flashed a generic flirtatious eye toward me. I only nodded because it was obvious he was not interested in meeting me. He was all up Azmir's butt.

"You've always had that buttah taste in the ladies, D. This one is really fly."

I didn't find that comment appropriate but somehow didn't feel the need to become offended because Mike struck me as heedless; I knew he wasn't attempting to be offensive.

"Really? I don't think I've ever come across anything as beautifully rare as Ms. Brimm," Azmir cleaned up though it was unnecessary. I knew this Money Mike character had put his foot in his mouth. His facial reaction to Azmir's remark confirmed it.

"Yup, you right, D! Y'all hitting up *Marqui* tonight. A lot of heads gonna be there. I heard it's off the damn chain right now. Jay and all 'em headed over there."

"Yeah. He's hit me up since I've been in town. Maybe we will roll through. The night's still young." Azmir peered my way for approval. I shrug my shoulders in agreement.

"But wait! Before y'all bounce I want you to meet Ragee, man." Mike turned and demanded a young female to go and grab Ragee right away and she quickly scurried off. Turning back to us he implored, "Yo, D, I really need all the help I can get with this one, man! The label is putting alotta dough behind him because I promised I could get people like you to push work."

While Mike pleaded, Azmir held an insusceptible face giving an occasional nod. My poor Azmir wasn't interested. He was getting hassled, and it didn't look good.

See, MirMir, this is why I don't like you buying me things. I don't want you to ever get the impression that I only value what you do for me materialistically. I wished I could explain this to him and soon.

"Yeah, man. I heard what you did for *RinRin*. That marketing plan was genius." Azmir's arms tightened around me again. He was uneasy.

"Money, man...my hands ain't been that deep in the industry in a minute. I'm in a different industry all together."

"Yeah, I heard that, D, man...but you still got radio connects in LA. I just need you to vouch for me. This why I want you to meet him, man."

And as if on cue, Ragee walked up on Mike and tapped him on the shoulder. When Mike turned over to him telling him who Azmir was, I whispered to Azmir, "I'm going to the ladies' room and when I return, I'll be ill and need to leave." I nodded slowly and he winked at me conspiratorially. I walked off just as Mike started his introductions.

I strolled over to the bartender and asked to be pointed to the restrooms, to which he did. *No line. Great!* I walked right in. I really didn't have to go and didn't want to leave Azmir out there too long but figured I'd excrete what I could, considering there would be more drinking and socializing after this gig. When I walked out of the stall, I washed my hands and refreshed my lipstick before returning to my tortured friend.

As I approached him, I noticed his eyes were already fastened to me. I employed my pouting face and began the show.

"Sweetheart, you don't look so good," Azmir consoled.

"No, I'm feeling a little nauseous. I need some air. I'm sorry to cut your time so short." I gave a convincing moue.

"A'ight, capo. That's my cue. Have your people call me. There are a couple of events coming up over there that you may wanna represent at," Azmir bode.

"A'ight, big homey! Don't forget about me, man. I can use this push," Mike pleaded as we headed out the door.

When we arrived at *Marqui*, man, was it star studded! We headed straight to VIP with our security behind us. I really didn't understand why we needed muscle. I didn't understand who was

Azmir that he was so acclaimed in the music industry. He's not an artist nor a musician. I knew his talents were boundless, but this really had me stumped.

What was even more fortuitous was the caliber of celebrity in the building. And I mean high roller entertainment figures! I was further blown away at how much love they showed Azmir. Several of them were at his birthday party a couple of months back.

All eyes were on us—mainly him. Azmir gripped my hand through every handshake, dap, and hug he gave. I was so relieved when he didn't attempt to introduce me. I was overwhelmed. I saw people on their *Blackberries* and others dancing.

To my left was a beautiful caramel complexioned woman who I swore licked her lips at me. My head swung to my right, and I walked up so close to Azmir my breasts touched his back. Other VIP patrons nodded and gave pleasant smiles to which I returned.

We sat on a plush leather sofa and were immediately offered *Ace of Spades*. Azmir took two and handed me a glass. I had no idea what *Ace of Spades* was but followed suit and sipped from it. *Delicious.*

"Are you okay?" Azmir asked while he thrummed the skin that was exposed in the cut-out portion of my dress. His eyes read contrite and whatever anxiety I was feeling had dissipated. I nodded my head, and he flashed his coochie creaming smile.

The night ran smoothly. The music was empirical and that was, of course, because we were in likely one of the hottest clubs in NYC.

People started filing in the VIP section and it was interesting to see the various fashions going on, some trends were novel, and others were on the more eclectic side, but all were vibrant. Mostly everyone spoke familiarly to Azmir including these two women with strong New York accents.

They both hugged and *oooh*'ed and *ahhhh*'ed at his presence, not in a flirtatious manner but a genuine platonic one instead. They sat next to me and spoke over me to Azmir. The one girl, Liz, had a short, tapered hair cut with spikes on top of her head. It was bold but she pulled it off well, probably because it seemed to have matched her personality. She was a shade above brown, nearly my complexion and her accessories dangled when she spoke.

"I can't believe my brother is here! I been tryna call you all week, yo! Oh, my gawd! I'm so gassed you're here!"

Liz eventually turned her attention to me as Azmir was waltzed into other conversations.

"So, you're the doctor, right?" Liz asked with a calming smile begging for me to lower my guards. I was intrigued as to how she knew about me. Azmir had never made mention of her.

"A physical therapist," I shouted over the music as she craned her neck into my personal space so she could hear me.

"Oh, right! I thought you guys are considered doctors."

"No. Lots of people confuse us. So, are you from The City?" I asked, trying to get to know her.

"Yeah, I grew up with Divine. Him and my brothers used to hang out as kids all the damn time. Even though he's moved around we've managed to stay tight."

"Oh, okay. Are your brothers here?" I wanted to make a connection. Azmir knew so many people but only had me around a select few.

"Nah. One lives out there in L.A. with Divine. The other one lives in Atlanta. They're all still close though."

He lived in L.A., and I hadn't met him? I knew she wasn't being literal when she said with Azmir. I wondered who he was.

Liz continued, "I was just out there for his birthday. He told me about you. I was happy as hell he got rid of that last girlfriend of his. She was a true bitch...not wanting him going anywhere without her but never wanting to be with his friends—"

Liz was interrupted by the friend who had walked in with her. I soon learned her name was Tionne. "Who y'all talking about?" Tionne screamed over the music as she stretched her body over Liz's lap to interject herself into our chat.

"Divine's last girlfriend. I couldn't stand that bitch. Remember when he brought her to the Garden for *Jay's* show? Ughhhhh?" Liz's thick New York accent could not be missed.

"Yooooo! That bitch was so stuck up," Tionne exclaimed and made sure to give me direct eye contact. "If you ain't a celebrity or in the industry she don't want nothing to do with you. I knew Divine wasn't happy. I was surprised it lasted as long as it did." She and Liz exchanged gazes proving solidarity. "I couldn't believe when I heard she cheated on him with that rapper. I can't front; I was happy as hell she wrote a check for him to dump her prissy ass!"

Liz shot Tionne an admonishing glance. Clearly, she'd spoken too much. My mouth dried. Azmir never told me about Tara cheating on him. I didn't know what to think.

"What? I'm sure she knew. She his new lady," Tionne spoke in a guilt-free tone.

Liz wasn't so confident. Immediately I broke a smile to ensure it was no big announcement. I wanted to know more.

"See!" Tionne sang. Liz's expression softened when I gave her a friendly nudge to further assure her. I don't know where the keen manipulation came from. No, I did—Azmir. He made me do and feel things I'd never cared to before him.

Liz's eyebrows lifted, "He wasn't even that dope of a dude to be tripping out on Divine for. But T is right. I was so fuckin' happy when she did that shit 'cause I knew he wouldn't stay with her after that."

Tionne's head shook enthused at Liz's thoughts. I couldn't believe *Tara cheated on Azmir!*

"Ain't she pregnant now?" Tionne asked.

Liz's protectiveness flared as her body jolted and she declared, "That is not Divine's baby! If it was, he would keep it one hundred and take care of his business. That bitch is lying her ass off!"

They both looked to me for contribution? A reaction?

Errrrr...

"Every dark secret has its day in the sun, right?" I squeezed out conspiratorially. I found myself in a giggling concert with the girls.

My thoughts went to what I'd just learned. Tara cheated on Azmir with an aspiring rapper? When was this? Most importantly was that the cause of Azmir's repellant attitude toward Brian Thompson? This definitely explains his jealous tendencies. But he didn't react that way when he learned I was at the industry party with Sebastian before he'd discovered the nature of our affairs. Could that have meant he'd developed feelings for me recently?

No—he's never said.

With the many questions causing the cogs of my mind to churn, I'd decided to put them to the side and get through this time in New York with Azmir. The bottom line was his affairs with Tara were just that—*his* affairs.

I entertained more chatter with Liz and Tionne for a while though no discoveries were as enlivened as the one about Azmir and Tara. They eventually made their way around the party and then left promising to keep in touch.

Sometime later, I was nestled in Azmir's back there on the sofa. His hearty laugh jolted me from my sleep. Azmir never laughs. *He chuckles.* I didn't want to disturb his seemingly fascinating conversation. So, I kept nuzzled into his chiseled back as he lay his hand against my folded leg laying against him, too. Much of my time listening was spent trying to decipher where I'd recognized his friend's voice from. It sounded familiar, but not in a personal sense. Their conversation was pretty generic, they were catching up. Azmir asked his friend about his latest business ventures and people from their past.

Somewhere in between my sleep and conscious state, I heard his friend say, "Serious, I see."

I felt Azmir's head pivot and assumed he gestured asking if his friend was referring to me. I didn't hear a confirmation.

"Seems like it. Could be over for me," Azmir replied.

"My nigga!" his friend cheered. "Old broad?"

"Forgotten," Azmir's tone was resolute.

"You handle that with ol' dude?"

"Wasn't worth my time. She wasn't about shit and had sealed her own fate before he entered in the picture."

"He was your saving grace." His friend gave a hearty, high pitched laugh—that familiar trill. That's when I placed the voice. It was the one opening my performance at Azmir's birthday party!

Is he and Azmir that close of acquaintances?

"Indeed." After a beat Azmir continued, "Let me get her in the bed."

"Oh, no doubt."

There was a little more mumbling going on before Azmir gently tapped me. "Brimm, baby. It's time to go."

Groggily, I rose with his help and ambled out of the club with his long arms cradling me into his side all the way to the car awaiting us outside. Before the driver could pull off, I was out, falling into slumber yet once again. The next thing I remembered was being lifted out of the car by Azmir, making his way into the hotel. As much as I wanted to tell him it wasn't necessary to carry me, I enjoyed being in his arms.

The elevator stopped on the fifth floor, letting our security detail off.

"You good, boss?"

"Yeah, man...eleven o'clock," Azmir murmured.

"A'ight, Divine."

At this time, I was pretty much awake but kept my sleepy eyes closed. I felt Azmir's cool breath on my face as he held me like a feather. My abdominal muscles tightened, and I involuntarily exhaled deeply. The next thing I felt was his lips next to mine, but he didn't kiss me. I opened my eyes to see what the holdup was and caught his wanting eyes drunken with desire looking down on me. He slowly blinked and when his eyes opened, he had applied a new coat of willpower. I moved my hand to the back of his head to initiate an embrace, but the sound of the elevator bell snapped me out of my trance. Azmir broke our gaze and carried me out of the elevator.

What!

Once inside he sat me on the bed and headed into the bathroom to draw a bath. He came back out to have me stand and helped me undress. He asked me to turn around and when I did, he unhooked and pulled the zipper of my dress down to the small of my back. I felt his gentle hands against my spine and my nerves went completely haywire.

How does this man have such an effect on me? He pulled the dress over my head and stepped back as I turned to face him. His eyes reflexively traveled down my body and in an instance, he turned on his heels.

"Finish undressing and come into the bathroom," he muttered while walking away.

What was that all about? I wondered to myself as I quickly doffed my bra and panties.

As I nervously walked into the bathroom, I challenged myself to just tell him I was in desperate need of him though deep down inside I knew Azmir was not only aware of my desires, but also had his. How he was able to abstain up until this point was beyond me.

He stood from kneeling over the tub as he watched me enter the bathroom. I noticed he was still dressed which meant he wouldn't be joining me. He took my hand to help me into the tub. I slowly descended trying to acclimate myself to the temperature of the water. Azmir grabbed the sponge and body wash and to my sensual surprise he washed me, something he typically did *after* a long and gratifying lovemaking session.

He didn't skip a beat as he started at my shoulders and took his time down my back, over to my belly, up my breasts and out to my arms. I barely but miraculously stifled my pending moans. He scooted himself down to the opposite side of the tub and lifted my leg out of the water so he could wash it from hip to ankle and repeated the same tantalizing torture on my other leg. Once he was done, he squeezed gel into his hand and rubbed them together into a lather before taking my foot and washing it. His strong hands felt unearthly licentious against my foot. *Azmir does foot rubs...and well!*

With his thumb he kneaded into the center of my foot over and over and over again. Every time he pushed with his thumb my pelvis jumped beneath the water. The alarming sensations running through my body tripled as I looked into his beautiful face. His expression was stoic as he was trying to gain mine. *Oh, no, Jacobs. I am not giving you the satisfaction of expressing my pleasure!* He moved to my other foot and delivered the same delightful sinuous treatment.

After he was done, he went over to the towel rack to grab a washcloth. He foamed it with soap before spreading my bent legs in the water and reaching down to wash my private area. He moved slowly and steadily, not ignoring my pearl. My poor pearl was so attentive and responsive to his touch *it* gave away my secret. Every time he swept against it through the washcloth, my pelvis jumped again. This time it couldn't be hidden. My body was coming alive, building itself in preparation for release. I closed my eyes as my mouth dropped agape. He rubbed against my sex over and over again applying mild pressure. In no time I was losing control.

All for Azmir to stop and mutter, "All done here. I'll let you get dressed and go to bed. I'm gonna hit the shower. I'm fucking exhausted." He sauntered out of the bathroom leaving me alone to wither in heat.

What? Was he serious? This has to be some type of joke!

Fuming, I rose from the tub in search of a towel. I dried off and went over to the vanity to wash my face. I was emotional and out of breath as I tried to hold back my looming tears. What was going on between us? *Should I confront him with concern or go ape on him completely?*

Confusion took over my mind and heart as I applied toothpaste to my toothbrush preparing to clean my teeth. I refused to cry, even if Azmir was now in the shower unable to see or hear my sobs.

I sauntered into the bedroom in search of my pajamas. Pulling the slip over my head, I let it fall down to my thighs and grabbed my phone from my clutch. *Goodness!* It was four fifteen in the morning. I crawled into bed weighed down from my bruised ego, throbbing clitoris and broken heart. The sheets felt so good against my now over-sensitized skin from the parching bath.

I heard the shower go off and minutes later Azmir was out of the bathroom. I kept my back to the bathroom so I couldn't see what he was doing. It really didn't matter because whatever it was, sex wasn't on his agenda—that much had been abundantly clear.

When he got into bed, he crawled over until his skin met mine. At this time repose had set in and I was fading fast. Per usual, Azmir buried his face into the back of my neck intensifying my randy state. In this moment, I could truly appreciate the phenomenon of my body and mind being at war. My mind was shutting down, but my body had its needs.

"Goodnight, baby. Thanks for hanging out with me tonight," Azmir whispered against my sensitive skin. After a sharp pull of air into his lungs he whispered, "You looked so luscious tonight...hell—all day."

My eyes shot up in the air!

Azmir

I'm inside of Rayna, plunging balls deep, relishing in her warmth moisture. She's pulling my face into hers and sucking my tongue out of my mouth while matching my thrusts from underneath me. Abruptly, she pauses and declares, "I love you so much, Azmir. This is where I want to be for the rest of my life...in your world. Always." I felt the buildup in my groin. I was preparing to explode, but then I heard a ringing sound in the background, annoying the hell out of me. It was loud and alarming. I mean *really* fucking loud, spoiling the moment.

"Azmir... Azmir, baby. It's the phone," I hear Rayna calling out. Why is she thinking about the damn phone at a time like this?

"Ignore it."

"No, it's late we have to get up."

"No. I'm not done yet."

I felt a jerk and it wasn't my pending orgasm. My eyes opened to daylight breaking through the curtains of the room. My arms and legs were draped around Rayna with my dick pinned dead-smack in the middle of her ass. My head swung up and I saw Rayna rubbing her sleepy eyes.

"Your phone is ringing, Jacobs. It's almost eleven."

I knew then I'd been dreaming.

Shit.

I jumped up and went for my phone. I saw two missed calls. One was from Tara and the other from Marcus, my security. I rung Marcus back, who was asking for a time check.

"We'll be ready to roll in forty minutes."

"Alright. I'll be in the lobby then. I'll call the driver to tell him the same, sir."

"Indeed."

Rayna scooted up on her arms in the bed asking, "We need to be ready in forty minutes?"

I took my time to answer, "Yes."

Even in my groggy state I knew my body was calling for a "Rayna relief." I had allowed my pride to lead my judgment since we'd arrived in New York and hadn't indulged with her. *In her.* I shut down on her somewhat, which is something I promised myself I wouldn't do in this relationship. I used to fuck with Tara's head a lot using that tactic. Now, I was lying in this comfy bed with my wood in my hand and my lady dragging herself into the bathroom, likely mad as hell at me for leaving her hanging these past few days.

Quickly, I decided I had to eat it. I was running late for a meeting with a woman whom I hadn't seen in damn near twenty years. My mother.

A little over an hour later, we were pulling up to a neighborhood favorite, *Momma D's Soulfood* restaurant in Brooklyn. I agreed to meet Yazmine here because it was a familiar place to both of us. Almost every trip home included a stop here to grub.

I spent a lot of my evenings here as a youngster when my mom would help Momma D with the cooking back during its first year or so of business. Mom would leave her full-time job and head straight to the restaurant to help free of charge. It was my parents' way of demonstrating helping our own to get ahead without expecting something in return. Momma D would sneak me her sweet cornbread every night and tell me to keep it between us. I had no doubt Ms. Brimm would enjoy it, too.

Once seated in the humbly scaled restaurant, I observed Rayna's body language. In worse terms this place is a step up from a hole in a wall, but she seemed relaxed yet aware of the modest eatery. The place can hold about twenty-five people. The thin gold picture frames displaying those considered patrons of importance were clearly outdated. Some of the leather chair pads were torn and the laminate floors were worn, but the food was sinfully delicious from aged recipes.

I watched as Rayna took it all in. She glanced at the dignitaries framed above our table as she sat her purse on the chair next to her. She wore cropped blue pants, a white blouse, and blue suede wedges. Her hair is up in a ponytail and her makeup was very modest. It was almost as if she knew what costume to wear today, this entire weekend for that matter. I liked her style.

"Momma D and my parents were good friends back when I was a kid. My mother put in crazy hours, free of charge, to help start up this place. She would waitress and cook, doing whatever needed to be done. I try to come here as often as possible to keep in touch. I wasn't surprised when my mother requested to meet here."

Her eyes widened in surprise. "You're meeting Yazmine here?"

I nodded, slightly amused by her apparent unease. She shifted in her seat. Momma D's yelping, "Azmir Divine! I remember when the doctors pulled you from your Momma's snatch and held you in the air. You was the biggest baby I ever saw and look at you now, living just as large!" woke me from my thoughts.

I could recite her greeting word for word. It never changed. She always came out of the kitchen to greet me with the same fervor. Momma D's smile was so big and bold, her eyes glistened with pride and joy. Rayna's eyes widened and danced, caught off guard by Momma D's gregariousness.

I stood as she smothered me in her gripping embrace. Her Jheri curls touched my chin as she was just a few inches shorter than me, an amazon of a woman.

"You look as splendid as ever. Who's been courting you? I see the glow," I teased.

Per usual Momma D ate it up, blushing from ear to ear waving me off. Her eyes traveled over to Rayna who was watching in amazement.

"Now who is this?" Momma D asked curtly. This was my first time bringing a woman to the restaurant.

Rayna looked tensed but maintained a gracious smile. Her beauty and poise never escaped me. I was grateful to have her there with me—for me during this monumental turn of events in my life. The last thing I wanted was her put off. She sat genteelly and demurely. I was suddenly caught up just looking at her.

"This here is Rayna Brimm, a valued friend. Ms. Brimm, this is the illustrious, Momma D."

Rayna stood and extended her hand to Momma D. It seemed like minutes had passed before Momma D budged, but Rayna didn't crack, she waited respectfully.

"Uhh-huhn. She ain't too tiny like them other Hollywood types. I see a lil meat on her," Momma D's tone was suspicious. She reluctantly reciprocated and greeted Rayna.

"Momma D, that's because I'm not from Hollywood. I'm from right across the bridge...Jersey," Rayna cajoled. "It's a pleasure to meet you. Azmir has had so many good things to say about you. I hear you're a woman about your business. I'm ready to throw down." She continued stroking Momma D's ego and with much success.

Momma D turned around to Ed, her younger brother, who followed her around like a shadow, and shouted, "Eddie, get this girl here a number four." She jerked her head back to Rayna who is now wearing an expression nothing short of confusion and asked, "You eat cheese on yo grits?"

Rayna slowly nodded and quickly informed, "...and eggs."

"Shit!" Momma D popped back in excitement. "Eddie, make that a number four wit' cheese all the way."

Rayna had won her over. Maybe this was a great idea after all. Momma D was special to me. She reminded me of happier times in my life. In fact, whenever I felt low about not having a family, I would occasionally pop up here around the holidays for comfort food. It was always *home* here. I made sure she met her expenses and when things cut close, I'd throw her a couple of bucks to stay afloat. She probably had no idea of my motive, but I knew why I valued her.

"Whatchu' gone have, baby?" she snapped at me.

"My usual, princess."

"Eddie, get Azmir Divine two sunny side up with blueberry cakes and beef bacon. Light on them eggs," she turned and shouted.

After taking our drink order, she excused herself. Momma D didn't wait tables unless someone of special interest was there, which wasn't every day. It was nice to be made felt special.

"She calls you by your full name," Rayna observed with a soft smile.

"Always has."

"It's nice to encounter people who *know* you."

I chuckled at the thought. Very few actually knew me. How badly I'd wished Rayna knew me. I often found myself living in fear of her knowing all there is to know about me. I wanted to protect her from my truths forever while I spoiled her with all the happiness she deserved.

Minutes later our food came out. Rayna appraised her catfish, grits and eggs with cheese. My blueberry pancakes were on point as always. The sated feeling I got from devouring them never got old. Rayna, to my surprise, cleared her plate.

"Someone was hungry," I teased.

"Someone has to impress Momma D. I know you caught her sizing me up," Rayna shot back.

"I'm the only one around here sizing you up. And I so happen to know you taste better than the food once on that clean plate in front of you."

She gasped as I heard Momma D yell out, "Yeah, Yazzy, he over there finishing up his food. Go on!"

I turned and looked behind me to find my mother sauntering over to our table. I rose from my chair and turned toward her. She looked exactly how I remembered her, only aged. She was just a few pounds heavier, but her posture was now lax. She now had a fixed defeated scowl on her face. She wore a velour sweat suit and black classic Reebok sneakers. I couldn't believe she still wore a gold nose ring and her head covering. Her expression initially was phlegmatic but the closer she got the more her face fell into a dark emotion. My heart trembled in my chest. My knees quaked.

By the time she reached me, tears were flowing from her eyes and her mouth hung open to release hard sobs. She stopped inches before me and wept from the grounds of her belly. It took me some time to raise my weighty arms to hold her. As my arms ascended, I felt a gentle touch on my back, oddly, willing me strength to comfort her. I knew it was Rayna. I didn't have to see her with my eyes. I had become that familiar with her touch. Though I didn't know until this moment she possessed so much strength.

I had held my mother for what seemed like an eternity. Momma D brought over a glass of water and Rayna handed Yazmine a few napkins to help with her tears and mucous. We must have gained attraction because out of nowhere, I heard Momma D telling her customers to look the other way, nothing bad was going on there.

Yazmine eventually found the rhythm to her breathing and broke our embrace.

"Perhaps we should go someplace more private," I suggested.

"You guys can have my office in the back," Momma D suggested.

By this time, Rayna was giving me short comforting strokes on my back.

"Nah, that's alright, beloved. We good here. Im'ma calm down," Yazmine assured while wiping her face as she turned to sit.

"Im'ma get y'all some coffee. Just sit and relax," Momma D commanded.

Suddenly, I felt soft tugs at the hem of my T-shirt. I turned to see Rayna with a look of strong regard.

"Azmir, I'm going to have the driver take me back to the hotel. Marcus can stay here with you, and I'll be fine alone there," she whispered. Her eyes shifted with concern, and I knew she was pleading with me.

I wasn't expecting that. "Are you sure?"

As the words left my mouth, common sense hit. Yazmine and I would likely discuss sensitive matters concerning Big D and our business, which shouldn't be done in front of Rayna.

I didn't want distance from Rayna. I'd grown that dependent on her energy. My manners kicked in amongst the myriad of emotions that I was experiencing.

"Before you leave, let me introduce you," I whispered before I turned to Yazmine. "This is a friend of mine, Rayna. Rayna, meet my mother, Yazmine Jacobs."

Rayna's brown round eyes slowly left mine and traveled over to my mother's with a polite smile in tow. She appeared discomposed.

"Hi, beloved," Yazmine greeted. She looked up at me and asked, "Is she your girlfriend?"

"Nice to meet you, Mrs. Jacobs. The resemblance is amazing," Rayna abruptly greeted, not giving me an opportunity to answer, as they shook hands. Suddenly, I'd wished we were in a perfect world and Rayna knew every detail of my life, eliminating the need for her to leave. I wanted her next to me.

"She's beautiful, Mir!" Yazmine beamed.

Damn. Do I know.

Coincidentally, my mother knew Rayna and I shared an intimate relationship. This shit was crazy. I was feeling emotions so unfamiliar to me, and I didn't know the protocol. I had my Earth, whom I hadn't seen since I was sixteen years old, here before me. Then I had this frustrating woman who suddenly showed more substance, support and grace than I thought she was capable of and thought I'd ever need in my corner at such a vital time. It was something to behold.

"Thanks," I responded to Yazmine as my gaze was pinned to Rayna who begged me through her eyes not to fight her on this.

I turned to face Rayna, as an act of privacy, "Okay. But if you need anything just pick up the phone," I heeded.

"Agreed. Go have your moment," she bade before leaving me alone with Yazmine.

I turned to watch Rayna's gait out of the restaurant. On her way out she paid rave reviews to Momma D on her culinary talents and told her she had hoped to be back soon. My chest squeezed as she hit the door and walked out to the car. Rayna frustrated me like none other, but the lowliness I felt from watching her leave me at this critical time scared the shit out of me. It spoke things I could no longer deny or defer to time. Time had caught up, and I could no longer refute the fact of her owning my heart. Suddenly, I had desperately wanted her to be in my destiny as well.

Fuck!

"Just a friend?"

I turned to find my mother's dubious eyes on me. I knew it was fucked up for me to give Rayna a nondescript title, especially with the feelings I'd just uncovered. I glanced over to Yazmine and offered a slight smile, embarrassed by my nonchalant introduction.

"Friends don't have you standing here watching her like you debatin' if you want to be without her for the next few hours, beloved. Only love do," Yazmine muttered before she sipped her water.

She's right. How could I have missed it all this time? *I don't get this shit.*

I watched the car pull off before resuming my seat now across from my mother, telling myself as soon as I returned to L.A., I would do some hard thinking about this thing with Rayna.

"It's good to see you."

Yazmine nodded very humbly. "It's good to be seen by my only child."

I could tell she was choking back a cry. Time had lapsed without either one of us knowing what to say. I still hadn't dealt with what having my mother back in my life actually meant. I mean, I didn't think she'd been dead all these years, but the truth of the matter was I didn't know. At some point in life, I put my need of her and the questions I had about her hasty departure from my life somewhere in the recesses of my mind. I'd been so focused on building an empire I didn't consider what I didn't have. I made it my mission to obtain those things I *could* control like money, power, and prestige.

I didn't need people for emotional purposes, just for functional ones, which is why Rayna had my head fucked up. *How could my mother service my needs?* This is the question I asked when vetting people for my life—to enter into my realm.

"Have you had her long?" Yazmine broke our silence.

My eyebrows met my forehead when I realized *that* was a question with a simple answer. Rayna wasn't that simple, but the answer to how long she's been in my world was.

"No. Just a few months."

Her eyes closed in pain and her forehead wrinkled in disgrace. I didn't understand—what had I said wrong?

"Who's been in your corner? Daryl's wife?" Yazmine sounded desperate.

As I pondered her question, I shook my head. I immediately understood what she was trying to gauge, who was serving in a maternal capacity in her absence. But my answer brought revelation even to me in the wake of my response to Rayna's leaving the restaurant just a few minutes ago.

My eyes flickered as I murmured, "No. No one."

Patricia was extremely nice to me and always met me with a soft hand, but I'd always felt it was because she wanted me for her daughter. Her motivation was for her daughter's future and lifestyle, not for my benefit.

"Allah as my witness, Mir, if there was something I could do I would've. There wasn't a day in there I didn't think about you or miss you. I swear it to you," she pleaded.

On a deep exhale and with raised hands I muttered, "It's okay."

Immediately, I felt that was an inappropriate and inadequate response. My mother was apologizing for her extended absence and begging me to accept how she'd missed me, and I spoke to her in the same tone used with my assistants. I didn't mean to be formal in my response but couldn't find any other way to express my forgiveness of the situation.

"I've had a very fortunate life. Once I got my head around not having parents, I learned how to survive without. I am a blessed man." I implored with my eyes as they bore into hers. "I just don't want to quickly get us into a place where you feel you have a debt to pay to me. I'm sure your conscious is loaded with far more pressing things. As it turns out, you were set up and put in a situation where you were separated from me. We know this. Now we spend this time agreeing what we move on to."

Yazmine's tears began to spring again. I didn't think I was being too forceful.

"I know, baby. You're right. I'm glad you forgive me. Now I need to forgive myself for getting so caught up back then and putting us in a situation where you had to live a life without me and here, I've been breathing all this time." She sobbed.

It really was okay. I'm sure I could recall when things weren't okay right after she disappeared, but today I was okay. I've seen and accomplished more financially at the age of eighteen than most men do in their entire lives. I've worked hard and long and probably at the expense of having those core relationships, but I have no regrets. Though, I now fear mistakes moving forward. More specifically, I feared mishandling this thing with Rayna.

On the one hand, I wanted her more than I wanted every penny

I had. I craved her. Adored her. Worshipped her. But on the other hand, I didn't want to fuck up what we were building by giving it a generic title of "girlfriend" or "love." I'd done that shit in the past and neither of them worked. What I felt for Rayna went beyond what I could give a name to. It was more than what my heart had ever held. The shit felt so good it hurt.

"I hate that man just as much as I do the devil," Yazmine hissed, snatching me from my trance.

I chuckled. "Let's talk about Daryl Harrison and how you'd like to see him dealt with," I suggested in an attempt to properly navigate this meeting. Yazmine's eyes darkened, filled with contempt. We spent the next few hours discussing things we *could* control and not braising in regrets.

I rushed into the suite in search of her. I'm not sure why I acted as if she wouldn't be found there. It was where she agreed to be until I returned. She was right in the living room packing up my paperwork. As I turned the corner off the foyer, I halted in my strides. I took a minute to adjust my eyes to her beauty. I stood there just staring at her.

"Ummmm...when I realized you'd be late I thought to start packing. We leave so early in the morning," Rayna offered up nervously.

She wore the hotel's plush robe and her hair in a high ponytail. My eyes were fastened to her as if she was my lodestar.

Continuing her anxious gaping, she asked, "Did all go well?"

I exhaled and gave a calm nod.

"Did she answer all of your questions?"

I gave another nod.

"Are you feeling satisfied having spoken to her?"

I nodded, this time more emphatically.

"Well, what's the matter, baby?" she asked with grave concern in her tone.

I shot my chin towards her.

"Me?"

I swallowed, "I've been neglectful...a little malicious even."

She inhaled deeply and her eyes fluttered in relief. She caught the reference immediately. "You...you haven't touched me in days."

I launched at her with remorse twisting in my chest. I needed to make things right. Grabbing her, I swung her around, gently pulling her head to the side as I nibbled on her neck and across her clavicle. I felt her shiver against me as I untied her robe with her back still against my chest.

"I thought there was someone else," Rayna blurted out breathlessly. How ridiculous a thought.

I pulled the robe down until it hit the floor exposing her bra and underwear, pink lace. With soft and wet lips in tow, I gently scraped my teeth down her back and unhooked her bra. Her breathing grew uncontrolled, further twisting my guilt.

As I removed her bra and clasped her breasts, I whispered directly in her ear, "I'm sorry. I've been so upset, feeling I'm not good enough for you in spite of my hard work over the years to build an empire. You can't penalize me for having money," my voice was rasped as I was making a plea.

She reached back and grabbed my wood, catching me off guard. She was in need. I was ready to deliver. I turned her over to face me, picked her up to spread her on the desk where I removed her panties. Pulling them up to my face, I inhaled her personal fragrance and grew further aroused. Rayna was overcome by my passion as her eyes slanted naturally. I pulled her face into mine and kissed her ferociously. I placed my index finger inside of her trying to test her waters. I moaned at the touch of her moisture.

She was so ready, causing me to insert a second finger as we were still intertwined in an oral embrace.

With her arm she hooked my head and shoulders, forcing me into her. I pulled back to lower my head down to her full breasts, softly pulling her nipples into my mouth. *Shit. She tastes so good.* Rayna thrust her pelvis into my hand as I continued plugging my fingers in and out of her, around and around.

"Ah!" she yelped sharply. I felt her stiffening around me and withdrew my fingers. When I pulled away from her grasp, she looked up at me confused and wanting.

"You've missed me?" I needed to know and would soon learn how much.

"Yes," she breathed as I unbuckled my pants, slowly freeing my cock. I stroked it, teasing her and she was taken. Her eyes shot down to him as she lustfully licked her lips.

"Wanna taste him?" I asked while stroking him long.

"Ummm-hmmm," Rayna cried as she nodded.

"Maybe later. Right now, I want to unwind you."

I placed the head plus a few more inches of my cock inside her, circling around and around. She relinquished immediately, collapsing her torso onto the desk. Her soft pants turned into loud groans, as I teased her relentlessly.

"Azmir, stop...I can't take it!" she cried.

When she could no longer endure, she quickly wrapped her legs around my hips attempting to push me into her, only it didn't work. I slipped my index finger in her mouth and as if on cue she sucked it, moaning loudly. After some time, I withdrew my wet finger and flickered it on her nipple driving her crazy.

"Azmir, I can't..." she screamed.

"You ready?" I goaded.

"Yes, please!"

That's when I pushed myself all the way into her before slightly pulling back and grinding. I pushed in again...pulled back, twisting my hips. Pushed in and quickly pulled back, and on my fourth thrust she came violently beneath me succumbing to a torrential orgasm. Rayna's body jerked so harshly I had to slow my plunges to be sure she was okay. Once I was able to resume, I felt the first tingle in my balls and in no time, I followed suit taking off into space.

She reached up to grab me as my body was calming, hugging me so close and tight. I knew there was meaning behind it. I wasn't done with her. I needed more of her to make up for my haphazard attitude. So, I lifted her from the desk and carried her into the changing room portion of the closet bypassing the bedroom. I'd thought of having her in there the day before and this was my chance.

In the closet, I let her down onto the floor and had her face the mirror. She looked a little confused, but she was certainly ready for whatever I had to bring. I stood behind her as we were both on our knees facing the mirror. She stiffened at the sight of her image.

"You're so beautiful, you must know this," I muttered as I scraped my teeth over her left earlobe. Her breathing hiked when I grabbed her breasts massaging them firmly. Her mouth became slightly ajar, but her eyes closed.

"As resplendent as you are, how could I in my right mind lay with another? Where can I go to get something this delicious other than from you?"

My left hand made its way to her valley to stroke her clitoris. She swayed her hips from side to side.

"*Mmmmmm...*" she moaned in agonizing pleasure.

"I'm going to pivot you, but I want you to watch. Okay?"

Rayna nodded her head anxiously as her soft body slightly trembled against me.

I nudged her to turn to her left and bent her over, then entered her slowly.

"Damn, Brimm. You're so tight. I love this," I whispered through clenched teeth.

I could see her in the mirror trying to focus her eyes. It turned me on watching her, watching us. Her mouth was wide open, and her brows narrowed. She was inebriated in lechery, just the way I liked her. Rayna was subdued and, in moments, confirming I could devote my life to this woman if she'd just let me into her heart the way she did her body. She was vulnerable and in need of me and in times like this I knew I could take her places. She could balance me —if she'd just trust me. As I peered at her in the mirror, I wondered what was going through her mind.

Her breasts were clapping to their own rhythm adding to the erotica. I was trying to maintain my composure, so I didn't explode too soon. I kept my stride in plunging, pleading with her to let me into her heart while locking eyes with her in the mirror. Rayna must have sensed my efforts. She muffled her moans as her mask flipped and suddenly, she was enduring and ironclad to survive my attempt at breaking the walls to her heart. I needed her, couldn't get enough of her, and wouldn't allow her to get away if she begged me to. There was a force of wills happening, a battle I refused to lose and would pledge my life to conquering her. All of her.

I saw her face soften in the mirror. I increased forceful speed as I pounded into her. Her eyes glazed and collapsed.

"Open!" I shouted just as forcefully.

Her heavy lids flew open, and her eyes fastened to mine through the mirror. I took her at the shoulders and deepened my thrusts. Balls deep and she took all of me. My soldier. I felt the sweat beads form over my entire body as every last muscle worked together to bring her pleasure. In no time I felt her tightening around my cock. I immediately grabbed her breasts, pulling and pinching her tauten nipples. Rayna started to cry out as she melted all around me.

Explosive.

"Open your eyes! Look!" I commanded.

She did as she continued to scream, "*Oooh!*"

In as many times I'd seen Rayna orgasm she seemed to be on

another planet this evening, furthering my remorse for holding back on her, but making clear of the battle I'd just won at getting one step closer to her eternity. This experience slapped me with the revelation I shouldn't play games with someone who I realized I wanted around for more than a long time. I wanted her forever.

"I'm so sorry, baby," I declared as I released inside of her, filling her with my seeds.

I collapsed on her back in complete exhaustion, and she took us down for a gentle landing on the floor the way only she could skillfully do. I rolled us over gripping her in my chest, wanting to remain inside of her, never letting her go. We lay there until our heartbeats stabilized.

As Rayna showered, I took the liberty of ordering dinner in the room. I didn't want to go out. It was close to eight and I was feeling a bit exhausted and wanted to end the trip quietly.

At the table eating dinner, Rayna asked, "So?"

"So, what?" I asked as I took in a piece of broiled lobster. By the ardent flicker in her eyes, I could tell she was going somewhere with her question but wasn't exactly sure where.

"How did it go with you and Yazmine?"

Ahhhh... I sat up in my seat a little surprised by her rare interest.

"Well, I believe...as you know, things started out quite emotionally and it took some time to get her to calm down but when she did, she was extremely apologetic. Most of the details behind her disappearance were discussed previously, and I didn't want to rehash it. But she seemed so..." I was at a loss for words.

"Fragmented...bewildered...galled?"

I was blown away by her accuracy. I put my glass of wine down. It was as if she could read my mind.

"Yes. Precisely."

She looked as if she was battling something internally. How did she know?

"My uncle did a seven-year bid when I was eight. He was so

vibrant and charismatic. He would play with us kids for hours on in. I'd never forgotten him; he was that cemented into my heart. When he came home, he was so withdrawn and timid. It has never set well with me."

Her tone was somber. Rarely did Rayna discuss her past. I wanted to ask more to clear up the mystery of her but felt in my gut it wouldn't have been a good move. So I continued talking in hopes of her feeling comfortable enough to reciprocate eventually.

"Yeah, she seemed so lost and unsure of herself."

"Where is she living?" Rayna asked with a hint of concern in her voice.

"With a family friend. She's working at Momma D's restaurant for pennies. I have to think of what to do to help."

She slowly reached her arm across the table to caress my hand. "We'll think of something."

"It's not that I can't hook her up, but it's just that my life..." my voice trailed off.

"No... I know." Rayna shook her head softly and sympathetic to my undertone. "You have to think of a way to include her. Throwing money at her isn't the best solution. She must be carefully integrated if this has a shot at working."

Rayna was on point more than she knew. That was exactly what I was feeling, along with the fact of keeping my mother away from my street life as well. She was, after all, being monitored by the FEDs and I needed my distance from her for that reason alone. *Speaking of throwing money...*

"Rayna, I... I'm sorry for my...reclusive behavior this weekend."

Her eyes shot up to me like a child in need of affirmation from its parent. *Fuck!* It confirmed my actions affected her. But I felt she had some level of culpability there as well.

"It's just that when you...flout me for spending money, it makes me feel rejected and I'm not good enough. Hell, I now know how defeated a broke man feels when he can't approach a high maintenance woman or one who out earns him. I just want to make you happy, and more often than I prefer, I feel I'm not the man for the job."

She looked confused across the dining room table with the now cold surf and turf between us.

"Azmir, you're more than good enough," she muttered just above a whisper in a *"don't-go-there"* manner as her eyes met the table. She seemed so torn. After a beat, she nervously scratched her eyebrows while her gaze was fixed on the table.

"There was this girl back at home...older than me—Corinne. And Corinne was sought out by the flyest dope boy in the game. He had the money green Beamer and the fattest gold rope with matching teeth. Whenever he pulled up into the projects his sound system would announce his arrival, and everyone would be looking down from their terraces or coming from around the building to check him out." I saw a hint of a smile on her flawless and makeup free face.

"Well, he had his eyes set on Corinne, a quiet, polite...beautiful young girl. It took him months to win her over. He'd buy her every color of the Classic *Reeboks*, the latest *Jordan's*, the gold-plated necklaces and bamboo earrings with her name inscribed—you know...hooked her up!" Rayna exclaimed with a bellyful chuckle. I had to laugh myself at the visual.

"Her parents moved south and of course, Corinne wasn't leaving him. So, she stayed behind, and he got her an apartment in the same building as me and we all saw when the sleek money green leather sofas were delivered and when she pulled up in her red baby Beamer matching his. They were living the life! Every girl wanted to be Corinne back then. She was the hood princess. But he got knocked a couple of months after Corinne got her apartment. It wasn't that long before we saw the repo man come get the car and management evicted her because she had no means of maintaining her lifestyle without ol' boy." Rayna took a long swig of her wine before continuing.

"She had to stay with people until her parents could afford to send for her." She snapped out of herself and muttered, "Anyway, a far-reaching story, but it has a lot to do with why I said I never wanted to become so dependent on a man I couldn't function on my own in his absence. So, a man with money wasn't in my dreams...*if* I had dreams of love." A frown darkened her face.

Was she saying she had no hopes of a relationship?

She snorted, "Or a drug dealer."

Oh, fuck! I froze in my chair. Although her revelations didn't derive from my life it felt like a warning shot.

"Azmir, you look horrified. No...no! With us it's a little different. I have my own, but I...I just don't want you to assume the role in my life as a provider. I can fend for myself. You've gone far above mere material things in my life. You've...you've made me look at myself and want to be a better Rayna. Shoot..." She snorted as her eyes were still south of her face, "...you talk about not being good enough—it seems like since I've met you, I've been able to identify all things that are wrong...broken in me."

At this moment, she was beautifully broken, and I didn't want her to wallow in this on my account. Silence coursed between us for some time. Eventually, I decided I couldn't bear it anymore. I reached over the table and began moving dishes to either side of the two lit candles in the center. I started with my side, worked my way to the center serving dishes and then I reached her side. She eyed my every move inquiringly.

I rose from my chair and walked around to her. Her mouth hung open in surprise and confusion. When I arrived at her, I stood her up by taking her hand, lowered myself to her racing eyes, and cupped her face as I gazed into them, got lost in them. Even in her bewilderment she was gorgeous. I moved my head to hers and tasted her lips. Her soft lips taste of tangy *Riesling*. She let out a groan. I felt her hands grab the wings of my back as I tipped her head back to kiss her neck. She smelled of citrus.

I yanked on the belt of her robe causing it to fall and the coat itself slightly opened. Grabbing her by the waist, I lifted her onto the dining room table, carefully placing her in the path I'd created just moments earlier, in between the candles. I turned on my heel to turn off all the lights in the room before returning to Rayna.

She lay there with her legs propped up and frontal view exposed from the robe splayed out on the table. I stood before her, piercing down at her hungrily. Her panting and relaxed eyes told me she was exactly where I liked her; mild-tempered and wanting. I reached over to the consignments display on the buffet table along the wall and grabbed a packet of honey. When I mounted the table with my legs astride her, I opened it and poured small amounts on her turgid nipples, carefully making sure not to leave a messy trace from one to the other. Hovering down over her, yet with my weight pressed into the table and not touching her, I flickered my tongue over her left nipple, stirring the drop of honey over her areola. She squirmed and let out a long throaty groan.

"You have to be still for this to work," I ordered.

She stilled. And then I went back to the same breast and licked the honey off. My lapping eventually turned into sucking and pulling of her nipples.

"*Ahhh!*" she cried out while thrusting her pelvis up to me.

I looked up and hissed, "You're not cooperating, sweetheart."

Once her left nipple was honey-free, I moved on to her right breast issuing the same treatment. Her mouth was agape, and her eyes closed as she hummed through her nostrils. Rayna assumed more self-control this time around.

"Good girl," I affirmed as I poured a drop of honey into her private crevices and scooted off the table. "I don't need to add too much honey to this. It's sweet as it is...no good for my teeth."

I dipped my head and went in. I knew Rayna was ready to explode so I let her. After eight seconds of me twirling my tongue around her clit, she convulsed into my face, grabbing my shoulders, neck then head.

"Uuuuh, Azmir!" she sang out almost incoherently.

When I knew she was too sensitive to touch, I inserted my

fingers below into her wet folds providing her body a reprieve and softly blew onto her button. Seconds later, I went back for more sensual torture. Licking, flicking, and twirling my tongue viscously on her clit.

"No...no. I can't. Wait!" she begged, trying to push me away at my shoulders.

"Trust me, baby girl," I calmly urged her in a whisper.

I loved performing cunnilingus. It comes as close to puppeteering as anything else. I enjoyed watching a woman, especially one as guarded as Rayna, become undone under my ministrations. This was one act guarantying her submission to me. Sex did as well but there were times when she wanted to take lead. This is the one thing she couldn't. I also was aware of the fact that I knew of things that would bring pleasure to her body that she was unaware of. I knew secrets of her chambers that were completely unknown to her. I could almost countdown to her next orgasm.

5-4-3-2...

"*Uhhh! Uhhh! Uhhh!*" she screamed like a mad woman.

My tongue retreated inside her walls and flapped rapidly, but for less a period of time and went back up to her clitoris.

"No! I can't Azmir! My body can't...handle. Another. One," she protested under libidinous siege.

"Okay...last one," I whispered as I grabbed her breasts and began stretching her hardened nipples. And in seconds her hips started swinging in the air and her hands squeezed into my deltoid muscles. Her breathing stopped and her ass collapsed back on the table. She was done.

"*Holy...holy...Shhh...!*" she blurted out with ragged breathing.

I gave her some time to gather her bearings, resting my head on her thigh. I could have played on her body a little longer but knew she was overwhelmed. Suddenly, I felt things inside causing my chest to tighten. I couldn't articulate what I was experiencing but knew it was associated with panic because I was falling deeper and deeper for a woman who wouldn't let me in completely. I wanted to love her hopelessly. Possess her totally.

After some time when I noticed her breathing had slowed, I whispered, "Okay?"

"Yeah," she breathed.

I helped her up from the table and when she was on her feet, I took to her eyes and murmured, "If you didn't see it with your own eyes, hear it with your own ears, or feel it with your own clit, don't make assumptions."

I turned to walk off to the bathroom, but not before I caught her mouth hitting the floor. Not sure if she caught the double entendre. I was referencing her ability to have multiple orgasms consecutively *and* her story about the young girl and the drug dealer. I needed a moment to settle my feelings from the story she'd shared. I needed to calm the sharp pains I felt in my chest from the amount of emotions quickly collected for this flighty woman.

The next morning, we were seated in the first-class lounge. I had to initiate a few e-mails to settle my staff until I was able to return to the rec and *Cobalt*. I was a tad bit tired yet renewed from the connection I believed I'd made with my mother. The prospect of having her around was invigorating. I knew some would have believed I needed time on a psychologist's couch behind these latest developments, but I would have abstained. I knew I'd only have to take it one day at a time.

"Hey, you," Rayna nudged me. She was all smiles and giddiness.

"Hey yourself, young lady."

"You're always working. When do you catch a break?"

"*Hmmmmm*... Let's see." I went to embrace her. "Ah! When I'm inside of you. Nothing else seems to matter."

She batted her eyes, clearly physically affected by my admission. "You shouldn't say that in public places," she whispered.

"Don't challenge me," I winked.

"You're nasty."

"You like it," I quipped.

With a heavy blush she turned her head away. I chuckled to myself.

When she returned, she shared, "I was thinking last night, maybe Yazmine could stay at my place. You know...until she gets on her feet."

"Really? I wouldn't want to put you out. I have a few rental properties and can have my assistant look into vacancies—"

She interrupted, "You do?"

I gave a firm nod. "I have real-estate properties...a few here and there." Then it hit me in my rambling state, I muttered, "I even have one in Manhattan and another in Jersey, but those I contract out to corporations for their transient executive staff. So that wouldn't work."

Hmmmm...

"Oh." Rayna's eyes danced with the speed of the cogs of her brain churning.

Shit. She freezes at the talk of my money.

Feeling the need to shift the mood I offered, "I think that'll be a good idea."

"Really? You don't have to feel obligated. I just thought you'd at least know she's safe, and who wouldn't like being by the water. But I didn't know you had rental properties..." her voice trailed off.

"No. I like the idea. It's more personal staying at your place rather than some random apartment. I'm sure she'd view it as being closer to me."

"Okay. It's totally up to you." Rayna looked down at her phone and I noticed the narrowing of her eyebrows.

"Hey... What's wrong?"

"Oh..." She turned back to me, realizing I'd caught on to her internal processing. "You remember the group Pastor Edmondson suggested I join to help me connect with others in the church?"

"Yes," I nodded.

"I've been going for a few weeks now and people volunteer their homes to host. I was asked to host and last week I declined but now I'm feeling like I don't have my *"get out of jail"* pass any more. The coordinator is asking again if we could do it at my place."

"I think that would be cool. Why the apprehension?" I knew she wasn't feeling the idea. Rayna wasn't the most outgoing person. She had no friends.

"You know I'm a very private person. And this is a church group."

"And?"

"And? We're living in sin," she muttered embarrassingly.

"Does your pastor know we live together?"

"Yes, I've told him."

"Then if you've gotten past that fact with him—the leader—no one else matters." I didn't want her dwelling on shit possibly coming between us. Who cared about us living together? We were living in the fucking twenty-first century.

"I know but, I don't want to subject myself, or what we have, to church folk prattle. Besides, at the end of the day, it's your place, and I've noticed that you never have people over. I wouldn't want to impose."

"Rayna, it is just as much your home as it is mine. I haven't had company because I work dog hours. Aside from that, when you're there, I don't need anyone else."

She looked at me as if I had two heads. This woman is a damn walking jigsaw.

"Look...have it at the crib. If it turns out you're not feeling them, don't invite them again."

As she gazed into the distance she agreed by uttering, "Yeah. You're right. Okay."

Problem solved.

CHAPTER 9

Azmir

The sound of my cell phone ringing continuously woke me out of a deep sleep. After being in a daze for a minute or two, I decided to answer. Half asleep, I didn't think to look at the number.

"I've been trying to get you all week. Where in the hell have you been? Do you think it's a good idea to continue with ignoring me? Your daughter had another round of shots a couple of days ago. It would have been nice for you to have come. Whatever's going on between you and me has nothing to do with Azina. I can't believe how selfish you've been over the past two weeks since she's been here. You bastard!" Tara spewed.

To say I wasn't expecting this call would be an understatement. Her voice traveled so far, Rayna, who was to the left of me, began shifting beneath the covers and turning over, toward me in the bed to figure out where the noise was coming from. She removed her hair from her sleepy face and tried to focus in on the source of the sound. *I have to get this chick off the phone before a problem occurs.* I'd barely recovered from their previous encounter.

"Are you still there?" Tara yelled.

"Listen, it is too damn early in the morning for this shit," I returned, not exactly aware of the time.

"Too damn early? It's ten in the damn morning!" she shouted. "Where the hell have you been?"

I didn't realize it was so late. Being away only one weekend had my body totally off. I had gotten adjusted that quickly to the time zone. I was really fucked up in the head this particular morning. Either way, I didn't want to hear this bullshit. Tara was getting out of hand with this baby shit! And this was a bad time to come at me with this with Rayna right here.

"Azmir!"

"You got one more time to yell in my ear and you're gonna be talking to a damn ghost!" I gritted through a clenched jaw. "Did you sign the paperwork for the test? I thought I made it clear there will be nothing going on until that's done."

"Are you on that bullshit again, Azmir? Are you really going to subject this little girl to all that probing just to find out something your pride won't allow you to admit? Yes, I've made mistakes, but I know who the father of my child is. Please don't continue to disrespect me!" she demanded.

"Again, until that's taken care of don't have any expectations of me. And another thing. Don't call me again until it's done. Are we clear?"

"Azmir..." Tara cried.

"*ARE WE CLEAR?*" I shouted furiously. I had to bring it back in because this conversation was lasting longer than I needed it to and I knew Rayna was going to follow up with her concerns about it. I didn't need this bullshit.

There was silence at the other end. I took it to mean she understood this conversation was over. In a much calmer, yet firm tone I advised, "Fill out the papers and we'll be in touch from there."

I disconnected our call then took a deep breath to prepare myself for what was coming. But Rayna was silent. I laid back on my pillow, brushed my face in exasperation with my hands and exhaled. She slowly got out of bed and walked towards the bathroom door.

"Where you going?" I asked with fury because I knew what was coming.

She was closing up on me. I can honestly say I prefer for her to bitch and scream because at least I knew where her head was and, most importantly, her heart. When she gave me the silent treatment, I got confused and insecure as a motherfucker!

"Work," was her one word answer.

I knew it was just an excuse. We were both exhausted and had only slept a few hours. I mean, we didn't have plans to spend time together once we returned and even, I had a little running around to do but I knew this abrupt exodus was because of Tara's call. I could have addressed the issue, but I was too damn tired to explain for the millionth time Tara was just dragging out our breakup. Hell, she'd been almost a year into this denial thing. Tara was either psycho or knew what she was doing, which was fucking with me!

I had a lot of shit on my plate. Business was plentiful and therefore stressful as hell; Tara was dragging her feet with the fucking DNA test so I could get her the hell out of my life forever or have my legal team help me to co-parent without the drama from her, and I'd been uncovering Big D's fraudulence. If the baby turned out to be mine, I don't know if Rayna could fly with it. I could ask her to but couldn't force her. That would be some shit I would have to eat.

I had to brush the shit off and get up my damn self. Big D had been pushing me to meet with him since our discoveries at the Santa Monica Pier. He'd called several times and left messages. He said I didn't allow him the opportunity to speak about the "incident" and we should. I told him I would meet with him today before leaving for New York.

I had done a great job at pushing the magnitude of his betrayal to the back of my mind. The truth be told, I was deeply wounded and dazed by it. I had vivid memories of my dad being a devoted husband, loving father, and an overall generous man to all those he came into contact with. I'd always been at peace with his absence because of Big D's paternal guidance. And to think the only man who I'd looked to as a father murdered my biological father. Big D might not have pulled the trigger, but the deed was done under his orders. He hadn't stop there; he set my mother up on drug charges, had her sent to prison for damn near twenty years, effectively separating us. All of this and he'd never made any mention of it.

This man was beyond insane. He was depraved.

Rayna

My night to host the women's Bible study had arrived. The women started trickling in just after seven in the evening; there were seven of them in all and I was nervous. I was not accustomed to having people over to my place and to make matters more nerve-wracking was having them over to the place I now shared with Azmir. We'd managed to have little to no visitors up to this point.

I knew the evening would be somewhat difficult for me, but I pushed through the challenge. I asked Chef Boyd to prepare a light spread he put his foot into and upheld his moxie. He prepared delicious finger foods, salads, and desserts I would've never thought of. It was truly impressive. I used the dining room table to set a beautiful display of his culinary artistry. Azmir informed me he'd be playing ball this evening and likely wouldn't be home until well into the night. I didn't hear much from him all afternoon or evening but chalked it up to him being busy.

LaWanda, our women's Bible study group leader, facilitated the session as usual and picked up where we had left off the previous week on the nine fruits of the Spirit. According to the Bible, there are nine fruits we are to challenge ourselves to take on in order to live full godly lives. I found this particular series to be quite interesting. Pastor Edmondson had been teaching it during his Sunday morning sermons and had arranged with the various subgroups of the church to take it on in their sessions in order to personalize it.

Holy Deliverance Tabernacle Church was fairly large, making intimacy among the parishioners somewhat limited. So, they came up with the idea of small groups to encourage fellowship. This women's group was comprised of about thirty women or more. Not one time had all the members shown to a meeting I'd been to. I had no idea why Pastor Edmondson recommended this group to me. Other than all of us being women, I wasn't sure what we had in common. Much of it was because I'd never gotten to know them enough to ask about their personal lives.

LaWanda picked up her phone from the coffee table to peek at the time. "It's time for us to start wrapping up, but before we close with prayer, I want to summarize tonight's lesson: the fourth fruit of the spirit—peace. When Jesus left for heaven He said, I leave with you, my peace. I believe He said this to remind us that trouble would be a part of our journey. It's inevitable; think about our current economy, the divorce rate, the statistics of incarceration and re-admittance into prisons, terrorist attacks, and the list goes on and on. He knew there'd be trouble and therefore left a helper, which is the spirit of peace. This fruit, like the other eight, is a supernatural phenomenon capable of presenting itself when we were troubled.

"Keep in mind we have to *choose* it. The Word tells us to put on the fruits, which means we have to decide we want to employ them. In this case, if you need peace you must decide to call upon it. When there is trouble in your life or things worrying or concerning you, you must decide you won't worry or waste in anxiety over it. Instead, you're going to call on the spirit of peace. It's a choice, and one you must declare and actively pursue. I will leave you with second Thessalonians, chapter three, and verse sixteen. *"Now may the Lord of peace Himself give you peace always in every way. The Lord be with you all."* Let's bow our heads in prayer...."

She closed in prayer. After we uttered *Amen* in unison, the ladies gathered back in the dining room where several of them packed food to go. I couldn't blame them and was quite grateful none of it went to waste. Boyd had really outdone himself. Before I had realized it, we somehow had gathered in the kitchen and started chatting.

"Whew! Everything was good tonight...the food and the Word! I'm sorry I have to get home to my Jimmy and those three rough boys of mine. Rayna, this is a nice place you have here. We should come every week!" Tanya stretched out her arms and shrieked.

Now, I knew Tanya was married to an automobile repairman and had children because she often spoke about how overwhelmed she was with it all. I liked her and thought she was sweet and easygoing. She often shared her struggles, most of the time causing me to shiver at the details of her life because she seemed to put up with so much. They struggled financially though her husband worked like a dog, and she stayed home with her youngest children.

"You always running out of here to those boys and that husband of yours. You should relax and hang out a bit. Me and Lisa going to that jazz club over in Hawthorne. It's a nice place to meet people," Rhonda announced. She was always on the prowl for a man. And I didn't know why she even suggested that to Tanya.

"Girl, I am married. I ain't got no business hanging out in no club with a whole bunch of single people! I got too much stuff to do at home," Tanya protested.

"You don't have to be looking for a man because you at a jazz club. It ain't like you at a dance club. It's nice and mellow," Rhonda rolled her eyes, clearly affronted.

"Well, I'm willing to go! I'm tired of looking at the same men Sunday after Wednesday after Sunday after Wednesday. I was so happy when we started these groups! I would rather look at a whole bunch of women than look at the same men in that church!" Lisa growled causing us to burst out in laughter.

She was extremely petite, having to be no more than five feet and a hundred and ten pounds, wearing turquoise fitted jeans with a paisley shirt to match. She kept the same hairstyle, a bun in the back with a blunt cut bang. Lisa had a permanent scowl etched into her face. Rarely did I see her smile, but she was very outspoken. "I'm serious! Name one man in that church that's single and desirable."

Trying to muzzle her laughter, LaWanda defended, "There are several eligible bachelors in *Holy Deliverance Tabernacle Church*. You have Mark that plays the keys—" All the women blew air from their faces or made some type of noise with their mouths in disagreement. "Okay. Paul the deacon and Greg the usher." The ladies went up in roar.

"Yeah, right!" one yelled.

"Come again?" another demanded.

"Is she serious? Paul picks his boogers during service and Greg flirts with everybody that he ushers to a pew!" Yolanda screamed.

LaWanda, wanting to belly over in laughter, waved her finger in the air instead. "Y'all women gotta stop being so picky! God can be calling Deacon Paul to you, and you worried about something as petty as his booger picking habit instead."

I liked LaWanda. She was beautiful with her almond complexion and bouncy natural afro, layered at least nine inches out. She was tall and slim and always wore oversized clothing. Her style resembled a hippy. LaWanda always seemed to be leveled and focused. She initiated this particular group. In one of our previous meetings, she mentioned her degree in Political Science, and she'd been pursuing a graduate degree in Public Administration. I could see her gathering and leading people to the promise land with her passion. I kind of envied her confidence and initiative. She'd been consistently warm and friendly. I'd heard from Yolanda's rants one week how she was seeing the bass player from the church.

"No! I'm not picky just because I'm not desperate enough to take on just any man flicking his eye at me! Shoot. It's hard being single, but I got me a mechanical device to pass the time," Karmen blurted out with the roll of her eyes while she rested her elbows on the marble countertop of the island we'd all retreated to. The kitchen was divided with half silence and half hi-fiving her. I was a neutral party and watched.

"Now, Karm, you know any sex outside of marriage is a sin, right?" LaWanda admonished. I guess she felt the need to be responsible since she was the group leader.

Holy crap! Time to get everybody out of here!

"That ain't sex. It's call self-preservation until God sends my Boaz!" Trina declared. There was another round of laughter in the room, and I went to one of the cabinets to grab small plastic bags for them to carry their containers in.

"No. Penetration or stimulation period should only happen in marriage, Karmen. You sat at the First Lady's conference this spring when she spoke about the conduct of the Christian woman. She shared a huge part of your faith is abstaining until God sends you a man. You know this," LaWanda calmly scolded.

"Well, I got faith and while I'm fighting it, Im'ma keep my rabbit charged and ready!" Rhonda huffed surly. Again, an uproar of opinions erupted.

"There are many of us who are fully abstaining. Abstinence is extremely difficult, but we can overcome anything through faith." LaWanda fought. I dropped the salad serving bowl in the sink trying to rinse it for the dishwasher. It was loud and somehow quieted the room.

"Rayna, you're always quiet during these talks. I know you're a medical professional and I can see by this expansive pad you got here you're doing well. I also know you're not married. What can you share with these women who are clearly divided on how a single woman of God should keep herself busy until she finds a man? You seem to have your head on straight and Pastor Edmondson speaks highly of you. Please share." LaWanda's big brown eyes implored.

In slow motion, all heads flung in my direction awaiting a response. My heart fell into my stomach, and I felt an anxiety attack coming on. *I knew this wasn't a good idea! I swear, I'll never host a Bible study again.* I felt cool air invading my mouth, telling me it was open and wide.

"*Errrrr... Errrrr...*I really don't know."

Rayna, surely you can come better than that! "Ummmm... Everyone's walk is different. I'm no better than anyone in this room. We all have needs and desires, but we're all on individual and singular journeys. Who am I to say?" I smiled sheepishly, hoping no one could detect my embarrassment and the riddle in my answer.

"Well, are you dating?" Lisa demanded with the twirling of her head and crossed arms.

Crap! Crap! Crap! No, not me...get the spotlight off of me!

"Ummmmm...dating? Maybe not. I—" I was cut off by the ever boisterous Rhonda.

"Everybody wants to know do you have a boyfriend, sleeping with somebody's man, gay...what? You be so quiet we don't know much about you. Now we see your sharp place that can fit a hundred elephants and...well, *inquiring minds wanna know!*" Rhonda's eyes were big and almost scary. I gazed around the oversized rectangular island to see all eyes searing me, including LaWanda's!

Really?

I was not about to sit there and talk to virtual strangers about my personal life. Wasn't it enough that I'd invited them over? They wanted me to draw blood, too!

I don't think so!

"I do have a...friend, yes. I'm sorry, I'm a little reserved and don't mean to be standoffish. I've always been a private person." I supplied the softest smile I could employ.

"Well, is it serious?" Sheila, the schoolteacher who was just as quiet in these groups as I had been, had the nerve to ask me. How dare she! I didn't probe into her personal affairs. This led me to wonder if they'd discussed me previously in my absence.

"What he do? Does he make good money like you?" Ronda blurted out.

"Or is he intimidated by all of this?" Lisa gestured with her hands referring to the lush apartment. "Because you know they can't handle it when we make more than them! *Humpf!*"

"Yeah!" a few of the women agreed, not giving me a minute to think.

"Whew," I verbally sighed to make them aware of my uncomfortable state. "Errrr...yes, I believe it's serious. He has his own career and has no need to be intimidated by my measly salary," I spoke slowly, trying desperately not to offend anyone, yet let down my guard a quarter of an inch to dispel their opinion of my quietness.

Thankfully LaWanda caught the hint. "Guys, that's enough. I feel like we're interrogating Rayna, and we shouldn't. She's our sister in Christ. She invited us here to fellowship and if we want to be invited back, we should show a little class and not badger her." With an added wink she instructed, "Let's give Rayna a round of applause for this awesome place and delicious spread!" LaWanda sounded as if she had led the charge of troops. They all fell in line and clapped. I thought it was unnecessary and quivered on the inside at the attention.

I just want to shower and sink into bed calling this a wrap!

Minutes later, after everyone had taken as much food as they could pile into the containers I thought to buy, we were in the foyer discussing who would host next week. No one quickly volunteered, but LaWanda, and reluctantly.

"Ladies, if no one offers up their place we'll be forced to meet at the church losing the intimacies of a home setting. So far four people have hosted and last I checked there were more than four people in this group." LaWanda scolded in her cool and non-offensive way.

I quietly handed out parting gifts, the book *"The Power of a Praying Woman"* by Stormie Omartian. I had read it a few weeks back and thought it would be nice to share with the group. I tied a pink ribbon around each book and stuck a pen beneath the bow giving it a classy spin. The women *ooooh'ed* and *ahhhhh'ed* affirming my efforts.

"We can do it again here next week," Tanya suggested in jest... or was it?

Just in case it wasn't I spoke up, "Sorry, next week wouldn't work well here. I'm having work done." This was slightly true, just not in that timeframe. Next week, the lighting was being re-wired but that was on Monday.

"Come on, guys!" LaWanda implored.

"Oh, alright! We can do it at my place," Rhonda sulked. I sighed in relief. "It ain't near as fancy as this one level mansion and I have cats, but if we need a place, we can do it there. And don't think Im'ma have food and gifts like we had tonight because I can't afford all of this!"

I knew no one typically served food or gave out favors for attending, but I also knew no one stayed in this area and all traveled considerably far so I thought to extend my hospitality.

LaWanda exhaled, "Cool. Do me a favor and text me your address and I'll send it out to everyone in the group by—" her words were halted by the opening of the door, and we watched Azmir's gait as he strolled in on the phone.

My surprise *and horror* didn't allow me to catch much of his conversation, but I did hear, "I'm home now and about to go into my office to take a look at the numbers. They have to come better than that. This is a seventeen million dollar deal we have on the table."

The silence in the room made me want to crawl into a hole and never return. The group of women were all standing at attention of Azmir's tall frame wearing a light gray suit with a white shirt unbuttoned at the top. He had his gym bag strapped to his shoulder and his phone glued to his ear. He exuded all things alpha male in a place where estrogen dominated, making him prey.

He looked up and stopped in his tracks with wide eyes, but didn't jump like I thought he would, instead he played cool and flashed his charming smile. I was all too familiar with that smile. It's the one that made your vajayjay cry in need. His face registered embarrassment once he realized what he'd walked in on. And all you heard was a chorus of gasps and appraisals.

"Jesus!"

"Oh, my gawd!"

"Who is...?"

"*Mmmmmm!*"

"Is *that* her man?"

"Oooooh!"

"Rich, I gotta go," he ended his call and surveyed the vestibule. His eyes landed on me apologetically. "Hey," he managed.

"Hey!" I stated in an overtly contrived manner, waving my hand with a faux smile.

"Hello, ladies," Azmir beamed, trying to lessen the awkward moment.

"*Hiiiiiiii!*" the chorus sang in unison—*this time.*

I couldn't believe there was an ounce of unity in this group, *but of course it would be for a man.* I discovered Azmir's natural comfort of being in front of strangers. His response was graceful, and it seemed he was doing a bit of harmless flirting to soften the blow of my pending punishment for him coming in during the session. He unleashed his infamous coochie-creaming smile. I wondered if it was done purposely or just a common facial expression having lecherous effects on all women. It was uncanny witnessing the reactions of the women knowing he'd had the same influence over me.

"I'm sorry. I didn't mean to interrupt you. I thought you'd be done," Azmir was still addressing the crowd. I had a leading suspicion he'd forgotten about them coming over.

The choir broke into sections. "No, it's okay."

"You're no bother."

"We were just leaving...?" LaWanda prompted him for a name.

Azmir paused, looking at me to gauge my lead. I was still in shock and had nothing to offer. His six-feet four-inch frame stood at the foot of wolves ready to devour him. Heck—even I was a little turned on by his presence after being in a room with a bunch of women for the past three hours or so. His beauty was really a sight to behold, even after coming from playing ball.

"I'm Azmir," he replied to LaWanda with his gaze fixed on me, still trying to read me. "I'm happy you guys came and trust you were able to share and impart a little knowledge on each other." His eyes then ran across the crowd giving them individual attention and genuineness.

"Oh, yeah! We had a *really* good time!" Lisa's buoyancy was on full blast. *Wipe your mouth, girl! You're drooling.* A few other women echoed her sentiments, at least those who were able to speak and had come down from their lustful discovery.

Azmir's gaze rested on me. I guess he picked up my alarm. "Well, I'll leave you to it. Have a wonderful evening and safe travels home, ladies." He turned and headed down the corridor to his office.

"Bye!" They all seemed to sing in concert with just a few stragglers.

Mortal shock coursed through me at their audacity to watch him amble down the corridor and into his office. Thank goodness he didn't proceed to the bedroom, which was at the far end of the hallway, prolonging their gaping.

"Ummm-hmmm!" I coughed in an attempt to call their attention away from my man and back to their pending departure. "Ladies, it's late and I know some of you have to travel further than others." I shot LaWanda a look hoping she could help reel them back in. It took a minute for her to snap into action as she was fighting *her* good fight of faith, trying to crawl out of her bed of immoral thoughts, which clearly included Azmir as well.

"Oh! Yes, ladies, where were we?" LaWanda was a little disoriented.

"We were just about to ask is that your man or your gay roommate because if he's your roommate, I can stay and lay hands on him to set him straight," Rhonda bellowed.

"Rayna, you living in sin?" Lisa asked.

"Wouldn't *you* if you could do it with *that*?" Sheila challenged.

"How tall is he?" Tanya asked.

"Oooh, did you hear the business he was talking on the phone? He was talking millions! What he do for a living, girl?" Karmen chimed in.

"All I'm asking is does he have a brother?" Trina asked.

All I could do was shake my head in disbelief. They somehow all quieted down to give me the opportunity to respond like earlier in the kitchen and I was nice *then*, but *now* I had to be a little more forceful.

"Ladies, this has been a wonderful meeting. LaWanda, you were great this evening. As usual, I've learned quite a few things I can use and take on my journey with me. Now, I'm going to have to say goodnight." I smiled but with a convincing enough tone informing they had to go without learning another detail of my life.

"Oh, okay. Okay! I don't want to not be invited again. I can take a hint," Rhonda hissed as she began collecting the bags she'd managed to drop on the floor when Azmir came in.

The others more or so repeated her expressions and filed out. LaWanda and Tanya slipped me their numbers offering up their friendship. I couldn't fight the accusation of their motives conjuring in my mind. After seeing them out and locking the door, I returned to the kitchen, drowning in exhaustion, to finish cleaning up. I knew Azmir relied totally upon his cleaning staff to tidy up this place, but I hadn't become accustomed to it and wasn't sure if I wanted to ever be.

While washing, sweeping, and organizing the trash, I began to reflect on the lesson and attempted to apply the principles of the spirit of peace to my personal life. I quickly thought of several ways in which I didn't actively pursue peace and how I could improve upon it. My thoughts were so deep and engaged that before I realized it, I had the living room, dining room, and kitchen back in place and spotless.

After turning off the lights, I sauntered back to the master suite feeling comatose. As I passed Azmir's office door, I saw it was almost closed and I was too tired to stop in, so I kept my stride to the back. I was beyond thrilled it was Friday, and I didn't have to get up so early the next morning.

While in the shower I mentally rolodex my plans for the following day. I had planned to meet up with Chanell at the mall. She was trying to put together an outfit for Kid's birthday party in Vegas next week and wanted to hang out, so I told her I'd tag along before my dance class. I dried off in the mirror, taking note of my pink eyes. I really needed to get some rest. I could swear I looked at least ten years older from being so tired.

I saw a white undershirt Azmir must have tossed onto the bench recently, and I couldn't resist. I grabbed it, held it up to my face and filled my lungs with the delicious fragrance of Azmir. Per usual, it was laced with his natural body oils, fabric softener and cologne—altogether a heady concoction. I had a not so hygienic inclination to wear Azmir's worn undershirts. They were comfortable, sensual, and well fragrant. Whenever he was due to leave town, I found myself collecting enough for the duration of his time away to keep me feeling near to him in his absence. Tonight was one of those nights he was home, but I couldn't resist.

When I walked out into the bedroom, I found Azmir sitting on the coffee table in the sitting room poring over papers and watching the plasma television hanging on the wall above the fireplace. He was shirtless in only his basketball shorts and black ankle socks, no doubt partly engaged in his sports channels. He ran several channels at a time on one screen. I didn't understand how he could concentrate on more than one at a time. As I walked over to him, he smiled with knitted eyebrows.

"What are you wearing?"

I ran my hands over the front of the T-shirt, slightly embarrassed. "You."

"I don't get it," he murmured when I reached down to peck his soft lips quickly and wetly.

"I have a nasty habit of wearing your used tees." I smiled, mildly embarrassed.

"Habit? This is news to me." He still looked confused. I plopped down on the couch to the side of him stretching my legs on the coffee table, right behind him.

"That's because I usually do it when you're away."

"Why tonight? And *why* the tees? What type of predilection is that?" he chuckled before diverting his eyes back to the television, hearing something beckoning his attention.

I waited patiently for his attention to return to me. And when it did he offered, "I'm sorry. I thought I'd just heard something that would defy all sports ethics," he shook his head slightly, brushing off the thought and then turned his body to me. "Well...?"

"Well...it's arousing for one." I giggled pathetically. He chuckled in response. "And...I don't know...it makes me feel closer to you."

"Un-huhn..." He was bemused but entertained me.

"It brings me peace..."

"Peace?" he squawked sarcastically with eyes wide, and mouth opened.

"Yes, silly. It's one of the nine fruits of the spirit. We're learning about them and tonight we discussed peace. God left us with the spirit of peace to comfort us in our times of need. Tonight we discussed peace is a state of the mind and heart you choose...something that has to be deliberate during hard times or inconvenient circumstances. Since the girls left, I've been *meditating* on it trying to see ways I can implement peace into my everyday life."

"And wearing my T-shirt—deliciously by the way—brings about peace? I should sell them in a bottle," he teased all throatily.

"It brings a bit of peace to me, yes, but there's something else I should decide on, too," I added. He reached for the remote and muted the television, giving me his full attention.

"Okay...?" he spoke nervously.

"No. No bad news. These are all positive changes I am undergoing to repair myself, Azmir," I tried to calm him.

"*Hmmmm*... Okay." His face softened. "Well, what is it?"

"Well, here's the thing...one of the biggest points of contention in our...friendship is the money spending thing...on me. The superfluity. You like to lavish me with considerably expensive things, and for some reason it makes me uncomfortable. We've fought over this on numerous occasions, and you've been adamant about wanting to do nice deeds for me and to take care of me. I still don't think I need to be cared for in that manner, but I don't want to change you no more than I can stand for you to change me. I'm not used to all of this...your wealth and eagerness to tend to me. I've never had it, but clearly it's here—smack-dap in my face, all six feet four inches of it which can't be ignored." I transitioned it to a joke to lighten the moment.

"I'm pretty sure he's longer and stronger than four inches." Azmir flashed a roguish smile I couldn't begrudge.

I gasped, "Azmir!" though unable to hide my shameful blush. "We're talking about holiness here. Don't."

With a more serious and straightened face he nodded in agreement.

"Anyway, I will no longer reprove of your supererogatory ways —" he cut me off.

"Supererogatory? You always make it take on a negative connotation."

"No...no! It's not negative at all." I sighed. I didn't mean for this to morph into such a serious conversation. "Can I be completely honest for a second?"

"I hope you would. That's all I ever want to be with you." Azmir's eyes were intent, and he was trying to take in this deep conversation.

"I think the reason I've given you so much grief over it is because I feel like I can't reciprocate. I don't have the means to *play* on your level and quite frankly, I don't know how to make myself useful in your world." I raised my hands in the air. "Please don't try to placate my insecurities by explaining your feelings for me. It's useless and unfair to do on the spot. More than that, I feel like it's something I have to figure out on my own *before I screw this up*," I choked on my last few words, but caught my tears before they pooled in my eyes.

Azmir sat there speechless but evidently still in the moment with me. I managed a little chuckle to put him at ease. He eventually grabbed my hands and kissed them gently. I smiled at his loving gesture.

Breaking the moment, I rose to my feet and exhaled. "Now, it's time for me to hit the sack. I've been dreaming about your cozy, tempered, firm, and snuggly bed all day. I must go meet with it." I laughed.

"Our bed, Ms. Brimm. You said you're on the path of peace and it starts with accepting me and all that comes with me. I'm yours and so is the bed." His voice was solemn and commanding. I so wish I was ready to receive that. I reached down and kissed him on the lips. I didn't want an emotional brawl; it was late, and I was too exhausted.

En route to the bed portion of the grand room he shared, "This *so* didn't end the way I thought it would."

"What do you mean?"

"I thought I was going to get a verbal lashing about coming home too soon and blowing your *shacking* cover," Azmir admitted while organizing his papers and laying them at the opposite end of the coffee table so that he could sit on the couch and put his feet up.

"Oh, I haven't forgotten about your monumental mishap. You're so busted! You forgot they would be over. Didn't you?"

He raised his arm in the air giving me that coochie creaming smile.

"Oh, and there it is!" I pointed my index finger towards his face. "Did you really have to flash those teeth and bat those lashes at them? You weren't playing fair. You were supposed to slip in and out of their view if anything," I fussed.

"I thought I did. Hey...I'm not used to us having company. I was caught off guard, too!" he played affronted.

"You knew what you were doing when you saw them at your feet salivating, willing to lick the tips of your shoes. I don't know how I'm going to face them until this dies down." I massaged my temples.

He shrugged his shoulders apologetically trying to hide his smile.

"Thanks, Mr. Jacobs!" I hissed and turned on my heels toward the bed.

He called out, "No, seriously...are you going to be okay if it gets back to your pastor? I thought you said he knew we cohabitated."

It was sweet of him to be so concerned about my spiritual developments as well as my religious concerns considering he was of a different faith. Azmir never made light of the restrictions and rules attached to the Christian walk I was pursuing. I knew deep down inside he feared me moving out or pulling back on sex, but I hadn't arrived at a place where I felt the need to address those issues. I had found a spiritual leader who said he wanted to start repairing my heart to make room for God, and God would urge me to transform in ways regarding my lifestyle. And for that, I was relieved and felt compelled to stay on this therapeutic passage.

"He does. It's just I don't feel the need to give people too close a view into my life. I like our solitude. Our bubble. It's been my refuge."

He smiled contently, "It's been working for me, too."

I walked off, crossing the suite, peeled back the sheets and climbed into bed feeling the cool firmness yielding to my curves.

Ahhhhhhhh!

The following afternoon I was out shopping with Chanell, and she was sure not to disappoint with the gossip. She told me how Kim had just learned Petey had a twenty-three-year-old lover, a Mexican PYT—*pretty young thang* as she termed it—he'd paid for to go to school.

Whoa!

She also mentioned how Kid's oldest daughter, by a woman he had cheated on Syn with when he was eighteen, had entered into college this fall and Kid bought her a baby Beamer, much to Syn' dismay. I guess the lavish gift was warranted seeing she was a sixteen-year-old whiz kid who was entering into college two years early. Apparently, Syn never forgave Kid for stepping out on her so long ago and has deeply resented this young girl.

"Yeah, but Syn can't be mad because Quadasia caught a full

ride to *USC* because she smart as hell!" Chanell exclaimed, smacking food in her mouth.

"Quadasia?" I asked as we sat in the food court eating lunch.

Chanell downed a tempting looking cheesesteak while I had a paltry salad. I was pissed I had a dance event coming up and needed to lose a couple of pounds to fit into my costume perfectly. I'd have much preferred eating what she had. Since being with Azmir, I'd rarely had the opportunity to eat sinfully.

"Oh, that's his daughter's name. You know Kid's government name is Quadir, right? That bitch, Heather, wanted to stick it to Syn's ass bad as a muthafucka and named his first seed after him."

"Didn't know that."

There was never a dull story leaked from Chanell. She was honestly a sweet girl who valued my friendship for reasons beyond who I was in Azmir's life. And I had to admit her prattler ways had its benefits, even if they were reduced to this mindless, hood bulletin.

"So how old will Kid be?" I asked.

"The big three-five! And I can't believe he that old. I remember when his ass used to beg for dry pussy. Word up!" she nodded her head. "Shit! That reminds me I gotta call the strippers for Friday."

"Strippers?" I asked as she went for her phone.

"Yeah. Petey got his hands full wit' that jump off shit wit' Kim so he asked me to book the strippers for Friday in a suite in the hotel we staying." She pulled out a small piece of paper I soon realized was the number of the *Tip Down Drills* for the strippers. "You know 'dem dudes love 'dem sum fuckin' strippers. They like to bring 'dem to their room instead of going to the clubs cuz' sum of 'dem mufuckas' wanna fuck. I be in there buggin' the fuck out at 'dem drooling' ass fuckas!"

All types of alarms went off in my head. Azmir hadn't mentioned Kid's birthday bash to me. I knew he was leaving again for business tomorrow but was due back on Thursday.

"So, the ladies are invited to these birthday bashes?" I tried so bad to downplay my hard-pressed curiosity and rising anger.

"The cool ones, yeah. A couple of the broads from around da way come wit' me, but not too many. They gotta be approved by Petey. Now 'dat Divine's big and shit they don't be wantin' shit leaked. 'Dem bitches from around da way be waitin' on a chance at all 'dem ballers."

As desperately as I wanted to inquire about Azmir's activities there, I didn't think I could handle the gut blow if I'd discovered his indiscretions. So, I kept my mouth shut, and in good timing as I heard Chanell make the arrangements for ten strippers to appear to a suite at a specified casino Thursday evening. My mind spun and heart tightened at the chunk of information from today's shopping and lunch.

Insecurity, no matter how buried, is a bitch and I think it might have bit me in the rear.

The following day, after church, Azmir called me on my way home telling me he'd made reservations for dinner at a restaurant in Malibu with a great view of the water before catching his red eye out of town to Atlanta. I flew through the door, headed straight to the closet to slip into something less formal and we headed right out. I hated seeing him leave for so many days at a time. Who was I fooling? I hated seeing him leave—period! But dinner was nice and held all the ambiance a woman could ask for considering the circumstances.

The lights from soft lamps and candles bounced off the ocean surface as the sun started to set and soft music was mellow and inviting. I'd been sipping on red wine too soon after an empty stomach, feeling a little tipsy. I hadn't eaten since breakfast before church. I was elated once our food arrived. I didn't prefer filling up on breads and salads.

"So, are you excited about your trip?"

"I guess there's nothing *not* to be excited about when you have big money on the table. Anxiety is more like what I'm experiencing. We've been in talks with this particular company for nearly eight months now. Finally, they're ready to play ball. In addition to that, Rich informed me this morning we may have to video conference a telecommunications company out in Canada who actually sought us out. They're tiptoeing on the sale though. We'll see."

"And there's Florida...next week?" I quizzed, hiding my disapproval, though loving his ease at sharing.

He sipped his drink. "Yup." Azmir had caught on to my contempt. "It won't always be like this."

"That's good to know," I murmured, holding my breath. I didn't want him to know how affected I was by his absence. How attached I'd grown to his presence. I've never been needy yet felt a semblance of it when he was away. I didn't like it.

"I remember, years ago, reading an article with Brian McKnight and his wife...*could've been Ebony...Essence...JET—I don't recall*...and she shared something along the lines of her not believing their marriage would survive if he did *not* travel as often as he did while working." My eyes traveled to find his. "They're now divorced, so how on par was she with their need for space?" I asked rhetorically. Melodramatic—but transparent of my heart, thanks to liquid courage.

He shifted in his seat. "I don't think spending time apart preserves a relationship. At best it gives time to reflect and evaluate it, but it certainly doesn't help to edify it."

Is he saying he didn't like being away from me like this? I had suddenly become so confused.

"How long will this last...you know the traveling?"

"I'm not sure. It's a part of the business. Is it becoming a problem for you, Brimm? Please be honest and tell me," he implored.

I didn't know how to respond. Heck, no, I didn't like the separation periods, but there was no way I'd come in between him and his business. I wasn't worthy of it; no one was.

"I'm fine, Azmir. How were the scallops? They looked as tasty as I am," I quipped trying to change the subject. The waiter was removing our plates.

It earned me a slow chuckle from him.

"Not quite as, but they were good. How was your eggplant?" he gave a bashful smirk. He wasn't expecting my jest.

"Really good."

The waiter asked if we wanted to see the dessert menu. I declined, not wanting to take up too much of Azmir's time. I knew he had a plane to catch, besides I felt I'd overdone it with my main entrée and didn't want to tip the scale later on. To my surprise, Azmir asked to see it and ordered sorbet.

"Thanks for relieving me of my Sunday meal responsibilities." My forehead wrinkled as I was, that quickly, hit with revelation. Clearly, wine didn't slow my brain. "You know, I don't think you've taken me to a bad restaurant yet."

He smiled. "And I don't endeavor to. Tell me, what are your plans for the week?"

I took a sip of my wine before answering, "The usual: counseling, dance, and church. Oh, and awaiting your return on Thursday," I flirted with a salacious narrowing of the eyes and a slow licking of my top lip.

"Good. As you should," he smirked in a way I didn't think I'd seen him do before. "My mother is flying into town next week."

"Oh, yeah? Where to?"

"I've arranged for her to stay at a hotel for a little while until she gets a lay of the land."

This was news to me. I recalled offering my place for her to stay indefinitely.

"Isn't a hotel a bit impersonal? I mean, you just said you don't know how long she'll be out here."

He raised his head and put down his napkin. I had hoped I hadn't offended him and didn't mean to intrude, but I knew this town could be a lot to take in.

"I mean, what are you going to do about her transportation? Is she coming alone? How will she get around or know where to go? With your schedule, you're unlikely to be around for assistance."

With narrowed brows he muttered, "I didn't think about all of that. The hotel plan wasn't permanent, but I figured it was the only way to start. I could take her around to my vacant properties to see if she likes one of them, but she'd need time to consider it and get to know the town. I hadn't thought about transportation. I could arrange for car service," he sounded doubtful.

"Azmir, car service may be a means to getting her around, but it won't resolve the issue of knowing *where* to go. It's not a personal touch. Why didn't you think to have her stay with us? Heaven knows there's plenty of room."

He steeled in place, looking me square in the eyes, "Our bubble."

I understood immediately what he meant. We had no visitors until this week, not even Petey had come through, at least since I'd been there. However, this was a special circumstance, it was his mother.

"I think that could be breached...temporarily. Just until she gets settled. Or you could consider my original offer and let her stay at my place. She could stay as long as she likes."

His eyes were suspended in the air at the thought. "We have a few days until she arrives. Give me some time to think about it."

I didn't understand what he meant, but immediately caught on to it being the end of the discussion. I suggested my place to him last week in New York and didn't know if he had ruled it out or simply forgotten about it.

"How was service today?" Azmir asked before taking a sip of his *Grande Marnier*.

I saw a hint of a smile on his face and rolled my eyes. I knew he was referring to the women in my Bible study group.

"The morning sermon was good, but I had a few new pew neighbors ask about my morning...*and previous night*. I can't believe that Rhonda asked if we go to bed at the same time!"

He squinted his eyes in confusion. "How did you answer that?"

"Are you kidding me? I didn't! She was out of line for that one. Lisa had the gall to *casually* ask about your measurements. She wanted to know how tall you were and your shoe size. I swear, I felt like your little sister instead of..." My words failed me and once again, my private truth piqued. I had no idea what I was to Azmir.

"Instead of what?" his lips twitched as if he found humor in my bemusement. He knew my hesitation and wanted to probe at it. *I don't think so!* I didn't want to damper the moment but didn't know how to change the course of the conversation.

"What's so funny? Do you think I'd say your wife or something?" I scoffed and rolled my eyes at the thought. Deep down inside I didn't view it as a joke, rather an impossible task.

With his eyes widened and in a look of total disarray, he asked, "What's so funny about *that* idea?"

Crap! Did I offend him? I didn't intend to. The thought of marriage caused me to cringe because I knew I could never be a valued partner to anyone. It would also cause me to reflect on how dedicated a partner my mother was to my father. It was to a fault, and he didn't appreciate it. I could never put myself in a position to let someone walk all over me and leave when it suited them.

"I don't know. What do you think?" I was at a loss.

The waiter served Azmir his sorbet in a fancy bowl with an obscurely shaped spoon. *Too rich for my blood.*

Azmir nodded in approval, dismissing the waiter and resumed our conversation.

"Well, it's what I know." He spooned his ice cream and scooped it in his mouth. *That mouth.* "But I won't tell. That'll have to be between my wife and me."

Though my neck stayed in place, my face fell to the table below. That stung. The thought of Azmir having a connection with another woman made my stomach churn and my chest tighten in anguish. He was mine and I didn't want to ruin what we had and allow another woman an opportunity with him. I downed the last of my wine in an attempt to blur the pain I felt in my heart. I was close to drunk and was happy about the shield it provided.

He reached over the table to share his dessert. I didn't want it, I was too wounded to be sentimental, but I humored him and ate from his spoon.

"Would you conduct your affairs with your husband any different from how you are with me now?" *Where's he going with this?*

"That's unfair to ask, Azmir. I'm far out of bounds where we are now. Unlike you, I've never been in a serious relationship." I shook my head in frustration. "Let's not talk about this."

He gave his confident chuckle and signaled for the waiter to bring the check.

Panic struck.

"Azmir, I'm not mad. I don't want to end dinner or rush your dessert."

Reaching for his wallet he muttered ever so smoothly, "Oh, nah, we *have* to go, Ms. Brimm. The way I see it is I have three hours before I leave for my flight." He handed his credit card to the waiter and motioned he didn't need to see the bill. "This gives me three hours to provide you with an idea of what sex would be like for my wife."

To say I wasn't expecting that wouldn't fully express my shock. After he cleared the check, we left for the marina.

I woke up in a daze. My mouth was dry, and my head was slightly spinning. It took seconds for me to realize Azmir was gone and recall he'd caught a redeye flight out to Atlanta. My mood immediately turned somber. I looked at the time on the nightstand and it read three thirty-three in the morning. It was hard to believe he was just here a few hours ago making wild barbarous love to me until I fell asleep in his arms—actually, I had collapsed from total satiation, and he wrapped me into his arms just before I dozed off. He was so...bestial I'd hardly recognized him. I grew aroused as I reminisced.

My thirst unpleasantly drug me from memory lane. I slid off the bed to go get something cool to drink. When my feet hit the floor, I winced from the pain sapping through my lower back radiating into my hip. *That man was wild last night!*

After taking a much needed trip to the bathroom, I made my way into the kitchen in desperate need of something to quench my thirst. I rested against the island and marveled at the sensation of the chilled orange juice traveling the full-length of my esophagus. *Mmmmmmm!* The advent of O.J. was divinely inspired.

Once back in the master suite, I checked my phone and saw nothing from Azmir. I couldn't deny the twinge of disappointment I felt from it, but decided to return to sleep before crazy thoughts crept in and took over.

A few hours—and five eight ounces of water—later, I was in the hustle and bustle of my day finishing up on staff evaluation interviews for the morning and preparing for lunch. Ben Shivers, one of my new PTs had just exited and closed the door of the conference room where I'd been conducting the evaluations when the phone buzzed, and Sharon informed me of a call on line two.

"Rayna Brimm speaking, how may I help you?"

"I think you just did. I miss the sound of your voice...but you sound a little hoarse. Are you coming down with something?"

Azmir's soothing voice dripping over the line was full of concern. It rendered me under siege, suspending my brain. His voice always awakened everything carnal in me.

I sighed. "I'm hoarse, deliciously sore on the inside, achingly sore on the outside and have been reprimanding myself for drinking so much yesterday."

"Yeah, you *were* throwing them back," he chuckled.

"And you were throwing *me* last night. I had no idea you had those positions in your arsenal. I'm still reeling from the things you pulled off!"

Azmir released the sexiest laugh I'd ever heard from a man. Nothing melted my heart and lowered my guards like his chortle did. He didn't do it to be sensual, it naturally was. It led me to my next question, the one I swore I wouldn't ask but he put me into such a comfortable state already in this call it got the better of my judgment. I leaned in and whispered into the phone, being sure to keep my voice low.

"How long have you been having sex?"

"What?" he gasped.

"You know...when did you become sexually active?"

He took a deep breath and let it out before giving me a sexy chuckle once more.

"Come on. Inquiring minds wanna know."

"I don't know, man. Ten—eleven, maybe? Why?"

"How many?" I shot back before I could think twice about it leaving my mouth.

"*How ma*— Are you sure you want to have this discussion? I am about to go into a meeting with a lucrative deal on the table and you want to have the conversation that will likely end up in you learning something you thought you wanted to know and could handle, but in reality, you can't?" I heard the laughter in his undertone.

That was a mouthful! But I had put it out there and there was no turning back.

"Number!" I ordered.

"Why? Please tell me why you must have this knowledge of my past?"

My conscious started roaring. He was right, I would *never* give him my number, so it was unfair to ask for his, but I still wanted to know.

"I just do, now tell me!"

"You're starting to remind me of how you felt Rhonda and Lisa hassled you in church yesterday with their insanely exploratory questions. But I'll play your little game. Are we talking about smashing or what I do with you?"

I could hear him speaking to someone about contracts in the background. *"No, the phrase on page twelve needs rewording. Yes. I agree with that as well. Thanks."*

"I'm sorry... Are you there?" he returned to our conversation.

"Yeah. You were just about to tell me how many women you've penetrated."

"Oh, right," he agreed wryly, quickly catching on to my slyness. "I've had my fair share of those I've smashed, but only a handful of those I've made love to." Azmir was the crafty one. He answered me indirectly. I knew him well enough to know that was his final answer.

Okay.

"How many of us have you pulled the tricks on you did with me last night?"

I had no clue why I was torturing myself. I hated the thought of him being with another woman the way he was with me last night —or any other time.

"Last night was a mixture of techniques, *and quite fun by the way*. There were a few things I've been wanting to try with you and some I did—and very successfully. I was testing your flexibility."

"And did I pass?"

"With flying colors." He didn't skip a beat.

"Yikes! I was nervous for a bit. I feel sorry for your wife if those are the tests she has to look forward to 'til she's old and gray," I teased.

"Don't worry. She'll be just fine. Tyler will make sure of that." I giggled at that one. "Seriously, are you okay? You were quite inebriated last night and...responsive," Azmir growled the last word out. "At some points, I thought I was hurting you until you made it clear that it was to the contrary."

Last night was freaking amazing! Are you kidding me!

"*Ummm*... Other than lingering soreness and paw bruising on my hips, I'm fine."

"Paw bruising?"

"Yeah. Your finger marks are on my backside and my hips and my thighs. I should try going home and explaining that to my husband," I picked up our joke from the previous night over dinner about being married to other people.

"Fortunate for me, and lucky enough for him, you don't have a husband." By the arctic sound of his tone, I could tell he didn't find my joke amusing.

He went off talking to someone else in the background again. "*Huhn? Okay.*"

"Ms. Brimm, that's my roll call. Gotta go make these donuts." Although I understood he really had to go, it really stung ending our conversation like that.

"Okay, knock 'em out of the park. And Mr. Jacobs?"

"Yeah?"

"Tyler won't have time to train your wife because he'll be preoccupied with me, helping me build my stamina so we can do last night again and again and again," I whispered seductively, I couldn't help myself. That's what Azmir brought out of me. Fieriness.

"*Ahhhhh*...you're hurting me, and just before I walk into my meeting," he growled.

"Later." I giggled.

"Indeed."

I smiled on the inside and outside after hanging up the phone. That man had the ability to make or break my day. I didn't think I liked him having that type of talent, but I was in over my head and just powerless at this point. My elated state didn't linger for long when my cell rang and moments later, I was chatting with Chanell.

"Guuuurl, 'dat tight ass skirt from *BCBG* ain't fit me! I told you I couldn't get into no size ten! Im'ma have ta' take 'dat shit back!"

"Oh, no! I was sure it would work. I'm sorry, C. When are you planning on going back to the mall?"

"I 'on't know. 'Dats why I'm calling you. I thought we could roll together. You ain't never pick up ya' gear."

What Chanell didn't know was I didn't know anything about Kid's birthday bash in Vegas until she brought it to my attention lunch. I thought Azmir would bring it up to me last night and he most certainly didn't mention it moments ago during our brief conversation. So, I had no need to shop. I didn't like the idea of him being danced on by strippers and I sure as heck had no desire to watch them.

"Chanell, I have no interest in watching strippers. I see enough moves by women in my dance class every week."

"Oh, nah!" she exclaimed. "'Da strippers is for Thursday. He having a big ass party down there on Friday night. He got the major hook up. There's gonna be performances and celebrities in 'dat bitch!" she shrieked.

"I don't know, C. We'll see. Did you arrange for the dancers?"

I couldn't lie. I had to know if Azmir would be in that suite with a horde of naked, sweaty, and thirsty women, wiggling for dollar bills.

"Yeah, 'dat shit is official right about now."

We wrapped up our conversation with me inviting her to text me a picture of a larger size skirt on and me giving her my deliberations that way. I didn't really care to make so many trips to the mall. Saturday was more than enough for me for a while.

The evening went by so slowly. The energy balance in the apartment was so off when the man of the house was away. He called to tuck me in, so to speak, but it didn't cure my blues for him. I took note he still hadn't mentioned Kid's party. I found it very strange considering how close they were. I had started to believe he simply didn't want me in on that part of his bachelor's life. But when I thought about how his time in Vegas would detract our limited time together in between his heavy traveling, it tore at my heart.

CHAPTER 10

Rayna

The following day went by a little quicker. Work came with its peaks and valleys, but because I had a session with Pastor Edmondson, it accelerated once I punched out.

Pastor Edmondson informed me he knew about my women's group discovery last Thursday. He, of course, didn't disclose his informant but did say he explained to "them" he was well aware of my living arrangements and had made it clear to me that, though he didn't condone my decision, he respected my walk with Christ enough to allow God to evolve my perspective on it.

He was totally honest. Pastor Edmondson lovingly demonstrated, biblically, why God disapproves of two people living together unwed, but made very clear it was not his intention to force a change of my lifestyle, only to infuse me with godly principles which would change my heart and from there *I* would willingly change my lifestyle. I didn't quite get it at that time, but it never left my memory.

He laughed apologetically about the encroaching questions I got and sympathized with Azmir for coming home to the likes of

Rhonda and the others in his living room gawking at him. My pastor was easy to talk to and uncompromising in his beliefs. I deeply respected him for that.

Wednesday, as I was writing reports to wrap up my day before heading to dance class, I got a call from Azmir. He sounded agitated.

"Hey, you! What's up?" I tried masking my panic.

"I just spoke with Petey who reminded me Kid's thirty-fifth birthday party is going to be in Vegas this weekend starting tomorrow." I was thrown partly because I'd already known and also because he seemed to have not!

"I was planning on coming home Friday and heading up to Santa Barbara with you for a quick overnight stay but shit, I gotta check on his birthday gift and at least be there for his birthday party on Friday night.

"It's okay. Kid is special to you. I wouldn't be upset if you went to celebrate a milestone occasion with him."

Did I sound like the proverbial understanding girlfriend or what! I wanted to see him on Friday—no, scratch that. I *needed* to see him on Friday!

"No, I need to see you this weekend," he muttered, quickly dismissing my offer and sounding more like he was thinking out loud than he was talking directly to me. I was happy he felt the same. "I'll be on a plane on Monday and away for almost another week again." There was a pregnant pause before he spoke again. "Would you mind hoping on a plane Friday when you get off and meeting me in Vegas? I'll have Brett book your flight and arrange for car service to the hotel. I won't arrive until Friday night because we have a meeting scheduled here first thing that morning."

"*Errrr...*" Wow! Talk about a turn of events.

"I'll have you home at a decent enough hour on Saturday so you can be ready for church on Sunday morning..." he pleaded. I could tell he was earnest in his offer.

This was a tall order. "Mr. Jacobs, the expense for me to get ready for this party... As it stands, this week I would have paid my monthly expenses, my mortgage..."

"Did you spend the money I had deposited last month? If so, I'll have funds deposited into your account by lunch tomorrow. Please. I'd really like to see you, Brimm." Okay now I hear desperation.

I had totally forgotten about the money he had put into my account. "Ughhhh...you know how I feel about—"

He cut me off again. "You just committed to not fighting me when I treat you to things. This would really be for me. I've screwed up my dates and am now inconveniencing you. Please cut me some slack and have *peace* about this," he seared me using my recent spiritual commitment against me. I sighed in concession.

"Okaaaaaaaaay," I sang softly in the phone sounding of defeat.

"Indeed," he breathed in his Brooklyn twang.

I heard a feminine voice in the background saying something to him.

"*Ms. Taylor*," rolled familiarly off his tongue, similar to the flirtatious manner he'd say my last name.

She must have walked up on him because I clearly heard her say, "*Mr. Jacobs...our table is ready. The host is calling for us,*" so velvety with a hint of seduction almost.

Something wasn't right. I didn't like the cordialness in their voices.

"Alright. I have to go, Brimm. Brett will contact you with your travel info."

"O-okay," I uttered with somewhat of a cracked voice. I was still trying to wrap my head around the cozy exchange he'd just had with this mysterious Ms. Taylor.

"Aye..." he called out, snatching my attention. "I expect you to fully expend the amount necessary to make you feel as good as you look. If you need more just let me know...*though I doubt you would be so liberal*," he was a bit mocking with his last few words.

He knew I wouldn't ask him for more money. There was no

ensemble I could think of exceeding an eighth of the astronomical amount he'd shoved into my account.

"Azmir...you know this is all new to me. Give me some time," I exhaled, frustrated and now feeling a headache coming on from hearing their suspect exchange *and* anticipating spending his money.

"Indeed. I'll call you after your class."

We ended our chat there. As much as I wanted to ponder my feelings over what I'd just heard, Azmir's knowledge of my evening schedule without me informing him pushed those contravening thoughts to the back of my mind. But they didn't evaporate. Instead, I sat there trying to map out a plan of preparation for my time in Vegas. Coincidentally, it would be my first visit. I wanted to look the part and make Azmir proud to have me as his arm candy. I finished my reports and made a call to Adrian for an emergency hair appointment.

The next morning when I had awakened and checked my phone for any correspondence from Azmir, I found an e-mail from his assistant, Brett, detailing my flight and car information for Vegas, making it a reminder for me to make all the arrangements necessary on my end to make this trip happen.

Later in the morning, after calling the luxury kennel to book an overnight stay for Azna, I sent a text to LaWanda telling her I had to fly out of town at the last minute for a friend and I wouldn't be able to attend this week's Bible study group meeting. After assuring her it had nothing to do with the girls' reaction to Azmir, she let me off the hook.

I hurried over to the salon to get my hair done on my extended lunch. Graciously, Adrian had me in and out in just under ninety minutes and I tipped him well for his expediency. I called Chanell to let her know she'd be seeing me on Friday and not Thursday night with the strippers. I was happy to know Azmir wouldn't attend that part of the celebration either—though I didn't share that piece of exciting news with her. She was just happy to know she'd be seeing me.

After work, I rushed through a couple of boutiques on a mad quest to find the perfect dress for this event. I was grateful money wouldn't be an issue when shopping. I'd only known the appropriate places to go to shop from Azmir's recent and generous shopping stints for me. I paid close attention to the names on the bags and receipts—when he didn't hide them.

I'd made it to my *third* boutique when I landed eyes on the perfect white *Sass & Bide* stretch bodycon dress, decorated with gold and silver beaded jewelry, stitched from the collar to the outline of my breasts and hips, accentuating my curves. Even the shoulders were decorated beautifully with silver jewels and the back was cut a little low exposing a bit of scapula bones. The dress was long sleeved and stopped inches below my behind.

I paired the dress with metallic gold *Christian Louboutin* twist-front platform pumps. I knew the look would go perfectly with my simple ponytail with a bit of a poof on top of my head. I chose gold brass-like stud earrings, feeling like I didn't need to go heavy on jewelry considering the jewels already in the dress. I had just hoped the ensemble would impress Azmir. By the time I was done with shopping, I luckily had just enough time to slip into a chair at the nail salon to get a mani and pedi. The evening ended perfectly and hearing from Azmir before closing my eyes was the icing on the cake.

Friday, I worked through lunch knowing I had to leave a little early to head straight from work to the airport. Brett texted me the hotel information. I didn't actually speak to Azmir as he spent half of his day in a meeting and the other half traveling. My flight was extremely short. *"What a tease in first class,"* I thought. My driver was there waiting for me holding a sign with "Brimm/Jacobs" plastered on it. *How cute.*

When I arrived at the hotel, the ambiance was nothing short of *A.D. Jacobs spectacular* in terms of decor. The Vegas energy hit me right away as I walked into the elegant lobby and found my way to the front desk where there was a note from Azmir, no doubt written by the concierge, instructing me to make my way down to the spa for a massage and facial. I thought the gesture was beyond thoughtful and did as he asked.

I was on the table, enjoying the stretching of my muscles when he texted me, checking in. Azmir shared he would have to meet me at the club because his flight was delayed. I noted it was seven. The plunge in my anticipation level accelerated at record speed at that discovery. I was looking forward to arousing him in one of the two pieces of lingerie I'd purchased for the evening. I tried my best to shake it off. I did so successfully by falling asleep during my massage.

Two hours later, I was back in the glorious and spacious suite preparing for the party. Chanell sent a text asking to meet, but I declined. I had no desire to roll with her girls to a party I would end up with Azmir at anyway. I took my time properly placing my lace undergarments and applying my make up. I loved my hair. The ponytail allowed for the highlight of my cheekbones, giving them more definition. I applied a burgundy shade of *MAC* lipstick and liner. Taking a deep exhale in the mirror, I appraised my final look. I was grateful it all came together.

Wheeeeew!

I just hoped Azmir felt the same.

At the door, I felt the drawing energy before stepping into the club. There was an enlarged poster with the faces of the birthday celebrants outside of the main entrance. I smiled when I saw Kid's high yellow complexion with neatly braided cornrows. He was fairly tall, trim and always warm to me.

I walked in and scanned the main room. Unsuccessfully, I tried spying the VIP section, but it was strategically and obscurely positioned so those in the common areas couldn't see the activities of those elite patrons. I didn't see anyone I knew, so I made my way to the bar to order a drink.

Before I could do another read of the room in search of my party, a handsome Caucasian man with glowing green eyes and dark blonde hair sat on the bar stoop to the right of me with a gorgeous smile. I had encountered quite a few undeniably good-looking Caucasian men since being on the West Coast, had even gone out with a couple. I quickly assessed this one would have definitely won my attention if I were available.

"You're stunning in that dress. The designer should be paying you for the advertisement. You're hot!" he charmed.

I blushed at his cute attempt. "Why, thank you."

"Aaron." He extended his hand for me to shake it. I obliged.

"Rayna. It's nice to meet you, Aaron." Over his shoulder I thought I had seen Wop, but it turned out to be a look-alike.

"Are you looking for someone?" He couldn't ignore my distraction.

I smiled politely. "Yes, I'm here attending a party for a friend, and I can't seem to find anyone I know."

"Are you sure you're at the right club? It would be something if you were supposed to be at a different casino altogether."

I shook my head. "No, I'm at the correct place. I saw his picture outside."

"Which of the birthday boys? Sam, Man, or Kid?"

I was surprised he knew them.

"Kid. How do you know him?"

"I coordinate and promote the parties here." He handed me his card, and I placed it on the bar next to my clutch. I had no need for it, but he didn't have to know that.

"How do *you* know him?" he asked with flirtatious eyes. He was being a little forward. I noticed his chiseled chin. Very handsome.

"We have mutual friends." That was true when you considered Chanell *and Azmir*.

"Oh, okay because I was hoping you weren't a *close* friend of his and he didn't properly inform you his party would be in a VIP area." His chin was tilted making it clear he was flirting.

Oh! That's where they are?

I wondered if Azmir had even arrived yet or was, he up in the suite preparing to come down.

"Oh, no! We're not that type of friends." I shook my head again. I immediately realized the more I shook my head and the less I used my words, the *more* he thought he had a chance with me.

"That's good to know." He winked his eye and I laughed at his persistence.

"Ah! She laughs! Now, I'll walk you up to the party if you promise I won't find out you are a *good* friend of his and break my heart."

"Pinky swear." I wiggled my pinky finger at him.

He winked again. I pivoted to grab my clutch and suddenly smelled the most familiar and erotic scent. I turned my head completely to the left and found Azmir leaning on his side, into the bar flickering Aaron's business card in between his fingers and wearing a cunning smirk. I gasped. He was dressed in a dark suit, and I automatically wondered if he had even been up to the suite to change out of his business attire.

"Azmir! How long have you been standing there? I've been looking for you guys." My heart rate had accelerated from his startling presence. He didn't say anything or remove his smirk. He slowly tilted his head to get a sight of Aaron on the other side of me. I jumped, figuring I should do the honors. I scooted back enough to allow a clear view for them to see each other. "Aaron, this is—"

"Mr. Jacobs!" Aaron seemed to have been more shocked than I was to see him. "Is this...?" He couldn't even complete his sentence. Wearing the same entertained expression, Azmir nodded in accession of Aaron's summary of the situation. "Oh, man! I am sorry. I had no idea," he tried to sound convincing.

Finally, Azmir rose from the bar and proffered his hand to Aaron, "Shit happens, Aaron. She's a beauty. I can't knock your ambitions—I have my own." Azmir then took my right hand, kissed my fingers, and helped me to my feet. Aaron watched, still shell shocked.

"*Errrr*... I trust everything is to your expectations up there?" Aaron asked referring to the VIP section.

With his eyes surveying me from head to toe Azmir replied, "It is now, Aaron. I had to find where she had lost her way."

My face split a dorky smile and a giggle slipped. He could be so impassioned when he wanted to.

I turned to say, "Thanks, Aaron. Have a good evening."

He nodded; I'm sure finding it best not to put his foot in his mouth any more than it seemed he just had. Azmir and I walked off with his hand gripping my waist, pulling my body into his. He whispered, "You look absolutely stunning, Ms. Brimm," reaching down to kiss me behind my ear, causing me to shiver.

"Funny. That's what Aaron said. See what the exuberate amount of money you had deposited into my account bought ya?" I teased.

He smiled as we took for the stairs leading to the VIP area and spoke even closer into my ear, "The only thing I would spend more money on is peeling you out of this ensemble." I puffed, shocked by his sensual wit in public. Then I heard bellowing and roars from Kid's birthday guests. It was Petey, Kid, Chanell, and the crew, apparently relieved I'd been located.

"There she go!" Kid yelled out clasping a bottle of champagne in his hand. He stood at our entering his arena. I could tell he was wasted already. Who could blame him, it was after all his day.

"Yo, Rayna!" Petey greeted. His short chunky frame and fluffy persona always warmed my heart. I saw Kim seated next to him waving excitedly and wearing a broad smile.

"Where was she?" Chanell howled over the loud music.

She was with a gang of slightly familiar faces I'd seen over the past few months at local events. Some were friendly and others were downright rude and ghetto as all get out. They gawked and mumbled to each other, clearly talking about me. It never seemed to faze Azmir, so I turned a blind eye to it as well. I greeted them all with hugs, one by one.

Kim was adamant I sat next to her. I could see she wasn't close to Chanell and the other girls this particular night, which was a bit unusual. It also seemed clear Azmir sat near Petey and Kim before taking off to find me. I adored Kim and didn't mind at all being by her side. We started our girl chat right away.

Minutes later, Syn came into the section with about a half dozen girls. When she landed eyes on me, she visibly grimaced. I had no idea why she didn't like me. I thought we would have been past it by now. Kid didn't seem to pay her much mind. He was soaking up the energy from the electrifying atmosphere. There were so many people in the building. I couldn't count on one hand the number of celebrities that walked through our VIP section or passed by us.

The performances were great. Azmir was in his element, leading the conversations in his urban vernacular. It always struck me how he could go from boardroom to hood corner with his lingo. He would whisper things in my ear from time to time, being sure to give me attention. He said he liked my lipstick and how it matched my nails and toes. I appreciated the observation, and it made the agony of selecting my colors well worth it. I guess he felt it was dutiful considering these were his friends, but truth be told, a handful of them were mine, too. Azmir ordered me a cocktail and made a playful toast with me. I could tell he'd really missed me and liked my look. I was so relieved.

I sat there for a while enjoying the energy and catching up with Kim, trying to adjust to all the camera flashes going on by people in the VIP section—candid and professional, and by those outside trying to see who was inside. I noticed Syn's girls she sat and snickered with while pointing at me had taken a few shots of me, too. I thought it was rude but would never cause a scene at Kid's party with his girl and her friends.

Eventually, Chanell motioned for me to come over to talk with her and I did. She caught me up on the latest gossip and inadvertently reminded me of Kim's recent discovery of Petey's co-ed lover, which answered why she played him so close. She had seemed to clock his every move all night. Apparently, Kim was salty with Chanell and some of the other girls there because they knew and hadn't informed her. I was just happy to see her out with Petey because it meant she was still with him. I guess I overstayed my time with Chanell at some point because Azmir motioned for me to return to him. It appeared a little possessive, but I didn't care. I was in Vegas to be with him.

A performer was being announced, and Azmir pushed me into his pelvic area as he stood against the railing overlooking the stage and the crowd. Seconds later, Kid generously and forcefully invited us to sit closer to the front of the VIP section where we'd have a clear view of the stage. It was a white leather sofa chair, but it seated just one. Azmir sat and gestured for me to sit on his lap. I didn't know how it would fair considering I had on such a short dress, but Azmir's legs were so long the stoop wasn't very low. My position didn't allow for snuggling but was fine since Azmir and I weren't in the habit of PDA anyway. Or, so I thought. We sat and watched the performance.

When the songs were over the crowd went bananas. I clapped with approval along with nearly everyone else. Kid got a few birthday shout-outs from the performers, making him smile and slowly nod in his drunken state. The patrons below settled back on to the dance floor while the D.J. spun the latest tunes. Azmir pulled out his pocket watch for the time, which I found odd. Why does the time matter at a club in Vegas? I looked up for Chanell but didn't see her. I figured she'd made a potty run.

I then turned to Azmir and chatted about the latest performer, and he agreed it was awesome and told me a story of the first time he'd met her and the work he did with her people. He didn't fail to continue sharing his salacious thoughts when he droned, "I can't wait to smear that lipstick off your lips. You should refresh it first. The heavier, the more on me when I wake in the morning." My panties began to become drenched from my liquefied libido. I smiled at him with slanted eyes approving of his sensual talk.

Abruptly, I saw dark nails gripping his round shoulder, trying to get his attention. My eyes slowly trailed the arm up to find a tall, beautiful woman with dark chocolate skin, wearing an azure blue fitted, one shoulder, mini dress with silver sandals and matching silver and diamond accessories. Her hair was full of bouncy curls, falling just above her shoulders. I could quickly tell she was about her diva. Her eyes beamed in excitement at the sight of Azmir. Initially, she didn't even look at me, she was so caught up in him.

"Ms. Taylor. Wow! It's good to see you." He seemed surprised by her presence. He flashed her a coochie-creaming smile I'd become accustomed to sharing with other women. I still hadn't decided if it was his charisma or just simple good looks causing it to be so alluring.

"Hey! We thought we'd fly out and chill. Thanks for putting us on. This place is popping!" she exclaimed, sounding like a valley girl.

She gave a clear view of her nicely whitened teeth under her dark red lipstick and alluringly lined eyes. And I could tell immediately she was completely taken by Azmir and all his glory. Could I blame her?

I could find reasons too!

"What a surprise. I thought you guys had, had enough of me. Where's Shayna?" Azmir asked quizzically.

I noticed he referred to her as *Ms.* Taylor but her friend by her first name. *So, this was the woman with the familiar "touch" I'd picked up over the phone...hmmmmmm.* I stood to get a better view and he rose from the chair and remained next to me. That's when she finally acknowledged me and gave me a once over. I realized I was squinting my eyes in reaction to it.

Azmir must have taken notice of her gaping at me. "Ms. Brimm, this is Dawn Taylor. Dawn, this is Rayna Brimm."

She offered up a snobbish half a smile and I gave a slight nod not knowing how much more I should have given providing she was not happy with having to share Azmir's air with me.

Suddenly, another woman joined sides with her. This one a lot shorter with straight hair horribly styled, wearing a figure-fitting red dress. She didn't look as put together as Dawn at all, but she was more pleasant when we were introduced.

"Azmeeeeeeeeeeeeeer!" she sang in anticipation of him being surprised by her being there.

"Hey, Shayna. You two sure do get around the country, don't you?"

"It's our job and you better know it!" She acknowledged me right away unlike her friend who still was mesmerized by the Adonis of Azmir. *Foolish girl!*

"Shayna Bacote, this is Rayna Brimm." She extended her arm and shook my hand graciously and I returned the favor.

"This place is nice! Do you come often?" Shayna asked. Dawn looked every which way but mine, she made frequent eye stops at Azmir, of course.

Before he could respond I heard, "Yo, Divine, who 'dis?" Wop and a few other guys came in to break up the reunion.

In the corner of my eyes, I could see Petey standing off at a distance, sipping on his drink closely watching, almost as if he'd orchestrated the diversion. Wop and the others would never intrude on Azmir's conversation without permission. They respected him like a leader and Petey was his deputy sheriff. Something was fishy.

"These are friends of mine from Atlanta. Show them some Southern California hospitality. Ladies, we'll be in touch," Azmir bade, excusing himself. It was clear he was trying to end the conversation.

Out of nowhere, Chanell appeared, "Divine, y'all wanna do a round of shots?"

In the midst of all the shouting over the music my senses were acute. I couldn't help but observe how Dawn's eyes were locked to Azmir, though we were now a couple of feet away from her and Shayna who had become swarmed in by members of *The Clan*.

"Oh, nah. Ms. Brimm here has seen enough for the night. I'm gonna take her upstairs now," Azmir responded to Chanell over the music, causing me to snap out of my eagle eyeing mode. I saw so much was going down at one time, even if I wasn't exactly able to piece it all together right there on the spot.

"Okay! Im'ma see y'all tomorrow at brunch at the restaurant, right?" Chanell asked.

I looked up to Azmir, who now had his hand splayed across my belly cradling me against his hard thigh, causing my backside to be nearly buried in his pelvis had he not been so tall. I could swear he was lifting me to make his target.

"Yeah, twelve thirty, right?" he answered.

"Yup. Peace y'all," Chanell bode.

Azmir released me just enough for me to hug her goodnight. *He's in an unusually jolly mood.* He even playfully lifted me in the air, gently swinging me like a rag doll over to Kim so I could do the same.

Kim and I both agreed to sit together at brunch the next day and Azmir chimed in saying, "Only if I can sit on the other side of her." Kim slapped him in a maternal manner on the arm before reaching up for a hug. He obliged but didn't let me loose from his left fastened grip. He and Petey nodded at each other but didn't do anything more, which was extremely weird, almost unheard of. As we exited the VIP section, I tried looking back over to Dawn Taylor but couldn't find her.

In the elevator Azmir gave me a penetrative gaze with his

tongue pressed into his molars. I shot a gaze right back at him as his long frame rested into the corner of the elevator. I was on to him, even if I hadn't quite figured out what had just taken place. He tilted his head to the side suspiciously gaping as if there was a problem.

"You barely had one drink tonight."

Ahhhh! He was also observant. "I think I drank enough the last time I was with you. I could use a little dry time," I tried hiding my discomfit from the episodes of the club.

"Ahhh-ha," he nodded.

I'd lied; my reason was experimental. Why I abstained from drinking was because I was familiar with the way my body succumbed to Azmir's expert sexual skills. But I needed to know the influence of alcohol had nothing to do with it. I knew Azmir and I would be intimate tonight, I just had to see just how much he contributed to my sexual arousal and satiety.

Once at the suite, Azmir moved to the side so I could use my card to open the door. Again, I wondered had he been to the suite at all. *I guessed this meant he hadn't.* I pushed open the door and walked in to find an immediate glow from a pathway of candles lit from the door to well into the suite. I turned around to ask Azmir for answers to have him close the door and pin me up against it and kiss me breathlessly. I was shocked by his abrasiveness considering I was still coming down from the various suspicious incidences taking place downstairs but warmed up to it almost immediately when his trained tongue swept against mine. I eventually became cognizant of the effort he must have taken to surprise me with the romantic set up there. Suddenly, nothing else mattered, no one else was considered or was a factor in our solitude. Our bubble.

Ripples of pleasure moved fiercely from my feet to the top of my skull and within just seconds I was caught up in orbit with him. Our tongues wrestled furiously, expressing things mere words could not. This man wanted to devour me; he needed me even more than I needed him. It was certainly one of those moments when *I* couldn't deny his unadulterated interest in me. Even if I didn't understand it specifically, the emotion was undoubtedly there.

A moan escaped my throat waking me out of my trance. I pulled away and pierced his hooded eyes. He gazed down at me entrenched in desire as his hand was still cupping the back of my head. I wasn't quite sure I'd ever seen him so beside himself in passion. I couldn't let the moment fleet us without saying something.

"What is it? What's all of this?" I was all pants.

"I've missed you, Brimm." He was out of breath himself and searching my eyes for a possible problem.

My feelings were all over the place from my concerns of Dawn Taylor to Petey's covert operations, but I wasn't about to broach the subject. I broke our gaze and ambled further into the suite to see how far out he went with the ambiance. From the foyer the trail took two paths, one into the living room and the other into the bedroom where there were dozens of rose petals covering the bed. The glow of the room reminded me of the one in Azmir's bathroom the night we made love for the first time since our breakup. I stood about a foot into the doorway frozen, trying to settle my mind. I felt him come from behind, kissing my neck, clouding my judgment. My body shivered at the touch of his deft tongue. He went from one side of my shoulder to the other.

"Do you know how good you look tonight? I almost brought you up here at the sight of laying eyes on you. I didn't want to ruin the surprise." Azmir's voice was hoarse, saturated in desire. "You are the most enthralling woman I've ever encountered."

His hands ran down the front of my thighs, pressing me into him so I could feel his log of an erection. My eyes closed in forfeiture of my will. He was ready. And my body instinctively reacted. His hands ran up to my belly and over my breasts, massaging them through the dress. My mouth opened but I was unable to make a sound. His hands rounded to the back and unzipped my dress, slowly planting soft kisses down my back as far as my zipper went. When he finished, he peeled the dress off exposing my strapless bra. His hands traced around my breasts missing my swollen nipples. He pulled the dress down to my ankles and sauntered around to face me but keeping a short distance. He took me in from head to toe before walking up to me.

He wrapped his arms around me, brought his mouth down to my ear and whispered, "Do you know how bad I want you?"

I shook my head *no,* being totally honest.

"I've been craving you since Monday morning when I woke up without you. You're the first thing I think about when I rise and the last thing I desire before I slip into slumber." My breath hitched. I wasn't intoxicated from liquor, but certainly was by his words.

"Yeah. That's how I feel!" he continued to whisper in my ear referring to my body's response in breathing and heart rate increase.

I felt his heart pump through his pectorals as he pressed me into his chest. So far, alcohol did *not* contribute to our chemistry. I wanted this man.

He removed his suit jacket, tossing it over the path of candles and onto the lounge chair in the corner and then started undoing his shirt all while gazing deeply into my eyes. It was all taking too long for me, so I helped by unbuttoning his shirt from the bottom, quickly and steadily. When I was done, I unbuckled his belt, then pants until they dropped to the floor, all the while looking him in the eyes.

He stepped out of his boxers and pants, discarding them along with his shirt. I raised his T-shirt over his head, breaking our mutual gaze to admire his chiseled chest. So badly I wanted to run my tongue from his clavicles past his sternum and down to silky pelvic trail leading to his long and heavy appendage, which was now poking me. He tossed his T-shirt and promenaded behind me.

"Step out," he ordered. I took two steps forward, leaving my dress behind for him to throw over into the chair as well, finding it amazing how he didn't miss the chair not one time. I stood in my heels when he hooked me at my belly and pushed my shoulders down bending me over. I felt his mouth on my backside as his lips trailed down it and onto the back of my thighs then back up, pulling my lace panties down with his teeth. I held onto my kneecaps trying to maintain my equilibrium during the heat of the moment. He had me step out of those before unsnapping my bra and releasing my throbbing breasts.

As his large hands massaged them, pulling at my nipples, he whispered in my ear, "You're so fucking perfect."

I was turned out! I'd never heard Azmir narrate our lovemaking so. *What is going on?* I wasn't complaining because his words *and* deeds sent me over the edge, but I have to admit I was taken by surprise.

He walked me over to the bed prompting me to crawl onto it and bend over. With my heels on and down on all four, Azmir opened and clutched my cheeks licking me from back to front until I moaned his name half past manic. I didn't climax and I don't believe he wanted me to. When he stopped, he sat up behind me pushing my neck into the mattress with one strong hand and ran his thumb the full-length of my spine pressing gently into it with the other. My body convulsed and it wasn't orgasmic, ending my thoughts of alcohol being the cause of my sexual demise with Azmir. I was every bit of sober and floated on cloud nine.

The only difference between this night and any other I was under the influence was my heightened intensity, making me feel like I was floating in orbit looking down to view the experience. Tonight, I was living in each moment and boy, was it good! Entering me from behind and causing my body to shiver as he coursed through me, Azmir made sweet and adoring love to me, and I rode out each second of each moment of passion. It was rough. It was hard. It was loaded. And it was impassioned.

The next morning, I broke out of my sleep early—too early. I fought my daze trying to recall where I was. It helped when I turned to find Azmir lying next to me on his back recovering through sleep from the party last night. *Was he drunk?* I'd hoped not. I was completely naked, remembering how just a few hours ago, I went through the suite blowing out each and every candle after Azmir passed out, not wanting the place to catch fire. After that task was complete, I showered and washed the makeup from my face. Finally, I got into bed and reflected on how romantic and intense he was before falling asleep myself.

I fought the urge to hit the bathroom when I looked over to him in awe of his sexy profile. *Seriously, no man should be this beautiful!* Thoughts of last night's events started flashing through my brain, from seeing this place illuminated from the candles to him climaxing behind me, blurting out I was the best he'd ever had on a feral cry. Out of nowhere, I became aroused wanting that same energy and matched passion from last night. I could never satisfy my need of Azmir, his hands, his mouth, his thirst for my needs.

I knew he was bare beneath the sheets, so I ducked between them until my mouth found his semi-erect appendage and pulled him in. I applied soft bites, pushed and pulled, stroked and sucked until he was fully awake against my tongue. I could hear him stir and moan, waking from his deep sleep and I worked diligently for his full consciousness.

In seconds, I felt his hands on the back of my neck directing my movements. I was feeling so alive and ready myself, enjoying his need of me. I pushed greedily until I felt him in the back of my mouth and then let out a moan; I was so turned on. Azmir pushed the covers from over my head giving me fresh air to breathe, much to my relief. It inspired me to work harder. I worked him over until his hips were thrusting in my face and he yelled through clenched teeth, "Ray, baby, I'm about to blow." That was music to my ears *and tried jaws,* challenging me to grip more and faster. Seconds later, his hips were pumping into my head so fast, and I felt warm trickling down my throat. It was a lot to take on, but oh, so arousing to hear him sing my praises in his most vulnerable state. I watched his abs heave and applied a roguish grin I'd learned from him. He was too caught up to respond to it.

Once he was done, I skipped to the bathroom to relieve myself and to wash my face and brush my teeth. When I returned to bed, I saw it was only six forty-five giving us plenty of time before Kid's birthday brunch. Azmir was wide awake and waiting for me.

"Good morning," he greeted with an appreciative smile and the delicious morning graveled voice of his, arousing me every time. I think he knew by his chuckle when I responded.

"Oooh! Yes, it is." I was smiling from ear to ear.

"You're up early." He gently stroked my cheek as he gazed into my eyes with sated approval.

"I have to savor every moment I'm next to you."

He looked at me with a smile. "Nice, Brimm," he stated wryly. Though I knew he was joking, it implied I was being insincere, and I wasn't, I needed him far more than I'd ever realized. I hated myself for not being able to tell him. I just wasn't ready.

I took to my pillow on my belly, trying to resume the comfortable position I'd awakened from. My hands gathered underneath the pillow when I felt an odd object. It was long and leather. *Jewelry box?* Slightly startled, I pulled it from beneath and examined it. Surely, it was a long rectangular box fit for jewelry.

My eyes shot over to Azmir who watched with a blank face as he laid flat on his belly with his head on the pillow, exposing the striations in his strong triceps. He nodded his head inviting me to open it, so I did. Inside was the most breathtaking four-tiered diamond bracelet glistening so brightly.

My head shot over to Azmir who advised, "For your ankle."

I didn't know what to say. I'd just hoped he didn't take my recent resolve to his spending as the green light for going overboard. It was enough he'd paid for my wardrobe to come down to Vegas. The bracelet was no doubt beautiful, and I couldn't be so churlish, so I whispered in awe, "Thank you, Azmir. I don't know what else to say. This is absolutely gorgeous."

"Not as gorgeous as you are. You're very welcome. And thanks for being gracious," he supplied, flashing that panty snatching smirk. I knew he was referring to my reception of the luxuriant gift. I told him I'd work on my attitude, and I planned to do just that.

"May I put it on you for size?"

"Sure," I breathed, still taken by his gesture.

As he rose from the bed and worked his way down to my feet, I couldn't help but ogle his deliciously chiseled frame, his pronounced pectorals, his bubbled abs, and the well-defined V marking his private zone. My eyes landed on his beautiful, mildly erect penis, but he caught my attention when he asked, "What type of student were you?"

Huhn?

"Student? What type of question is that?"

"One of many I think about when I'm away. I realize I know too little about the person you were prior to moving out to Cali." The ardent look in his glistening post-coital eyes told me I should play along.

"*Ummmmm...* In my formative years I was an average student. I brought home mostly Bs and when I became distracted by sports or indifferent about a particular subject, I'd slip and get an occasional C. College was totally different. I used school to escape and viewed Cs as failures. Needless to say, I did well."

I was still thrown by his inquiry but for the sake of conversation, I threw the question back to him. "How about you? What type of student were you?"

"Well... That depends on what period of my life we're talking about. From the start of school, I was a straight A student and got an occasional B for the same reasons you mentioned." His eyes furrowed while he paused. "But all that changed when my father died. I skipped school and ran the streets with my boys."

I scoffed. "I don't see Yazmine going for that."

I heard the snap from the bracelet. "There you go."

I marveled at the brilliance of the diamonds showcased on my ankle. It had the semblance of a leash, though a very expensive one. The thought was unpleasant, but I couldn't deny the beauty of it.

"Looks even better than I thought it would. I'm glad it fits." He kissed my lower leg, sealing the deal. I smiled to hide the lurch of my belly reminding me I still had needs to be met thanks to the BJ I'd just bestowed upon him.

Azmir slowly took back to his pillow and seamlessly continued with the conversation. "She didn't. The only reason I got away with it was because of her mourning my father presented a distraction. She was the reason I'd received honor roll every marking period from the time I got letter grades. When she snapped out of her depression, she packed us up and moved to Chi-town. And when I got there, she worked hard with me to regain my focus. I played the game and made sure I brought home amendable grades to get her off my back, but the streets were calling, and I answered the door." His brown eyes markedly traveled over to mine.

"You ended up at Stanford, so you were wise to play her game."

"Oh, *that* came from making a deal with Big D. He didn't want to transfer me out of the school system so quickly, so he promised to take care of me if I agreed to lay low in school. Laying low to me meant hitting the books. It earned me several scholarships to schools across the country. I chose Stanford for the location. To me it was in the cut, and I could stay out of trouble."

Lucky enough for me he chose the high road. I couldn't see Azmir as a knucklehead. He seemed too suave for that.

"Softball?"

"Huhn?" His question threw me.

"You said you played sports. Did you play softball? Or did you cheer?"

I sucked my teeth. "Whoa! Why does it have to be one of the two? Back to your chauvinistic ways, I see!" I feigned offended.

"I don't mean to be chauvinistic. I was just using deductive reasoning. Did you run track?"

"No!" I swung, catching him in the right pectoral.

He belted a hearty laugh. Trying to catch his breath he asked, "Well? What did you play, Ms. Brimm?"

"Basketball!"

"Get the hell outta here!" He couldn't stop laughing.

"Yes, point guard! Varsity!" I hissed over his loud amusement.

"Okay! Okay! I believe you. It's just I can't picture you in a uniform. That's cool though. I played a bit myself throughout school. I wasn't the star of the team, but I partook."

"Really? Now, see I can see all the girls lined up around the corner at your Tuesday night game, hoping to get a drip of your sweat flung at them." I teased.

"Nah. Not necessarily in that order." He smiled at the ceiling. After calming himself, in a more serious tone he asked, "Did your boyfriends come to your games?"

"I didn't have *boyfriends*, Mr. Jacobs. What type of girl do you take me for?"

"Well, I guess I'm asking did you have a lot of boyfriends coming up."

"Oh, no! I am not about to share *my* number with you, buddy! That's personal!" I declared.

"I would never think to ask you that question. My heart would never be able to stand an obscene number. I'm asking how many times you have been in love."

Oh. That's more reasonable.

"Ummmmm...I only had one boyfriend. I've told you this. I

guess I was in love at the time...considering my age and lack of life experience. It was a train wreck of a relationship."

"Are you still in touch with him?" His head turned to me.

"Oh, no! Absolutely not. We are worlds apart and I would rather keep it that way." I chuckled at the thought of a man of O's caliber approaching me at this point in my life. He would get the same half a look as Azmir's younger Clan members.

"What's so funny?"

"I don't know. I don't think about my past often and some things about it are hilarious." I turned on my side to face him. "I'm content with where I am now. I have only a few regrets and hope it never changes."

Azmir's eyes went back toward the ceiling, "Indeed."

We sat in silence, I suppose recounting our exchange, or at least I was. The silence was peaceful. I guess it was agreeable to the early hour. But it didn't last too long.

Azmir asked, "How do you know when you're in love?"

My head swung up to catch his expression.

What an odd question...and coming from Azmir Jacobs. I was askew and didn't have an answer. I'd been getting by for so long without a legitimate relationship I had no clue.

"I have no frame of reference," I muttered, answering when the revelation hit me, and I rolled back on to my back. I really didn't know. "I guess that's something I could take on in a session with Pastor Edmondson. *Hmmmmm*... What *is* being in love?" I tried the question out for size.

Feeling it would somehow start answering the question for me as well, I turned my head to ask him, "How do you know when *you're* in love?"

The next thing I knew Azmir lunged at me, pressing my body into the mattress using his full weight. He kissed me, pinning my head between his hands and in one rapid swoop from his arms, he pulled me on top of him. He shifted the covers so there was nothing between us, just skin on skin. His aged cologne was still present and intoxicating. I couldn't ignore it as he ran his hands up and down my back while using his mouth to claim my tongue.

His kiss caused a blur in my mind and appealed to my heart, consuming me completely. It spoke secrets of Azmir's being, filled with deep passion and unexpressed needs. I tried to keep up, blocking out the fear from his exposure. I didn't want to run from it. He was raw and unshielded, something I envied. His actions were so arousing, immediately my juices began to flow. He worked me onto his steely erection pushing me down, burying himself inside my flowing depth. He held me close to his chest, just as he did the first time we made love in my house. I loved it because I could feel his increased heartbeat. And suddenly, I wondered the point of it. Did he want me so close, I felt what was going on inside of him?

He pulled and pushed me into him to the point of me losing control of my rhythm from the overwhelming sensation of him being so deep inside, tapping my frozen heart. He pulled my hair, forcing my eyes to meet his. And in this moment, the atmosphere charged between us. It was electrifying, and he knew what was happening and demanded I acknowledge it as well. Only, I felt the charge, but didn't fully understand what it meant for us. All I knew was he couldn't be close enough no matter how deep inside of me he was. He couldn't warm me enough, no matter how much heat emanated from his divine touch, thawing my chilled chambers. I wanted more of him. All of him.

It was frightening and all consuming, but I yielded to him. To *it*. Azmir and I made love, hard, with unerring precision and with no regret until our energies were spent, and we fell sound asleep.

A rapid movement of my head jerking woke me from my sound sleep. When I opened my eyes, I discovered Azmir's index finger flickering my bottom lip was the culprit. He was across from me, at the same distance and in the same position as he was when we were having our pillow talk. He lay on his stomach smiling adoringly at me.

"It's a quarter to eleven. I don't know how long you'll need to dress but I'm gonna have to beat you to the bathroom. The throne is calling. I have a few calls to make about Kid's gift while I'm in there. See ya in a bit." He kissed me softly on my head before sauntering out of bed and into the bathroom. And I undoubtedly enjoyed his sexy gait until he was out of sight.

I stretched in the bed wishing there was no place to run off to, though I missed Azna. I was excited about picking him up later and wrestling with him on the Persian rug in the living room. He enjoyed rubbing his back into it. It was so delightful to watch.

So much had happened in the previous hours. Azmir was great...*but different.* He seemed more attentive and affectionate, even in public. I wasn't used to it and didn't know how to take it. I allowed my mind to fantasize about life as his wife. *Would he be this affectionate? Would he make love to me this frequently? Would he remain this romantic? Oh, the possibilities!* I didn't force the thoughts for too long because I felt even the possibility was a world away.

I needed to get myself together, so I didn't blow the opportunity of this...*friendship* we were building. *He asked me about my childhood! He said he wonders about it when I'm not around!* That swelled my heart. It felt good knowing I was thought of by a man without motive—at least that was my assumption. I took him at his word.

My stream of thoughts was interrupted by the alerting of a text above my head. I slid up the bed to the nightstand and grabbed my phone, but I saw no notification. I looked up at the nightstand again and saw Azmir's identical phone there. His phone didn't have a case like mine, but apparently, we had the same generic text tone.

Hmmmmm...he must have his Blackberry in the bathroom with him. How could he talk on the phone while taking a dump? Ewwwww! But how hot was it that he was handling business in every sense at the same time.

I laughed to myself and was interrupted when the phone

alerted of a text again. I understood Azmir was a busy man and his phone never slept, but today's a Saturday and this is his personal line. *Why the high activity now?* It hadn't buzzed all night or morning. I heard the sound of the shower starting to run and figured he wouldn't be coming out any time soon. Curiosity and annoyance got the best of me, and I picked up the phone. My primary mission was to silence it until he came from the bathroom.

I saw a text notification from Petey and then one from Dawn Taylor. *What?* I unlocked the phone, went into the text app and saw his exchange with Petey. They seemed to have been discussing Kid's birthday, but much of their conversation was encoded and I couldn't decipher it. What was clear was Azmir informed Petey his ringer had been off purposely so he could not be disturbed—*DND* —but he would be turning it on.

Okay, that explains why the sudden vibrating activities, but what does Ms. Taylor have to say to Mr. Jacobs? Without thought, I went to their exchange and read.

Gr8 c'ing U last nite...but not 4 as long as I'd hoped. How long R U N town? Can we meet 4 breakfast (ALONE)?

A stinging sensation flashed through my chest upon reading her words. She didn't say anything inappropriate, per say, but I knew she was interested in Azmir. A *woman knows*. Her attraction to him was undeniable from the way she gawked at him the night before in the club. But what could I do? I wasn't his keeper...just someone he slept with and who kept his bed warm—*every night*. All the fittings of a bed-buddy.

I couldn't deny the twinge of jealousy spiking through my heart. All my recent inclinations of progressing to a deeper place with Azmir were quickly dissipating and I could feel the frosting in my heart so intensely my body shivered, and goose bumps surfaced.

I heard the shower water stop and assumed Azmir would be done soon so I tightened the sheet around my bare breasts in preparation of skirting back up the bed to return his phone to the nightstand. I could have never survived being caught.

The phone pinged again. It was Dawn. *Again.*

Shit! Shayna just reminded me of a conference call that we have at 11:30. How bout lunch? I need 2 ask u about the woman u were with last night. Is she a "friend" of yours? I have my personal reasons for asking which is Y I wanna meet alone. :) Hit me up. Where R U? Which CASINO R U staying at?

That was as forward as it gets. She wanted Azmir. The emotions—the pain I felt were some that hadn't surfaced since I was kid experiencing perfidy from O and Keysha. The distant memory from the sting of betrayal was still acute.

I reached up to return the phone to the nightstand and immediately started experiencing hot flashes. From chilled goose bumps to hot flashes in a matter of seconds. My arm pits excreted sweat and my heartbeat increased. Azmir opened the bathroom door and I practically jumped out of bed in search of a few toiletries before gustily sprinting into the bathroom.

I felt it.

As much as I thought I'd improved on my responses to unfavorable situations, the familiar urge to shut down, run, and protect myself was too tempting—too easy. I was quickly slipping into self-protection mode, a place where Azmir wouldn't survive.

Rayna and Azmir's love journey to be continued...

NEXT UP...

LOVE UNCHARTED

from the *Love's Improbable Possibility* series

Available now!

~LOVE ACKNOWLEDGES:

Love's Betas: My first official audience. Thank you! And to Kelly, Tondi, Karmen (*L.I.P.'s Marketing VP – 300...400 Like marks*), Patrice, Angela (book club junkie) and Yorubia, thank you for your assistance in promoting the L.I.P. series. You ladies rock!

Tina Baker: You may not consider it much, but I appreciate the time you took, on several occasions, to offer resources and advice. It is my prayer that one day I can return the favor in any form presented. God bless you!

Marcus Broom of DPI Designs: Thanks for your talented artistry.

Brandy of Momma's Books: I have no words! When you come across absolute strangers in your pursuit of success and they *enthusiastically* take you to the next level, giving your career a boost, you must know that it's God-orchestrated. It's His favor. Thank you sooooooooooooo much!

Tanya Keetch - The Word Maid: Thanks for your editing services as well as linking me into your circle. You have the warmest energy. Thanks for everything!

In-house editor - Zakiya Walden of *I've Got Something to Say*

Incorporated: Your tireless dedication to our team has been nothing short of rare blessing. Thank you from the bottom of my heart, boss (insider)!

Tina V. Young: Thanks so much for helping me comb through this baby for a good cleaning. I'm sure we'll do it again. LOL!!

Juaquanna Gaines-Sams: You have been more than a friend – try a manager, a designer, an editor and my first L.I.P. fan! I'm just glad you haven't cut your fangs into anyone yet. LOL!!

MDT: The depth of our partnership is so precious...when people see me shine they are experiencing the inner glow that you ignite with your unwavering dedication. #TeamMKT

To my **Master**, my **Jireh**, my **Rohi**, *2 Corinthians 9:10-15*. Your praise shall forever be in my mouth.

~OTHER BOOKS BY LOVE BELVIN

Love's Improbable Possibility series:
Love Lost, Love UnExpected, Love UnCharted & **Love Redeemed**

Waiting to Breathe series:
Love Delayed & **Love Delivered**

Love's Inconvenient Truth (Standalone)

Love Unaccounted series:
In Covenant with Ezra, In Love with Ezra & Bonded with Ezra

The Connecticut Kings series:
Love in the Red Zone, *Love on the Highlight Reel, *Determining Possession, End Zone Love, Love's Ineligible Receiver, & *Pass Interference (*by Christina C. Jones)

Wayward Love series:
The Left of Love, The Low of Love & The Right of Love

Love in Rhythm & Blues series
The Rhythm of Blues & The Rhyme of Love

The Sadik series

HE WHO IS A FRIEND

The Muted Hopelessness series:
My Muted Love, Our Muted Recklessness, & Our Reckless Hope

The Prism series:
Mercy, Grace, & The Promise

Low Love, Low Fidelity (Standalone)

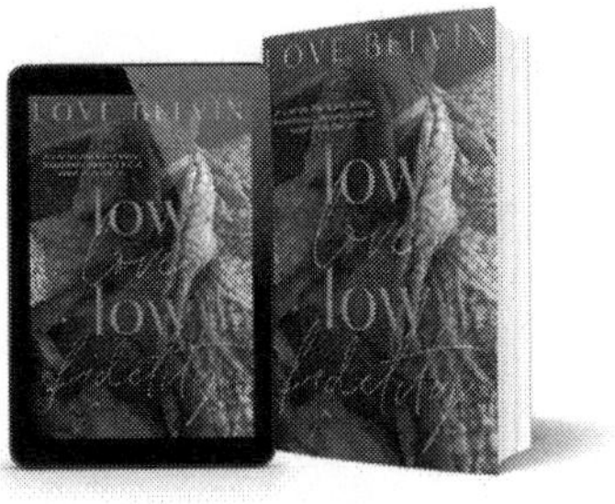
LOVE BELVIN

~EXTRA

You can find Love Belvin at www.LoveBelvin.com
Facebook @ Author - Love Belvin
Twitter @LoveBelvin
Goodreads: Love Belvin
and on Instagram @LoveBelvin

Join the #TeamLove mailing list to keep up with the happenings of Love Belvin here!

Made in the USA
Middletown, DE
10 March 2025